ANOTHER MAN'S CHILD

Celia Mulligan is in love with farmhand Andy McCadden, but her father refuses to let his daughter marry a mere labourer. Celia elopes with Andy and they take a ship to England. While on board, Celia meets Annabel, a demure young woman who tells her in confidence that a friend of her father forced himself upon her and she is pregnant. Annabel asks Celia if she will accompany her to Birmingham as her lady's maid. Andy encourages Celia to accept – he can find employment for himself and save for their future. But soon Celia is forced to choose between the man she loves, and the love of a vulnerable child...

ANOTHER MAN'S CHILD

ANOTHER MAN'S CHILD

by

Anne Bennett

Magna Large Print Books
Long Preston, North Yorkshire,
BD23 4ND, England.

British Library Cataloguing in Publication Data.

A catalogue record of this book is
available from the British Library

ISBN   978-0-7505-4407-8

First published in Great Britain in 2015 by HarperCollins*Publishers*

Published in Large Print 2017 by arrangement with
HarperCollins Publishers

Magna Large Print is an imprint of Library Magna Books Ltd.

Printed and bound in Great Britain by
T.J. (International) Ltd., Cornwall, PL28 8RW

I dedicate this book to my cousins,
Martin Logue of Redditch in the
West Midlands, and Michael Mulligan
from Dublin, with all my love
and best wishes.

ACKNOWLEDGEMENTS

I am always grateful to have such a strong team behind me at HarperCollins because without them the books would never hit the bookshelves at all, so heartfelt thanks go to my editor, Kate Bradley, and Charlotte Brabbin, Amy Winchester and Ann Bissell. A sterling job was done by Rhian McKay and special appreciation must also go to Susan Opie, who does such a marvellous job copy-editing my work, and to my agent Judith Murdoch, who is always there for me should I need her help or advice. It is very reassuring for a writer to have such a comfort blanket at their back and I owe a debt of gratitude to you all.

I am also grateful I can rely on the support of the family too: my husband, Denis; my three daughters, Nikki and her husband Steve, Tamsin and her husband Mark, Beth and my son Simon and his wife Carol and, of course, the five grandchildren. All of you are immensely dear to me.

But the most important people are you, the readers, for without you there would be no point to what I do and I value every single one of you. So thank you from the bottom of my heart and I sincerely hope you enjoy this book. I love it when you write to me and tell me what you think.

The title *Another Man's Child* was thought up by

my agent and so an especial thanks again to Judith. You know how rubbish I am at titles. As always I did a lot of work on research and the internet is a wonderful tool and I could not manage without it. From there I obtained a timeline of the Black and Tans roaming Ireland at the time. But I also used books such as *Rekindling a Dying Heritage* by Evelyn Ruddy, a book of rural Ireland at the time, *Catholics in Birmingham* by Christine Ward Penny and *Life on the Home Front,* which is a *Reader's Digest* publication. However I found a lot of information for this book through my cousins – Martin Logue, who lives in the Midlands, and Michael Mulligan, who lives in Dublin. Both of them have been researching the family tree for some time and there is also now a Facebook page, 'The Logues of Tawnagh', so I can ask questions if there is something I'm not sure of. I have found it such a valuable resource in writing this book that it is being dedicated to both of them.

ONE

It was Norah Mulligan walking alongside her sister, Celia, who noticed Andy McCadden first. It was the first Saturday in March and the first Fair Day of 1920 in Donegal Town.

It was a fine day, but March living up to its name of coming in like a lion, meant it was blustery and cold enough for the girls to be glad they were so warmly clad. They were still wearing winter-weight dresses, Celia's in muted red colours and Norah's muted blue, and they were long enough to reach the top of their boots so the thick black stockings could not be seen. Over that they were wearing Donegal tweed shawls, fastened by Celtic Tara brooches, and their navy bonnets matched the woollen gloves that encased their hands.

Celia knew Norah considered bonnets old fashioned and babyish but Celia was glad of hers that day and also liked the blue ribbons that tied so securely under her chin. 'Anyway,' she had reasoned with her sister when she had complained again that day as she got ready in their room. 'You'd have to have a hat of some sort – and just listen to the strength of that wind. Any other type of hat you had today would be tugged from your head in no time and in all likelihood go bowling down the road, however many hat-pins you had stuck in it. You running to retrieve it would cause great entertainment to the rest of

13

the town and I doubt that would please you much either.'

Norah said nothing to that because she did agree with Celia that bonnets were the safest option that day, especially when riding in the cart with their father where the wind was even more fierce. Given a choice she wouldn't have gone out at all, but stayed inside by the fireside; however, their mother, Peggy, had given them a list of things to buy as they were going in on the cart with their father who had some beef calves for sale. They did go in often on Saturdays because the Mulligans' farm was just outside the town and Peggy always said her gallivanting days were over, so the girls each had a bulging shopping bag as they crossed the square – shaped like a diamond and always referred to as such – to the Abbey Hotel where they were meeting their father.

The beasts for sale were in pens filling the Diamond and the pungent smell rose in the air and the noise of them, the bleating and grunting and lowing and squawking of the hens, just added to the general racket, for the streets were thronged with people, the shops doing a roaring trade.

As usual on a Fair Day the pubs were open all day. Some might have their doors slightly ajar so the two girls might get a tantalising glimpse inside. That was all they would get though, a glimpse, and if any men were standing outside with their pints, they would chivvy them on, for respectable women didn't frequent pubs and certainly not young ladies like Norah and Celia.

The cluster of gypsies was there too as they were every Fair Day, standing slightly apart from the

14

townsfolk. They'd always held a fascination for Celia, the black-haired, swarthy-skinned men who often had a jaunty manner and in the main wore different clothes to most men of Celia's acquaintance: light-coloured cotton shirts, moleskin waistcoats and some, mainly the younger ones, bright knotted handkerchiefs tied at their necks, and they were not above giving girls a broad wink as they passed. The women seemed far more dowdy in comparison, for they were usually dressed in black or grey or dark brown with a craggy shawl around their shoulders and more often than not there was a baby wrapped up in it, while skinny, scantily dressed, barefoot children scampered around them.

Suddenly, Norah gave her sister a poke in the ribs, taking her mind from the gypsies as she said, 'Will you look at the set of him,' and she jerked her head to the collection of people at the edge of the fair at the Hireling Stall who were in search of someone to take them to work on one of the farms or as servants in the house. As the Mulligans needed no outside help, Celia had never taken much notice of them and she cast her eyes over them now. There were, however, a few young men and she said, 'Which one?'

Norah cast her eyes upwards. 'Heavens, Celia,' she cried. 'Do you really need to ask? The blond-haired one of course, the one smiling over at us this very moment.'

'I'm sure you're wrong, Norah,' Celia said. 'It can't be us.'

'Celia, he's looking this way and smiling so he must be smiling at someone or something,'

Norah retorted. 'No one but an idiot would stand there with a wide grin on his face for no reason and I tell you he is the least idiotic man that I've seen in a long time. Quite a looker in fact.'

Celia stole a look at the man in question and did think he was most striking-looking and she took in the fact that he was tall, broad-shouldered and well-muscled and the sun was shining on his back, making it seem like he had a halo around his mop of very blond hair. She couldn't see the colour of his eyes, but she did see that they were twinkling so much it was like light that had been lit inside him and she felt herself smiling back. She looked away quickly and felt a crimson flush flood over her face. She saw that Norah had noticed her blush and, to prevent her teasing, said sharply, 'Mammy will wash your mouth out with carbolic if she hears you talking this way.'

'Better not tell her then,' Norah said impishly.

'I just might.'

'No, you won't,' Norah said assuredly. 'You're no tell-tale.'

'All right,' Celia conceded. 'You're right, I'd never tell Mammy. But talking of men, I was wondering the other day about you wanting to go to America and all. Whatever are you going to do about Joseph O'Leary?'

'What's Joseph O'Leary to do with anything?'

'You're walking out with him.'

'Hardly,' Norah said. 'We've just been out a few times.'

'Huh, more than a few I'd say,' Celia said. 'But it doesn't matter how long it's been going on, in any-one's book that constitutes walking out together.'

16

'Well if you must know,' Norah told her sister, 'I'm using Joseph to practise on.'

'Oh Norah, that's a dreadful thing to do to someone,' Celia cried, really shocked because she liked Joseph. He was a nice man and had an open honest face, a wide generous mouth and his fine head of wavy hair was as dark brown as his eyes, which were nearly always fastened on her sister.

Norah shrugged carelessly. 'I had to know what it was like. I am preparing for when I go to America.'

'Does he know your plans?'

'Sort of,' Norah said. 'I mean, he knows I want to go.'

'Does he know you're really going, that Aunt Maria said she'll sponsor you and pay your fare and everything?'

'Well no,' Norah admitted.

'Poor Joseph,' Celia said. 'He'll be heartbroken.'

'Hearts don't break that easy, Celia.'

'Well I bet yours will if you can't go to America after all and Mammy could stop you because she's great friends with the O'Learys.'

'Mammy will be able to do nothing,' Norah said confidently. 'She has made me wait until I'm twenty-one and that was bad enough, but I will be that in three months' time and then I can please myself.'

'She doesn't want you to go.'

'I know that and that was why she made me wait until I was twenty-one.'

'And that doesn't worry you?'

'It would if I let it,' Norah said. 'Now you worry about everything and in fact you would worry

17

yourself into an early grave if you had nothing to worry about. You never want to hurt people's feelings either and, while it's nice to be that way, it could stop you doing something you really want to do in case someone disapproves.'

'Like you going to America?'

'Exactly like that.'

'But I'd never want to leave here,' Celia said, looking around the town she loved so much. She loved everything, the rolling hills she could see from her bedroom window dotted with velvet-nosed cows calmly chewing the cud, or the sheep pulling relentlessly at the grass as if their lives depended upon it, and here and there squat cottages with plumes of grey smoke rising from the chimneys wafting in the air. Their farmhouse was no small cottage however for it was built of brick with a slate roof and unusually for Ireland then, it was two storeyed. Downstairs there was a well-fitted scullery with a tin bath hung on a hook behind the door and leading off it, a large kitchen with a range with a scrubbed wooden table beside it and an easy chair before the hearth. It was where the family spent most of their time, for though there was a separate sitting room it was seldom used. The stairs ran along the kitchen wall and upstairs were three sizeable bedrooms; her parents had their own room, another she shared with Norah and Ellie and the other one was for Tom, Dermot and Sammy.

It was all so dear to her, familiar and safe and she couldn't see why anyone would want to leave it. She said this to Norah and added, 'I'd never want to go away from here.'

'Never is a long time,' Norah said. 'And you're only seventeen. I felt like that at seventeen. But by the time I was twenty I felt as if I was suffocating with the sameness of every day.'

'But don't you want a husband and children?'

'Not yet,' Norah said emphatically. 'Why would I? I intend to keep marriage and all it entails at bay or at least until I meet and fall madly in love with a tall and very handsome man, who has plenty of money and will adore me totally.'

Celia burst out laughing. 'Shouldn't say there's many of them about.'

'Not in Donegal certainly,' Norah conceded. 'But who knows what America holds? The country may be littered with them.'

Celia laughed. Oh, how she would miss her sister for, since leaving school, she saw her old friends rarely. She'd meet some of them occasionally in Donegal Town, but it wasn't arranged or anything, they would just bump into one another. They seldom had time for any sort of lingering chats because all the girls would usually have a list of errands to do for their mothers. The only other time to meet was at Mass on Sunday but no one dawdled after that because most of the congregation had taken communion and so were ravenously hungry, for no one was allowed to eat or drink if they were taking communion. So the two sisters had relied on each other – and Peggy wasn't the only one to hope that Norah would change her mind in the months till her twenty-first birthday.

Celia opened her mouth to say something to Norah about how much she would miss her, but there was no time because they had reached the

19

Abbey Hotel and their father, Dan, was waiting on them. Celia thought her father a fairly handsome man for one of his age; his black curls had not a hint of grey and he had deep dark brown eyes just like her eldest brother, Tom. Only his nose let him down for it was slightly bulbous, but his mouth was a much better shape. Tom was just like a younger version of him. Dan was a jovial man too and as they approached his laugh rang out at something someone in the crowd had said and it was so infectious that Celia and Norah were smiling too as they reached him.

He had told them on the way in that if he sold the calves early enough, they could wait on and he'd take them home in the cart, but if the calves were not sold, he might stay on and they would have to make their own way home. Celia wondered why he even bothered saying that because she had never known her father come home early on a Fair Day and his delay had more to do with the pubs open all the day and old friends to chat to and gather news from than it had to do with selling the calves.

Norah knew that too, but both girls went on with the pretence. 'Have you sold the calves, Daddy?'

Dan took a swig of Guinness from the pint glass he held before he said, 'Might have. Man said he'd tell me this afternoon when his brother has a chance to look them over. So you must make your own way home. Tell your mother.'

'Yes, Daddy,' the girls chorused, though they knew their mother wouldn't be the least bit surprised.

They passed the Hireling Stall again on their way out of town and Celia saw the blond-haired man talking to Dinny Fitzgerald whose farm abutted theirs in many places. 'Looks like Dinny's hiring that chap,' Norah remarked.

'Well Daddy said he would have to hire someone after his son upped and went to America,' Celia said and added, 'Huh, seems all the Irish farms are emptying of young men going to that brave New World.'

'Yes and I might want to nab one of those men for myself in due course,' Norah said. 'That's why I have to practise on poor Joseph.' And her tinkling laugh rang out at the aghast look on Celia's face.

It was some time later when Dan Mulligan came home, very loud and good-humoured, which Peggy said was the Guinness effect. He brought all the news from the town though, including the fact that Dinny Fitzgerald had indeed taken on a new farm hand.

'Must be no sign of his son retuning then,' remarked Peggy. 'America seems a terrible lure to the young people.'

'Aye,' Dan said. 'But sure it's hard for a man when he has only the one son who will inherit the farm and who has so little interest in it he is away to pastures new, and so Dinny has to have strangers in to work it with him.'

'Maybe the lad didn't take to the life,' Norah said. 'You know, maybe he doesn't want to be a farmer.'

'Take to the life,' Dan said with scorn. 'What's whether he likes it or not got to do with anything?

21

People can't always do as they please and in this case there is no one else and it's his birthright. Is he not going to come back and take it on board after Dinny's day, let the farm fall to strangers and after it being in the family generations? Tell you, I'd find that hard to take.'

'Well not every man has the rake of sons you have,' Peggy said. 'So if our Tom here didn't want it, then Dermot might or even wee Sammy, for all he's only seven now. Or Jim might come back from America and take it on if there was no one else. Mulligans will farm here for some time to come I think.'

Celia, listening as she washed the dishes in the scullery, knew her mother was right. She knew too most farmers wanted more than one son but the eldest inherited everything and the others had to make their own way. That's what Jim had said when he left for America's shores. It had been five years ago when he had decided. He had been twenty-three then, two years younger than Tom and, knowing his future was in his own hands, he had written to Aunt Maria who had sailed away to New York many years before with her new American husband and was quite a wealthy woman now, but a childless one. She had been delighted to hear from Jim, and agreed to not only sponsor him but also pay his fare and said she would do the same for all who wanted to follow their brother.

Peggy hadn't liked to hear that bit and she watched the restless Norah growing up rather anxiously and was glad and relieved when she settled with Joseph O'Leary, but not as settled as she might be, because just a few months before she had claimed it wasn't serious between them. There was no understanding, Norah had said and it was just as well because she wanted to follow Jim to America.

'If you throw Joseph over you'll get your name up, girl,' Mammy had said at the time.

Norah had not been a bit abashed. 'Maybe here I might,' was her retort. 'In America they wouldn't care a jot I bet. According to what Jim says, it's much freer there and you don't have to marry a man you go for a walk with.'

Peggy's sigh was almost imperceptible for she knew another child was going to cross the Atlantic.

Celia too wished Norah would fall madly in love with Joseph O'Leary and declare she couldn't bear to leave him, but she had to admit that didn't look the slightest bit likely and she knew Norah was every day more determined than ever to sail to America. She had marked her twenty-first birthday on the calendar in the room they shared with a big red circle and each day she marked another day off. Thinking about it now as she swirled the dishes in the hot water Celia felt very depressed and wondered if one by one they would all go away.

Two years before, her sister Katie had married a Donegal man but he was a wheelwright and had a house and business in Greencastle in Inishowan, a fair distance from Donegal Town, and that's where Katie lived now. So they hadn't visited her since the wedding, not even when she had her first child that she named Brendan.

Maggie might have stayed and married a local

man for she was the prettiest of them all and had a string of admirers. Mammy would shake her head over her and said she would be called fast and loose, as she would accept gifts pressed on her by men, without any sort of understanding between them. She was in no hurry to settle down, she said, but Maggie had taken sick with TB a year after Jim had left for America. To protect everyone else she had been taken to the sanatorium in Donegal Town and died six weeks later when she was nineteen years old.

That had been a sad time for them all, Celia remembered, and for herself too because she hadn't really had to deal with death before and certainly not the death of one so young and pretty and full of the joys of life. It seemed like the whole town had turned out for her funeral, but afterwards the family had been left alone to deal with the loss of her.

Time was the great healer, everyone said, and Celia wondered about that because for a long time there had been an agonising pang in her heart if she allowed herself to think of Maggie. She imagined it was the same for her mother for, though Peggy had never spoken about it, Celia had seen the sadness in her hazel-coloured eyes and the lines pulling down her mouth were deeper than ever and there were more grey streaks in her light-brown hair. Eventually, though, time worked its magic and they each learned to cope in their own way for life had to go on.

'Have you not finished washing those pots yet?' Peggy called and her words jerked Celia from her reverie and she attended to the job in hand.

24

Monday morning they were expecting Fitzgerald to send over his bull to service the cows, for their father had told them the night before, but as the cart rumbled across the cobbles outside the cottage door, Celia, peering through the kitchen window, was surprised to see Fitzgerald's hireling driving the cart pulling the horse box.

'Why should you be so surprised?' the man replied when Celia voiced this as she stepped into the yard to meet him. 'I have been doing farm work all my life and driving a horse and cart is just part of it.'

'I saw you at the fair on Saturday,' Celia said.

'And I saw you,' the man said with a slight nod in her direction. 'And I was interested enough to ask someone your name so I know you to be Celia Mulligan. And mine,' he added before Celia had recovered from her surprise, 'is Andy McCadden and I am very pleased to make your acquaintance.'

He stuck out his hand as he said this and Celia would have felt it churlish to refuse to take it but, as their hands touched, she felt a very disturbing tingle run up her arm. It made her blush a little and, when she looked up into his face and saw his sparkling eyes were vivid blue, she found herself smiling too as she said, 'I'm very pleased to meet you, Mr McCadden.'

'Oh Andy please,' the man protested and he still held her hand. 'And may I not call you Celia? After all, we are neighbours.'

Celia knew her father probably wouldn't see it that way but her father was not there, so she said, 'Yes I think that will be all right.'

25

There was a sudden bellow of protest from the bull and she said, 'Now we'd better see to the bull? My father is in the top field separating the cows. I'll show you if you get the bull out now.'

'You'll not be nervous?' Andy said as he began unshackling the back that would drop down to form a ramp for the bull to walk down.

'Not so long as you can control him,' Celia said.

'Oh I think so,' Andy said. 'Mind you,' he said as they went out down the lane leading the bull by the ring on his nose, 'I'm surprised you haven't your own bull on a farm of this size.'

'Oh we did have our own bull one time,' Celia said. 'It was long before I was born and my parents were not married that long and Mummy was expecting her first child. The bull pulled away from Daddy and charged at Mammy who had just stepped out into the yard. He gored her quite badly and she was taken to the hospital and there she lost the child she'd been carrying and nearly lost her own life too. Even after she recovered, the doctor thought she might be too damaged inside to carry another child. At least that has proven not to be the case, but she would never tolerate a bull around the place afterwards.'

'Sorry about your mother and all,' Andy said. 'But I can't help being pleased that you haven't your own bull.'

'Why on earth would that matter to you one way or the other?' Celia asked in genuine surprise.

'Because this way I get a chance to talk to you,' Andy declared.

Celia blushed crimson. 'Hush,' she cautioned.

'What?' Andy said. 'We are doing no harm talk-

26

ing.' And then, seeing how uncomfortable Celia was, he went on, 'Is it because I'm a hireling boy and you a farmer's daughter?'

Celia's silence gave Andy his answer and he said, 'That's hardly fair. My elder brother Christie will inherit our farm and after my father paid out for my two sisters' weddings last year he said I had to make my own way in the world. He has a point because I am twenty-one now and there are two young ones at home for them to provide for and I would have to leave the farm eventually anyway.'

'I know,' Celia said. 'That's how it is for many. Tom will have the farm after Daddy's day.'

'Have you other brothers?'

'The next eldest to him went to America where we have an aunt living.'

'It's handy to have a relative in America.'

'It is if you want to go there, I suppose,' Celia said.

'You haven't any hankering to follow him then?'

Celia shook her head vehemently. 'Not me,' she said. 'My sister Norah is breaking her neck to go, but Mammy is making her wait until she's twenty-one.'

'And is that far away?'

Celia sighed. 'Not far enough,' she said. 'It's just a few months and I will so miss her when she's gone.'

'Have you no more brothers and sisters?'

'Yes,' Celia said. 'Dermot is over three years younger than me, so he is nearly fifteen and left school now and then there is Ellie who is nine and Sammy who is the youngest at seven.'

'Not much company for you then?'

27

Celia shook her head. 'I'd say not,' and then she added wryly, 'Mind you, I might be too busy to get lonely for I will have to do Norah's jobs as well as my own.'

'You can't work all the time,' Andy said. 'Do you never go to the dances and socials in the town?'

Celia shook her head.

'Why on earth not?'

'I don't know why not,' Celia admitted. 'It's just never come up, that's all.'

'Well maybe you should ask about it?' Andy said. 'No wonder your sister can't wait to go to America if she is on the farm all the days of her life. There's a dance this Saturday evening.'

'And are you going to it?'

'I am surely,' Andy said. 'Mr Fitzgerald told me about it himself. He advised me to go and meet some of the townsfolk and it couldn't be more respectable, for its run by the church and I'm sure the priest will be in attendance.'

Celia knew Father Casey would have a hand in anything the Catholic Church was involved in – particularly if it was something to do with young people, who he seemed to think were true limbs of Satan, judging by his sermons. And yet, despite the priest's presence there, she had a sudden yen to go, for at nearly eighteen she was well old enough and she wondered why Norah had said nothing about it. Tom attended the dances but she never went out in the evening and neither did Norah, not even to a neighbour's house for a rambling night, which was often an impromptu meeting, spread by word of mouth. There would be a lot of singing or the men would catch hold of

28

the instruments they had brought and play the lilting music they had all grown up with and the women would roll up the rag rugs and step dance on the stone-flagged floor. She had never been to one, but before Maggie died the Mulligans had had rambling nights of their own and she remembered going to sleep with the tantalising music running round in her head. She didn't say any of this to Andy for she had spied her father making his way towards them across the field and saw him quicken his pace when he saw his daughter in such earnest conversation with the hireling boy.

So Dan gave Andy a curt nod of the head as a greeting and said, 'Bring him through into the field.' And as Andy led the bull through the gate Dan said to Celia, 'You go straight back to the house. This is no place for you anyway.' And Celia turned and without even looking at Andy she returned to the farmhouse, deep in thought.

TWO

'Why do we never go to the socials or the dances in the town?' Celia said as she and Norah washed up together in the scullery.

Norah shrugged. 'What's brought this on?'

'Just wondered, that's all,' Celia said. 'Heard a couple of girls talking about it in the town Saturday.'

'Did you?' Norah said in surprise. 'I never heard anyone say anything and I'd have said we were together all the time.' Her eyes narrowed suddenly and she said, 'It wasn't that hireling boy put you up to asking?'

'He has got a name, that hireling boy,' Celia said, irritated with Norah's attitude. 'He's called Andy McCadden and he didn't put me up to anything. He asked if I was going to the dance and I said, no, that we never go.'

'What was it to him?'

'God, Norah, he meant nothing I shouldn't think,' Celia said. 'Just making conversation.'

'Well you were doing your fair share of that,' Norah said. 'I watched you through the window, chatting together ten to the dozen. Very cosy it looked.'

'What was I supposed to do, ignore him?' Celia asked. 'I was taking him to find Daddy and he was leading a bull by the nose. Not exactly some sort of romantic tryst. Anyway, why don't we ever go to the dances and the odd social?'

'Well Mammy would have thought you too young until just about now anyway.'

'All right,' Celia conceded. 'But what about you? You're nearly twenty-one.'

'I know,' Norah said and added with a slight sigh, 'I went with Maggie a few times; maybe you were too young to remember it. When she took sick and then died I had no desire to go anywhere for some time and then we were in mourning for a year and so I sort of got out of the way of it and anyway I didn't really want to go on my own.'

'Tom goes.'

'He's a man and not much in the way of company,' Norah said. 'Anyway he'd hardly want me

30

hanging on to his coat tails. After all he went there hunting for a wife.'

'Golly!' Celia exclaimed. 'Did he really?'

'Course he did,' Norah said assuredly. 'No frail-looking beauty for him, for he was on the lookout for some burly farmer's daughter, with wide hips who can bear him a host of sons and still have the energy to roll up her sleeves and help him on the farm.'

Celia laughed softly. 'Well he hasn't, has he?' she said. 'Though no one said a word about it, everyone knows he's courting Sinead McClusky and she is pretty and not the least bit burly.'

'Maybe not but you couldn't describe her as delicate either and she *is* a farmer's daughter.'

'What about love?'

'You're such a child yet,' Norah said disparagingly. 'What does Mammy say? "Love flies out of the window when the bills come in the door." Tom will do his duty, as you probably will too in time.'

'Me?' Celia's voice came out in a shriek of surprise.

'Ssh,' Norah cautioned. 'Look, Celia, it's best you know for this is how it is. If I stayed here and threw Joseph over, apart from the fact my name would be mud, Daddy might feel it in my best interests to get me hooked up with someone else and of his choosing. This might well happen to you and it isn't always in our best interests either, but it's done to increase the land he has or something of that nature. And it will be no good claiming you don't love the man they're chaining you to for life, because that won't matter at all.'

'What about Mammy?' Celia cried, her voice

31

rising high in indignation. 'Surely she wouldn't agree to my marrying a man I didn't love?'

Norah shrugged. 'Possibly the same thing happened to her and it's more than likely she sees no harm in it.'

'Well I see plenty of harm in it,' Celia said. 'You said something like this before, but this has decided me. I shall not marry unless for love and no one can make me marry someone I don't want.'

'Daddy might make your life difficult.'

Celia shrugged. 'I can cope with that if I have to.'

'Well to find someone to take your fancy,' Norah said, 'you need to go out and have a look at what is on offer, for I doubt hosts of boys and young men will be beating a path to our door. And so I think we should put it to Mammy and Daddy that we start going out more and the dance this Saturday is as good a way to start as any. You just make sure you don't lose your heart to a hireling man.'

Celia expected some opposition to her and Norah going to the dance that Saturday evening when Norah broached it at the dinner table the following day, but there wasn't much. Peggy in fact was all for it.

'Isn't Celia a mite young for that sort of carry-on?' Dan muttered.

Celia suppressed a sigh as her mother said, 'She is young, I grant you, but Tom will be there and he can take them down and bring them back and be on hand to disperse any undesirable man who might be making a nuisance of himself.'

'And I will be there to see no harm befalls

Celia,' Norah said. 'It isn't as if I'm new to the dances – I used to go along with Maggie.'

Peggy sighed. 'Ah yes, you did indeed, child,' she said, a mite sadly. She had no desire to prevent them from going dancing, particularly Norah, for if she wasn't going to marry Joseph maybe she should see if another Donegal man might catch her heart and then she might put the whole idea of America out of her head.

And so with permission given, the girls excitedly got ready for the dance on Saturday. They had no dance dresses as such but they had prettier dresses they kept for Mass. They were almost matching for each had a black bodice and full sleeves. Celia's velvet skirt was dark red, Norah's was midnight blue. Celia had loved her dress when Mammy had given it to her newly made by the talented dress maker and now she spun around in front of the mirror in an agony of excitement at going to her first dance.

'Aren't they pretty dresses?' Celia cried.

'They are pretty enough I grant you,' Norah said. 'It's just that they are so long.'

'Long?'

'Yes, it's so old fashioned now to have them this long. It is 1920 after all.'

'Let me guess?' Celia said. 'I bet they're not this length in America.'

'No they aren't,' Norah said. 'Men over there don't swoon in shock when they get a glimpse of a woman's ankle.'

'How do you know?' Celia demanded. 'That's not the sort of thing Jim would notice and he certainly wouldn't bother to write and tell you.'

'No he didn't,' Norah admitted. 'But Aunt Maria did. And she said that the women wear pretty button boots, not the clod-hopping boots we have.'

'Well pretty button boots would probably be little good in the farmyard,' Celia pointed out. 'And really we should be grateful for any boots at all when many around us are forced to go about barefoot.'

'I suppose,' Norah said with a sigh. 'Anyway we can do nothing about either, so we'll have to put up with it. Now don't forget when you wash your hair to give it a final rinse with the rainwater in the water butt to give it extra shine.'

'I know and then you're putting it up for me.'

'Yes and you won't know yourself then.'

Norah knew Celia had no idea just how pretty she was with her auburn locks, high cheekbones, flawless complexion, large deep brown eyes and a mouth like a perfect rosebud. She knew her sister would be a stunner when she was fully mature. She herself looked pretty enough, although her hair was a mediocre brown and her eyes, while large enough, were more of a hazel colour.

She sighed for she wished her mother would let her buy some powder so she could cover the freckles that the spring sunshine was bringing out in full bloom on the bridge of her nose and under her eyes. However, she had heard her mother say just the other day that women who used cosmetics were fast and no better than they should be.

She imagined things would be different in America, but she wasn't there yet and Celia, catching sight of Norah's forlorn face, cried,

'Why on earth are you frowning so?'

Norah shrugged and said, 'It's nothing. Come on, Tom will be waiting on us and you know how he hates hanging about.'

Celia did. Her brother wasn't known for his patience so she scurried along after her sister.

The church hall was a familiar place to Celia and she passed the priest lurking in the porch watching all the people arriving. She greeted him as she passed and went into the hall, where her mouth dropped open with astonishment for she had never seen it set up for a dance before, with the musicians tuning up on the stage and the tables and chairs positioned around the edges of the room while still leaving enough room in there for the bar where the men were clustered around having their pints pulled, Tom amongst them. Celia knew respectable women and certainly girls didn't go near bars though. Tom would bring them a soft drink over and Norah said that was that as far as he was concerned.

'If you want another we shall have to go and find him,' Norah said.

'What d'you do if you haven't come with a man?' Celia asked.

Norah shrugged. 'If you haven't got a handy brother or male cousin it's often safer to stay at home,' she said.

'Safer?'

'Yes,' Norah affirmed. 'Some men are the very devil when they have a drink on them.' And then glancing at the door she said, 'Oh Lord. Here's Joseph come in the door and looks very surprised to see me, as well he might be.'

Celia turned and saw Joseph's eyes widen in surprise at seeing Norah, yet Celia saw that he was anything but displeased about it because his face was lit up in a smile of welcome. 'I expect I will have to go and be pleasant to him,' Norah said.

'I'd say so,' Celia said. 'Look at that smile and it's all for you. I'd say he's really gone on you.'

'Yes,' Norah said. 'I wish he wasn't.'

'Well he can't help how he feels, can he?' Celia said. 'And anyway it's partly your fault. You should have been straight with him about your intention to emigrate to America from the start.'

Celia saw from the reddening on Norah's cheeks that what she had said had hit home and watched her walk across towards Joseph. Celia turned away, wondering what it would feel like to have a man smile just for her in such a way.

And then she saw Andy McCadden at the bar smiling at her in much the same way. It made her feel slightly light-headed and before she was able to recover her senses Andy was by her side and saying, 'I thought you said you never came to the dances, Miss Celia Mulligan.'

Before answering him, Celia took a surreptitious look around. Tom, she saw, was talking to Sinead McClusky and Norah was away talking to Joseph and so she faced Andy and said, 'We don't. This is the first one I have been to and I wasn't sure I would be let go and it was only because Norah was here to keep an eye on me and my brother was walking us down and back again that made Mammy say I could go.'

'And where are your protectors now?' Andy

36

asked in a bantering tone. 'Not doing their job very well, I would say. Leaving you stranded in the middle of the room without even a drink in your hand. I can remedy that at least.'

'Oh no,' Celia cried. 'Really it's all right.'

'It's not all right,' Andy said. 'I have a great thirst on me, which I intend to slake with a pint and I can hardly drink alone. I'm afraid I must insist you join with me.'

And before Celia was able to make any sort of reply to this, Andy wheeled away and left her standing there. She felt rather self-conscious and looked round to see if she could see Tom or Norah, thinking that she might have joined them, but so many people were now in the hall she couldn't see them. And then Andy was back with a glass of Guinness in one hand and a glass of slightly cloudy liquid in the other which he held out to Celia. She didn't take it though and, eyeing it suspiciously, said, 'What is it?'

'Homemade apple juice.'

'You mean cider?'

'No. If I meant cider I would have said cider,' Andy said with a smile. 'I would never offer anyone of your tender years alcohol. This is what I said it was, apple juice plain and simple, and it will do you no harm whatsoever. Take it.'

Celia had barely taken the glass from him when Norah pounced on her. She had felt guilty for leaving her to her own devices to talk to Joseph and hadn't meant to be away so long. Now she said sharply, 'What are you up to and what is that in that glass?'

'I'm not up to anything,' Celia retorted. 'Why

37

should you think I was? And all that's in my glass is apple juice.'

Norah was still looking at it suspiciously and Andy put in, 'It's true what Miss Mulligan said. I found her looking a bit lost. I believe it is her first time at an event like this.'

Norah knew it was and that was the very reason she shouldn't have left her high and dry as she had and so when Andy went on, 'I was buying a drink for myself and so I offered to buy one for your sister and it is, as she said, apple juice,' Norah couldn't say anything but, 'Thank you for looking after her so well, Mr...'

'McCadden,' Andy said, extending his hand. 'Andy McCadden.'

'Norah Mulligan,' Norah felt obliged to say as she took hold of the man's proffered hand. 'And you have already met my sister, Celia.'

'Yes indeed.'

'And now you must excuse us,' Norah said. 'There are some people I want Celia to meet.'

Andy gave a sardonic smile as if he didn't believe for one moment that there were people Celia had to meet but he said, 'Of course.' And then, as they turned away, he added, 'Perhaps I can claim you both for a dance later?'

Celia didn't answer for she had seen Norah's lips purse in annoyance and then Norah answered in clipped tones, 'We'll have to see, Mr McCadden. I can make you no promises.'

'There was no need to be rude to Mr Mc-Cadden,' Celia hissed through the side of her mouth to her sister as soon as she was sure they were out of earshot of the man who was standing

38

watching them walk across the room.

'I wasn't at all rude,' Norah protested. 'I was perfectly polite.'

'You were stiff and awkward, like,' Celia persisted. 'And it wasn't as if he did anything wrong – unless talking to me and buying me a drink is wrong. I did look round for you and Tom and couldn't see either of you.'

'I can't answer for Tom, but I stepped outside with Joseph,' Norah said. 'After what you said, I decided to tell him once and for all about America. I thought I had strung him along enough and he deserved that I tell him the truth. He was a bit upset, wouldn't accept it you know, so I stayed talking to him longer than I intended. I did think Tom might have checked to see you were all right and though I think Mr McCadden was pleasant enough he is not the kind of person that you should encourage. And now here's Tom coming with a drink for each of us. Put the one McCadden brought you on the table quick before he sees it.'

'Why? It's only a drink, Norah.'

'Will you do as I tell you,' Norah hissed. 'There are things that are not done and accepting a drink from a man unrelated to you and almost a stranger to boot is one of them. You are going the right way to make Tom tear him off in no uncertain terms for being familiar and Tom won't care how rude he is.'

Celia thought Norah was probably right and so she slipped the drink Andy had brought her onto the table beside her, just as Tom came into view, smiling jovially at the two girls. 'Enjoying yourselves?' he asked.

'We've only just got here,' Norah pointed out, but Celia said, 'I think it's quite exciting. It's nothing like the church hall is normally.'

'No indeed it isn't,' Tom said as the band struck up the music for a four-hand reel. He asked, 'Now will you be all right? I promised Sinead a dance.'

'Then go on,' Norah said. 'There are lots of people I want to introduce Celia to.'

Tom left them as Norah slipped her arm through Celia's. 'Come on,' she said. 'There really are lots of people I want you to meet, men as well as girls, and I think I can guarantee that, looking as you do, you will be up dancing most of the night and won't give a thought to Mr McCadden.'

In a way Norah was right for Celia proved a very popular girl. She was slight in build, the sort of girl that the men she was introduced to wanted to protect, and so light on her feet as she danced the set dances and jigs and reels and polkas that she loved. Not even Father Casey looking about him with disapproval could quell Celia's enjoyment. And yet she couldn't get Andy McCadden quite out of her mind and every time she caught sight of him his brooding eyes seemed to be constantly fastened on her.

They lined up for the two-handed reel and Andy suddenly left the bar and joined the line with another woman. It was the sort of dance when the girls started with one partner but danced with different men in the set until they ended up back with their original partner and so at one point Celia was facing Andy. As they moved to the centre Andy spoke quietly through the side of his mouth, 'Your sister is trying to keep us apart.' Celia didn't answer – there wasn't time anyway – and the second time they came near to one another he said, 'D'you ever walk out on Sunday afternoons?' and the third and last time they came close he said, 'We could meet and chat.'

Before Celia had time to digest what Andy had said, never mind reply to it, she was facing another partner and the dance went on and she was glad that she knew the dance so well and didn't have to think much about it because her head was in a whirl with the words Andy had whispered to her. As the dance drew to a close and she thanked the man who had partnered her, she had to own that Andy was right about one thing: Norah had taken a distinct dislike to Andy McCadden and was going to do her level best to keep them apart. Celia thought she had a nerve. Norah was prepared to swan off to America, upsetting everyone to follow her dream, and she had told Celia she was too fond of trying to please people and she had to stop that and look to her own future. Now Celia wasn't sure that Andy McCadden would be part of that future, she was a tad young to see that far ahead, but what was wrong with just being friends or, at the very least, being civil to one another? Norah didn't have to treat him as if he had leprosy.

She was sitting at a table alone for once, a little tired from all the dancing, and she scanned the room for Tom and Norah, just in time to see Tom leading Sinead outside. Norah was nowhere to be seen and suddenly Andy was by her side again with another glass of apple juice in his hand.

'Thank you,' she said as she took it from him without the slightest hesitation and drank it gratefully.

'You look as if you were in need of that,' Andy said as he sat on the seat beside her.

'I was thirsty,' Celia admitted. 'It's all the dancing.'

'And tired, I'll warrant.'

'Yes a little.'

'That's a pity.'

'Why?'

'They are playing the last waltz,' Andy said. 'I was going to ask you to dance with me but if you are tired...'

Celia hesitated, for she knew the last waltz was special and she shouldn't dance it with a man she hardly knew. Andy saw her hesitation and said, 'Or perhaps you think your brother and sister would not approve.'

Andy wasn't to know, but his words lit a little light of rebellion in Celia's heart. What right had Norah and Tom to judge her? All she was proposing to do was dance with a man she had spoken to a few times in open view of everyone. It wasn't as if she was sneaking outside like Tom with Sinead, who might well be up to more than just holding hands, and she had no idea where Norah was. And so she smiled at Andy and, at the radiance of that smile, Andy felt a lurch in his stomach as if he'd been kicked by a mule.

'I'm not that tired, Andy, and I would love to dance with you,' Celia said.

She stood up and Andy took her by the hand and she glided into his arms. As he tightened them around her she felt a slight tremor that began in her toes run all through her body. Andy felt it too and it aroused his protective instincts and he held her even tighter. 'You're shivering. Are you afraid?'

'No,' Celia answered, 'I've never been less afraid than I am at this minute. I don't know why I'm trembling so much, but it isn't unpleasant.'

'Oh that's all right then,' Andy said with a throaty chuckle and swept Celia across the floor with a flourish and that's what Norah saw as she came back into the hall.

Had Norah heard the conversation between Celia and Andy McCadden she would have been further upset because, as she re-entered the hall, Celia was looking at Andy as if he had taken leave of his senses as she said, 'I can't just take off like that on a Sunday afternoon.'

'Why not?'

'It would be thought odd,' she said. 'It's not something I ever do.'

'Don't see why not,' Andy persisted. 'It's a normal thing to do, to go for a walk on a Sunday afternoon. What do you usually do?'

That was the rub, Celia thought, for she normally did nothing; that is, she worked harder than any other day in the week and so did Norah and their mother, for from the minute they returned from Mass, lightheaded with hunger, they would be cooking up a big breakfast and barely had they eaten that and cleared away than they started on the dinner. The washing-up after that Sunday dinner seemed to take forever and while Celia and Norah tackled that Peggy would make some delicacies and pasties to be served after tea.

Then sometimes Norah would take up the embroidery she was so fond of. The young ones would be playing outside, Dermot would be going to meet with other young fellows in the town like himself, Tom off to see Sinead, and her parents would doze in front of the fire. Celia loved to read but all she was allowed to read on Sunday was the Holy Bible and she thought it the dullest day in the week and suddenly going for a walk seemed a very attractive prospect.

And yet she hesitated, for she knew however bored she was on Sunday, walking out on the hills with a man would not be viewed as a viable alternative. 'I don't know you,' she said at last.

'You do,' Andy insisted. 'I am Andy McCadden, second son of Francie McCadden and trying to make his way in the world.'

'That's not it,' Celia said. 'I mean, I know who you are but that is not the same as knowing a person.'

'Well wouldn't we get to know each other better if we walked and talked?' Andy said. 'Isn't that what it's all about?'

'Mm, I suppose,' Celia conceded and then shook her head. 'I wouldn't be let.'

'Well that's a real shame,' Andy said as the waltz drew to a close and he continued to hold Celia as he went on, 'I would say bring your sister but she seems to hate my guts – she's looking daggers at us now.'

Andy was right. Celia glanced across at Norah and saw her eyes smouldering in temper. She felt her stomach give a lurch for she knew she was for

44

the high jump and then, as Norah gave a sharp jerk of her head, she said, 'I'll have to go.'

'All right,' Andy said. 'But if you are ever allowed to make your own mind up about things, I shall be walking around Lough Eske tomorrow afternoon if the weather is middling. Dinny and his wife tell me it's a beautiful place to walk.'

As Celia trailed back towards her sister, she thought it probably was but she had never seen it herself, even though it was only a few miles away. They never walked just for the sake of walking, they walked only to get somewhere and she had never had an occasion to visit Lough Eske.

They had barely left the church hall before Norah started on Celia, saying she had made a holy show of herself dancing the last waltz with the hireling man and it was the first and last time she would take her to the dance if she was going to get up to that sort of carry-on.

Celia was really angry with her sister, but was unable to answer her because Tom had joined them and they both knew better than to involve him. He appeared not to notice any constraint between his sisters and was in high spirits himself. He asked Celia what she had thought of her first dance.

Celia ignored the glare Norah was casting her way and answered that she had thoroughly enjoyed herself. 'Well I would have thought you would,' Tom said. 'I saw you up dancing a number of times.'

Celia glanced at her brother but he still had a smile on his face and the words weren't spoken in any kind of a pointed way and so she relaxed and they fell to discussing the dance as they walked home together.

It was as they got in the house that Celia realised how weary she was. Her parents were already in bed and Tom, mindful of the milking in the morning, went straight to bed himself. Though Celia had intended to say something to Norah when they reached the semi-privacy of their bedroom, she fell asleep as soon as her head touched the pillow.

THREE

When Celia awoke she didn't forget how outraged she had been by what Norah had said about Andy the previous evening, which she'd thought grossly unfair, but she didn't get a chance to get her to herself until they were walking to nine o'clock Mass. The day promised to be a good one; a hazy sun shone in the blue sky, only broken by the fluffy white clouds scudding across at intervals blown by the slight breeze, and she couldn't help thinking that Lough Eske would look lovely with the sun shining on it.

Strictly speaking, Celia and Norah weren't really alone for they had charge of Ellie and Sammy. Neither of them liked to walk sedately though Peggy insisted they did on their way to Mass because it was more seemly and they would be dressed in their best clothes. However, that morning it suited Celia to let the two youngsters run

46

ahead down the lane because she wanted to have it out with Norah who she accused of unfairness with regards to Andy McCadden.

'How do you work that out?' Norah asked.

'Because you're so snooty when you talk about him being a hireling boy,' Celia claimed and demanded, 'Would you feel the same way about our brother, Jim, for Andy McCadden is in just the same place as the second son of a farmer? It's just that he doesn't have a rich relative in America willing to sponsor him.'

'I know that,' Norah conceded. 'And yes it probably is unfair but that's life and it still doesn't mean Mr McCadden is suitable for you.'

'Why not?'

'He has no prospects.'

'Oh for heaven's sake...'

'You can scoff and roll your eyes all you like but from what I've heard fresh air isn't very nourishing,' Norah said.

'Look, Norah, I only danced with Andy,' Celia said. 'I didn't give him my hand in marriage or anything, and at least the man has a job.'

'That's just it,' Norah said. 'He has a job and incidentally I hope you're not referring to him in that familiar way. He should be Mr McCadden to you.'

Celia looked at her sister incredulously and then, head on one side, she asked, 'You sure you're ready for America, cos things are a lot less formal there, Jim says? And while we are talking of America, who is going to police you and make sure you only mix with suitable people, cos Jim says that Aunt Maria is much more relaxed about things

47

than Mammy and Daddy? And if you're honest that's one of the major reasons for you busting a gut to go to America.'

Norah was silent because she knew her sister was absolutely right and Celia went on, 'Anyway you are telling me off but you're not so squeaky clean yourself. You played with Joseph till he thought you two had a future together and then threw him over. I think that is far worse than me being friends with a hireling boy.'

Again Norah didn't answer Celia but instead, as the church came into view, she called to Ellie and Sammy to tell them it was time to calm down and enter the church in a respectable manner.

There was no time to speak of this again for they were greeted by fellow parishioners as they approached the church.

It was much later, after the big roast dinner and apple pie and custard was eaten and the mountain of washing-up done, that Celia had time to think of Andy McCadden and where he would be that afternoon. She knew she would be in big trouble if it was ever discovered that she was slipping out to meet a man on her own and especially when that man was a hireling man.

Celia listened to the ticking of the clock and the settling of peat in the grate and she looked around at the others in the room. Her father was already snoring and her mother almost asleep. Tom had long gone, she could hear Dermot and the young ones playing football in the yard and Norah had finished her embroidery and was looking as bored as she was. Suddenly Celia felt stifled and a spirit of recklessness seemed to run all through her body and she leapt to her feet and said, 'I fancy a walk.'

'A walk,' repeated Peggy, jerked awake as if such a thing was beyond her understanding.

'Yes, a walk,' Celia said. 'It's such a nice day and a shame to spoil it staying inside. Are you coming with me, Norah?'

'Yes,' Peggy said, coming round to the idea. 'It will do the pair of you good. I used to walk miles at your age.'

Norah could hardly say then she didn't want to go, not without betraying Celia, because she was well aware that this was no innocent walk; she knew her sister well and her face was very expressive. However, she said nothing for she felt a little like a hypocrite because once she was in America and away from her parents and the insular Catholic community she intended to have as much fun as she could. Maybe then she shouldn't judge her sister for squeezing a bit of happiness out of life for herself. Nothing could come of it and, although Norah wanted no part in deceiving her parents, she knew she had to go along with Celia to make sure no harm came to her.

'So?' Norah said as they reached the lane.

'What do you mean, so?'

'Come on,' Norah said. 'I wasn't born yesterday and you have never suggested going for a walk before.'

'People can change you know. It isn't a crime.'

'Celia, stop playing games,' Norah said with a sigh of exasperation. 'Have you arranged to meet someone on this walk or haven't you?'

'All right,' Celia said. 'Nothing is arranged but Andy did say he fancied walking round Lough

Eske because Dinny told him how beautiful it was.'

'It very likely is,' Norah said. 'It's some time since I have been that way and I doubt it will have changed much?

'Well we'll soon see that for ourselves,' Celia said.

'Oh no we won't,' Norah said. 'Because that is the one place we must avoid at all costs.' And she stood stock still on the road.

'Why?'

'You shouldn't need to ask that.'

'Norah, you're the one that said I am too anxious to please,' Celia cried. 'And that I do things I might not want to do in case I upset people – and you're right. But sometimes you have to upset people for your own sake.'

Norah felt a bit guilty then for telling Celia what was expected of a farmer's daughter, for all it was true. 'All right,' she said. 'So what do you intend to do to stamp your independence?'

'I don't intend to do anything,' Celia said 'I mean I haven't got any sort of plan, but I will not let Daddy force me to marry a man he thinks is a good catch that I might not even like. And you said that means I have to meet other men and one of those who's very pleasant is Andy Mc-Cadden and I am going down to Lough Eske and if he is there we will walk together and talk and you can please yourself. And,' she went on as she saw her sister open her mouth, 'if you say one more time that he's a hireling man, like he is some lesser kind of human being, I will be very angry with you.'

'I wasn't going to say that,' Norah protested, running to keep up with her sister, who was making her way in the direction of Lough Eske at a tidy pace. 'I was going to say you don't know him.'

'I know enough,' Celia said. 'I know, as I told you, that his parents own a farm, which his older brother will inherit. Added to that there are two younger than him at home and his two older sisters were married this year, which was very expensive for their family, and so, knowing he would have to leave the farm anyway, eventually he decided to go sooner and not be a further burden for his family. I think that's quite enough to be going on with and anything else I wish to know I can ask him when and if we meet.'

'When did you find all that out?'

'Mainly when we were walking the bull up the lane,' Celia said.

'Well he's a quick worker I must say.'

'Norah, it wasn't like that,' Celia protested. 'Honestly, we were just making conversation. Why don't you take off your stuffy, disgruntled face and come and meet him? I'm sure if you judge him fairly you'll find him as pleasant as I do.'

Norah knew that she shouldn't agree to this. Not only should she refuse to see him, she should tell Celia not to be so foolish and either drag her away or, failing that, go home now and tell her parents of Celia's intentions. But she did none of these things and found herself nodding as she said, 'All right, I'll meet him, but I will make up my own mind about him and will be honest with you.'

51

That seemed to satisfy Celia but Norah went forward with some trepidation because, however nice this man might be, she knew it would all end in tears when it was discovered that Celia had met and walked and talked with a totally unsuitable man and one she had no sort of understanding with. And they were bound to be spotted – you couldn't sneeze in this place without everyone being aware of it – and she knew without doubt that that discovery would happen before either of them was very much older.

However, she was pleasantly surprised by Andy McCadden. It was easy to see why her sister had been so taken with him for not only was he incredibly handsome, he also had a pleasant disposition and was quite likeable in fact. His face took on a beam of happiness when he saw Celia, but he looked at Norah ruefully as he said, 'I am surprised to see you, Miss Mulligan, for I know you don't really approve of me.'

Norah didn't deny it but she qualified it by saying, 'It's nothing personal, Mr McCadden. It's just that we are farmer's daughters while you...'

'While I am just the hired help,' Andy said.

'Basically yes, that's it.'

Andy didn't speak for a moment, but looked across the lough before saying, 'Dinny and his wife were right about this place, it is very beautiful. Shall we take a turn around it?'

Both girls would rather that than stand in an uncomfortable silence but when Andy offered his arm to both women Norah hesitated, but eventually, seeing Celia had no qualms, she put a tentative arm through his. To cover her slight embarrassment she returned to the subject of the lough. 'In the spring it's beautiful right enough with the sun shining on the water and the reeds and rushes sighing in the breeze,' she said.

'I bet it's a different place in the winter though,' Celia said. 'All desolate and bleak.'

'Have you seen it that way yourself?'

Celia shook her head. 'I told you I have never been here, winter or summer, we hardly ever come here and I don't know why as it's on our doorstep.'

'Oh that's often the way things are,' Andy said.

'Celia says you came to Donegal from Killybegs looking for work?' Norah said. 'You didn't want to go further afield? England perhaps?'

'No,' Andy said. 'I mean, I might change my mind later, but at the moment Ireland serves me well enough and I do think it's incredibly beautiful.'

'So do I,' Celia said.

'But so dreadfully boring,' added Norah.

'Only in your opinion,' Celia retorted.

'Your sister tells me you want to go to America,' Andy said.

'Yes, that's true.'

'I'm told the situation is very different there,' Andy said. 'There is none of the outdated class system we have here and a man is judged for who he is rather than what he does and that goes for employment too.'

Norah knew that was true for Jim had said as much in one of his letters:

It's having a job that's praised here and a man who

53

works is respected, whether he waits on tables, or empties bins, or, is a shopkeeper or banker. No worker is looked down on.

'That is mainly true,' Norah said to Andy. 'My brother who is over there says a similar thing.'

'So then how can you feel the way you do about Andy just because he's a hired man and has no farm of his own?' Celia demanded.

'I feel that way because I don't live in America yet,' Norah retorted. 'And neither do you and like it or not you have to go with the culture of the place.'

'Even if you don't agree with it?'

'Even then.'

'Then how are things ever to change? How are we ever to be free?'

Norah sighed, 'All changes to life here come very slowly.'

'Like the mills of God,' Andy said. 'But eventually all people will see how constrained their lives are and change will begin to seep in.'

'D'you really think so?'

'I more than think,' Andy said. 'I know so. People's dissatisfaction will challenge the old order. In semi-remote areas like this it might take longer but it will happen regardless.'

'It won't change quickly enough for my parents to sanction you and Celia having any sort of friendship, never mind anything more.'

Andy nodded. 'I agree.'

'Well I don't,' burst out Celia. 'And stop talking about me as if I'm not here.'

'I was going to go on to say that I know if your

parents were aware that we were meeting and talking this way then they would be upset,' Andy said. 'They might be very angry and it may be that you have no wish to annoy your parents in that way. And if you really feel that, I will not press you and this will be the first and last time we'll meet this way.'

Celia chewed on her bottom lip. Once she had wondered if she could do something that her parents so strongly disapproved of, but that was before she had met Andy. If she told him to go now she would be behaving like a coward, letting someone else choose her future for her, and she thought of all the single farmers round and about and there was not one that had the slightest appeal for her. The thought of being married off to one of those without the least regard for how she felt about it did not fill her with joy. She intended to marry only for love, as she had already said to Norah, and in the meantime be friends with whoever she liked.

The silence had stretched out between them without her being aware of it as she walked along the side of the lake with thoughts tumbling about in her head and when she glanced at Andy she saw his face creased with concern and so she spoke firmly. 'As a child you try to please your parents, but as an adult, though you don't go out of your way to oppose them and make them cross and worried, you can't live your life just to please them because that might not be what you want to do. We get one crack at our future. Norah is spending hers in America and I want to spend mine here and find someone I could love enough to marry and so

I am going to continue to be friends with you because that is another thing I want to do.'

Andy wasn't totally happy with that because he was quite taken with Celia and had begun to hope that he might be the special one in her life. But for all her almost eighteen years, she was like an inexperienced infant in matters of the heart and he knew he had to tread very carefully so as not to scare her and so he squeezed her arm a little tighter and said, 'I'm pleased.'

Norah said nothing but feared for Celia, because despite the brave words she had never stood against her parents about anything. Everyone knew that Celia hated arguments and she wondered if her sister had the moral fibre to withstand the fallout from this.

But, then Norah reasoned that if she hadn't and if her sister caved in as soon as her father found out, forbade her to go on with it as she knew he would, Celia would in all probability say a tearful farewell to Andy McCadden. And if she was upset, then she would get over it and it would be the best solution all round – and anyway by that time Norah would be in America and away from all the unpleasantness.

So, working on the assumption that the little chaste affair would be discovered and stopped sooner rather than later, she declared herself on their side. Celia was delighted. 'What changed your mind?'

'You did,' Norah said simply. 'For what you said made sense and I think marriage is hard enough without being chained for life to someone you actively dislike – and that could happen.'

56

'What about you saying I should do my duty like Tom?'

'Well I never said you should. I just thought you would go ahead with any plans Daddy may have for you because you have never defied him before. But you have said you will only marry for love, so stick out for that.'

'What about Tom?'

'Tom will inherit,' Norah said. 'So it's his job to marry suitably and, if they love each other as well, that's a bonus for them both.'

'It all seems very clinical,' Celia said.

'It probably is a bit,' Andy said. 'But even if the words aren't actually spoken they're understood. My brother Chris knows what he must do too.'

'Do you regret not being the eldest?' Norah asked.

'I did,' Andy admitted. 'But then I got to thinking about it and I've got more freedom being the second son, freedom to go where I choose and marry who I choose and when I want as well and not at my father's urging.'

'Oh I can see that,' Celia said. 'And my brother Jim seems happy enough. I mean, Tom might have liked to go to America as well, but I doubt he would have been let go, at least not without a fight.'

'I'll be happy enough when I get there as well,' Norah said. 'Can't come quick enough for me. And just for now we shall have to get back fairly soon, so if we are going to walk around the lake we shall have to put our back into it.'

And they did and later, as they made their way home, Norah acknowledged what good company

Andy McCadden was and thought it a damned shame that it couldn't work out between him and her sister.

FOUR

Six more weeks passed. Easter came and went and Celia turned eighteen and the relationship between Celia and Andy blossomed. Celia dreamed of Andy almost every night and woke with a smile on her face and at odd moments throughout the day his face would float into her mind and a warm glow would fill her being. Celia often wondered if she was falling in love with Andy, but she wasn't sure. She thought it odd that, though it was the thing often sung about and written about and all, no one explained how you would feel and it wasn't a question you could ask of anyone, least of all Norah. But Celia was well aware that life without Andy would be much bleaker and lonelier and more especially so when Norah sailed for America when she imagined it might be harder to see him as often.

She trembled when she imagined her father's rage when he found out about their relationship and yet he had to know because she hated meeting Andy in secret. In fact she seldom met him at all in the week for they both had jobs to do and their absence would be noticed, but every Saturday she and Norah would make for the town with the list of things their mother wanted and always meet Andy on a similar errand for the Fitzgeralds and they would take a turn about the town together and, though Norah was there too, she often would take an interest in a shop window or have a chat with some of her old friends and let them wander off together.

Andy was always grateful at her doing this, though he too hated the subterfuge and from the first had wanted to call on Celia's father and ask for his permission to walk out with her, but Norah and Celia had begged him not to. But as each day passed, Celia was becoming more and more important to him and he had seen the love light in her eyes when she looked at him, though he had never touched her, much as he wanted to, for he couldn't bring himself to until it was known to her family.

But, oh, how he longed to hold her hand as they walked the town, or take her in a tight embrace and give her a kiss – not a proper kiss for he imagined that would frighten the life out of her – but just to put his lips on her little rosebud mouth would do for now. The dance that she came to with Norah every week, when she danced virtually every dance with him, was the only time he could legitimately hold her in his arms and it simply wasn't enough any more.

And that is what he told Celia that Saturday. 'You mean one hell of a lot to me, Celia, and I want to declare that, not conduct some sort of hole-in-a-corner affair.'

'And what if we tell my father and he forbids me to see you as well he might and you know that.'

'Then you must talk to him,' Andy said. 'He will

hardly prevent you from seeing me physically.'

Celia had never seen her father raise his hand to any of them and even when he had a drink he was a happy drunk, not a violent or nasty one, and so she shook her head. 'I think that highly unlikely.'

'Well there you are then, and remember we're doing nothing wrong and it would be better you tell him rather than he finds it out from someone else.'

'Yes,' Celia said, knowing Andy was right, and added, 'Norah thinks it a wonder he hasn't been told already.'

And Norah was totally amazed because people must have seen them walking around the town on Saturday and at the dances. Tom might have had his eyes dazzled by Sinead McClusky, but there were plenty of others who would have seen the way Andy McCadden monopolised Celia and that she seemed to be agreeable to this. Then there was the way she lingered after Mass for a word or sometimes, if the girls were walking together, having been sent on ahead to prepare the breakfast, Andy would join them on the road, out of view of the church. Norah could see that the presence of Andy McCadden with the two Mulligan girls caused great curiosity from the people in the cottages they passed, though they were all greeted as normal, and then in their Sunday jaunts they often passed people on the road taking the air too and she couldn't understand why no one seemingly had had a word with their parents about it.

However, that day the girls hadn't long reached the house when Dan arrived in a raging mood.

He had been in the town himself, having wheel rims replaced on the cart, and he had gone into the pub for a pint while the job was done and what he had been told there had caused fury to rise in him so that for a few moments he saw black before his eyes. The poor carthorse, Bess, had never been driven home at such a speed and it didn't do the new wheel trims on the cart any good either, rumbling so quickly over the rutted lane. However, Dan seemed not to care about that or anything else. Neither Tom nor Dermot had seen their father in such a tear and it was Tom, watching his father jerk the horse to a stop in front of the house, who said, 'What's up?'

'You'll know soon enough,' Dan answered grimly. 'See to the horse.' And so saying he bounded, up the steps and shut the door behind him with such force it juddered on its hinges.

'Whew,' Dermot said as he led the sweating horse towards the barn. 'Someone's for the high jump.'

Tom thought it was probably Norah who'd done something because even before this business with America she had been a bit wild, not like Celia who seldom put a foot wrong.

He would have been surprised then if he had seen that after ordering Celia upstairs Dan followed her up and pushed her into her bedroom. He faced her across the room. He was breathing heavily and Celia noted that his face was purple with rage and a pulse was beating in his temple as he almost spat out; 'Now I want the truth. Is there some sort of carry-on between you and Fitzgerald's hireling?'

61

Celia had never seen her father like this and she was nervous. The scathing way her father had said 'Fitzgerald's hireling' caused her heart to feel heavy, as if there was a lump of lead in it, and her voice trembled as she spoke. 'It's not some kind of carry-on, Daddy. We just meet and talk sometimes.'

'A lot of times from what I hear.'

'Not that many,' Celia said. 'And we are not doing anything wrong. We've just been talking, that's all, and most times Norah has been there.'

'Yes and she will get the rough edge of my tongue as well,' Dan said. 'She should have told me what was going on for I spoke to men today who have passed you walking with the hireling on Sunday afternoon on one of the walks you suddenly took such an interest in. You say you're doing nothing wrong, when you have wilfully deceived your parents to meet a man you knew I would heartily disapprove of.'

'How can you disapprove of the man?' Celia cried helplessly. 'You don't even know him. His family had a farm too but he was the second son like Jim and, not having a handy relative in America, he is having to make his own way in the world. It's not fair to be so against him.'

'I don't care how fair you think it is,' Dan said. 'Anyway, he is some man to go behind my back like this.'

'He wanted to tell you,' Celia said. 'He wanted to ask your permission to walk out with me, but I stopped him. I was afraid you would stop us seeing one another.'

'Well you were right there,' Dan said. 'For from

now on you will have nothing more to do with this man.'

'Oh no, Daddy,' Celia cried, covering her face with her hands while tears trickled down her cheeks from eyes filled with sadness.

'Oh yes, Daddy,' Dan mocked scathingly. 'You just think yourself lucky that I am not a violent man for I know many would horse-whip their daughters for behaviour like this, but I will lock you up if you disobey me, for until you are twenty-one you are under my jurisdiction.'

Celia had never been scared of her father before, but she was now, so scared that she felt her knees knocking together. But then Andy's lovely face filled her mind and she remembered her sister saying that their father could make life difficult for her if she opposed him. But what harm was she doing being friendly with Andy McCadden? So she lifted her head, which she had initially hung in shame, and faced her father and in a voice she willed not to tremble she said, 'I don't think you are being just at all here, Daddy. The only thing I have done that is wrong was deceive you and I did that to prevent you doing this and forbidding me to talk to someone who is a neighbour to us and who has shown both myself and Norah nothing but pleasantness. And yet you resent him out of hand, all because he is a hired man.'

'Yes and as such he is nothing to you.'

Now Celia was more angry than fearful and she said, 'Andy McCadden is a fine man and yet you choose to look down on him because of an accident of birth, a man you know nothing of.'

'I know enough to know he won't be earning

63

enough to provide for you and any family you might have.'

'Daddy, I'm not suggesting marrying Andy McCadden,' Celia declared, though she crossed her fingers behind her back because she knew she was fast becoming very, very fond of him. 'I don't want to marry anyone just now and Norah is always with me when we meet.'

'Then how is it,' Dan asked, 'that I was told that just this morning the pair of you were waltzing across the Diamond side by side with no sign of Norah?'

'I was with Norah,' Celia protested. 'If you ask her she will tell you the same, but she met an old school friend as we were crossing the town and stopped to have a chat. If whoever told you had watched a bit longer he would have seen Norah join us after a few minutes.'

'That apart, Celia,' Dan said, 'surely to God I don't have to tell you how unseemly it is for two young girls to walk unchaperoned with a man we know little or nothing about. I thought at least you knew how to conduct yourself respectably.'

'I am respectable,' Celia said. 'We were only talking. You said we know nothing about him and we didn't but we are finding out.'

'What he was or is or does is nothing to do with you,' Dan said. 'And as for talking to him and referring to him in that familiar way... Well here's an end to it. You are never to see or speak to this man again.' Celia gave a gasp, but her father hadn't finished. 'And I want your solemn word that you will not defy me in this.'

Tears were trickling down Celia's cheeks, but

she remembered Norah saying that often fathers decided the future of their daughters and so her voice was unusually firm as she said, 'You can forbid all the friendships you like, Daddy, and as you said I must do as you say until I am twenty-one, but one thing I will say, and it won't matter how old I am, I will marry for love or not at all.'

'Do you know who you are speaking to?'

Celia gave a defiant toss of her auburn locks as she said, 'Yes, I know. And I also know neither you nor anyone else can make me marry a man I do not want to marry.'

Dan was stunned for this was not the compliant, easy-going girl not long from childhood that he had thought her, but a determined young woman that knew her own mind and that fact had been made even more apparent when she refused to give her word not to see and speak to Andy McCadden again.

'Then,' Dan said, 'I must lock you in while I tell your mother what has been happening.'

Celia stared at her father in shock, not sure she had heard right, but her father meant every word and he closed the door firmly. She heard the key turn in the lock with a grating noise then his footsteps were going down the stairs and she had the urge to hammer on the door. She was proud of herself for not giving in to that, but as she gazed at the locked door a sudden sense of desolation swept over her and she threw herself on the bed and cried, broken-hearted, muffling the sound in her pillow.

Downstairs they were all waiting for Dan in the

kitchen, but he shooed Ellie and Sammy outside, for what he had to say was not for their ears, and he told the others what Celia had said, and it implicated Norah too for she had known and said nothing.

'I am disappointed with you,' Peggy said. 'You were the elder and it was up to you to turn her from this foolishness.'

'I'm really sorry,' Norah said.

'Is there any more light you can shed on this?' Dan asked her.

Norah was determined to say nothing further that would get Celia into more trouble and so she shook her head as she said, 'No, it's just as Celia said. We'd meet Mr McCadden sometimes and talk and that's all.'

Peggy knew Norah wasn't telling them everything and so she looked at her sadly. 'How could you do this?'

'I've said I'm sorry and I am,' Norah said. 'But I honestly didn't see much harm in it.'

'Not much harm in it,' Peggy repeated. 'Well we will agree to differ on that and I'm glad at least that you are sorry for your part in it, but you won't be half as sorry as you will be when I write to Aunt Maria and tell her about your part in all this.'

'Must you do that?'

'Indeed I must,' Peggy said firmly. 'She might decide she doesn't want a lying, deceitful girl living in her house.'

Norah saw her wonderful future slipping through her fingers. 'But, Mammy,' she cried. 'I haven't lied and I only deceived you by not telling you about Mr McCadden and I am truly sorry about that.'

'You know more than you are telling,' Peggy said. 'And, unless you are honest and tell us everything about the relationship between Celia and that man, I would say you can kiss America goodbye.'

Norah bit her lip for she knew that the way her mother would write such a letter would cast her in the worst light possible and Aunt Maria might easily say that she wouldn't take on the responsibility of such a bold and wilful girl. Suddenly she was angry with Celia, for she had told her from the beginning not to get involved with a hireling man and the fact that she had ignored that advice meant that her own future was now in jeopardy.

And yet she hated letting her sister down but her father was relentless in his interrogation of her and eventually the story was dragged out of her and they heard that it really began from the day Andy McCadden came with the bull and put it in Celia's head to go to the dance in the town that night. Reluctantly she told him of McCadden buying Celia a drink when Norah had left her unattended and that later her sister had danced with him. When she mentioned the last waltz she heard her father's teeth grind together.

'And where were you when this was going on?' Dan asked Tom, fixing him with a steely glare.

Tom looked a bit sheepish. 'I don't know,' he said. 'I noticed nothing untoward. I was with Sinead a lot.'

'Well, I'm surprised at you, Tom,' Peggy said. 'I expected you to look after your sisters better than that, Celia in particular.'

'Why didn't you tell me?' Tom demanded of Norah.

Norah sighed. 'Didn't want to get her into trouble I suppose,' she said and added, 'I did try talking to her about it.'

'But she didn't listen?'

Norah shook her head. 'She got worse,' she said. 'The next time she danced nearly every dance with Mr McCadden. The other men who might have wanted a dance with her never stood a chance. And it was at the first dance they arranged to meet on Sunday afternoon at Lough Eske.'

And then, because it hardly mattered now for she knew with dread certainty Celia's goose was well and truly cooked, as she had expected, it all came out about meeting Andy every Sunday afternoon and meeting him in town most Saturday mornings as well as attending the dances and even about the times he met them on the road going home from Mass.

'It's a catalogue of deception that's what it is,' Dan said angrily. 'Fine respect that is showing her parents. I bet everyone knows about this and I've been made a laughing stock and the only thing I am surprised about is that I wasn't told of it sooner.'

Norah was too, though she said nothing. She thought it better to keep a low profile and anyway her father was saying, 'The thing to decide now is what are we going to do about it and I will have to give that some thought. And meanwhile Celia will stay locked in the bedroom,' he said and then he glared at Norah as he said, 'And I want no one creeping up the stairs to talk to her and, Norah,

68

you keep Ellie and Sammy away too.'

'I will, Daddy,' Norah promised. 'And I'll not go near Celia, never fear.' She didn't want to face Celia because she felt she had let her down, though she didn't see what else she could have done when the news had leaked out anyway.

It was a few hours later in the byre as they were milking the cows that Dan said to Tom, 'That hireling man has got to be dealt with for I had sort of semi-promised Celia to Johnnie Cassidy.'

And although it was Tom he had spoken to, it was the appalled voice of Dermot that answered, 'You can't have promised Celia to him. Christ, Daddy, he's an old man.'

'When I want advice from you I'll ask for it,' Dan snapped. 'Till then hold your tongue. And what have I said to you about taking the Lord's name in vain? You're not too old for a good hiding and don't you forget it.'

Dermot was silent and though his face was red with embarrassment at being reprimanded his eyes still smouldered defiantly and Tom, hoping to deflect his father's anger, because he could understand how astounded his young brother had been, said, 'Dermot's right though, Daddy. Johnnie's a nice enough fellow but a bit long in the tooth. He must be over twenty years older than Celia.'

Dan nodded. 'Twenty-three,' he admitted. 'But it's a young wife he's after, one young enough to bear him plenty of sons that will help him when the farm work gets too much for him and one of his blood to take over after his day, otherwise he says it goes to some nephew in New York that he

69

has never met that hasn't been once to see the place he might well inherit.'

'Even so,' Tom said. 'That young wife needn't be Celia.'

'I doubt it will be now,' Dan said glumly. 'Before this business Celia was easy-going and eager to please, little more than a child, and I'm sure I could have convinced her it was for the best. We'd not lose by it once she agreed to marry him for he was giving us two fields almost adjoining ours and a gift of two pregnant cows when they married. He had a great fancy for our Celia.'

I bet he had, Tom thought but kept that to himself and instead said, 'You think she might still be persuaded if McCadden was off the scene?'

Dan shook his head. 'She says not. Says she'll only marry for love. Did you ever hear such foolishness?'

Tom lowered his head as he smiled for he was well aware of his father's views on 'love' and yet he was pretty sure he loved Sinead and she certainly loved him, but he'd hate to be forced or coerced into marrying someone he couldn't stand. No wonder Celia had said what she did. And yet it would never do for her to marry a hireling boy.

'What do you intend to do?' Tom asked his father.

'Get rid of McCadden for starters.'

'And how do you intend to do that?'

'Bribe him.'

'Bribe him?' Tom repeated and Dermot's mouth dropped open.

'Every man has his price,' Dan said. 'Tonight I

70

intend to waylay McCadden as he makes his way to the dance and ask him what is his price to go far away from here for good and make no effort to contact my daughter.'

'D'you think he will agree?'

'We'll see,' Dan said. 'But it will be the worse for him if he refuses because if he won't go by peaceful means, then he might have to be persuaded in other ways.'

The alarmed eyes of Dermot met those of his older brother, who had heard of the wild man his father had been in his youth, though that had been years ago. Now his father was known as an easy-going, even-tempered man and, though he was quite a strict disciplinarian, before this business Tom would have said that he was seldom unjust, never mind violent. And yet maybe any father might be moved to violence when his daughter's future was at stake. But it might never come to that, Tom told himself, for surely the man would take the money and run and that would be the last they would hear of him.

'And you,' Dan said to Dermot as he prepared to take the cows back to the field. 'You heard none of this, you hear?'

Dermot nodded. 'I won't say a word.'

'See that you don't,' Dan growled.

Dan began leading the cows across the yard. Tom smiled reassuringly at Dermot and heard him give an almost imperceptible sigh of relief, as they started to clean out the byre.

That evening Dan allowed Celia to come out of her room to eat the meal with them and an extremely uncomfortable meal it was, for she was well aware that her, father and mother were still greatly displeased and disappointed with her. That did upset her because they had never even been cross with her before and the little conversation they had was stilted and unnatural and even the younger children picked up on the atmosphere and were quieter than usual.

Norah knew there would be no dance for her or Celia that night, in fact Dan had told Celia he had an errand out that evening, which shouldn't take long, and she was not to leave the house for any reason in his absence. Celia had just nodded and so Dan barked out, 'You hear what I said?'

'Yes, Daddy.'

'And I have your word on that?'

This time there was slight hesitation and then Celia nodded again. 'Yes, you have my word.'

Dan knew Celia wouldn't break her word. In that way she had always been trustworthy and so he nodded, satisfied, as Peggy asked, 'What errand have you to make?'

'Ask me no questions and I will tell you no lies,' Dan replied and Celia knew exactly who he was going to see and she regretted giving her word to him for she knew he was going to see Andy McCadden and she had no way of warning him. Dermot knew where he was going as well, but he'd been charged with secrecy so when Celia asked in an urgent whisper, 'Has Daddy gone to see Andy tonight? Is that his errand?' he shrugged and said, 'Don't know.'

Later Tom went upstairs to change for he had to see the McCluskys, and Sinead in particular, and explain things and Dan went to him in the bedroom. 'Don't discuss this with Sinead and her family.'

'I wouldn't do that,' Tom promised, knowing how much his father hated family business being told outside of the family. 'I'll think up some excuse to satisfy her and her parents, but I must tell her something. We'll more than likely go for a walk then, for the evening's a fine one. I couldn't trust myself at the dance tonight anyway for if I saw McCadden I'd want to push my fist down his throat.'

'I know,' Dan said. 'But there'll be no need for any of that if he takes the money as I'm sure he will.'

After his father had left to waylay McCadden, Dermot sidled into the scullery where the girls were washing up. He knew it was his only chance to talk to them, with Tom and his father out of the way and his mother washing Sammy and Ellie in the big tin bath in the kitchen, where they were making a lot of noise about it. He said to Celia, 'I know why Daddy was so mad at you making eyes at McCadden.'

'I was not making eyes at McCadden,' Celia protested.

'Ssh,' Norah cautioned as Dermot said airily, 'Oh you know what I mean and it was because he had someone already lined up for you.'

'What did I tell you?' Norah said, but Celia ignored her and said to Dermot, 'Do you know who it was?'

'You bet I do,' Dermot said. 'It was Johnnie Cassidy, old Johnnie Cassidy, and I tried telling

Daddy he was too old for you and got my head bitten off.'

Celia seemed too shocked to speak She seemed unaware that her mouth was open and her lips pulled back in distaste as Norah cried, 'I'll say he's too old. It's almost obscene.'

'I heard Daddy say that he's twenty-three years older than you, Celia,' Dermot said. 'And he's after a young wife that will bear him plenty of strong sons that will help him on the farm as he gets older.'

'Yes,' Norah said in clipped tones. 'You'd have the body pulled out of you with a baby born every year and when your child-bearing years were gone you'd have an old, maybe senile man to care for as well as a houseful of children to cook for and clean after and you would be expected to help on the farm as well. If you married him, your life would effectively be over and you would be an old woman before you had a chance to be a young one.'

Celia gave a shiver at the thought, but answered firmly enough. 'That isn't going to happen because I am not marrying that man. I barely know him, for heaven's sake, and I have no wish to know a man old enough to be my father. I told Daddy I will only marry for love and I stick by that.'

'When you said that to me I said Daddy might make life difficult for you,' Norah warned.

Celia tossed her titian curls with defiance, though her heart trembled at the thought of unleashing her father's anger if she continued to stand against him. She still maintained though, 'He can't force me to marry someone I don't

74

want to marry.'

'No,' Norah conceded. 'But what are you going to do?'

'Why have I got to do anything?' Celia asked.

'Well I suppose you want to marry someday?'

'Probably.'

'Well who will it be?' Norah asked. 'And don't say Andy McCadden because I think we can take Daddy's reaction to mean he will never agree to that. And don't think after this you will be let go to the dances any more to choose someone more suitable. When I go to America it will be worse.'

'When I'm twenty-one I can do as I please,' Celia said. 'You said that.'

Norah nodded. 'It's three years away,' she said. 'But if you stick it out you can marry who you like – even your hireling boy, if that's who you want – but Daddy might say that he doesn't want to see you again, might disown you if you do. Would you be prepared for that?'

Celia gasped for she had never imagined being banished from her home and yet she could see it happening if her father was angry enough. Once he had made a decision that was that and he usually couldn't be shifted, though Peggy could sometimes coax him into a more reasonable response.

Celia loved her father and though she knew he was quite strict, it was what she was used to. His attitude to discipline had never affected her because she had given him no reason to censure her, for she had always done as she was told and until now had never answered back either.

Dermot could say nothing, but he wished he

could tell Norah that soon McCadden would be out of their lives, for he had no doubt that the man would accept the money his father would offer him and be on his way. Celia would undoubtedly be upset at first, but she would get over it and, with McCadden out of the way, she would be able to socialise more and meet suitable men, that weren't in their dotage. Then their father might be willing to accept one of them as a son-in-law and Johnnie Cassidy would have to look elsewhere for a wife.

However, he wouldn't dare say any of this. He had said enough in telling them the name of the man their father had marked down for Celia and that had only been because he wanted her prepared.

Suddenly, Celia said, 'Everyone goes on about respecting our parents. But I don't think it is respecting us very much, mapping out the only future we'll have to the extent of even telling us who to marry, and like you said before, Norah, it's usually for their good, not ours. Dermot, what will Daddy get if I was to marry Johnnie Cassidy?'

Dermot gave an ironic grin as he said, 'Two fallow fields and two pregnant cows.'

Celia covered her face with her hands for the proposal was preposterous enough to be funny. 'So that's my bridal price,' she said. 'Two fields and two cows. Huh, I'd say he was getting me cheap. If I married him at eighteen I could easily give him a dozen children before I was totally worn out and I'd say a fair few of them would be the boys he craves.'

'And he'll get a nurse to tend him in his old age

too,' Norah said. 'He wins hands down, I'd say.'

'Well Daddy can do what he likes, but I won't agree to that,' Celia said almost fiercely. 'Just at the moment I am happy as I am and I have no desire to marry anyone.'

'Don't blame you,' Norah said. 'And all I can advise you to do is stick to your guns.'

FIVE

Dan was late coming home that night, so late that Peggy was the only one up, for he'd gone to the McCluskys' house after his meeting with McCadden, knowing Tom would be there. He was welcomed warmly for the two families were friends and might soon be related for, though Tom hadn't proposed to Sinead, they all knew that it was only a matter of time till he did. There would be no obstacles to their marriage for Dan and Peggy thought the world of Sinead and her parents thought Tom a fine figure of a man, who could well provide for their daughter for he would inherit the farm. And so they sat and chatted easily together though they never discussed the problem of Celia forming an unsuitable relationship with Andy McCadden until Tom and Dan had left the house and were on the road home. When Dan told his son what had transpired that evening Tom looked at him in amazement. 'He refused the money?'

Dan nodded his head. 'He did. He said he was

settled here, that he had a job he enjoyed and had no intention of moving just because his face didn't fit with me.'

'How much did you offer him?'

'Fifteen pounds.'

'God, Daddy, that's a fortune,' Tom said. 'Not many people would pass that up.'

'Well he did,' Dan said. 'Said if I offered him four times that amount he wouldn't leave because he didn't want to. Mind, don't tell your mother this or I'll never hear the end of it.'

Tom smiled because his father spoke the truth. 'I won't say a word, never fear,' he said. 'But did McCadden say anything else?'

'Oh, yes,' Dan said. 'When I told him to stay away from my daughter he said he meant her no harm, but they liked each other and at her age she should be able to choose friends for herself.'

'Arrogant young pup,' Tom said. 'He certainly needs teaching a lesson.'

'He'll get one, don't worry,' Dan said. 'But I've been thinking about this and I know in the long run I won't be able to keep them apart if they are determined to meet. I can't police Celia every hour of the day and if McCadden really won't go from here nor agree not to see Celia, then for her own good Celia must go.'

'Go?' Tom repeated. 'Go where?'

'America,' Dan said. 'That's far enough away to keep her out of his clutches. I just need to convince your mother that that is the only workable plan if we are to keep her safe.'

Tom was quite shaken that his father proposed sending Celia away. Knowing how much his sister loved Ireland, and that she had never expressed any wish to go anywhere else, he had thought she would always be there, and he said, 'Daddy, it's one hell of a trek for Celia to make, especially as she won't want to go, doesn't want to leave Ireland really.'

'Well if McCadden won't do the decent thing and go from here and keep away from Celia then I have no choice but this,' Dan said. 'Maria will make certain she makes an advantageous marriage over there and to hell with whether she loves the man or not.'

'What about Norah?' Tom asked. 'She has her heart set on America. Are they to go together?'

'No,' Dan said. 'She will have to put aside any ridiculous idea of going to America now. She only has herself to blame for she colluded with Celia in this relationship. If she had told me in the beginning I could have nipped it in the bud before it got out of hand.'

Tom knew his young sister would be devastated but knew it was no good saying that to his father and so he said, 'Well I know one who'll be pleased that Norah isn't going to America anyway and that's Joseph O'Leary.'

'Well that's another thing that does me no favours,' Dan said. 'For she treated that man disgracefully. His father spoke to me about it for when she told Joseph she was definitely going to America he was terribly cut up, because he said they were walking out together. He thought they had some sort of understanding.'

'Aye, most people did.'

'And then he finds she hadn't taken it seriously

at all. I mean, she made a complete fool of the man.'

'Aye she has,' Tom agreed. 'I've felt sorry for him at times.'

'Well if she's staying here she will have to have him in the end,' Dan said. 'I'd say it will be Joseph O'Leary or no one, for none of the other men will likely have anything to do with her.'

Tom shook his head. 'They've seen the way she has treated Joseph and between you and me she is known as a tease. I didn't bother taking her to task about it because I thought she would soon be off to America.'

'Maybe even Joseph won't want her after all.'

'Oh he will,' Tom said with assurance. 'He's mad about her still.'

'We'll say nothing to her about this now for I know she will be upset,' Dan said as the farmhouse came into view and added, 'One contrary daughter is enough to cope with just at the moment.'

Tom took himself straight to bed when they arrived home and Dan was glad because he wanted to talk to Peggy on her own and he told her that he'd talked to McCadden whom he had met on the road. He said nothing of the money offered but did tell her of McCadden's reaction when he'd asked him to keep away from Celia. Peggy could see the problem, but couldn't immediately agree that the best solution was to send Celia away. She knew she wouldn't want to go to America whereas Norah did, so both would be distraught. She also felt Celia was too young and naïve to cross the

Atlantic all by herself. Norah, on the other hand, was older and more emotionally mature.

'Couldn't we let Celia marry this hireling man if she is so set on it and help them out with money and all till they're on their feet?'

'Oh so you would throw your daughter away like that, would you?' Dan sneered contemptuously. 'The man is a hired help and that's all he will ever be. He will never be able to provide for Celia properly and I will be the laughing stock of the place, letting her throw her life away on the likes of him.'

Peggy thought she would rather suffer the ridicule of the townsfolk than kiss Celia goodbye knowing she would never see her again. But she saw with a sinking heart that Dan's mind was made up and she was used to giving way to him for it was the only thing to do and so when he said, 'I want you to write directly to Maria and ask her to send the ticket as speedily as possible,' she nodded her head and turned away so that he shouldn't see her tears.

The next morning Norah saw the letter addressed to her Aunt Maria in her mother's hand and her heart sang for joy because she knew it was to ask her to send the ticket to America, where her life would really begin. Celia didn't see the letter sent and did wonder what her father was going to do to her for he wasn't one to let anything drop.

Walking to Mass, Celia was flanked between her parents and neither spoke a word to her. She was allowed to speak to no one at all, either before or after Mass, and though she was aware of Andy

McCadden sitting across the aisle, next to Mr and Mrs Fitzgerald, she kept her head lowered.

Andy had seen Celia's white face though and her saddened eyes, but didn't know if there was any way of easing the situation for her and for the first time he wondered if it would be better to leave as her father asked him to. He didn't want the money and the only reason he would consider leaving was if it would make life easier for Celia. It would hurt like hell, but it was obvious she wouldn't be allowed to even acknowledge him and he could only guess what the situation was like at home. Maybe he should just take off and that might at least give her a chance to find some other man that her irascible father might accept more readily. However, just the thought of leaving and settling someplace else and never seeing Celia again caused his heart to miss a beat and his stomach to give a sickening lurch. He told himself firmly he hadn't to think of himself but Celia; he had to give her the chance of a future of sorts and he imagined his heart would mend in time.

Dermot watched Andy McCadden's face and wondered what he was still doing there, for he thought he'd be well gone. He concluded in the end that he probably hadn't wanted to leave Dinny Fitzgerald in the lurch and so had agreed to stay on for a while until he got someone else. Still, he would be gone soon, he thought with relief, and life would return to normal and his father would not be going round constantly like a bear with a very sore head.

There was no conversation as Dan marched his wife and daughter home that morning and an almost silent breakfast was over before he said, 'You will wash up now with Norah and then you will be locked in your room until dinner. No one will fetch and carry for you so you can come down for meals and help Norah to clear away afterwards, but that is all. The rest of the time you will be locked in your room.'

Norah looked at her sister's stricken face and shot her a look of sympathy as Celia faced her father and said, 'How long for? You can't keep me locked up for ever.'

Dan gave a growl of anger. 'Don't you tell me what I can and can't do,' he said. 'You'll push me too far, my girl. I'm angry enough at the moment to give you the whipping you deserve and if you annoy me further I might do just that.'

Looking at her father's face, Celia knew he meant every word and thought it best to keep quiet – for now.

The worst thing about being incarcerated was the boredom. Peggy brought her work box up on Monday morning and a pile of mending and said she might as well make herself useful. Celia wouldn't have minded any amount of mending if she'd had company, but they'd all been forbidden to talk to her and that more than anything drained her spirit. After nearly a week of this she was a changed person. She had no hope for the future and as one day followed another she lost all interest in life outside her room, and although she could see spring, her favourite season, unfolding in the farm beyond her windows, it seemed to have nothing to do with her.

She lost any interest in food for she found it hard to eat. Family meals were conducted almost in silence for even Ellie and Sammy, both picking up the atmosphere, seemed constrained and didn't chatter as they used to; any conversation attempt seemed awkward and strained. Celia would feel her parents' reproach that lay heavy on her heart. Her father's every remark to her was delivered in a cold, curt way and although her mother's voice was softer, her sighs and the sorrowful look in her eyes made Celia feel guilty for she knew, she had caused her mother to be so sad. Norah felt immensely sorry for her sister for she hated to see her suffer so and knew she would be glad when the ticket arrived and she was on her way. Every time she thought of that frissons of excitement ran down her spine, which she tried to hide from Celia, for no such thrilling future was beckoning her.

Dan had decided that he and Tom would collar McCadden on his way to the dance on Saturday and teach him a lesson and so Tom headed up to Sinead's house on Friday evening as he doubted he would be seeing her on Saturday. It was much later, as he was on his way back, that he met Joseph O'Leary, also making for his home, and he saw straight away that the man had had a skinful, a state he had got into a number of times since Norah had told him she was definitely going to America.

Joseph greeted Tom, lifting his hand in a wave so that he overbalanced and would have fallen if Tom hadn't caught him. 'Here, man, you need to steady up.'

Joseph's voice was thick and slightly slurred. 'Why?' he said belligerently. 'Nothing to steady up for.'

'Norah's not the only pretty girl around.'

'She's the only one I want,' Joseph maintained. 'Would you have me settle for second best?'

Tom didn't answer for there was nothing for him to say, but he felt guilty that his sister's callous treatment of this man had reduced him to a sot for they were friends, despite the differences in their ages. So when he added, 'Every day that passes is one more day nearer the time that Norah will board that ship and sail away and I will never see her again,' Tom felt a bolt of sympathy for the man as he looked into his pain-filled eyes and he made a decision that he was to realise later was not a very sensible one, because he said, 'You can cheer up, Joseph, because Norah will not be going to America after all.'

Tom's words made Joseph stagger again and he desperately tried to focus on Tom's face and the words spilled from his mouth as he snapped out, 'Now what you on about?'

Immediately, Tom realised his error. You don't tell a drunken man something you don't want to be made public knowledge yet. However, the damage was done now and just maybe Joseph was too drunk to remember anything about it, so he said, 'It's true. Mammy sent for the ticket right enough but, though Norah doesn't know yet, it's for Celia.'

'Celia told me once she never wanted to leave Ireland.'

'She probably doesn't,' Tom said. 'But ... look, it

85

will probably be public knowledge soon enough anyway: Celia has got herself involved with someone unsuitable.'

'If you're talking about Fitzgerald's farm hand, that's news to no one who was at the dances and saw them together,' Joseph said.

'Wish someone had thought to tell me.'

'Well,' Joseph said, 'I shouldn't go blaming other folk if I was you, because you were usually otherwise engaged. You should really have seen it for yourself.'

Tom felt guilty that he had been too involved in his own affairs and so been neglectful of his sisters, but Joseph wanted to focus on only one thing. 'Are you sure Norah isn't going to the States?'

'Positive sure,' Tom said. 'To keep Celia from this man's clutches she is being sent away whether she likes it or not.'

'Norah will be upset.'

Tom nodded. 'She will indeed and angry too, I shouldn't wonder, but she'll get over it, people have to cope with disappointment. And then when she is over the worst of it, you can move in and comfort her, like.'

Joseph had a beam plastered across his face and Tom said urgently, 'It's important that you keep this to yourself for now. It's important Norah doesn't get to know just yet, so keep everything I have told you under your hat, all right?'

'All right,' Joseph said happily. 'I can wait for the main prize.'

They parted company there and Tom had a frown on his face as he watched Joseph staggering home, humming a little ditty to himself, and wished wholeheartedly that he had kept his big mouth shut.

The following day it was afternoon before Norah went into town because once the breakfast dishes were washed Celia was once again locked in the bedroom and it took Norah longer to do the jobs she had always shared with Celia in the past. On the way to town she ruminated on her sister's plight and decided she wouldn't have her sister's life for all the tea in China as she thought of her living her days out in that rural backwater. It was a desperate situation altogether.

She missed her sister's company and she knew Celia missed hers and sometimes cried in bed, though she muffled the sounds as best she could because of Ellie. Norah would put her arms around her, but there were no words she could say that would make things better so she didn't try, just held her tight. Celia had always been a bit on the thin side, but Norah was aware now how bony and delicate her sister was becoming and she seemed dispirited and lethargic. Eventually she told her mother that it was detrimental to Celia's health to leave in her room every day, but knew, even as she spoke, she might as well have saved her breath because she knew her mother would not go against anything their father said.

The walk to town that afternoon seemed longer without Celia to chat to and Norah hurried along, anxious to get the things her mother wanted quickly and get back home again.

Joseph was leaving Paddy McIvor's pub when he saw Norah. He was not quite sober but nowhere near as drunk as he had been the night before when he was talking with Tom. He dared not go home in that state again for his father had warned him as he helped him to bed that if he came home near paralytic again he would spend the night in the barn. Much of what had happened the previous evening was fuzzy to Joseph when he woke the next morning for a hundred hammers beat inside his head and his mouth was as dry as dust.

As he had milked the cows later, laying his head on the cow's velvet flanks, the throbbing pain settled to a dull ache and Tom's words had come back to him and he wanted to sing the news from the rafters. He didn't do that, remembering what Tom had said about secrecy for now.

When he saw Norah across the Diamond it was as if his thoughts had conjured her up. He sauntered across and she suppressed a sigh as she put the heavy shopping bags on the pavement beside her. She could afford to be gracious with Joseph.

'Hello Norah.'

'Joseph,' Norah said and inclined her head.

Joseph remembered that she knew nothing about the change of plan and suddenly he wanted to hurt her as she had hurt him, to know how it felt, for his heart had splintered into a million pieces the evening Norah had told him she really and truly was going to America and he realised that she had just been playing with him. It had all been for nothing, the endearments she had whispered were meaningless and the love he

88

had for her she had thrown back in his face, and so despite Tom telling him to keep the news to himself he said, 'Saw Tom last night.'

'Oh yes?'

'He was telling me about some trouble with Celia.'

Norah's eyes narrowed with suspicion. Surely Joseph was lying. 'Tom wouldn't tell you anything like that,' she said.

'Well he didn't have to tell me much, did he?' Joseph said. 'I mean, we all saw how she was with that hand at Fitzgerald's place. Anyway, she's cooked her goose right and proper for Tom was after saying that your father has decided to pack her off to America.'

Norah's eyes opened wide for that was news to her.

'America?' she said in surprise, not yet aware that this sudden decision by her father had any bearing on her plans in any way. 'Celia will hate that. It's me that's always wanted to go to America.'

'I know,' Joseph said in a sympathetic tone. 'Pity then that your plans have been scuppered by your sister.'

'What do you mean scuppered?' Norah snapped. 'It's all in hand. Mammy has sent for the ticket and everything.'

'I know,' Joseph said in the same consoling voice. 'But when that ticket arrives it will be for your sister, Celia, not you.'

Norah's cheeks drained of colour as she leapt from Joseph's side, her eyes in her bleached face looking as though they were on stalks. 'You're lying!' she said accusingly.

'What would be the purpose of lying to you?' Joseph said. 'Tom told me himself. Said it was the only way that they could keep Celia away from that McCadden chap.'

'It can't be true. It can't. They can't do that,' Norah cried as bitter tears of disappointment spurted from her face and dribbled down her cheeks and watching her Joseph was smitten with guilt as he realised there was no satisfaction for him in seeing his beloved so distressed. He felt worse than ever for blurting out something he had been warned to keep quiet about and for having done it in the middle of town, where all the people passing could witness Norah's wretchedness. Suddenly Joseph picked up the two bags of shopping with one hand and with the other guided Norah into an alleyway, away from the gaze of curious shoppers intrigued by the sight of the Mulligan girl crying openly in the street. And Norah continued to cry as the visions and plans she had made for when she got to America flitted across her mind and she groaned.

She refused Joseph's offer of the loan of his handkerchief and wiped the tears from her face with her hands as heartbreaking sobs racked her body over and over. Joseph stayed helpless beside her, longing to take her in his arms, but she was holding herself so stiff he knew she would reject him. Words too would be futile, so the only sounds were the agonising sobs and the gasps of Norah. And they seemed to pierce Joseph's very soul. It seemed they had been there hours before Norah eventually wiped her hands across her tear-stained face and said brokenly, 'You must have had some hand in it. You never liked the idea of me going to America.'

'No, I didn't,' Joseph admitted. 'But I was learning to accept it for I had no right to keep you here, but how I felt about things would have had no bearing on the decision your father made.'

Norah shook her head from side to side as if she couldn't quite believe it. 'I never thought that Daddy was so unfair, so cruel, and Mammy must have been involved too. They knew how much going to America meant to me. I've talked of little else for months. And,' she added fiercely, 'I'll never forgive them for this, never ever. And now I'm off to confront them.'

However, the tears she had shed had left her feeling faint and light-headed and her legs felt suddenly shaky and she almost fell over when she reached for the shopping bags. 'Let me,' Joseph said. 'I can carry at least one of them home for you.'

She didn't want him to, didn't want him anywhere near her, but thought it might be more embarrassing to fall flat on her face in the Main Street of Donegal Town. She gave a brief nod of her head and Joseph picked up the larger and heavier of the two bags and linked his other arm through hers and she was unsteady enough to feel a little grateful.

'I suppose you're glad about all this?' Norah said as they walked along, the road.

Joseph was ecstatic, but he knew Norah didn't want to hear that and so he chose his words with care. 'I would be lying if I didn't say that I am

91

happy that you are not going to disappear to America, but I know how much it meant to you and I hate to see you so upset. If I can help in any way just ask.'

Joseph's words made Norah feel quite humble for she knew how distressed Joseph had been when she had thrown him over and so she said, 'You are a much nicer person than me, Joseph O'Leary, for I know I hurt you badly and really thought you might hate me now.'

Joseph shook his head. 'I couldn't hate you,' he said. He gave a sigh and went on, 'You didn't want to hear this at the time and possibly don't want to hear it now but I will say it anyway, and that is that I love you, Norah. I can't really remember a time when I didn't love you and you don't stop loving a person because they don't feel the same way and you can't turn it off like a tap when that relationship is over.'

Norah was nearly reduced to tears again then, not for herself this time but for Joseph, who she realised loved her with a deep abiding love and she had taken him so much for granted. 'I'm sorry, Joseph,' she said. 'I never knew you felt that strongly.'

'You would never let me tell you,' Joseph said.

'Yes because I didn't want you to feel that way with my heart set on going to America.'

'I know,' Joseph said quietly. 'At least, I didn't know it all at first. I mean you were always talking about America and I knew you had a hankering for it, but I thought it was just a fantasy, especially when you agreed to walk out with me.'

'That was unkind,' Norah admitted. 'And it was

92

Celia said I had to be straight with you and I was and it hurt you.'

Joseph didn't deny it, but he did say, 'I had to know sooner or later and whenever you would have told me it would have hurt.'

They reached the head of the lane to the farm. 'I'll leave you here,' Joseph said. 'You will have to speak with your parents and they'll not want spectators.'

'Goodbye, Joseph.'

'Goodbye, Norah.' Joseph drew her gently into his arms. There was nothing sexual in the gesture and Norah submitted to it and reflected on what a good and selfless man Joseph was and it was a pity she couldn't bring herself to love him as he loved her.

It was as she reached the door of the farmhouse that she realised she had forgotten half the things her mother wanted and she supposed she would get into trouble for it but that mattered less than finding out whether what Joseph had told her was true or not. And it was and the only thing Peggy was concerned about was her being told in that way. Norah ranted and raved to no avail and Peggy just waited without saying a word until she was done.

'You can't do this to me,' she cried in anguish in a husky voice where tears still lurked.

'We can and we have.'

'But, Mammy, it's not fair,' Norah said. 'You promised when I was twenty-one I could go. Celia is only just eighteen and she never had a yen to go to America and I had and–'

Peggy suddenly lost patience with Norah and

she said sharply, cutting her off, 'It's about time you grew up. When you get as old as I am you'll realise that life is seldom fair, that circumstances change things and that is what has happened here. So despite what I promised you, and regardless of what Celia likes or doesn't like, she needs to go to America and you do not and that's what will happen and whatever temper or tantrum you get into it will not change the outcome one bit. And what's more that is my last word on the subject.'

'But, Mammy–'

'I said that was my last word on the subject, Norah.'

'Daddy–' Norah began hopefully.

'Your father will feel the same as me,' Peggy said. 'It was his ultimate decision. He has no desire to keep Celia locked up for the rest of her natural life.'

And Norah realised then there would be no America for her. Knowing it was hopeless she did appeal to her father but he just said the decision was final and refused to discuss it at all.

Now the news was out, the rest of the family were told as they sat round the table having their evening meal and Celia looked at her father as if she couldn't believe her ears. She felt shocked to the core and suddenly very frightened because she had never had any sort of desire to cross the Atlantic Ocean and go miles from her family.

'I don't want to go to America,' she said.

'Your behaviour means that what you want or don't want has no bearing on anything,' said Dan. 'I have said you are going to America and that is where you will go and you only have yourself to blame.'

Celia looked across at her mother's sorrowful eyes fastened on her and knew in her heart of hearts she didn't want her to be sent so far away, but her views would count for nothing either. Tom looked unhappy and Dermot couldn't understand why Celia had to leave the home she loved, when her father had said he was bribing McCadden to go away from Donegal. Ellie and Sammy didn't understand any of it and were asking questions they knew might not be answered. They had known for ages that it was Norah who was going and they couldn't understand why it was Celia who was now going and why she was so upset about it.

Celia in fact felt full of misery and she could hardly bear to look at her sister, who was completely silent and stiff. Celia knew Norah was holding her emotions together with difficulty and if she had tried to speak they would likely burst uncontrollably from her and she sighed for she had no idea that hurting those she cared about would cause her such anguish.

Dan seemed unaware of the bombshell he had released and in fact the only thing he seemed concerned about was how Joseph O'Leary knew it all to tell Norah. She explained that Tom had told him and Dan tore Tom off a strip for discussing the business of the family with outsiders.

'I did ask him to keep it to himself,' Tom protested. 'I didn't know that he was going to run slap bang into Norah the very next day. Anyway, I'm surprised he remembered anything I said, for he was well away when I saw him.'

Norah pulled herself together enough to say bitterly, 'Oh he remembered all right, and though he hid it well he actually took great delight in telling me my dream of going to America wasn't going to happen.'

'I don't want family business discussed with half the county.'

'It was hardly that,' Peggy said. 'Anyway, everyone will know about this soon enough. People can't just disappear, especially in a place this size, so our business will be known and discussed everywhere before long.'

Norah got to her feet and began stacking the dishes, noticing again how little Celia had eaten and thinking she would be worse now she knew. Celia had no desire to go to America and the thought of going there would take away what little appetite she had. Norah was amazed that no one else had noticed how thin her sister had become and how ill she looked.

She was still thinking of it when she climbed into bed beside Celia that night, trying not to get too close because she was incredibly bony, and she had resolved to say something to her parents the following day and make them listen because Celia was literally fading away. And then suddenly the solution for all their problems came to her. Celia could run away with Andy McCadden. Norah wondered why she had never thought of such a thing before. She was sure it could be done and had to be done quickly before the ticket came. Then Celia would have her hireling man and she could go to America as planned and everyone

96

would be happy, except perhaps Joseph O'Leary, but despite that thought, Norah went to sleep with a smile on her face.

SIX

There was a funny atmosphere in the house the next morning as they got ready for Mass. Celia thought her mother seemed vexed about something. She seemed angry with all of them and even Ellie and Sammy, sensing it too, were quieter than usual. There was no breakfast eaten before Mass on Sunday for the family would take communion so Celia was surprised to see her mother making up a tray with a bowl of porridge on it and a cup of tea. She exchanged a surprised glance with her sister and it was Norah who asked who the tray was for.

Peggy sighed. 'Well I suppose you'll know soon enough,' she said. 'Tom isn't well and he's having a morning in bed.'

Celia knew that wasn't true because their mother seemed almost cross that Tom wasn't well and for a minute wondered if he had taken a drop too much the night before, but she had known him do that before and yet he had never missed Mass over it. Anyway, if he had taken a drop too much, would he have wanted porridge and tea?

Celia watched her mother lift the tray just as Dan came in with Dermot and Peggy caught her husband's eyes and her eyes flashed fire. It was the sort of look the younger children dreaded for when it was directed at them it was usually the forerunner of smacked legs, but this time she was looking at their daddy that way. It was very strange and so was the very pointed sniff Peggy gave before she left the kitchen. Celia glanced at Dermot and he shrugged his shoulders and spread his hands and it was obvious he could shed no light on anything.

Later, as they made their way to Mass, Norah, Celia and Dermot walked ahead of their parents and Dermot said quietly, 'Don't know what's up with our Tom, but there was a bit of moaning and groaning when he got into bed last night.'

'Wasn't half,' Sammy agreed.

'You were asleep,' Dermot said disparagingly.

'No I wasn't,' Sammy protested. 'And if I had been I'd have woken up quick enough with all the turning and tossing Tom was doing.'

'What is it all about?' Norah said, perplexed. 'Daddy said nothing, I suppose?'

'Are you kidding?' Dermot said. 'Daddy has enough trouble bidding me the time of day on the normal run of things. And if I'd dared ask him, the mood he was in this morning, then I would have had the ears scalded off me?'

'But what did Tom look like?' Celia persisted. 'Did he look strange?'

'How would I know that, Celia?' Dermot said. 'It was dark when he came in and he didn't light the lamp and this morning when we got up the covers were pulled around him.'

'One side of his face was like black,' Sammy said.

'And how do you know?' Dermot said disbelievingly.

'Cos when you went downstairs he pulled the covers away a bit and I saw before he tucked them in again.'

'Well we'll likely know all soon enough,' Norah said.

'And we'd better shut up about it now because we'll be at church in a minute.'

Norah welcomed the silence that fell because all morning she had been thinking that it was all right to come up with this great idea about how she could make it to America anyway and also give Celia her heart's desire, but how it was going to be achieved was another thing. She needed to see Andy McCadden alone and see if he really loved her sister enough to take her away out of this before she was spirited across the Atlantic.

But they had reached the church now and were greeted from all sides by fellow parishioners. Among those that usually greeted them were Mr and Mrs Fitzgerald, but that morning they were ignored and Andy, who was usually with them, was not there. This didn't strike her as odd initially; Norah thought maybe he was running late and would join them later. But he didn't and when the Mass began she took a surreptitious look around but could see no sign of him. She concluded he had been taken with doing some jobs on the farm and would likely go to the later Mass and a sudden excitement gripped her as she realised that this might be the only chance she had to see Andy McCadden alone.

But had she the courage to walk out of church

in the middle of Mass? Not if she had been near her mother, she knew, but she was right on the other side of the pew. And her eyes were fastened on Sammy. He was sitting on the boys' side of the church with all the others but his mother always sat as close to him as she could because he was inclined to fidget and chatter and drop his collection money and make a great deal of noise and fuss retrieving it and sometimes he was better behaved after a good poke. So Peggy's attention was taken by her youngest son and beside her were Dan and Dermot, then Celia, and Norah was at the end. 'Cover for me,' she said to Celia out of the side of her mouth.

'What?'

'I need to leave Mass. There's something I've got to do.'

'What sort of something?'

'Tell you later,' Norah promised. 'When Mammy notices I'm not here, say I was taken sick.'

She slipped from the pew into the side aisle before Celia could reply to this and for the benefit of the parishioners, who were looking at her askance and who she knew would report what they saw to her mother, she bent her head as she scurried quickly down the aisle with her hand to her mouth. Once out of the church she continued to hurry for she knew she wouldn't have long. Her mother might not notice her absence until communion, but then she would miss her and quiz Celia and she might send someone to see if she was all right and it would never do if she was found anywhere near Fitzgerald's farm.

The day was fine and warm and the countryside had never looked lovelier, but Norah hadn't time to stand and stare and she cut across the fields which was quicker and where there was less likelihood of her being seen. She had expected to see McCadden in the field, or failing that the farmyard, but he was in neither place and she, reached the farmhouse door without seeing him and though she knew he slept in the barn there was no way she was going in there on her own.

Then she heard a noise from the kitchen, like the scrape of a chair on the kitchen floor, and though she nearly took flight she reminded herself what was at stake and knocked on the door tentatively. When it was opened, McCadden stood there with a towel over his arm and his face was one unholy mess, battered, bruised and grazed, one eye blackened and nearly closed up and his lip was split open as well.

'What happened to you?' Norah asked though she knew fine what had happened him.

'Give you one guess,' McCadden said in a voice slurred and a little indistinct because of the swollen lip.

'But who did it?'

'Huh,' McCadden said. 'Thought you might have figured out who that was. Even wondered if you'd come to gloat.'

'What?' Norah said, confused. 'What are you on about?'

McCadden gave an ironic laugh. 'You really don't know?'

'Know what?'

'It was your brother did this.'

'Tom?' Norah cried. She could hardly believe it

101

and her shocked reaction was genuine, McCadden saw. 'Tom did this to you?'

'Yes,' McCadden said. 'And he didn't get all his own way I can tell you. I left my mark on him too.'

'You did,' Norah said, remembering her brother's odd behaviour and what Sammy had told them about his blackened face on the way to Mass. 'He didn't get up for Mass this morning.'

'Well if your father had had his way, I might not be getting up at all,' McCadden said. 'I might still be lying in the ditch in the mangled mess they would have made of me because the two of them attacked me first and I said only cowards think it takes two men to attack one.'

Norah's eyes grew wide. 'You called my father a coward?'

McCadden nodded. 'I did.'

'Surprised he didn't kill you.'

'He didn't try because Tom said I was right and he would fight me fair and square.'

'Who won?'

McCadden shrugged. 'I did knock him down in the end, but I think we were fairly evenly matched. All in all, Tom gave a good account of himself.'

'And this was all over Celia?'

Andy nodded. 'To teach me a lesson, your father said. He could have saved himself the bother. I have already given my notice to the Fitzgeralds and not because of the money your father offered me or the beating he tried to give me.'

It was news to Norah that her father had offered McCadden money – to stay away from Celia, she presumed – and she was surprised by the lengths he was prepared to go to in order to protect Celia from Andy McCadden, as if he was some sort of monster.

'Unless I move on,' Andy went on, 'Celia will be given no life at all. I see how they have her at Mass and she is like a frightened little sparrow.' He shook his head sadly and went on. 'I can't do that to her.'

'How much do you care for her, Andy?'

'A great deal. I thought you knew that.'

'I had to be sure,' Norah said. 'Do you care for her enough to take her away from here when you go?'

Andy started for that was the last thing he'd expected Norah to say. Knowing she had not been that keen on him in the beginning, his eyes narrowed in suspicion. 'What rot are you talking? You know your father–'

'My father mustn't know,' Norah cried. 'You must sneak away.'

Andy shook his head regretfully. 'I can't do that,' he said. 'For all Celia is eighteen now, she's emotionally younger than her years. She needs to live a bit.'

'She loves you.'

'She has met no one else, that's all,' Andy said. 'When I am gone they will ease up on her and she will meet someone else your father approves of.'

Norah shook her head. 'She won't. She will be sent to America.'

Andy looked at her disbelievingly. 'There's no point in that if I am not here anymore. Anyway I thought it was you going to America.'

'It was,' Norah said with a sigh. 'Now, to keep

Celia out of your clutches, she is being sent there. I doubt it would help if you disappeared off the scene now because my father wouldn't know where you'd gone to and whether you'd be back. Celia's fate, I'm afraid, is sealed.'

'I still can't take her with me,' Andy said. 'It wouldn't be right.'

'Is it right to send her to America where she doesn't want to go?'

'Maybe not,' Andy conceded. 'But your parents have rights over Celia until she is twenty-one.'

Andy was silent and Norah heard the ticking of the clock and she felt quite desperate. This was maybe the only chance she would have to talk to Andy alone. She thought he would have jumped at the chance. The silence between them had begun to feel uncomfortable when Norah gave a shrug and said, 'That's that then. Celia will be going to America. That's if she's well enough to make the crossing.'

Andy's head shot up. 'Why wouldn't she be?' he cried. 'Is she sick?'

'In the mind only,' Norah said. 'She is locked in her room every day and let out only for meals, not that she eats much of anything put before her. Andy, her clothes are hanging from her and she looks pale and listless. It's like she is pining away and I think she is pining for you. Don't desert her now, Andy. It would be too cruel and might indeed be the last straw for her.'

Andy was greatly affected by Norah's words and they changed his mind-set completely. He had seen Celia's wretchedness and it was to help her that he had decided to leave, but if she was actually becoming ill and if Norah was right and his leaving now would not help the situation, then he had to do something else. And so, despite any misgivings he had about taking Celia with him because of her age and immaturity, and also despite the jurisdiction her parents had over her, he knew he had to get her away from her tyrannical father before he killed her altogether. How could he live with himself if something happened to her because he didn't act?

'Has the ticket for America arrived yet?'

'No and it would be well to be away before it comes,' Norah said. 'If now you've decided to take her with you?'

Andy nodded. 'I'll take her because I feel I must.'

'She will die if she stays,' Norah said. 'Either before she goes or on the crossing, when she will be completely alone. Once that ticket arrives I think Daddy will have her on that liner faster than the speed of light.'

'You're right,' Andy said. 'I will not be able to work my notice and I do feel sorry about it because the Fitzgeralds have been good to me. And I'll have to borrow Mr Fitzgerald's horse too, because we'll need a horse to get to Letterkenny by dawn to get the train down to the docks in Belfast before dawn and we daren't use the roads. The horse's hooves will sound in the night.'

'So how will you know the way if you don't use the roads?'

'We'll follow the rail bus tracks.'

Norah knew all about the rail buses, the little red trains that ran on narrow-gauge tracks that

105

people said had opened up the north of Ireland. 'I've never travelled on one of those.'

'Nor me,' Andy said. 'In fact I had never left home before I travelled from Killybegs to Donegal to look for work, but some in Killybegs had travelled on them and they said they go all the way to Letterkenny. The tracks pass through Donegal so if we pick them up and follow them we should get there all right.'

'And you're making for the docks?'

Andy nodded. 'We must make for England for there is nowhere in Ireland I would consider safe. If they were to find us they could demand Celia's return and I doubt I would have a leg to stand on. I suppose she is agreeable to all this?'

'She will be,' Norah said confidently. 'But as yet she has no idea.' And she explained how she had sneaked out of church pretending to be sick. 'I must go soon or I will be missed.'

'How will I know if Celia agrees?' Andy said. 'I will force her to go nowhere.'

'She will be agreeable, I tell you.'

'I must know. Can you get out with a message to me?'

'No I can't,' Norah protested. 'What possible reason could I give for leaving the house without arousing suspicion? I am not locked up like Celia but I am watched like a hawk.'

Andy thought for a minute and then suddenly said, 'I have it. If I get halfway down your lane I can see your house. Where's your bedroom?'

'At the front to the right of the front door.'

'Right,' Andy said. 'If Celia agrees to this, light a lantern and put it in the window tomorrow

106

night. And if that lantern is lit then I will be there to fetch her on Wednesday night at midnight.'

'Right, that's settled then,' Norah said. 'And now I really must be off before they send a search party out.'

Norah had felt a bit guilty as she walked home that morning because, though every word she had said had been the truth, she had been thinking about herself as well. She knew that Celia thought the world of Andy McCadden but she wasn't absolutely sure that the love her sister had for him would give her the strength to sneak out to go with a man who intended to take her to another country altogether, one which she had never expressed a wish to go to.

First though, she had to deal with the wrath of her mother who couldn't believe she had left the church without a word to anyone.

'I told Celia,' Norah protested. 'I hadn't time to tell anyone else. As it was I only just got out of the church before I was as sick as a dog.'

'So why then didn't you come back in?'

'Because being sick didn't make me feel any better,' Norah said. 'I went for a walk to see if it would help being in the fresh air.'

'Which it obviously did for you look as right as rain to me now.'

Norah thought it best that she didn't recover quite so quickly and so she said, 'My stomach still feels a little delicate.'

'Well I don't know what's up with you,' Peggy said, almost impatiently as if Norah had been sick to spite her. 'You've never been the sickly type and you've had nothing to eat that the rest of us haven't had. Still, if you say you felt sick then I suppose you did and I won't give you any porridge this morning – that'll give your stomach a rest.'

Norah's stomach was actually yawningly empty. She gave an almost imperceptible sigh for it was a long time until dinner and her stomach rumbled and grumbled in protest, but going along with the pretence of still feeling queasy she had to agree with her mother.

Watching the others eat the breakfast she would have enjoyed was agony to Norah and she was glad when it was over and she was able to escape to the scullery with Celia and clear away all trace of it. As they worked under the cover of the clatter of plates, she told Celia what had transpired since she had left the church and knew from her open-mouthed amazement that that had been the last thing that Celia had thought she would do.

Celia was incensed when Norah told her about the fight, especially when her sister said Andy would have been in a worse state if the two of them had set about him as their father had intended.

'I never thought Daddy to be a violent man or one that would join with Tom to beat another man up. I'm a bit disappointed in him to be truthful.'

'Your Andy McCadden didn't waste time being disappointed,' Norah said. 'He virtually told Daddy he was a coward coming at him that way and he would fight one man at a time and Daddy was raging apparently but Tom said McCadden was right.'

'But is Andy all right?'

'Basically,' Norah said. 'His face is a bit of a

mess, but he'll heal and at least we know why Tom is keeping to his bed today. Anyway, he said they were wasting their time for he's already given notice to the Fitzgeralds and is moving on.'

Celia gave a little distressed cry and her hands fluttered to her mouth while tears squeezed from her eyes and dribbled down her pasty white face as she said in a shaky whisper, 'Where's he going?'

'He's talking about making for England,' Norah said. 'But wherever he's going you can go with him if you want to.'

Celia's eyes that she fastened on Norah were filled with uncertainty as she said, 'What do you mean?' Norah told her the idea she had put to Andy McCadden and his reaction to it and while her sister spoke thoughts were tumbling in Celia's head. She wanted to go with Andy, oh she did, only she'd never thought about anything like this happening. Whenever she had thought about the future it had been like a big hole in front of her and now that hole was filled with tenuous brightness and hope.

She acknowledged that once she left her home the likelihood was she would never enter it again and to her parents it would be like she had died and despite everything that thought saddened her. But she had already made her choice and she trembled inwardly at the thought that her parents might get to hear of their plans and intercept them at the last minute and this was what she said to Norah.

Norah took hold of her hands. 'We'll take care that they won't,' she said. 'This is your one chance to have the future you want, Celia. So take heart and be strong and believe that this is going to happen, because it is.'

A fluttering began in Celia's breast and she realised it was the stirring of happiness and she smiled at her sister and it was so long since she had smiled at anyone, her mouth felt strange. 'Don't be too joyful all of a sudden,' Norah warned, 'or Mammy at least might smell a rat.'

Oh Celia knew that full well because she often thought her mother had some sort of sixth sense, so she sobered her face as they entered the kitchen and for the first time she was glad to be isolated in her room where she could smile to her heart's content or dance a jig of happiness if she felt like it.

Celia saw her brother's battered face for the first time the following morning as he came in for his breakfast after the milking and so did Norah, who thought he looked moderately worse than Andy McCadden. It was obvious he had been in a fight of some kind but no one spoke of it, which in itself was odd. And then Ellie and Sammy came running in dressed for school and Sammy skidded to a halt when he saw his eldest brother's face. 'Crikey!'

Dermot gave Sammy a kick under the table and shook his head for he had already asked the question he knew Sammy was about to ask when Tom had come into the byre that morning and his father had nearly bitten his head off for it. Sammy paid no heed to Dermot and turned to Tom. 'What happened to you?'

It was Dan who answered. 'That's none of your business,' he snapped.

'Yeah but Daddy–'

'Did you hear what I said?'

Peggy seldom spoke against her husband and never in front of the children, but she had been shocked at the sight of her son the previous evening, for Dan had had to half-carry him home and she knew it was at Dan's urging that they had gone looking for McCadden. However cross he might have been, Tom would never have picked a fight unless his father had or been at the back of it, and so she spoke sharply. 'Dan, it's obvious they're going to ask. It would be stranger if they didn't and if you are ashamed of the consequences you shouldn't have done the deed.'

'Who said I'm ashamed?' Dan roared. 'I'm ashamed of nothing.'

'Oh no you're not ashamed. You're the big "I am". Well you ought to be ashamed for encouraging two young men to beat each other near senseless, too battered and bruised to be at Mass yesterday. And for what? It will have achieved nothing and the Fitzgeralds seemed very vexed too.'

'They'll get over it,' Dan said gruffly for he had also noticed their testiness. Before Peggy could make any sort of reply to this, Sammy, who'd taken a great interest in the proceedings, despite shovelling porridge into his mouth, said to Tom, 'I knew you were in a fight, I could tell. So why did you fight?'

'You really don't need to know that, Sammy,' Peggy said. 'Just take heed that fighting never solved anything. And I'm sure,' she said, glancing at Tom, 'Sinead will feel the same way.'

'I went over yesterday and told her that Tom had a bit of a fever,' Dan said.

'As soon as she catches sight of him she'll know that's not true,' Peggy said. 'Tom, I think she will let you have it with both guns blazing and I won't blame her one bit.'

Celia didn't either and felt worried about Andy. 'Does he look as bad as Tom does?' she asked Norah as she took her up to their room.

'Slightly better I would say,' Norah said.

Celia shook her head. 'I can barely believe it,' she said. 'I wouldn't have said Tom was a violent man, nor Andy either.'

'All men are violent if they're given what they think is a just cause,' Norah said. 'It's just the way they are.'

As she spoke Norah recalled Andy's view of Celia and knew he had a point. She was incredibly naïve about the nature of men and even the ways of the world and maybe it was like feeding her to the wolves to encourage her into Andy McCadden's arms, but there really was no alternative. All she could hope was that he would be kind to her young sister and patient and gentle.

'What's the matter?' 'Celia said, seeing the lines of concern on Norah's face.

'Nothing's the matter,' Norah said brightly. 'What could be the matter? Anyway you'll be out of here and on your way in a couple of days.'

Celia wrapped her arms around herself with excitement. 'I know,' she said. 'Ooh, I can't wait.'

'Well keep a lid on it for now,' Norah advised. 'The fewer people know about this the better. Not a word with Ellie in the room, even if she seems to be asleep. What she doesn't know she can't tell.'

It was sound advice for Celia wanted nothing to stand in her way now. Even the problem of finding a receptacle to put clothes in was solved because when Jim was going to America he was bought a big bag to put his things in and when there was talk of Norah joining him there he had sent the bag back and Celia crammed into it all the clothes she could.

By Wednesday Celia was in such a fever of excitement she could hardly contain herself and she thought the clock had never moved so slowly. Even so, when she reached her bedroom that night after the evening meal, she looked around as if to commit it to memory. She hadn't expected to be leaving her home for some time yet, and not to leave Ireland at all.

Still, she told herself firmly, there was no point at all going on and on about it and she wished it was time to meet Andy for she knew that when she did meet him all doubts would flee. She thought of not bothering to get undressed, but knew that that might cause comment from Ellie if she noticed, so she compromised by slipping her nightie over her underclothes. And she had just done that and got into bed when she heard Ellie coming up the stairs and she closed her eyes and feigned sleep for though she was aware that it would be the last time she would lie beside Ellie, she dared not betray herself at this late stage. In any case, her mind was in far too much turmoil to talk in any sort of sensible way and she forced

113

herself to lie still until she heard Ellie's even breathing and she felt she could relax a little.

The next thing she was aware of was Norah shaking her. 'It's after eleven,' she whispered. 'You must get dressed and be on your way.'

Celia awoke muzzy-headed for she hadn't intended to go to sleep and she heaved herself from her bed as fingers of apprehension trailed down her spine and caused her to shiver. Knowing that it would be chilly at that hour and would get colder before they reached their destination she had laid out a winter-weight dress of dark green and dark blue checks, a blue cardigan and thick blue stockings.

'Carry your boots in your hands,' Norah advised. 'And don't forget your shawl.'

Celia did as she was bid and followed her sister. She never before realised the door opened with such a loud click of the latch, or that the hinges groaned as the door opened further or that so many planks on the landing creaked so much. Norah had come with Celia this far so that she could bid her farewell properly and so she could re-bolt the door, a job her father always did. If he'd discovered it unbolted he would have been alerted straight away that there was some sort of problem and it was important that Celia's disappearance was not discovered too soon. So she helped Celia on with her boots and embraced her, worrying now the moment was here whether she had made the right decision in encouraging Celia's flight from the house.

'I'll never forget you for this, Norah, never.'

'You are sure about this?'

Celia nodded her head. 'Certain sure.' If she had been absolutely honest, Celia might have admitted to a few lingering doubts, but Norah didn't need to know about those. She was immensely glad of the full moon shining down like a golden orb and the twinkling stars in the sky that lit the lane so effectively.

She stopped at the curve in the lane to wave and it was as Norah closed the door and drew the bolt that she realised that, in making it safer for Celia, she had made it more difficult than ever for herself because if the door was bolted someone in the house had not only known about Celia's escape, but had helped her, and her father would know full well the only one it could have been. She almost drew the bolt back again, but she knew if her father found out Celia had gone at half four or five when he rose for milking and saddled a horse and set off then he just might have caught up with them on the road.

She couldn't bear that, she thought as she tiptoed up the stairs, for she honestly didn't know what her father might do to Celia this time if he was to catch her, for not only had she run away from home, she'd run away with the very man her father had forbade her to even see. There would be no way back for her sister after this and, if Norah wasn't careful, she would be in hot water as well.

She reached the bedroom without incident and knew the only way she might get out of this was to make it look as if Celia had got away through the window. So, with a glance at Ellie to check she was still asleep, she crossed to the window, eased it up slightly and looked out. By the light of the moon she saw that anyone determined enough to escape could use the pipe which was fastened to the outside wall of their bedroom. It carried the rainwater from the roof to the water butt and could easily be reached by a person leaning out of the window. If Celia had thrown her bag out she could have shimmied down the pipe until she reached the scullery window and dropped to the ground from there. So Norah pulled the curtains but left the window open, and eased herself into bed beside Ellie, hoping she wouldn't be woken by the cold for then she would surely realise her sister was not in the bed and would rouse the house.

She gave a sudden yawn and realised how tired she was for she hadn't slept well since Sunday. She curled her body around Ellie to keep them both warm but sleep eluded her with the worry of what would happen the following day and she acknowledged how afraid she was of her father's rage when he found Celia missing. She tried not to toss and turn too much and eventually drowsiness seeped through her befuddled brain and she closed her eyes and fell into a deep sleep.

SEVEN

Andy was waiting for Celia at the end of the lane holding the horse by the bridle and his dazzling beam of happiness when he saw Celia approach chased away all of her doubts. He took the bag from her and took her in his arms and kissed her cheek gently as he said, 'All right?'

Celia nodded though she doubted she would ever feel all right again. This was such an alien thing for her to do, leave her home in the dead of night and be taken to God alone knew where, but when Andy said, 'You sure about this?' she nodded her head more vigorously.

'Right then,' Andy said. 'There's no time to waste.' And he tied Celia's bag to the saddle and then he lifted her on to the saddle and swung himself up beside her, jiggled the reins and as the horse moved forward his free arm tightened around Celia's waist. It made her feel a little uncomfortable and shy to be held so close to a man and yet she felt safer too, for though it was too dark for her to see the ground she knew Ned to be a big farm horse and so it was a long way down if she was to fall.

It was odd, she thought, that she felt almost shy of Andy but maybe it was better not to talk for their voices might carry in the still night and then Andy said gently, 'It'd be about twenty-five miles to Letterkenny and if we want to catch the early morning train to Belfast we need to go a little quicker than this. Shall you be scared if the horse goes fast?'

'Not half as scared as I am of my father catching us if we do not,' Celia said with the ghost of a smile.

'Yes,' said Andy in agreement. 'It's good to get as great a distance from your home as we can before they discover your disappearance.' He spurred the horse on, saying as he did so, 'We will follow the rail bus tracks so that we do not get

117

lost in the dark for I have never been this far from home before. Have you travelled much?'

'Not at all,' Celia replied.

'Now, you'll be quite safe for I'm holding you tight,' Andy said. 'You can even go to sleep if you want to.'

'Oh no,' Celia said. 'I'm not the slightest bit sleepy.'

'Here goes then,' said Andy.

However, Ned wasn't built for speed, but for strength and endurance, but he valiantly tried his best and trotted on as well as he was able and Andy was glad of the moonlight catching the odd glimmer of the rail tracks lighting the way for him. Celia asked why they weren't riding on the road and Andy said, 'The clop of a horse's hooves would sound loud in the night and might cause people to try and find out who it was abroad in the dark when all decent folk were in their beds. Wouldn't do to get careless,' he went on. 'For when the hue and cry goes up when they discover you gone we don't want anyone to remember the sound of a horse they'd heard.'

So it was a fairly quiet ride, and Andy warned they had to be really quiet as they approached and passed the rail bus halts because some of them were manned. They passed by the side of a lough that Andy said he thought was Lough Mourne and the moon gleamed on the slight swell of water and rippling waves as Andy slowed the horse to a walk. 'Probably it's very pretty in the day,' he said to Celia. 'But we shall have to take extra care for I don't fancy us pitching in there because we lost our footing or went too close to the edge.'

118

'Pleased to hear it,' Celia whispered back.

With the lough behind them they were facing Derg Bridge, which led down to Derg Halt, and once across the bridge, as they joined the rails now running alongside the road again, they saw in front of them two rugged boulder-strewn heaps stretching up into the skyline in the dusky light from the moon while the rail bus tracks and the road ran right between them.

'D'you think this is Barnes Gap?' Celia said in an awed whisper as they started through it.

'Must be I'd say,' Andy whispered back for while neither had seen them close up, though they were big enough to be seen from some distance away, they both knew about them because the adults were fond of telling children gruesome tales of the highwaymen who'd once ridden Barnes More Hills with impunity. In the past many travellers were nervous of going through the gap between the two towering, craggy peaks, and with reason, for highwaymen would often stop the coaches going through and kill the men without a thought and rob the women of all they possessed and often molest them too. 'Took your life in your hands going through in those days,' Andy remarked.

Celia thought it still seemed menacing to ride through the imposing rock faces to either side of her, the night darker than ever with the moon obscured by the rocks and the wind channelling through the gap caused Celia to gasp and tighten her shawl around herself. She was so glad to be out of it she breathed a sigh of relief.

'All right?' Andy asked.

'Mm, I am now,' Celia said.

There was silence then as they travelled on and, despite Celia assuring Andy when she had got on Ned that she wasn't a bit tired, she had become rather drowsy and must have dozed off because she was jerked awake by Andy saying, 'We're coming into Lifford now and it's a customs post so we'll have to leave the rail tracks and go up into the hills to cross the border. It will be a bit rough for a while and not a sound because this is quite heavily manned I should imagine. I'm going to lead Ned. Do you want to stay on?'

'No. I'll walk with you.'

'Righto,' Andy said and he swung his legs off the horse's back and lifted Celia down beside him. And then, mindful of the need for silence, she bit her lips to stop a cry escaping from her for she was so stiff and sore and cold. Andy could feel her trembling and could guess the rest and he whispered, 'You'll warm up and your legs won't be as stiff when you've walked a bit. Stay close to me.'

Celia wasn't sure if she had the strength to move those taut legs and when she tried they throbbed with pain, but she did her best to keep up with Andy as he toiled up the hill and was very glad when he eventually called a halt.

'Get your breath back here,' he advised. 'And then we'll cross and go down the other side and when we are far enough away we will join the rail bus tracks again. Letterkenny is just a step away now and can you see the sky lightening?'

'Oh yes,' Celia said, looking round and seeing the grey tinge to the horizon.

'We'll get to Letterkenny in good time to catch

the early train to Belfast and the docks I'd say.'

'What will you do with Ned?'

'Oh, I'll leave him in Letterkenny in stables,' Andy said. 'And they'll feed him and look after him and I'll send a telegram to Fitzgerald telling him where he is but not until we reach Belfast.'

'He's sure to be cross with you.'

Andy gave a chuckle. 'I'd say so,' he said. 'Especially as he will have to pick up the bill in the stables. But don't look so worried, Celia,' he went on when he saw the slight frown on her face. 'Why should I worry about Fitzgerald now when I'm never likely to see him again?'

'But the money he will have to pay, that surely isn't right,' Celia said. 'I mean, none of it is his fault.'

'Well no, I don't suppose it is,' Andy conceded. 'But I had no option but to take the horse. We wouldn't have got to Letterkenny this night without him. As for the bill at the stables, he can pay that in lieu of the wages he would have given me this Friday had I stayed that long.'

Celia felt better about the money Fitzgerald would have to pay out then and when Andy said, 'Are you ready to go on now?' she nodded her head eagerly, glad to be on the move again, for every step she took was one further step away from her father, for she guessed his rage would be fierce and she would be afraid to face him.

'I would hate Daddy to overtake us,' she said.

'He is hardly likely to do that,' Andy said. 'He might not have noticed you missing yet and when he does he will have no idea of where we are making, for we are so close to Letterkenny now.

121

When I am in Belfast and send the telegram telling Fitzgerald where his horse is, he might not tell your father straight away for he's not too friendly with him because of the fight I had with Tom. It was totally unnecessary, you see, because I had already decided to leave and he didn't want to accept my notice either. We've got on very well in the time I've been here, but I made him see in the end that it was better for you. Anyway,' he said, 'fighting never solved anything.'

'I agree.'

'Between you and me, he thinks your dad is a little old fashioned about deciding who you marry,' Andy said. 'For, as he says, his son could be carrying on with all sorts of people in the States and he'd not know and if he eventually brings home a totally unsuitable girl to marry, they will have to accept her, because she will be the son's choice.'

'He's right as well,' Celia said.

'Aye he's a sound man,' Andy said. 'And a sensible one. Now we're coming to the rail tracks on the other side of the border post and I think it's getting light enough for Ned to carry us from here.' Soon they were both mounted on the horse again and Andy guided him as he picked his way down the hillside. Once they reached the rails there was not a soul in sight and they continued their journey towards Letterkenny.

When they arrived in the town, they located the railway station and Andy left Celia in the waiting room on the platform while he went to settle the horse and buy the tickets. It was as he came back a little later that it was light enough to see his face fully for the first time and Celia felt quite ashamed of the damage her brother had inflicted and she said so.

Andy sat down on the bench beside her and told her not to worry, that he'd live.

'How can I not worry?' Celia said almost angrily. 'Tom has made one unholy mess of your face.' Andy knew he had and silently thanked God that he had got such good healing skin for if he applied for a job with his face still looking how it looked now, he doubted it would help his prospects. No one would want to employ a trouble-maker. But he wouldn't burden Celia with that small concern he had.

'And the further we go away from my home the more I see that Norah was right all along, and Fitzgerald,' Celia went on. 'I mean why do parents think they should have such a say in our lives and why do we allow them to go on thinking it? How would Tom feel if my father took against Sinead McClusky? Would he throw her over at my father's say-so and look for someone he did approve of?'

'Huh, shouldn't think so,' Andy said. 'Seems pretty keen on her to me. But why worry what your father thinks any more? You're getting away.'

'This must be costing you some money,' Celia said. 'And there is no way I can help you because I was never given any money of my own.'

'I'm all right for now,' Andy said. 'When I had to leave home my father gave me two ten-shilling notes in case I couldn't get work straight away but I did and Fitzgerald was a good payer because he said I was a good worker. I had all my meals at the house, even overalls provided, and as

123

I only went out on Saturday for a dander around the town and for the dance in the evenings I saved a good deal of my wages and I haven't touched my father's money at all. As long as I am set on as soon as we are settled somewhere, we should be all right.'

But though he assured Celia, Andy was worried for he knew there was a massive slump in England. And yet he knew he had to find work to provide for them both and there was the problem of finding somewhere to live, for he didn't want Celia to end up in some rat-infested dive of a place with no money coming in. She deserved better than that. He wanted to look after her properly and the worry that he might not be able to initially did gnaw at him at times.

Something else bothered Andy greatly as well and that was how Celia really felt about him. She thought she loved him, had left home to be with him, and he certainly loved her, he loved her too much to abuse that innocence and naivety for Celia had little experience of life. Even if she was ready for marriage – and Andy doubted that she was – she couldn't marry without her parents' permission for three years and during that time they could not really live as man and wife. He was very glad the waiting room was still empty as he attempted to explain this to Celia.

'Is it because you don't love me any more?' she asked plaintively.

Andy took hold of her shoulders and looked deep in her eyes and felt his heart turn over with love for this girl on the verge of womanhood. 'It's because I love you too much, my darling girl,' he said. 'I cannot take anything from you until I can make you my wife. It wouldn't be right.'

'Then what ... when...'

'I will still stay with you and take care of you always,' Andy said, lifting Celia to her feet and putting his arms tight around her. 'But for propriety's sake we should travel as brother and sister.' And he went on, 'Andy and Celia McCadden, alone in the world as our parents are dead and we have come to England in search of a better life. How does that sound?'

'All right I suppose,' Celia said in an uncertain voice.

'This is to protect you and your reputation,' Andy said. 'Do you mind very much?'

Celia shrugged. 'It isn't as I imagined,' she admitted and added, 'But I do understand why you want to do this.'

'And you'll go along with it?'

Celia nodded. 'I'll go along with it.'

They had a bit of a wait for the train to Belfast. The bustling station of Letterkenny, though not that large, quite unnerved Celia. And she was pleased when eventually the train clattered in on singing wheels and stopped at the platform with a squeal of brakes and a hiss of steam. There was soot-laden smoke spluttering from the funnel wafting in the air and Celia tasted the tinge of coal dust on her lips as she moved forward to get on.

They found a carriage very quickly but Celia thought the steam train went far too fast with the countryside flashing past so quickly it was hard to see anything and the train swayed that much that it was hard to keep her footing. Andy seemed

125

much steadier and when the train had been running for a bit he went off and bought cheese sandwiches for them both from the restaurant car. Celia, who hadn't had anything to eat for some time, felt suddenly famished.

'Ah,' she said as she finished the last vestige of her sandwich. 'My stomach was beginning to think my throat was cut.'

Andy let out a bellow of laughter. 'Well I haven't heard that one before,' he said. 'But I gather it means you were hungry and I am delighted to hear it because it looks as though you haven't been hungry for some time. Norah mentioned it, but then I saw it for myself.'

Celia nodded. 'I wasn't eating much,' she said. 'I couldn't work up any enthusiasm somehow and it wasn't that I was hungry either. I was full up of misery.'

'I'll try to see you never feel that way again,' Andy said but he had his fingers crossed in the hand he had behind his back and truly hoped he would be able to keep the promise he had made to her.

When Celia's disappearance was noticed, which was fairly early in the morning, everyone appeared astounded and Peggy was extremely worried. Climbing out of the window was the very last thing she would have expected any of them to do and Celia least of all. Both Ellie and Norah denied all knowledge of Celia's flight and both said they had heard no strange noises in the night, which was true in Ellie's case. It was Ellie who noticed the bag was missing from the top of the wardrobe and Peggy then went through Celia's drawers to find most of her clothes were missing too and faced the fact she had run away.

'But run away to where?' Peggy cried. 'There's no one for her to run to.'

'We must look for her, that's all,' Dan said.

'Look where exactly?'

'Well we'll start with the farm. She could be hiding out some place.'

'With a bagful of clothes?' Peggy said edgily. 'I'm just worrying that she might do something stupid. You know, harming herself in some way – for you do hear of girls doing that sort of thing when they were being made to do something they didn't want to do.'

Dan was dismissive of that. 'Celia wouldn't do anything stupid,' he maintained. 'She has too much sense for that.'

'I'd hardly call climbing out of the window in the dead of night sensible,' Peggy remarked.

'Anyway, didn't you say she has been better in herself these last few days?'

Peggy nodded her head. 'I did and she has been,' she said. 'But now she has disappeared and I can't help feeling that maybe she was more accepting because she had planned something to make sure it didn't happen.'

'Look,' Dan said, 'I'll use your argument; if she intended doing away with herself, she'd hardly bother to pack a bag of clothes for herself.'

'No, I suppose not,' Peggy said, wringing her hands in agitation. 'But where in God's name is she?'

'We'll find her, don't fret yourself,' Dan said

127

soothingly. 'We'll have a quick scour of the farm and if she's not found then I'll get the horse out and go after her. She can't have gone that far.'

Everyone was marshalled in to help with the search and Norah searched along with the rest, but in a desultory way, knowing her sister would not be found on the farm or anywhere near it. She wondered that they hadn't thought her disappearance was linked in any way with McCadden, but Dan had made quite sure Celia had had no contact with him, for even when she saw him at Mass, she was never allowed to talk to him.

Norah knew he would find out just how involved McCadden was and well before the day was over. It was like the sword of Damocles above her head, for while at the moment her father had a chance of believing she knew nothing about Celia's disappearance, the moment he knew Andy McCadden was implicated he would automatically believe Norah was involved in some way. She trembled inwardly and she knew she would bear the whole brunt of his anger. And all she could do was continue to protest her innocence, because to admit anything would not help her.

Ellie and Sammy were sent to school as usual, both protesting loudly that they wanted to stay behind and help find Celia. But Peggy was too distracted to listen to their grumbles and so was Dan, only warning them to say nothing about their sister's disappearance to anyone at school as he put the saddle on the horse and set off to try and find his daughter. Two hours passed before Dan returned with no success in finding Celia. Peggy was a nervous wreck by then and said that she thought the Guards should be notified, but Norah knew involving the Guards in family business was the last thing Dan would want to do. However, he knew it might come to that and, as the morning wore on, Norah began to wonder why Fitzgerald hadn't been to see her father, for she imagined he might think his missing farm hand and horse might have something to do with her sister.

However, Dinny didn't think that straight away for he didn't know Andy was missing until he'd gone to the barn to rouse him, surprised that he hadn't gone to fetch the cows in as usual, and found his bed hadn't been slept in. He was irritated that he had taken off without a word and left him in the lurch like that and complained to his wife about it as he had his breakfast after tackling the milking single-handed and she expressed concern. 'Maybe something's happened to him,' she said. 'It's not like Andy to let us down.'

'No, it isn't,' Dinny agreed. 'I mean, I know he was leaving anyway, but he gave notice in the proper way and agreed to stay on till I found a replacement and now this.'

'Like I said, maybe something has happened to him.'

'Aye, and I'd say that that might have something to do with that Mulligan girl he's sweet on.'

'If you're right maybe those Mulligan thugs have set upon him again,' Dinny's wife pointed out, for she had been incensed at Dan and Tom Mulligan beating up their farm hand for no good reason.

'Well I don't think he'd be able to do anything about her at the moment, however sweet he is on her,' Dinny said. 'Rumour has it the father has her locked in her room like some princess of old.'

'He can't do that for ever.'

'No he can't but I don't think he intends to,' Dinny said. 'He's shipping her to America as soon as ever he can.'

'Thought that was the other one, Norah – she that threw over that nice Joseph O'Leary because of it.'

'Well I don't know what they have decided. Maybe the two of them are going, but one way or another they are sending Celia away to keep her away from Andy,' Dinny went on. 'It's madness and I said as much to Dan. I mean she could take up with a right rascal in America, I hear tell there are plenty of them around, while Andy McCadden is a decent young man. Dan Mulligan has an inflated idea of himself. He thinks he's bloody royalty but he's only a blooming farmer same as the rest of us and it's madness to say that Andy McCadden isn't good enough for his daughter.'

'Dinny, while we sit here discussing something we can do nothing about, Andy might be lying injured somewhere about.'

'I bet he isn't,' Dinny said, getting to his feet. 'I think we might have seen the last of him and I don't know why he hadn't the decency to wait and tell me to my face. I would have expected that of him at least. But to put your mind at rest I will saddle up old Ned and have a look round.'

That was when Dinny discovered the horse was missing too and he was enraged. 'Going off is one thing, but stealing horseflesh is quite another.'

'What are you going to do?'

130

'The only thing to do,' Dinny said. 'I'm inform-
ing the Guards. Horses cost money and, anyway,
I've had Ned some years. I'd hate to hear of something bad happening to him. I want the Guards to
find him and bring him home and McCadden
deserves to be punished for taking him.'

Dinny went into the police station but it was
some time later before a policeman, on a bone-
shaker of a bicycle, bumped his way up the lane
and said he intended first talking to the farmers
of the area around to see if they had seen or
heard anything unusual in the night. He called at
the Mulligans' first and heard a tale of a young
daughter of the house who had climbed out of
the window in the dead of night and the policeman's suspicions were aroused. He told Dan and
Peggy of the disappearance of McCadden too,
and Dinny Fitzgerald's horse.

'It's my belief they went together on Fitzgerald's horse,' the policeman said. 'Have you
any idea where they would make for?'

Dan and Peggy were stunned. Inside Dan pure
rage was simmering, but Peggy just felt helpless.
She wondered if their harsh treatment of Celia
had led her daughter to flee her home in such a
way and with the last man in the world they would
have chosen for her and felt a wave of immeasur-
able sadness flow through her. But neither she nor
Dan had any idea where they would have gone to
and the girls also pleaded ignorance.

Dinny and his wife were no help either. 'Mc-
Cadden came from Killybegs way,' Dinny said.
'But he would hardly head for there, knowing it
would be the first place they would look for him.'

131

'There is more importance given to this now that the safety of a young girl is involved,' the policeman said. 'You don't think they might make for England?' he asked Dinny.

Dinny shook his head. 'I don't think I ever heard him express a wish to go there and Celia's family said truthfully that Celia had always said she never wanted to leave Ireland.'

'Even so,' the policeman said. 'It will do no harm to keep a watch on the ports. When I get back to the station I'll put a call through to the police in Belfast and they can take it from there.'

'Well, if they are apprehended,' said Dinny, 'ask McCadden what he's done with my horse.'

However, Dinny soon found out what happened to Ned for the policeman had only been gone an hour or so when a telegram was delivered to their door by a boy on a bicycle. Neither of them had ever received a telegram before and to their knowledge, telegrams usually conveyed bad news. Convinced it would tell of some catastrophe that had befallen their son in America, Dinny took it from the boy with hands that shook. But it wasn't from their son but from Andy McCadden who apologised for taking the horse and gave the address of where he was stabled and said Celia was travelling with him and that she was all right.

Dinny took the telegram to the police and when the Letterkenny police went to see the man at the stables he said truthfully he had never seen a woman, it had been a man who had delivered the horse. He had been polite and well-spoken and said his boss would be along for the horse later. He looked respectable and the man at the stables said he hoped he wasn't in any trouble and, no, he didn't say where he was bound for and it wasn't his business to ask.

Still, the search centred on Letterkenny, which was just as well for the police in Belfast said they hadn't the manpower to look out for a couple who just might be making for the boat. They didn't even know what these people looked like – did they in Donegal have any idea of the number of people crossing on each sailing? They would have the normal dockside police there anyway, but they wouldn't have the resources for anything further.

When Andy and Celia reached Belfast they had another wait to board the boat, as they were on the evening sailing. Celia wished the time would speed past for she knew she wouldn't feel perfectly safe from her father till she was on English soil.

She wasn't the only one to feel that way, for Andy too knew that he could relax more if a great expanse of water separated him from Dan. But as he could do nothing to speed up the process, he suggested a walk around the city. He had to send his telegram to the Fitzgeralds about the horse he'd left in Letterkenny anyway, and he did so at the first post office he came to. Otherwise, generally not knowing the city at all, they stayed close to the docks.

When they retraced their footsteps they saw the mass exodus of disembarking passengers and Celia felt excitement beginning in her feet and spreading all through her body. When the people cleared and they joined the queue of passengers waiting to board she saw the boat clearly for the first time. It was so big and imposing, standing clear out of the water with its three black funnels, that her mouth dropped open and she turned with a smile to Andy and his heart turned over, seeing her delight, and he reached for her hand and squeezed it gently. She squeezed back but knew that that really was the last time they would be able to make a gesture like that if they were to make people believe that they were brother and sister. From now on, and for the rest of this journey at least, she had ceased to be Celia Mulligan and become Celia McCadden, sister of Andy.

Andy had wondered if she'd be upset at pretending to be his sister but inwardly she had been relieved because she had been worried that Andy might want, even expect, her to submit to things she might not want to do as a sort of payment for getting her away from her father. She didn't really know how she should respond if he did that and the fact that he obviously wasn't going to press her filled her with gratitude.

There was a lot of activity on the docks and Andy had seen the police as they queued to board, but noticed they weren't scrutinising people intently and so he imagined it was just routine. He didn't mention it to Celia, feeling it might have unnerved her, but as they would soon be claiming they were siblings they didn't act like a couple. The dock police in Belfast had been told it was a couple that might be boarding so they would have taken no notice of them in any case.

The queue, hampered by heavy bags or cases, inched forward, the boat listing a little in the grey, slightly scummy water. It was secured, Celia saw, by big ropes as thick as a man's forearm wound tightly round bollards on the dockside and the boat was accessed by a wooden board with raised bits across it every so often.

'This is called the gangplank,' Andy whispered to her.

'How d'you know?' Celia asked but he hadn't time to answer for a man was saying questioningly to Andy: 'Man and wife?'

Andy shook his head. 'Brother and sister.'

The man gave a nod and directed Andy to the left and Celia to the right. 'See you in a minute,' Andy assured her, seeing the slight panic in Celia's face.

She nodded and fought to still the panic rising in her for it was too late for second thoughts; for her the die was cast now.

EIGHT

When Andy went looking for Celia later he was unable to find her. One of the other women asked who he was looking for.

'My sister,' he told her. 'Celia McCadden.'

'Is she red-haired and wearing boots and has a blue shawl around herself?'

'Yes.'

'Well I didn't catch her name or anything, but a young woman like that went to help the other one who collapsed.'

'Who collapsed?' Andy asked in alarm, thinking for a moment it was Celia the woman was talking about.

'This other one, don't know her name either,' the woman said. 'And she just sort of folded up in a heap on the deck. And,' the woman added, 'I'll tell you something odd though... I mean I didn't see that much of her, but the one who collapsed wasn't one of us, if you get my meaning. She looked a bit posh, like, not the sort of person you see travelling on their own. Usually they have a lady's maid and whatnot. You know the type?'

Andy nodded for he knew the type well enough. 'Suppose that's why she clung on so tight to the other woman who was probably your sister.'

'But where are they now?' he asked.

'Well,' said the woman. 'I heard her tell the ship's doctor who came to see if she was all right after her faint that she had come up the wrong side of the boat, because she had booked first class and that she had a cabin booked too. Hardly worth it for four hours' sailing, I wouldn't have said. But then it takes all sorts. Don't know where they went after that cos a steward came for them. You'll have to ask.'

'Yes and thank you.'

Andy did ask and explained the situation. The steward left him on the deck while he checked the first-class passenger list and spoke to the ship's doctor and then he returned to Andy.

'According to what you've told us, the lady who collapsed is a Lady Annabel Lewisham and she appears to have your sister with her,' he said. 'Come this way please, sir.' And he led the way to

136

the other side of the boat, and opened a set of metal gates that led to first-class accommodation and then down some steps to a small corridor. Before he knocked on the door marked 'Number Six', he said, 'What is your name, sir?'

'Andrew, Andy McCadden.'

'And your sister's?'

'Celia.'

And so when the steward knocked on the door and Annabel called out, 'Who is it?' he was able to answer, 'The steward, Miss and I have a chap with me the name of Andy McCadden looking for his sister, Celia.'

Annabel looked across the room to Celia. She knew her first name but nothing else about her at all and she said now, 'D'you know this man?'

'Yes, Miss,' Celia said. 'He's my brother.'

'Best see what he wants.'

So it was Celia who opened the door and she smiled at Andy as she said to the steward, 'Yes, this is my brother.'

The steward continued to stand there and Celia hoped he didn't want money for she had none to give him as she said, 'Is there anything else?'

'Yes, miss,' the steward said, obviously embarrassed. 'Your brother can't stay here. If you wish to talk to him you must move to second-class accommodation on the other side of the gate.'

'But I'm second-class and I'm here.'

'Yes but Lady Annabel Lewisham wanted you to attend to her and she's first-class and that's the difference.'

'Come on,' Andy said, seeing the steward's discomfort. 'The man's only doing his job. See if she

137

can spare you for a while because the second call has gone out for passengers not travelling on the boat to leave and we will be setting off in a minute or so. Thought you might want to come on deck and watch the shores of Ireland disappear.'

'Doubt she'll mind,' Celia said. 'It isn't as if I'm officially employed or anything.'

Annabel didn't mind for, as she said, she had virtually kidnapped Celia and hadn't even realised she had a brother travelling with her. 'You will come back though, won't you?' she asked. 'I realised when I took the boat over to Ireland that I am a very bad sailor.'

'Well I don't know how I am going to be myself yet,' Celia said. 'It's my first time on a boat of any description, but I will come back afterwards, I promise.'

As she joined Andy in the corridor she just stopped herself reaching for his hand as she realised that wasn't a sisterly action and they walked side by side to join the others on deck to find the evening air had turned misty. The engines began to throb and leaning over the side she saw the gangplank lifted and then the thick ropes that more seasoned travellers told her were called hawsers unwound from the bollards. Black smoke billowed from the funnels above them and the drone of the engines became a roar, causing vibrations all across the deck so the very rails were shaking as the boat eased itself away from the dockside and a little cheer rose from the crowd.

Celia understood that cheer, for only now could she let out the sigh of relief she hadn't even

138

been aware she was holding, and the smile she cast on Andy was warm and open. He had the urge to pick her up in his arms and spin her round, but fought the urge and stood with her at the rails as the shores of Ireland were swallowed up by the misty dusk. Celia felt a pang of homesickness for the land she never intended to leave but she didn't say any of this to Andy for she knew there had been no alternative.

Andy had been in the corridor and had overheard Celia agreeing to go back to the cabin to at least see how the lady was and she was glad when he reminded her of this now, for caring for someone else would probably stop her feeling sorry for herself. 'You'll not mind if she wants me to stay?' she asked Andy.

Andy did mind in a way because he had looked forward to sailing away together, but he realised it would be very easy to betray themselves as lovers and not siblings if they were together too much and that was what he whispered in Celia's ear and his words of endearment sent delicious trembles down her spine. Andy felt her body responding to him and he smiled ruefully and beat down any lingering resentment and said, 'I can't understand though why a lady like that is travelling without a maid.'

'I couldn't either,' Celia said. 'Because she is a true lady, Annabel Lewisham, and I asked her why she was travelling alone.'

'And what did she say?'

'She said she has to go to her brother's place in Birmingham urgently and her lady's maid was taken ill at the last minute.'

139

'And she couldn't postpone it until she was better?'

'Obviously not,' Celia said. 'And I can't really understand it and she's so young. I mean, she's very beautiful, but little more than a child I wouldn't have said. She's got jet-black hair and she has put it up, but not very well, and I thought she probably did it herself to make herself look older, I suppose, but she can't disguise her face. She has nearly white skin and big violet eyes and a nose so straight and long she could look haughty without really trying but her soft mouth saves her from that.

'Tell you something else, she had on a lovely wool coat with a hood and everything and when I helped her off with it ... Well, there's nothing to her. She has a wonderful dress on, like cream silk with flowers and lace and ribbons decorating it and a wrap sort of thing over that. Underneath there will probably be petticoats and camisoles and the like but you can still see just how thin she is and to my mind she needs looking after. I don't know what all this is about but I feel sorry for Lady Annabel, for all her privilege.'

'Then you best go back to her,' Andy said.

And Celia was to find that Lady Annabel was a terrible sailor. She had begun feeling sick almost as soon as the boat set off and by the time Celia returned and the boat was heading for the open sea she had begun heaving. Celia noted even her face had a greenish tinge and she handed her a bowl. And Celia saw the need for the cabin even for just a four-hour crossing because Annabel was violently sick over and over.

140

Celia, who was suffering no ill effects herself, felt immense sympathy for Annabel. During her bouts of sickness her hair had shaken itself free of the kirby grips and it cascaded around her face and tumbled down her back, making her look younger than ever, and still the vomiting continued. Celia held her hair away and bathed her face with cool cloths and always had water ready for her to drink. An hour passed and then another and eventually, though Annabel's stomach still churned and she still felt nauseous, the intense sickness had stopped and Annabel lay back on the bunk with a sigh. 'I am very grateful to you. You're very kind.'

'It's all right, Miss,' Celia said. 'I would do the same for anyone. You certainly do suffer.'

'Yes,' Annabel agreed. 'And I'll ensure it will be a long time before I go on a boat again.'

Celia laughed softly. 'Can't say I would blame you for that, my lady.'

Watching her, Annabel thought what a pleasant person she was and a pretty one too, especially when she smiled, and she made a decision. But first she had to find out a little bit about her and she said, 'Do you and your brother intend stopping in Liverpool?'

'I don't know,' Celia said and she didn't. She and Andy had really thought no further than arriving in England and she'd assumed they might talk about what to do next as they were crossing the Irish Sea.

'So you have no employment awaiting you?'

'No, Miss,' Celia said. 'It was just that there was nothing for either of us after our parents died and

141

we decided to try our hand in England.'

'We have a big enough depression in England too by all accounts,' Annabel said. 'But if you were prepared to travel to Birmingham with me I could find you employment as my lady's maid.'

Celia stared at her as if she couldn't believe her ears. 'But what of the lady's maid you left behind in Ireland?' she asked. 'Won't she want to return to you when she recovers from whatever it is that ails her?'

Annabel flushed a little and said, 'No, I can assure you she won't.'

Celia was still a little uncertain. 'Are you sure of that Miss, for I don't want to take employment for just a few weeks and then have to start searching again for something else?'

Annabel sighed. 'I see I have to be honest with you,' she said. 'The fact is there is no lady's maid left behind in Ireland. I have never actually had a lady's maid of my own as I have only just left the school room. My governess gave notice when I was sixteen as she said she could teach me no more, but until then I wasn't allowed to put up my hair and my governess used to deal with it. If I was required to dress for some formal occasion my mother would loan me her own lady's maid to assist me.'

'Had you lots of servants?'

'I suppose, but it's a big house,' Annabel said. 'You see, my father is really Baron Lewisham, but he thinks the title a clumsy one as his father did before him and my mother hated being called Baroness, so he calls himself and my mother Lord and Lady Lewisham and Henry is always referred to as Lord Henry, while I am Lady Annabel. That's how these things are worked out apparently.'

It quite unnerved Celia and she said, 'What about Henry's house? Are there lots of servants there too?'

Annabel gave a tinkling laugh. 'No, Henry just has an ordinary house in an ordinary road. He will inherit the Hall where we both grew up after my father is dead and become Lord Lewisham, if he chooses to use the title, or even live at the Hall at all.'

'Why wouldn't he?'

'At his work they know who he is, of course, but no one uses the title and they just call him Henry on his insistence,' Annabel said. 'He's always been that way inclined but has definitely been worse lately. He says the house is a mausoleum and it's almost indecent for all those servants to look after two people. They do so little for themselves he often says he doubts they'd have a clue how to look after themselves and he doesn't want the same thing happening to him. He didn't have to get a proper job, but he insisted on it as soon as he finished his university education.'

'So what's his house like?'

'It's big; red brick with gardens all around it. He says it's Edwardian, my governess agreed, and it has three floors with a couple of servants' quarters in the basements with room for just two or three people.'

'And that's where I will sleep?'

'No, I shall want you in the room adjoining mine where the governess used to sleep. It's a proper

143

room of its own but near to me, similar to the accommodation at the Adeiphi I always insisted on when I travelled with my governess. I would have hated relegating her to substandard servants' quarters probably located in some damp basement.'

Celia was glad of that, not because she had ideas above her station, but because she would be nervous of meeting more experienced staff who would soon discover that she wasn't a proper servant at all and so when Annabel said, 'Is becoming a lady's maid the line of work you were looking for?' Celia answered, 'Oh Miss, I am looking for any line of work. I wouldn't be too fussed what it was, but I don't know the least thing about being a lady's maid.'

'Remember I have never had a lady's maid of my own either?' Annabel said. 'Though I know some of what their duties are because of watching my mother, so I'm sure we'll manage. We'll learn together.'

'I don't even know what to call you.'

'That's easy,' Annabel said, 'I'm My Lady if you're speaking to me directly and if you are referring to me, I am Lady Annabel. Really Celia, you will be fine, I'm sure.'

Annabel's confidence in Celia's ability to do this alien thing of looking after a very young, titled lady had begun to rub off on Celia and she began to think that she really wanted to do this. She was quite drawn to Annabel who apart from her sea sickness appeared to be troubled in some way, but she had Andy to consider, so she said, 'Of course the decision isn't mine alone.'

'No,' Annabel said. 'And your brother will want to know that what I am offering you is legitimate and above board and quite right too. My brother Henry is a banker and he has recently been working abroad, setting up new banks and ensuring the staff were trained adequately when the team of British workers left. His work is at an end now though and he is on his way home. His house is in Erdington, just outside Birmingham, and he has never married, so I am going to stay with him for a while and I will be in dire need of a lady's maid.'

Celia wanted to say a very decided 'Yes,' because as the boat travelled closer and closer to England she had begun to wonder what they were going to do when they left it. 'I must talk to Andy, my lady, but are you all right for me to leave?'

'I don't think I'll be sick any more if I stay absolutely still,' Annabel said. 'My head is still pounding though and the sooner I am off this boat the better I will like it. But this has to be decided, so see if you can find your brother and put it to him.'

Celia found her brother soon enough, but she had only just begun to tell him about Annabel's proposal when she felt suddenly light-headed and she stumbled on the deck.

'Are you sea sick too?' Andy asked.

'No, hungry,' Celia said, for it had been hours since she'd eaten anything.

'Well,' Andy said. 'If you are hungry then you will eat. There is a canteen here that does delicious porridge because I had a bowl myself a little while ago. How does that sound?'

'Perfect,' Celia said.

Andy took hold of her arm and marched her across the deck to the canteen and a little later watched in amusement as Celia devoured a bowl of porridge, two slices of soda bread and two cups of tea, telling him between mouthfuls all about the plan Annabel had told her about.

Andy's initial feeling was that he hadn't brought Celia away to start life in service, but then what had he brought her away to? Most of the chaps travelling with him had plans or offers of jobs on building sites in and around Liverpool, whereas he had no plan, no job and very little money, no idea even where he would sleep that night. Left to himself he could sleep anywhere – even a park bench would do him for a night or two while he looked for work – but he couldn't inflict that on Celia. At least as a lady's maid she would have a bed to sleep in and food to eat and if he hadn't her to worry about her in that respect, it would give him time to get a job and somewhere halfway decent enough to live. Till then she could bide with this Lady.

It would mean moving to Birmingham, but that in itself wasn't a bad idea for if Dan Mulligan found out somehow that they had come to England and decided to follow them and force Celia home, Liverpool was where he would look, so it was best for both of, them not to stay long there. Also, one of the chaps travelling with him was going to Birmingham himself and he had told him what he knew about it because his uncle and aunt had lived there for some years. The man's uncle worked in the brass industry and he had put in a word for him and they had agreed to

146

try him out for a few weeks.

'Lucky you,' Andy had said.

'Well if you haven't got anything lined up,' the man said, 'Birmingham's probably a better bet than most places because my uncle said Birmingham is known as the city of a thousand trades, or it was before the war at least. So if I don't stay in the brass industry any one of them would suit me because I'm not a fussy chap.'

And neither am I, Andy thought and so as Celia finished the second cup of tea he said, 'Tell your Lady Annabel we will go with her to Birmingham and providing you feel all right about it you can be her lady's maid with my blessing.'

Celia gave an inward sigh of relief for she didn't know what to do if she rejected Lady Annabel's offer of employment for it wasn't as if they had a plan B. Anyway, she felt rather protective of her because she did seem incredibly frail and other-worldly somehow. Celia was feeling much better about everything as she left the canteen for it was amazing how much more confident a person feels when they have eaten well. When she returned to Lady Annabel and saw the lights of Liverpool and knew the boat was approaching the shores of England, she felt excited rather than apprehensive.

Lady Annabel obviously didn't feel the same and she groaned when Celia told her it wouldn't be long now till the boat docked.

'I thought you would be pleased to know that you will be off the boat soon.'

'I am pleased about that,' Lady Annabel said. 'Delighted in fact, but I feel that if I stand up my

147

head will explode and we will be staying in a hotel tonight and continuing our journey in the morning and I can't arrive looking like a scarecrow so I must somehow put my hair up.'

'I will help you, my lady, if you tell me what to do.'

Lady Annabel gave a slight nod. 'I will be glad of your assistance,' she said. 'And it's good to know how to do it for it will be one of your duties anyway.'

So between them they made Lady Annabel's, hair look more respectable and then Celia helped her on with her coat and inveigled her on the deck for she was sure the cool night air would make her feel a whole lot better. They stood together and watched England approach and the salty breeze revived Annabel somewhat and Celia was glad to see that it took the greenish tinge from her cheeks as she said, 'My brother, Henry, has an account at the Adelphi as it's where he stays when he's in Liverpool and where my father and I stayed before taking the boat on our way to Ireland. Henry will have phoned to make a reservation for me and told me to make for there and he will settle the bill later. Your brother will not be able to stay with us, though, and he will have to lodge elsewhere. It is a port so I would say there are many places a man may lay his head.'

Celia said nothing but marvelled a little at how the rich manage things, their lives and other people's.

They had to disembark in different areas and it was while Celia was waiting with Andy that she told him of the arrangements Annabel had made for their overnight stay in Liverpool. She felt quite sorry for Andy, but he assured her that he would have expected no more and as long as she was fixed up he could easily find somewhere for himself.

When Lady Annabel joined them though, she looked rather askance at Andy and said, 'What happened to your face?'

He had been asked this question by some of his fellow travellers and he said he had been riding a horse that bucked and had gone over the five-barred gate and landed in a prickly bush. He knew none of the male passengers believed it because they knew the marks of a fight on a person's face but he was grateful that they didn't press him, thinking it was his own business. Lady Annabel believed him totally and expressed sympathy and concern, but he said it was healing nicely.

They took a motorised taxi from the docks, another first for Celia and Andy, and when the cab pulled up before the sumptuous entrance to the hotel, a very smart man in uniform that Celia found out later was called a commissionaire stepped forward and opened the door for them, while another took all the luggage from the boot of the taxi.

'You have your usual suite, Lady Annabel,' the smart man said. 'And I see you have your maid with you,' he added. 'She can have an adjoining room if you wish it.'

'Yes,' Annabel said. 'And this,' she added, indicating Andy, who was standing beside them on the pavement, 'is my maid's brother who was kind enough to escort us from the docks and is now off to find his own lodging and then will be travelling back to Birmingham with us in the morning.'

'Yes, Lady Annabel,' the commissionaire said, taking her arm. She looked back at the door and said to Andy, 'Be at Lime Street Station at eleven a.m. tomorrow morning.'

'Yes, I'll be there,' Andy said. He wondered if he might be able to say good night to Celia and knew she thought the same and had taken a footstep towards him when Annabel said quite sharply, 'Celia, come along, do.'

Celia turned away with a rueful smile. The tone annoyed Andy slightly but neither he nor Celia were in a position to do anything about it – it was just the gentry pulling rank as the nicest of them were wont to do. Celia knew it too and with a slight sigh followed her mistress. Andy watched them go and then he slung his bag over his shoulder and with his hands in his pockets made his way through the dark, unfamiliar streets to the dock area where he reasoned most of the cheap lodging houses would be.

In the suite of rooms allotted to them Annabel sank thankfully into a chair with a sigh of relief as soon as the porter had left.

'Are you all right, my lady?'

'No, Celia,' Annabel answered. 'Though you were right and the night air did revive me a little, I am still very weary and my head is pounding.'

'Maybe if you eat something you'll feel better,' Celia suggested. 'Your stomach must be very empty.'

Annabel nodded. 'Yes,' she agreed. 'But my

stomach is far from right yet. I don't want to eat just to bring it back again. I think it's better to give it a complete rest for tonight and then it should have recovered by the morning. In the meantime I think I should have been honest in the beginning when I offered you the position of lady's maid and maybe when you know the truth you won't want to be my lady's maid after all, but I hope that isn't the case.'

Celia heard Annabel's voice rising in distress and saw her twisting her lace handkerchief between her agitated fingers and her heart turned over in sympathy for this girl so obviously deeply upset about something and she said, 'Don't fret about this, whatever it is. I won't leave you, I promise, and you can tell me whatever it is that's bothering you when you are feeling a little stronger.'

'No, I must tell you now,' Annabel insisted. 'We must be straight with one another.'

Celia felt a little guilty when she thought of the lies she had told about her and Andy being brother and sister. Even her surname was a false one, and she wasn't at liberty to confess any of this unless she could speak to Andy first because it affected him as well and so she pushed this to the back of her mind and turned her attention to Annabel.

'Go on then, my lady,' she urged. 'If you are determined to tell me I'm more than willing to listen to anything you have to say.'

'First I must have your solemn promise that you will not tell a living soul what I am about to say.'

'You have it, my lady.'

'I mean everyone,' Annabel said. 'Not even your brother.'

'No, I won't tell him either.'

'It's just that it's the greatest shame a woman can bear for I am expecting a baby and not married.'

Celia was shocked, but not by her words as much as the fact that she couldn't see how she could be carrying a child for she was more than thin, she was almost gaunt. 'Are you sure, my lady?'

Annabel gave a harsh little laugh. 'I'm sure, the doctor's sure and my father's sure. I'm expecting all right.'

'Who's... Who's the father?'

No doubt about Annabel's harsh tone now, as she said bitterly, 'Oh that's the best bit yet. The father is a great friend of my own father and he's nearly the same age. His name is Charles Timberlake and he was one of the crowd of men and some wives who would arrive periodically at the house for the shooting or a dinner party or some such. My home is almost a mansion, Manor Park Hall, near a little hamlet called Longdon which is the other side of Lichfield and many miles from here, thank goodness. It's set in its own grounds, acres and acres of farmland and pasture to exercise the horses, and there are always people coming to the house for they entertain a lot.'

Easy to do when you have a houseful of servants to do the work, Celia thought. She didn't say this, feeling it wasn't her place and waited for Annabel to continue.

'And the funny thing was I really liked this

152

man,' Annabel said at last and she glanced at Celia and said, 'Not that way you know, not sex. I just liked him. He talked to me and listened to what I had to say. That was a novel experience for me.' She broke off here and looked at Celia as she said, 'How old are you, Celia?'

'Eighteen.'

'And have you ever had a boyfriend?'

Celia knew she had to be careful and so she shook her head.

'Nor me,' Annabel said. 'I am sixteen and my father said I was too young to meet men. He promised me a ball when I was eighteen and he would invite all the eligible bachelors. He always said I would easily bewitch one of those men and be married by the age of nineteen. That won't happen now of course, in fact when I look into the future I see one big, dark hole.'

'Oh, Lady Annabel.'

'It's true, Celia,' Annabel said. 'Who will look at me now? And all because that man I liked, who I thought liked me as the daughter of his good friend, broke into my room one night when he was very drunk and raped me. It hurt like hell and he had his hand over my mouth so I couldn't make a sound. In fact it was so tight I thought I was going to suffocate. I was so very scared.'

Celia reached across and took one of Annabel's hands and squeezed it tight for she felt the tremors running all through her body as she re-lived that terrifying night.

'It seemed to go on forever, him pounding into me on and on and on,' Annabel continued. 'And when it was over he rolled off me and left the

153

room without a word and I was left drenched with sweat and blood.'

'Lady Annabel, this is terrible,' Celia cried. 'What did you do?'

'Nothing,' Annabel said. 'I mean, I did nothing about telling anyone. I jammed my chair against the doorknob lest someone else tried something similar and waited for the house to grow silent and when it did I lit a fire in the grate and burned the soiled sheets and the nightdress he had ripped from the neck to the hem and I crept along to the laundry room for more sheets but I had to turn the mattress because that was saturated too. Then I got dressed and went out into the dark night because I couldn't bear to see that man's face again. Fortunately, they were leaving that day which is why there had been such a boozy feast the night before and I stayed away from the house till I saw his carriage pull out through the gates. Of course I was scolded for my bad manners in not being there to bid our guests farewell, but I didn't care about that.'

'Couldn't you have confided in your mother then?'

Annabel shook her head. 'My mother is not the sort of woman anyone could confide in,' she said. 'She cares more for respectability and standing in the community than even my father does.' There was a small silence and then Annabel went on. 'I could maybe have told my governess, but she had left the week before. In fact it probably wouldn't have happened at all if she'd been there for her room was very close to mine and he probably wouldn't have risked her hearing and maybe

154

coming to my aid. As it was I had no one I could tell. Anyway, I wanted to forget the whole thing ever happened. But that was easier said than done. I was beset by nightmares so I was afraid to sleep, I had panic attacks in the day sometimes too when I felt I couldn't breathe and I lost my appetite and became listless.

'My mother initially thought I was pining for Henry who was abroad. I was too, for my mother never really cared for me and told me all the time when I was growing up that she had little time for daughters and all they were good for was marrying well. Henry was the apple of her eye and she would have been content with just him. I loved him too and he has always championed me, sometimes even against Mother, and I did miss him. It was much more than missing Henry, however, and when my monthlies stopped, the doctor was sent for because my mother was convinced I needed a tonic. When the doctor told her I was pregnant she fainted clean away.'

'You told them then who it was?'

'Oh yes and they believed that bit of it because they knew it had to be a visitor because I seldom left the house and never without at least one of them with me. I never had a chance to meet anyone.'

'So was he called to account, this man?'

'No, not exactly,' Annabel said and her face grew suddenly very sad. 'He admitted what he had done, and said he had been very drunk and that I had been leading him on all night when in fact I had hardly seen him and had gone to bed early. But my father was too drunk to remember

155

much of that night himself and my mother was little better and so they believed what the man told them. Even when he went on to say that I was waiting for him when he went to bed and I drew him into my room and I was naked and he was so drunk he couldn't help himself.

'My father told me all this later, he sort of threw the words at me. He actually said that the man claimed I had been gagging for sex, begging the man to love me properly and after all, my father said, he was only flesh and blood, like any other man, and too drunk to ignore the advances of a lewd and craven temptress. I tried to tell my father that every word Timberlake said was a lie and that I had done nothing wrong. He didn't believe me and looked at me with total disdain and said he was ashamed to have fathered such a slut. He went on to say the man admitted he had done wrong and he was prepared to pay something for the child's upkeep, but he said he couldn't take the total blame for what had happened when I had enticed him in the first place and been a willing, even an eager participant.'

'Oh my God,' Celia cried. 'Surely your father knew you better than that?'

'You'd think so, wouldn't you,' Annabel said. 'But neither he nor my mother would listen to my account of what happened and the recriminations went on and on. My mother said she couldn't believe she had given birth to such a wanton hussy without a shred of decency. Henry is the only one that might have believed me and he certainly wouldn't have let them send me away.'

'Where were you being sent?'

'To Aunt Agatha's,' Annabel said. 'She lives on the West Coast of Ireland and she takes religion to extremes and is completely intolerant of people who don't adhere to her strict regime of prayers and rigorous fasting. She would have had me on my knees all day every day and fed meagre amounts of food while she told me how sinful I was and God knows what would have happened to the child when I gave birth. Anyway, I couldn't stand it and it was unfair because I was being punished for something that wasn't my fault. So, when the boat docked in Belfast I pawned the jewellery I'd had the sense to bring.'

Celia's mouth dropped open. 'You pawned your jewellery?' she repeated incredulously. 'You went into a pawn shop?'

Annabel nodded. 'I had to because I had no money of my own.'

'I know, but I would be scared stiff to go into a pawn shop.'

'I was,' Annabel admitted. 'And it was a horrid little man who came to attend to me. At first he wanted to know the ins and outs of it all and how I came by so much jewellery and so on. I told him that that was none of his business and that all he needed to know was that I had come by it all honestly and it was mine to sell if I wished to do so.'

'So he gave you the money?'

'Of course he did,' Lady Annabel said. 'He wanted to get his hands on all that jewellery and he knew I had to have money and fast and so he probably fleeced me totally. No,' she said thinking back. 'It wasn't a pleasant experience and not one I'd want to repeat in the near future, but not

157

half as scary as being buried alive with Aunt Agatha.'

'Well all I can say is that you have some pluck, Lady Annabel.'

'Desperate situations call for desperate actions,' Lady Annabel said. 'I used some of the money to book a passage back to Liverpool. I had written to Henry as soon as I realised what my parents had planned for me. He said his business was complete and to send him a telegram in Belfast just before I got on the boat and when it docked, after a night in the hotel, to make straight for his house in Birmingham if he wasn't there to meet us at New Street Station. He also told me why our parents believed the man over me so completely.'

'Why?'

'Because it suited them to,' Lady Annabel said. 'Charles Timberlake is apparently a very influential man and extremely important to my father in business for the company needs his money to finance certain projects they are planning. Money and business is obviously more important to him than his own flesh and blood.'

Celia was appalled by what Annabel had told her, which was so obviously true and which she was still so affected by. No wonder she saw her future as a black hole for even Celia could see no way forward after this. Maybe housekeeper to her brother was the best she could hope for and as for the future of the child... Annabel had finished her tale and asked Celia if she wanted to continue to be lady's maid to her and Celia replied emphatically that she did.

Both Celia and Annabel were very tired but

Annabel explained to Celia that she couldn't go to bed with her hair fastened up with kirby grips and it all had to be loosened and brushed one hundred times before plaiting it. Then Celia took out Annabel's nightgown from the portmanteau and helped her into it and made sure she was tucked into bed before being free to get ready for bed herself.

She was so bone-tired she was sure she would sleep easily. However, once she was alone Annabel's words echoed in her head and she remembered how upset and agitated her young mistress had been in recounting the rape she had endured and felt such sympathy for her that, despite the fact that the bed in the little room adjoining Annabel's was perfectly comfortable, sleep eluded her as she tossed and turned. She felt quite helpless to ease the circumstances of what had happened to Annabel in any way and resolved only to be as good a lady's maid as she could be and maybe a measure of support for her young mistress if the occasion arose. Finally, as dawn was beginning to turn the sky a pearly grey, she fell into an uneasy doze.

NINE

The following morning Celia found that putting up Annabel's hair was far easier that it had been on the boat and Annabel was delighted and said that Celia had the makings of a first-rate lady's maid. Eventually, Annabel decided they were both fit to be seen and what a breakfast awaited them as they went down to the dining room. Both girls were hungry and tucked into a bowl of porridge with sugar and cream, followed by bacon and a fried egg followed by toast and marmalade and as much tea as they wanted. When she had finished, Celia sat back with a sigh and said, 'I have never had a breakfast like that in the whole of my life.'

Annabel, to whom such breakfasts were commonplace, was charmed by Celia's evident delight and she smiled at her as she said, 'I wonder if your brother fared as well in his lodgings?'

Andy could have told her he did not. He had very little money left and had to eke it out till he could earn more and so he had looked for the cheapest place to spend the night. Eventually he shared a room with two Irish navvies, who stank of beer, tobacco and sweat and snored all night long so he was almost glad when it was light enough to get up. The navvies told him that the seaman's mission did a good cheap breakfast and they were right for Andy found the porridge thick and filling, the bread and butter plentiful and the orange tea so strong he imagined you could stand the spoon up in it.

But Andy didn't linger over his breakfast for he didn't know how far away the station was and the result of that was he arrived on the platform half an hour before he was due to meet the others. And that's how he bumped into Seamus Docherty, one of the young men he used to meet at the dances in Donegal. He was delighted to see Andy and came over and shook him by the hand.

'Long time no see,' he said. 'Thought you were at Fitzgerald's place?'

'I was,' Andy said, hastily scanning the entrance to see if he could see Celia or Annabel. 'I gave notice.'

'Oh, so what you doing here?' Seamus persisted. 'In the station I mean.'

Andy had to think fast. 'Oh, I was acting as porter,' he said. 'Saw this family with loads of luggage and offered to give them a hand. They were very grateful.'

'Grateful enough to tip you?'

'Yeah and every little helps till I get a proper job.'

'What you looking for?'

'Thought I'd try me hand at the building,' Andy said. 'There seems a lot of Irishmen at it already.'

'There are,' Seamus agreed with a nod. 'And that's the point, isn't it? I'd say it's hard to get a job in the building. Anyway I thought you were set at the Fitzgeralds' – and didn't you have a thing going with Celia Mulligan?'

'Just a bit of fun.'

'Seemed pretty serious to me the way you were with her at the dances.'

'Not at all,' Andy said. 'She took it in the same vein.'

'Hope for your sake she did,' Seamus said and added, 'Women can be the very devil when a man tries to have a bit of fun that way.'

'Celia knew the score and knew there was no future for us,' Andy said. 'And as for the Fitzgeralds, I just fancied a change. What about you? What brings you to Liverpool?'

161

'My Uncle Phillip's funeral,' Seamus said. 'Moved some years ago and dropped dead the other day of a heart attack and before that Dad said he'd never had a day's illness in his life. He was the youngest brother so Daddy was nearly twenty years older than him but he's getting a bit shaky on his feet these days so I came in his stead.'

Andy was only giving half an ear to what Seamus was saying. Looking over his head to the entrance, he saw Annabel and Celia come in and said hastily to Seamus, 'Well, it's been lovely talking to you and give my regards to all those back home but I must be off now to do the tour of the building sites.'

'Oh, I thought we might go for a pint together.'

'No money for beer with no job.'

'My treat. You'd do the same for me.'

Andy was desperate to get rid of Seamus. Any minute Celia or Annabel would spot him and probably hail him and then the game would be up.

'Sorry, Seamus. Another time maybe?'

Seamus sensed Andy's preoccupation though he had no idea what it was all about. 'No likelihood of another time if you'll be biding in England now.'

'No, I suppose not,' Andy said. 'And I'm really sorry but I really have to go now.'

'All right. I'm not holding you,' Seamus said a little huffily and he watched Andy hurry across the platform and he saw two women, who he hadn't noticed before, turn as he passed, though he was some way away from them. One of them put up her hand as if to hail him and he gave a sharp, quick shake of the head and she dropped her arm, confused. Seamus moved closer and he saw clearly

162

who it was. Celia Mulligan and she must have run away with Andy McCadden, the sly old fox.

So intrigued was he that he slid behind a pillar for it was fairly obvious the tale about staying in Liverpool and looking for a job in the building was false. Andy McCadden and Celia and maybe the strange woman with them were bound further afield, for Andy had a bulging knapsack on his back and the two women were surrounded by cases.

When Andy returned to the station, looking round him to check that Seamus had gone, the train was ready to pull out and Annabel said sharply, 'You cut it fine.'

'You did,' Celia agreed. 'And that was because you went running out of the station just minutes ago. Why did you do that?'

Andy was busy loading everything onto the train and so he just said, 'I'll tell you when we are on our way.' Annabel had booked first-class seats for herself and Celia and Andy had booked third-class for himself and, as the train began to move forward, Celia said she would help Andy find his carriage because she sensed he wanted to talk to her. As they stepped into the corridor, Andy began telling her of his encounter with Seamus Docherty.

'Didn't he know what had happened?' Celia said. 'I would have said it would have been all around the county by now.'

'It may well be,' Andy said. 'But Seamus was travelling to a funeral at the time. No doubt he will be fully informed when he returns.'

'Does it matter?'

'Shouldn't think so,' Andy said. 'He didn't catch sight of you, I don't think.'

'That's why you didn't want me to wave.'

'Yes and why I didn't approach you at all. I told Seamus I was staying on in Liverpool to look for a job in the building like many of the men I travelled over with.'

'Did he believe you?' Celia asked.

'Think so,' Andy said. 'Why wouldn't he believe me? And if anyone comes looking for me working on a building site in Liverpool they will come unstuck for I will probably be doing something completely different and living in Birmingham.'

Celia let out a great sigh of relief. 'Yes and no one has the least idea where we're bound for.'

As the train left the station with a clatter of wheels and picked up speed, Seamus stepped forward from the pillar he had hidden behind and remarked to a passing guard, 'That train is in one almighty hurry. Where's it bound for anyway?'

'Oh that,' the guard said. 'Bound for New Street Station in Birmingham, that one. It'll hit on a few more stations on the way but that's where it will end up.'

And Seamus smiled, knowing that when he made his way home later that day he would have a fine tale to tell to everyone back home in Donegal.

The train journey was uneventful, but travel was such a novel experience to Celia that she was enjoying the views of the countryside flashing past the window. When the train had chugged through two small stations without stopping or even slowing down noticeably, though, she asked if the

164

train was stopping anywhere before New Street in Birmingham.

'We will stop at some of the bigger stations,' Annabel said. 'The first the train stops at after Liverpool is Chester and we will be coming to that very soon.'

And when they did, Celia didn't think it was that big at all. But the train didn't pause long before it was off again and when it next stopped it was at a place called Crewe, which was much bigger and so many people were waiting to join the train and almost as many got off.

'Busy station this,' Annabel said. 'It's a sort of junction where people going some place other than Birmingham can change trains at, but we don't have to do that.

'Now,' she said as the train started again, 'it's a fair distance to Stoke-on-Trent, which is the next stop, so what d'you say to fetching your brother and we'll go on the dining car and have a bite to eat?'

'They have a dining car on a train?' Celia asked incredulously.

Annabel gave her little tinkling laugh and said, 'Of course they have.'

There was no 'of course' about it, Celia thought as she lurched along the corridor to find her brother who was certainly agreeable to Annabel's suggestion. He was feeling the journey to be a tedious one and he was feeling peckish and not sure what to do about it and so in minutes there they were in the doorway of the dining car, which looked like a very plush restaurant and, despite the sound of the wheels on the rails and the swaying motion, it was hard to believe they were on a train. There were pretty curtains at the windows and the tablecloths were pure white and lace trimmed and the upturned glasses sparkled and the silver cutlery gleamed. Celia and Andy were rather over-awed by it, but Annabel took it in her stride and she stepped into the car and took the seat the waiter pulled out for her and took up the menu.

Celia had never been in such a restaurant in her life, never mind have a man pull out a chair for her as if she was someone of importance, but she tried to follow Annabel's lead though she felt awkward and she saw that Andy felt just as bad, totally out of his depth.

'I never imagined there were places like this on a train,' Celia whispered to Annabel.

'Well how many trains have you been on?'

'Oh not many,' Celia admitted. 'None at all until we decided to leave Ireland, but this is like a proper restaurant.'

'It is a proper restaurant,' Annabel said. 'And can be very annoying when everything is sliding all over the place. Now what shall we have?'

Neither Celia nor Andy could decide and so Annabel ordered tea and buttered crumpets. Celia and Andy had never tasted crumpets but found them delicious, especially spread with the delicious jam they brought too.

Later, Andy sat alone in the railway carriage with nothing to do and remembered what the fellows on the boat had told him about the slump in England and that many of them had jobs on the buildings lined up.

'A man came round the town looking for

labourers,' one had told him. 'Tell you, he was spoilt for choice for lots of us had no jobs, you know? Anyway he came down the pub and spoke to us and engaged us all on the spot. All we had to do was get here and report to him.'

'We were lucky,' another said. 'It's damned hard to get set on unless you know someone, I was told.'

Andy thought that what they intimated at was the truth because that morning as he'd made his way to the station he had seen groups of unemployed men lounging on street corners. There was no reason to suppose Birmingham was faring any better than Liverpool, whether it was the city of a thousand trades or not. He began to doubt the wisdom of leaving Ireland altogether when England seemed in as bad a shape or worse. They could have maybe tried Dublin. That was a good long way from Donegal.

But they were here now and so had to make the best of it and he knew he could find it easier to face hardship if Celia was protected from it, so it was a damned good job Lady Annabel had taken such a shine to her.

Celia too was realising her good fortune in meeting Lady Annabel and she felt rather protective of the young girl and thought it shocking that her family had taken the word of a visitor to their house over the daughter they had reared. She could only hope that her brother, Henry, who she set such store by, would not let her down too.

Annabel seemed to have no doubts about Henry and told Celia how good, kind and generous he was as the train thundered on.

'How far is it now?' Celia said when there was a break in the conversation.

'Not much further,' Annabel said. 'We're pulling into Stoke now and it's Wolverhampton next and from there Birmingham is no distance away.'

And so it seemed and, as the train neared New Street Station, Annabel hugged her with excitement.

'Soon I will see my beloved Henry,' she explained to Celia. 'And,' she added with absolute confidence, 'he will take care of everything.'

Celia fervently hoped that he would and waited to meet him with trepidation. When the train eventually drew to a halt with a squeal of brakes and a hiss of steam, Celia, standing in the corridor, was both fascinated and nervous. She had thought Lime Street Station busy and she'd had plenty of time to look at it as they had waited impatiently for Andy to arrive, but she had never seen anything the size and scale of New Street.

There was also a general cacophony of noise, the clatter of trains arriving at other platforms, the squeal of brakes and the odd ear-splitting screech from the hooters. As Andy joined them and they stood on the platform with their cases around them, Celia was aware of the announcer's voice trying to break through the hubbub, but what she was trying to say was indecipherable, as was the voice of the newspaper seller, drowned out by the general noise. People were greeting others, talking, laughing and shouting and there was the steady tramp of feet as people made for the exits. None of this seemed to bother the porters who weaved

168

apparently easily through the milling hordes, warning people to 'Mind your backs please.'

Andy was wondering if he should try and bag one of these porters to carry all their luggage to the taxi rank outside when suddenly on the platform, through the soot-laden steam that wafted in the air, appeared the most handsome man Celia had seen in the whole of her life. He was also the best dressed man. Back home in Ireland the men would wear suits for Mass, but many looked constrained and uncomfortable in the formal clothes. This man was at ease in his navy suit with the pristine white shirt, and his tie fastened with a golden pin, matching the handkerchief in his top pocket and polished leather shoes on his feet.

Annabel gave a small shriek. 'Henry,' she cried and leapt into his arms with a cry of delight and as his arms tightened around his sister, Celia caught the flash of gold cufflinks at his wrists. She realised that, though Henry might be all that Annabel had said he was – good and kind and generous – he had something else too and that was his air of authority, which he wore so easily. He was courteous enough and shook her hand very cordially when Annabel introduced them and Henry soon organised a porter and all the luggage was packed on a trolley ready to be pushed to a waiting taxi.

Celia was astounded by the many shops that lined the streets as the taxi eased its way out of the station and into the city centre traffic and some of the shops were so big. Magee's was the biggest shop in Donegal Town, not that she had ventured in there much for their mother had always said it was too expensive and not for the likes of them anyway, but some of these stores she passed in the taxi would dwarf Magee's.

The sheer volume of people thronging the pavements unnerved her a little, never mind the traffic, even when the city centre was left behind them. And then there were the clanking swaying monsters that ran on rails set into the road that Annabel told them were called trams and here and there cyclists dodged between the traffic. The road seemed too narrow for the amount of vehicles on it and yet everything kept moving.

Here and there Annabel would point things out to Celia and Andy, like the big green clock that stood on an island on its own in a place called Aston Cross. Aston Cross had other things as well: a mass of shops lining both sides of the street and then a large building on one side that Annabel said was Ansell's Brewery as they drove alongside it and, on the other side, a lot of small houses that looked squashed all together.

'Back to backs,' Annabel said almost dismissively, but didn't explain what 'back to backs' were. As they crossed over what Annabel called Salford Bridge, Celia caught a glimpse of water. 'It's the canals,' Annabel told her when she mentioned this. 'There is a big canal network here and when we're over the bridge one branch of the canal will run alongside the lane.'

Annabel was absolutely right. Once over the bridge the driver turned right and they were in the countryside and they bowled along now and then Celia saw the gleam of water.

'We're coming to Holly Lane soon,' Henry

suddenly told them both. 'Look to your right as we pass and you'll see a hump-back bridge that's over the canal and Fort Dunlop is beyond that – where they make the tyres, you know?' Celia did not know and wondered if Andy did, but she nodded knowledgably enough. The canal veered to the right after that and they turned into Holly Lane.

'How much further?' Celia asked.

'Oh no distance now,' Annabel said airily. 'Henry's house is on Grange Road and that leads off Holly Lane. We shall be there in minutes.'

And they were. The taxi drew up before two ornate gates and, as the driver got out to open them, Celia noticed with slight amusement that there was a lion atop a pillar on either side. It was, however, a fine house of red brick and three stories high as Annabel had said, with a great many windows and chimneys and steps at the side that led down to a cellar and Celia wondered what a man on his own was doing living in such a large house with so many rooms. 'Must rattle round like a – pea in a drum,' she thought as the taxi, with a splutter of gravel, drew up before the house where three marble steps led up to an oak studded door. Henry got out and began to pay the driver, and only Celia noticed the concerned frown between his eyes. She guessed he was more worried about his sister than he was showing at the moment and no wonder because whichever way you looked at it, Annabel was in one hell of a fix.

Celia was right for Henry was thinking of his sister. He knew Timberlake, and he had never doubted her once in the letter she had sent him which had told him everything. He had no time

171

for the man who appeared to possess no morals at all, because Annabel wasn't the first girl Timberlake had raped, and yet Henry had never thought for one moment that he would sink to raping the daughter of a friend, especially when he was accepting hospitality from that friend.

However, he also knew with a sinking heart that, even if he could get his parents to admit Annabel's innocence in this, which he doubted, she would still have to bear the shame of having an illegitimate child. It was rare for a young woman of the privileged classes to find herself in such a dilemma as they were usually well protected from predatory men. If the unthinkable did happen then usually a worker on the estate would agree to rear the child for an agreed sum of money.

He imagined that his father would be thinking along those lines once he knew that Annabel wasn't being buried alive in the wilds of Ireland. With such arrangements in place, after the birth, Annabel could forget this distressing incident ever happened and get her life back on track. In the meantime though, she needed someone with her for he had a job to do and Celia McCadden would do as well as anyone, not least because his sister had taken to her and she didn't take to everyone.

They stepped into a large hall with black and white tiles on the floor and a sweeping staircase led up the carpeted stairs. As Henry had no staff, Andy helped him carry all the cases up the stairs and along the landing where Celia felt her feet sink into the carpet as she passed numerous doors, wondering what was behind them all. Annabel ran ahead for she had her own room in the house, chosen because of its size and because of the adjoining room where the governess used to sleep.

'And now you can, dear Celia,' she said.

Celia glanced at Henry, for he might have had different ideas, but he said, 'It would be better to be near Annabel if you don't mind that, Celia. In case she needs you in the night, especially as her pregnancy progresses.'

Mind? Celia thought as she had a peep in the room assigned to her. What was there to mind?

Celia's room was spacious. The large and ornate bed dominated the room although there was also a bank of wardrobes, two chests of drawers, a dressing table and a handsome desk. The room was also attractively decorated and there were gorgeous drapes at the large picture windows that overlooked the garden.

'This is your room,' Annabel said leading the way to it and wrinkling her nose as she said, 'I'm afraid it's not very big.'

'Oh Lady Annabel,' Celia cried, 'I've never had a room of my own before and to be honest it's like a little palace to me with the lovely thick carpet on the floor by the bed and the bed itself looks very welcoming and comfortable. And I won't know myself with all the storage. I haven't the clothes to nearly half fill the drawers in the chests, let alone the wardrobe and dressing table I have all to myself.'

'So you're happy with it then?'

'Oh, Lady Annabel, much more than happy.'

Andy was brought to see it at Annabel's insistence, so he could see where his sister was going to sleep and Celia, busily unpacking Annabel's

173

clothes, could see that he was impressed.

'Proper fell on your feet here, Celia,' he hissed as he passed her and though she was unable to speak because Annabel was approaching, the beaming smile she cast him was answer enough.

When everything was done Henry wondered what they should do for something to eat, for neither Andy nor Celia were dressed well enough to eat in the establishments he was used to and they would maybe feel awkward if he took them there and also they were weary from the travelling anyway. He had never told his mother for she would have been horrified how many times he had eaten fish and chips, introduced to it by fellow soldiers and even officers in the army. His mother thought such things common but then his mother had never lived a proper life and he thought fish and chips would be the best option for them that night anyway.

So Henry said, 'Now we have no cook, though I intend to remedy that as soon as possible, but for now how would you like me to go out and bring fish and chips in?'

Annabel had never had fish and chips from a shop and such things were alien to Celia and Andy as well. But they were all hungry and prepared to eat anything and so they said that that would be fine for them and Henry set off to fetch them for he knew where the shop was and he didn't want Andy getting lost.

When Annabel told her that they would likely be wrapped in newspaper, Celia went into the kitchen to organise plates and then stood still in the doorway for she had never seen a kitchen so

174

big. A scrubbed table stood in the middle of the room with chairs arranged around it and against the wall was a large range and above it on hooks were copper saucepans of every size and shelves ran from floor to ceiling on one side of the range and on the other was a series of drawers. The shelves were filled with crockery and all manner of cooking dishes and in one of the drawers Celia found cutlery. Annabel, who had followed her in, told her that the door to the left was a pantry but the shelves in there were woefully bare. By the time Henry came back the table was laid and the kettle was singing on the range.

Celia was to find that fish and chips made a delicious meal and while she was eating it she asked Henry, 'How is it that your house is so clean? I imagined at the very least a film of dust everywhere if not cobwebs festooning every nook and cranny.'

'I employ an agency,' Henry said with a smile. 'There are plenty of small households like mine who don't want to leave staff in the house, often for an indefinite period, and so an agency come in once or twice a week according to what you require and air the place and keep it clean. I sent them a letter cancelling their services when I knew when I was coming home.'

'Well they've done a good job, I'd say,' Celia said. 'For the place is lovely and the beds made up too, I noticed. It must be nice to have the money to have your life made so comfortable.'

'If they hadn't done a good job then I would complain and then people might lose their jobs,' Henry said. 'They wouldn't risk that. And you have helped me too.'

'How?'

'Well first, I am very grateful for the way you looked after Annabel, especially when she was so sick on the boat,' he said to Celia. 'And now she's here she has need of a lady's. maid and, as you have agreed to do that, it is one less thing to worry about and I'll see that you don't lose by it.'

He knew he had to do something for Celia's brother for he had seen his slight animosity and the man had obviously been in a fight of some sort. He knew plenty of Irishmen who were big drinkers and handy with their fists and he wanted neither type in his employ, but possibly Celia would not stay long without her brother. He spoke in an off-hand way, turning to him and saying, 'As for you, a house this size always needs a handyman. You can do all the jobs that need doing and fill in where necessary and help keep the garden tidy and things like that.'

Celia clapped her hands with glee, so happy and relieved that they had both found work so quickly and easily in a country where so many were unemployed.

She was so happy that she was unaware that Andy hadn't spoken, for he had no intention of being a lackey to some jumped-up Englishman. Henry represented everything that Andy hated and he had no intention of working for him, but he said nothing and Henry thought everything had been sorted out.

Andy didn't sleep much that night for he wrestled with his conscience and that kept sleep at bay. With Celia's future secure he had to leave sooner rather than later when he still had a little money to tide him over for a wee while at least. He knew that Celia would be devastated if he was to just disappear and yet that's what he must do.

He felt more confident in leaving her now that Henry had arrived because, though he didn't like the man, two girls alone were in need of male protection. Celia had told him Annabel had no intention of going home, telling him only that she'd had an awful row over a man her parents wanted her to marry that she didn't care for and Andy accepted that.

However, even as he decided he must leave, a little voice of reason advised him not to look a gift horse in the mouth. 'Surely,' it said, 'any job is better than no job.' He ignored that voice because in his mind's eye he wanted to learn a trade so that when he married Celia in three years' time he would be trained, or nearly so, and earning enough to support them both. And even if Celia were never allowed to go home again he would know he had done right by her.

Andy had been housed in the basement and he was glad of this when he rose in the early hours with a heavy heart for he knew he would miss Celia as much as she would miss him. But trusting he was doing the right thing, the only thing, he packed his knapsack.

He couldn't just walk out of Celia's life without leaving her some sort of note though. He hadn't anything with him to write any sort of letter but in the dining room where they had eaten their fish and chips he had noticed a bureau set against the window and he made his way there on stockinged feet, carrying his boots in his hands. The desk dropped down when the bureau was opened and inside Andy found both paper, pens and envelopes. In his haste to sit and write the important letter he dropped one of the boots and it landed with a dull thud on the thick carpet and, though Andy waited a while and listened, he was fairly convinced the noise wasn't loud enough to disturb anyone.

It had woken someone though. Annabel's room was above the dining room and she had been lying awake going over and over the night Timberlake raped her and she heard the thud of the boot hitting the floor at an hour when no one should be abroad. She crept to the door of Celia's room but she was fast asleep. She thought of rousing Henry, but then she told herself it might be nothing and she decided to see for herself first and so she stole down the stairs silently and on bare feet.

The dining room door was ajar and she pushed it open further to see Andy bent over the desk scribbling furiously. She watched as he signed the letter and then folded it and put it in an envelope which he sealed. He looked around the room, as if deciding where to put it, but when he strode from the room a little later Annabel, secreted under the stairs, saw he still had the letter in his hand as he made for the kitchen. Annabel followed and saw him slip the letter behind the clock on the mantelshelf above the hearth. He gave a heavy sigh and then he opened the door and was gone.

Annabel was across the floor in minutes to retrieve the letter and stood holding it in her

178

hand, wondering what to do with it. Andy had run out on his sister, that much was clear, and Celia would be bitterly upset. Any sister would be, because he had given no indication of what he had intended the night before. Annabel imagined the letter would explain it all. But what if that should further distress Celia? Had Annabel the right to find out? In her heart of hearts she knew she hadn't and that it should be given unopened into Celia's hand. Even knowing this, Annabel filled up the kettle and put in on the range.

She was to find that steaming letters open isn't as easy as people would have you believe in books and she scalded her hand in the steam and still the glue wasn't that accommodating. She ripped the edge of the flap in her attempt to ease it up and so she knew Celia would know she had opened it. Thinking she might as well be hung for a sheep as a lamb she stuck her finger in the hole she had made and sliced it open, withdrew the letter and as she read it her eyes opened wide with astonishment.

My dear, darling Celia,

I'm heartsick to leave you this way, my darling girl, but you seem set with the Lewishams and if you stay there, will have a guarantee of food to eat and a roof over your head and a wage, while, I at present can offer you none of those things. I need to establish myself in some sort of job and find somewhere to live as well, so please bide there with patience, believing that we will be together very soon and then the future will be ours to savour. Never doubt my love for you. I am leaving you because I love you and I will be in

*touch again as soon as I am financially secure so that
I can care for you properly.*
Your ever loving Andy

From the content of the letter Annabel knew
Andy McCadden was not Celia's brother, but
her lover. That put matters on a different footing
altogether for she knew then that any time Andy
could come and take Celia away, he'd said so in
the letter, and just at that moment her need for
Celia was greater than his. Annabel had found
few people to trust in her life. Henry was one and
Celia another for, although she was of the servant
class, she was the only female confidante Annabel had and so she decided it might be better if
she didn't see the letter.

What to do with it was a problem because the
fires had not been lit at the moment, nor the
boiler, and Annabel knew she'd probably be
unable to burn something in the range without
being seen, so she took the letter to her room.
There was a desk in her room very similar to the
one her father had had in his library and it had a
secret panel in it that had fascinated her as a
child. She used to leave messages for herself in
there Henry knew this and so when he had been
choosing bedroom furniture for the guest room
to match the rosewood wardrobes that were already fitted in he bought a desk to please Annabel, as well as the chest of drawers and fancy
dressing table. Annabel remembered how
enchanted she had been by the desk but that had
been when she was young, before the nightmare
had begun.

However, now she thought it would do to hide the letter in for now. The secret drawer was operated by a little lever at the very back and she felt around until her groping fingers found it and she pushed it to the right. There was a click and the front panel to the side of the main desk slid open just like her father's used to and she put the letter inside, the compartment. Then she pushed the lever to the left and it shut so completely that you would never guess that one side would open and she knew the letter would be safe there for the time being.

She went back to bed but, though it was still very early, she was unable to sleep because she did feel guilty about hiding the letter. But she hardened her heart when she remembered the way Celia and Andy had deceived her by saying they were brother and sister. And yet she knew by concealing the letter that she would cause Celia extreme pain, more pain than if Andy had really been her brother because she had obviously fled her home to be with him. She must have loved him very much, for she had put her reputation on the line and it would be in shreds if he left her without a word and Annabel knew that's what Celia would think when she found him missing.

Annabel wondered for a brief moment what she would do if Andy turned up as he'd said he would when he secured a job that could keep them both. However, she knew there were not many of those kind of jobs in Birmingham at that time so it might be an age before he returned for Celia. And by then she might have fallen out of love with him, especially if she thought he had let her down, and at any rate she might be too angry and distrustful of him to leave Annabel. Anyway, Annabel decided to cross that bridge when she came to it and when she heard Celia moving about in the next room she lay down and closed her eyes.

'Good morning, Lady Annabel,' Celia said as she crossed the room and pulled open the curtains.

Annabel gave a sigh and rubbed her eyes sleepily as if she had just woken up as Celia went on, 'It's a lovely day, my lady, already sunny and warm. Makes you glad to be alive, a day like this.'

'Are you always so cheerful at this hour, Celia?'

Celia laughed. 'I suppose I am, Lady Annabel. I know everyone's not the same, but you get in the habit of rising early growing up on a farm so you sort of get used to it.' She looked at the clock and thought that her father and brothers would have the cows milked by now and the byre washed out and be sitting down to their breakfast porridge. She nearly said this. But then she realised in time the lies she had told Annabel that she had to continue with and she had a sudden longing to see Andy, for just to see him would still any doubts she might have and he always was optimistic about the future. And if they should be alone and he could put his arms around her, that would be even better.

But there was a lot to do before she had a chance to even catch a glimpse of Andy and the first thing she had to do was help Lady Annabel dress. Celia had never been in service before and could see no reason why she had to help an adult woman dress herself, but apparently that's how the rich and privileged liked things and Henry was giving her five shillings a week to act as lady's maid to his sister and so she bit back her irritation.

When they went downstairs it was to find Henry coming in the door with a bag of oatmeal under his arm.

'In the absence of a cook at the moment,' he said in explanation to Celia, 'I thought you may be able to cook porridge.'

'I can cook most things if I have the ingredients,' Celia said. 'My mother insisted on it. She...' She broke off, knowing it was safer not to talk of her life in Ireland, but Henry put her hesitation down to sadness over her mother's death. To distract her he said, 'I looked for your brother to fetch the oatmeal but I couldn't find him.'

'What d'you mean, you couldn't find him?' Celia asked. 'Wasn't he in his room?'

'Not when I looked.'

So Celia went to look herself and what she saw chilled her to the marrow. Even accepting the fact that he wouldn't have taken many clothes out of his knapsack the previous night, there should have been some indication that he had slept in the room, but there was none. The sheets and blankets were neatly folded on the end of the bed, his jacket was gone from the back of the door and there was no sign of his knapsack and no clothes, even dirty ones, left on the floor.

Celia knew with dread certainty that Andy had left her, here alone in a strange country with people she had only just met. She thought he loved her and she had left her home so that they

183

could have a future together. 'Oh God!' she thought. She was fearful of the future without the man she loved beside her. Tears flowed from her eyes as she cried at the black betrayal of Andy and suddenly her legs refused to hold her up and she sank to the floor in a paroxysm of grief.

TEN

Celia opened her eyes and then wished she hadn't bothered because Andy's betrayal and his lack of thought for her struck her afresh. What a fool she felt now and she gave a low groan.

'Oh thank goodness,' said Annabel's voice and Celia turned her head slowly and was surprised to see that she was lying on her own bed and Annabel was crossing the room towards her from the window. 'How did I get here?' she asked.

'Henry carried you,' Annabel said. 'Golly, you gave us both a start. We heard you give a cry and Henry and I went down to see what the matter was and there you were in an unconscious heap on the floor. He carried you up here and sent for the doctor.'

Doctors hadn't been sent for unless there was a dire emergency in the Mulligan household, for doctors cost money, and so Celia said, 'Really there's no need, I'm fine now.'

It wasn't strictly speaking true and anyway it did no good.

'There is every need,' Annabel said. 'And

Henry said he might as well look me over as well because since the doctor who told my mother about my pregnancy I've been seen by no one medical and Henry said I must be checked over to make sure everything's going as it should.'

'Yes, I suppose it would be as well,' Celia said. 'Though where I lived in Ireland the doctor only came if there were problems. A neighbour woman would help and usually that was enough.'

'I doubt you would find a woman willing and able to do that behind the lace curtains in this road, do you?' Annabel asked with a smile.

Celia found herself unable to smile back for she felt benumbed by sadness as she replied, 'I suppose it would be difficult.'

Annabel looked at Celia's woebegone face and she felt shame wash over her. 'Ah Celia, are you very upset about your brother leaving?'

'Of course I am,' Celia cried. 'Who wouldn't be upset? It was the way it was done.' And then a thought struck her. 'I suppose there was no note explaining everything?'

Annabel lowered her head to hide the flush she felt burning her cheeks as she said, 'No. That was the first thing Henry thought of and as soon as he had carried you up here we both searched. But, as I said to Henry, we didn't need to be really thorough, because if your brother had gone to the bother of writing a note to you, he would have left it in a fairly prominent place – otherwise what would be the point of writing it?'

'There wouldn't be one,' Celia said. 'And it isn't as if he has anywhere to go for this is his first time in England and he knows no one.'

Annabel, remembering what Andy had written in the letter, suggested, 'He might be going to try and find employment and a place to live before coming back for you.'

Celia shook her head. 'He could have had employment here, it was offered to him and he'd have found some way of letting me know if that's what he intended. I think I must accept the fact that he has gone and that's that. That's why he didn't accept your brother's offer of employment. He is telling me that there is no place for me in his life any more and I have no idea why he felt that way.' She looked at Annabel and her eyes were like pools of sadness as she said, 'I am truly heartbroken to tell you the truth.'

Deep shame filled the whole of Annabel's body and she had an actual pain in her own heart and she very nearly confessed to Celia what she had done, but she stopped herself just in time because she had the idea that if she was to tell Celia what she had done and show her the letter Celia wouldn't stay with her. She might go and see if she could find her lover and Annabel knew that to be all alone day after day would scare her to death.

'What is it?' Celia asked, because she knew Annabel was agitated about something.

'It ... it's Henry,' Annabel said. 'He wants to see you, ask you something, but I don't know that you are up to it yet.'

'What does he want to ask me?'

'I'll let him tell you himself,' Annabel said. 'Are you feeling strong enough to get up if I help you?'

Celia didn't feel strong at all. She felt as if none of her body was connected and her head was filled with cotton wool and her heart was as heavy as lead, but she agreed to see Henry, knowing she didn't really have a choice because her life was linked to Lady Annabel and her brother.

'I'll manage,' she said.

However, when she got out of bed she felt decidedly shaky and Celia was glad of Annabel's arm as they crossed the room and went down the stairs where they found Henry. He was pleased to see Celia so much better, but he also noticed the pallor of her skin and asked if she was well enough to be up, but she brushed his concerns aside.

'I'm well enough,' she said. 'Annabel said you wanted to speak to me?'

Henry nodded. 'I did, yes,' he said but what he went on to say made her look at him in amazement for it was the very last thing she expected him to say. 'So,' he went on, 'it would be a tremendous favour for you to agree to do this.'

'But why would you want me to change my name?'

'Because Lewisham is a very well-known name in certain circles in Birmingham. And those are the circles Annabel has to move in when she is back in society. It is important that there is no scandal attached to her if she is to get the chance to marry well. If you change names with her for now it will help enormously.'

'But I speak with an Irish accent and what about my clothes?' Celia cried. 'You can call me anything you like but I'll never be a grand lady like Lady Annabel.'

'If explanations should be needed we could say that you grew up in Ireland,' Henry said. 'As for clothes, Annabel has plenty and most of them she will be unable to get into soon anyway.' And then as she still hesitated he cried, 'Please, Celia, if you care for Annabel at all, please do this to help her?'

Celia looked across at Annabel, who was biting her lip in agitation in a way that made her look even younger than her sixteen years, and she felt such sympathy for that young girl, having to go through such an ordeal, and yet she shook her head.

'It won't work, Lord Lewisham. There's a saying that applies in this case and it's that you can't make a silk purse out of a sow's ear and that's right enough. You put me in Annabel's clothes and call me Annabel Lewisham, but it will fool no one. It will be like I was dressing for some sort of game because inside I will still be Celia Mul–McCadden and that will be proved when I opened my mouth.'

'You don't have to fool anyone, Celia,' Henry said. 'You and Annabel are going to live very quiet lives here and, apart from my parents maybe and the doctor, there will be no callers. But I must engage a cook and cleaner and someone to look after the gardens and because they have time off I don't want them talking about Lady Annabel Lewisham being pregnant. My parents are too far away to hear a whisper of this, of course, but someone else might and, well, that's how rumours start and reputations have been destroyed on less.'

'Can you see how important it is?' Annabel said. 'If it gets out that I gave birth to an illegitimate baby, my life will be over.'

188

Celia heard the desperation in Annabel's voice and saw her face ravaged with anxiety, and knew that she couldn't refuse to do this.

'Please,' Henry said again. 'I know it's asking a lot.' His dark brown eyes were fastened on Celia in a way that made her feel quite weak especially as she could see the concern in them and so she nodded her head and saw Annabel sigh in relief.

'But what about when the baby's born?' Celia asked. 'You can't keep that baby a secret for long.'

'Well what usually happens in cases like this – and this is not the first time an unmarried girl from a good, respectable home has found herself pregnant – the child is given to some worker on the estate to bring up. I wrote a long letter to my parents last night and told them that Annabel is here and will stay here until it's over.'

'Will they come for her?'

'Oh no,' Henry said. 'It will suit them for me to have her here while she is in this "interesting" condition. If I'd been in the country, Aunt Agatha might not have become involved at all. As it is I'll have to send her a telegram telling her things have changed and her services won't be required.'

'Will she be annoyed?'

'I suppose,' Henry said. 'But then she's annoyed most of the time. You wouldn't know what you'd have to do to please her. And any baby brought up in any way by Aunt Agatha would have a terribly wretched childhood,' he went on. 'That was probably only proposed because I wasn't here. Mark my words. Once our parents know I am virtually hiding Annabel away till the deed is done, they'll look round for a likely couple to be the child's foster parents. Now let's get our stories together before the doctor gets here.'

'I could do with some breakfast too,' Celia said. 'I am more than just hungry.'

Henry laughed. 'Come on then,' he said. 'Let's have a forage in the kitchen before we talk.'

By the time the doctor came, Celia had had her breakfast and was dressed in a red dress that had once belonged to Annabel.

'From now on,' Henry said. 'You will be my sister, Annabel Lewisham, newly returned from Ireland where you have lived for many years and with you is a good friend, Celia McCadden, who has recently been widowed and has then found after her husband's death that she was expecting his child. You all happy with that?'

'I'm not happy with the name Annabel,' Celia said. 'It's too fancy a name for the likes of me. And I know for now we're pretending that I am someone else, but the name doesn't rest easy. I don't mind Anna.'

'I agree,' Annabel said. 'I don't want to be called Celia either. It's like taking someone's whole identity. I want to be called Cissie, Cissie McCadden.'

Celia bit her lip as she remembered McCadden was an assumed name too and she'd been happy enough with it when she thought her future lay with Andy. But now she wanted no truck with it and she was glad to get rid of it and become Lewisham, even if it was for just a few months.

Dr Tranter didn't appear to doubt the story at all and said the girl he called Miss Lewisham

190

would have no ill effects from the faint.

'You're too skinny for my liking though,' he said. 'Are you sure that you are not in the same condition as your friend Mrs McCadden?'

'Oh no, doctor,' Celia assured him. 'There is not a chance of that.'

The doctor gave a small sigh of relief because the girl had no ring on her finger. Annabel, on the other hand, had her grandmother's antique wedding ring that her mother had given her when she was sixteen – one thing she wouldn't pawn because she had loved her grandmother very much – and now it sparkled on her finger, giving her the right to be pregnant.

Dr Tranter had commented on the loss of her husband and her so young and asked how he'd died. That hadn't been discussed so Annabel said the first thing that came into her head: that he was a soldier and had just returned to his regiment after a spot of leave and had sailed almost directly for India and been killed there in a skirmish on the second day. The doctor was impressed with her stoicism and said so while he examined her and she said it had been tragic at the time, but she had the baby to think of. Celia, watching Annabel, was amazed at the tales spilling from her lips. It was almost as if that actually happened and she knew it would be hard for anyone to doubt that she was a grieving widow carrying her beloved husband's child because she played the part so very well.

'All in all,' the doctor told Celia as he reached the hall and was preparing to leave, 'she's not bad considering what she has been through. Shouldn't think her appetite has been of the best, but now she needs good solid food and plenty of it because according to her dates that baby seems small to me. She needs plenty of fresh air to get the roses back into her cheeks too, so take a long walk out every day. She needs to keep active because it will be better for her in the long run.'

'Yes. I'll see to it, doctor.'

'Good girl,' the doctor said approvingly. 'Mrs McCadden is lucky to have such a good friend. Everyone needs someone with them at a time like this.'

If it was hard for Annabel to treat Celia as an equal, it was even harder for Celia to adapt. Though she had never been in service before, she was used to being at the beck and call of those at home. She and Norah had little free time as they grew up because they would be always helping their mother and so she slipped into the role of lady's maid naturally. Now though, the positions had been reversed and she didn't know how she would be able to convince anyone that she was Lady Anna Lewisham and was thankful that Henry had said that from now until the baby was born they would meet very few people.

'I suppose I should really call you Lady Anna,' Annabel said later that day.

'Oh, no,' Celia said. 'We are supposed to be friends, aren't we? I shouldn't think you use titles between friends, do you?'

'How would I know?' Annabel said. 'I've never had a friend.'

'Haven't you?' Celia said. 'How awful. Didn't

you make any friends at school?'

'I was never allowed to attend school,' Annabel said. 'Henry was, but my mother said schools for girls were totally unnecessary, so I had a governess, a Miss Amelia Clovelly and I suppose in the end she became a sort of friend though she was such a meek and mild person, the sort that wouldn't say boo to a goose, and she was terrified of my mother and she always called me Lady Annabel.'

'Well she would,' Celia pointed out. 'However friendly you became, she was still an employee. Where is she now?'

'She applied for a position in Northumbria,' Annabel said. 'Teaching the daughters of a vicar. She wrote once and said she was happy and settled, but the vicar's three daughters were proving more of a handful than I ever was. I replied at once for I missed her more than I realised and she has probably written again, but I was banished from home so I'll never know.'

'Shame you may have lost touch,' Celia said. 'Was she with you some time?'

Annabel nodded. 'Yes,' she said, 'she came when I was five. She thought when she left my mother might send me to some sort of finishing school. I thought so too and hoped she would, but she said that a finishing school would not be needed and that she was to teach me the social skills I needed. I was also allowed to put up my hair and join my parents for dinner each evening and I was there with my mother when she was "at home" to visitors or when she held her soirees for the select few.'

'What did you do there?'

'Make social chit-chat with total bores mainly.'

'You didn't enjoy it then?'

'No,' Annabel said emphatically. 'No I did not. I thought it a pointless exercise. There was talk of me coming out when I was eighteen, but I wasn't looking forward to that either.'

'What's "coming out" mean anyway?'

'It's a marriage market,' Annabel said vehemently. 'You are taken to all these elegant balls and extravagant parties in order for you to meet eligible men. At the end of the "season" you are expected to have at least a marriage proposal, that's what Amelia told me. But before I could start on any of that I had to learn to dance and my mother was making enquiries about dance classes just before that horrid man raped me. I don't think I'd have minded learning how to dance for at least it would be something to do. Can you dance, Celia?'

'Yes,' Celia said. 'I learnt when I was just a child, but they wouldn't be like the dances you do. It was reels and jigs and the like.'

'And have you ever been to a dance?'

'Oh yes,' Celia said. 'They had a dance of some sort most Saturdays and I went often. They were run by the Catholic Church.'

As she said that she bit her lip because it was now Saturday and she had to find a Catholic church and go to Mass or she would have a mortal sin on her soul.

'I need to see your brother,' she said to Annabel now. 'D'you know where he is?'

Annabel nodded. 'He's gone to the recruitment

194

place in the town to try and get staff. He said he'd be back just after lunch and it's almost lunchtime now – my stomach says so anyway. Are you hungry, Celia?'

'Not starving, but I could eat something,' Celia said. 'Let's see what's left in the kitchen.'

'It doesn't matter what there is, I couldn't make anything with it,' Annabel said flatly.

'You mean you can't cook anything?'

'Don't know the least thing about it. There was never the need.'

'Well there is now,' Celia said. 'Even if Henry manages to engage a cook it's hardly likely she's going to work straight away and seven days a week and you need to know something about cooking yourself if you are ever going to discuss meals with her, I would imagine. I bet your mother used to do that.'

Annabel nodded. 'She did but she never showed me how. I wouldn't know where to start. Anyway, what if they won't take me back?'

Celia did wonder that herself, for they'd been willing to exile her to the wilds of Ireland and an Aunt Agatha, who Henry hadn't a good word for. 'Henry won't stand for that,' she said assuredly. 'Anyway, whatever happens you need to know how to cook some simple dishes at least and no time like the present. Come on, let's go and look in the kitchen.'

However, she found little to make a satisfying meal for Henry had only bought very basic things, but she found oats and flour and there was butter in the dish so she made a big pile of oatcakes and made Annabel watch how she did it.

Henry came in before she was finished and was delighted that she could cook.

'I have hired a young girl as housemaid,' he said. 'Her name is Jackson, Janey Jackson, and she isn't working at the moment and is anxious to start work and earn money straight away so she is beginning next week. The cook, however, who is called Sadie Phelps, has to work a fortnight's notice and I wasn't sure how we were going to manage.'

'I can cook most standard things,' Celia said. 'Not much fancy or anything. I can't cook without ingredients though,' she added. 'So we need to go shopping as soon as we've finished these oatcakes.'

'Write a list of everything you need,' Henry suggested. 'Erdington Village is just a step away and it has every kind of shop and you will be able to get anything you want there.'

The three of them went together and Celia found it just as Henry had said. Every shop she could need – a butcher's, grocer's, fishmonger, greengrocer's and a bakery – were all grouped around the village green, less than fifteen minutes' walk from the house. They came back home with laden bags, though Annabel was allowed to carry nothing heavy, and Celia set to work straight away to make a hearty Irish stew served with oaten bread, taking Annabel into the kitchen with her and showing her how to chop the vegetables.

Everyone was hungry by the time it was ready and they attacked the meal with gusto and eventually Henry wiped the last piece of oaten bread round his plate and put down his spoon with a sigh. He sat back in his chair and said, 'That was delicious. This is really very good of you, Celia.'

'It's all right,' Celia said. 'I don't mind cooking and I like to keep busy.' That was true, especially now, for every time she thought of Andy she felt a pain in her heart and so the less time she had to think the better. She remembered that when her sister, Maggie, had died eventually the intense pain had settled to a dull and manageable ache and knew she would feel that way about Andy eventually. But life still had to be got through and this was her life for now. 'What did, you do normally for meals?' she asked Henry.

'What d'you mean?'

'Well there must have been times when you were here on your own and there was no resident cook, so what did you do?'

'Well I'm not completely helpless,' Henry said. 'I can boil eggs, make porridge and anyone can knock up a sandwich. For everything else I would go out. There's plenty of restaurants, or my club in the town which has a damned good chef, but we can't do that now because it's important that Annabel is not seen by anyone who might recognise her.'

'Oh, I can see that,' Celia said and then she said, 'Oh I nearly forgot, I need to find the nearest Catholic church, because tomorrow is Sunday and I have to go to Mass. We passed an abbey today on the way to Erdington Village so that will be it, I suppose.'

She had never imagined there would be any sort of problem. Henry was quiet for quite some time and when he spoke at last it was regretfully. 'I'm really sorry, Celia, but I cannot agree to that.'

'But you must. It's a mortal sin if I miss Mass.'

'I know and I am really sorry, but you risk blowing this subterfuge to protect my sister's name wide open if you go to a Catholic church. Do you see that? You are supposed to be my sister and we are not Catholics and so, until the child is born and everything is settled, you will be unable to attend your church.'

It was like a hammer blow to Celia. All her life she had been frightened of committing a mortal sin for the Catholic Church had drummed it into her that if you died with a mortal sin on your soul you would burn in the flames of hell forever. She turned to Henry to tell him that she couldn't do it, that he was asking too much, and she saw his deep brown eyes were full of anxiety and his brow was furrowed. She felt her heart give a flip. His earnest concern for his sister was evident and she knew she couldn't have borne it if she brought danger on these people she relied on.

So she gave a slight nod of the head as she said, 'All right then.' She closed her eyes tight for a moment and then in a voice a little above a whisper went on, 'I quite see I can't go to Mass at the moment.'

'Oh, Celia, I am so relieved,' Henry said with a sigh.

Annabel had seen what it had cost Celia to make that decision and she put her arms around her as she said, 'Thank you and thank you again because I know that wasn't an easy decision to make.'

'No it wasn't,' Celia said. 'But I quite see it was the only one to make and as I am not going to Mass tomorrow I will have the time to show you how to make a roast dinner.'

Henry roared his approval. 'This I've got to see. Roast dinner eh?'

'Yes,' Celia said and admitted, 'This will be a bit of a learning curve for me too, because I have never made a full roast dinner myself, though I have helped my mother often, so I sort of know what to do and I'd like the chance to have a go at it.'

'Well now is your chance,' Henry said. 'Once the cook is installed, if she is anything like every other cook I have ever met, you will virtually need her permission to even enter the kitchen, never mind actually cook anything in it.'

'That will be a really odd thing for me,' Celia said. 'But I suppose like everything else it is something for me to get used to.'

Andy was also getting used to new things and one was that he didn't think it was going to be as easy as he had thought to get a job and he was missing Celia a great deal more than he'd ever imagined he would. And though he could do nothing about it at that moment, when almost a week had passed, he thought that he ought to try and ascertain that Celia was happy because the Lewishams were perfect strangers and he told himself that once he knew that she was all right he could put all his energies into finding a decent, proper job.

And so early the following morning he made his way from his dingy lodgings in Erdington to

Grange Road. After leaving the way he had, he had no desire to meet Henry and, though he guessed by the time he arrived there Henry would have left for work, he decided not to approach the house directly to be on the safe side. Instead, he secreted himself away behind a stout oak tree outside Freer's farm, which was virtually opposite Henry's house. He hoped he might catch sight of Celia on her own and have a word with her, but for some time there was no movement at all.

He had begun to wonder how long he should wait, when he really should have been out looking for work, when suddenly he was rewarded by the sight of two young ladies coming out of the house together. It took a few minutes for him to realise that one of the young ladies was his Celia, for she was as elegantly dressed as the other one, who he recognised as Lady Annabel. Celia seemed well nourished too and happy, for as she emerged she was laughing at something Lady Annabel said.

Both girls carried shopping bags and he imagined they were making for Erdington Village and he was surprised that Lady Annabel was carrying anything. Any carrying was usually left for the servants and her carrying a bag as well made them look like equals. This was compounded when Lady Annabel slipped her arm through Celia's and they sauntered down the road as two friends might.

Andy was suddenly shy of calling after Celia as he had intended. He was very puzzled and while one part of him was relieved Celia had so obviously fallen on her feet, another part of him was concerned that this new Celia in the fancy clothes and footwear was like a stranger to him. He knew he would have hated for this new Celia to see the straitened circumstances he was in for his digs were spartan to say the least and he'd little opportunity to wash himself or change his clothes either.

The Celia he had come away with would have been sympathetic for his plight, but he thought the well-dressed, self-assured Celia he had just seen might just cast him a look of disdain and contempt. For a split second he had the urge to run after Celia and drag her away from the Lewishams before they tainted her altogether.

'But to what?' said his saner, inner voice. And he couldn't answer that question because he had no viable alternative to offer Celia if he tried to force her to leave the comfort of the Lewishams' place.

Even his own future was uncertain because he had little cash left and, unless he found work soon, he wouldn't have enough to pay rent on the squalid room he had and would have to take to the streets. Did he want to risk imposing that on the girl he loved? No, of course he didn't and as he, sloped away he castigated himself that he should be so churlish about someone treating Celia almost too well. Instead, he should be pleased he'd made the right decision in leaving her behind with Lady Annabel and her brother, Henry.

He tried to feel relieved and happy, but he couldn't totally ignore a knot of worry lodged in his heart that Celia was being pulled away from him. He had the feeling that the gap between them would widen the longer he was out of work until that gap would become an unbridgeable gulf and he couldn't do anything about that either.

Back in Donegal, Norah was depressed and despondent and she knew in her heart of hearts then it was her own fault. Dazzled by thoughts of America dangling before her, she had encouraged and helped Celia escape without thinking through the implications for herself.

Dan Mulligan was no fool and knew Celia must have had help to run away for she was too closely guarded to make arrangements for herself and he also knew that the only one who would help her had to be Norah. She denied all knowledge of it of course, but her father didn't believe her. Appealing to her mother was no good either because she thought the same way as her father and for a while she was treated like a leper.

No ticket came for America because Peggy had written and explained Celia's flight and Norah's suspected part in it and Aunt Maria quite understood that Norah couldn't be trusted to leave her home just now, but suggested that perhaps Dermot might like the chance. Peggy read the letter to Dan, expecting him to pooh-pooh the whole notion of Dermot going so far away. She had no desire for any more of her children to go to America, that godforsaken place, in the knowledge that when they went aboard that ship she would never see them again.

To her utter amazement Dan said, 'That's a fine opportunity Maria is offering for a young man. It will be a wrench though, for the lad has become a real help on the farm now he's grown up a bit.'

'Dermot is far too young to be sent so far away,' Peggy snapped. 'I am surprised at you for even considering it.'

'And what if he was to up and join the IRA?' Dan said quietly. 'As lads as young as him and younger are doing?'

Peggy knew Dan was right because as news of the brutality of the Black and Tans spread through the land, boys were joining the IRA and calling themselves Freedom Fighters in droves. And yet she maintained, 'Dermot would never do such a thing. He's far too sensible.'

Dan shook his head. 'Sense doesn't come into it when passion is aroused and in the young the passion is very close to the surface. You mind Jerry Maguire, Dermot's best friend, who was never away from Donegal when they were wee boys together and a kinder, more even-tempered boy it would be hard to find?'

'Of course I remember him,' Peggy said. 'Don't say he's involved in this?'

Dan nodded his head. 'His parents are destroyed for they know once a person joins that organisation there'd be no getting out of it later. Not unless they want to spend the rest of their lives with busted kneecaps or worse. I would rather my son had a chance in America than be an IRA recruit and have his life snuffed out by a British Tommy gun.'

Peggy was silent. She still was not keen on Dermot going so far but Dan was right when he said passion among the young was to the fore. It was passion of a different kind that had caused

Celia to run away. Never would Peggy have thought her daughter would have done anything like that, so there you are, you never knew what any of them might do, whatever upbringing they had, seemingly.

'Shouldn't we ask Dermot?' Peggy said. 'I have never heard him say a word about America, so maybe he has no desire to go.'

Dan nodded. 'We'll ask him certainly.'

'And there is to be no pressure, Dan,' Peggy warned. 'If he says no it stays as no.'

Dan lifted up his hands. 'Promise you. No pressure.'

Peggy was right, Dermot was sensible, far too sensible to hanker for things he couldn't have and so that evening after the meal when his parents asked him to come into the sitting room, a room used only rarely, he had no idea what it was about. Norah was left to the task of washing the pots and she was no wiser either, so when Dan asked Dermot if he would like to go to America as Norah wasn't being allowed to go, he was literally struck dumb for a moment or two. It was the very last thing he had expected his parents to say.

'You serious?' he asked his father.

'Course I'm serious,' Dan said.

'But how will you manage? Sammy is too young to be of much help to you.'

'Sammy will grow,' Dan said. 'He is nearly eight. And you won't be going for a while yet. The summer is not the time for a farmer's son to leave the land with everything ripening in the fields. Once the harvest is gathered in and the turf collected before winter sets in, that's when you'll be going,

204

and for now take Sammy around with you as much as possible and show him what to do. But you must grasp this chance with two hands for such an opportunity will not come again.'

Dermot knew that well enough, but he was not expecting to leave his native soil for a long time yet, though he was well aware he'd have to make his way in the world eventually.

'For all this is a marvellous opportunity for you,' Peggy said, 'we will understand, both of us, that you feel yourself too young to leave home yet and we will respect your decision.'

Dermot knew that was his mother's way of saying she didn't want him to go, but he remembered the things Jim had written to his sister to sort of prepare her for life over there and he had made it sound a very exciting place to live. While Dermot would undoubtedly miss his family and would have hated to be cast on America's shores alone, he already had an older brother who would look out for him and an aunt who would be ready and willing to welcome him and the more he thought of the idea, the better he liked it.

'Yes please,' he said. 'I think I would like to go to America.'

He heard his mother give a heartfelt sigh, but his father clapped him on the back in approval.

'Good man, Dermot, I think you've made the right decision. If you'd decided against it now, you may have regretted it all your life.'

'I know,' Dermot said. 'I felt that way too.'

He knew though that Norah might be further hurt by the fact that he was going to America and he was sorry that he would have to hurt her afresh because he was very fond of her. However, working on the assumption that, as she had to know anyway, it was better sooner rather than later, he sought her out as soon as he left his parents. When he told her of the offer from Aunt Maria that his parents approved of, he saw her eyes open wider for the disappointment at the loss of her dream was lodged in her heart like a raw pain and she felt as though a knife was turned inside it at Dermot's words.

And yet she did her best to smile at her young brother and tried but didn't quite succeed in keeping any resentment out of her voice as she said, 'Congratulations.'

'Maybe later I can send for you?'

Norah smiled ruefully. 'I think not, Dermot. My chance is gone.'

ELEVEN

All in all, though Celia remained hurt and confused by Andy's behaviour, she was getting over it. She did enjoy Annabel's company and there was plenty to occupy her because every morning they would decide on the menu for that day and then go into Erdington Village to buy all the things they would need. Once home again, at first Celia would show Annabel how to make dishes she was familiar with and so Celia would make bacon and cabbage, colcannon, coddle and Irish stew together with fruit cake, and apple pie and rhubarb crumble. Annabel felt better than she had in ages and was proud of the fact that an appetising meal she'd helped make was put in front of her brother when he came in from work each evening.

When Janey Jackson started work Celia thought it the strangest thing to watch a young girl – for she was only fifteen – do the jobs she thought of as hers. And she didn't have to just watch her, but also give orders to her and Celia found that well nigh impossible at first. Annabel said she had to get over it for though many things were routine in the day, often Janey might have to be told to do certain jobs.

'You'll leave her rudderless if you don't,' Annabel said. 'She won't know what to do if you don't tell her.'

'You could do it.'

'Don't you think that might look dashed odd if I gave her orders when you are supposed to be Henry's sister?'

'I suppose.'

'If I were you I'd get used to issuing orders to Janey,' Annabel said. 'Because you'll have to deal with Cook soon and that will be harder because she will be older than you and if she's anything like the cooks at the hall that I had experience of, she's used to reigning supreme in her kitchen and you will have to discuss menus and plan meals with her. You should be grateful that we are such a small household.'

'Oh this being a toff is not all it's cracked up to be,' Celia groaned and Annabel laughed at the disgruntled look on her face.

While Celia was getting to grips with coping with Janey Jackson, Andy was almost penniless, and now he was no longer able to pay the rent on his dodgy, down-at-heel lodging house, there were just the streets left. Never had Andy thought for one moment he would end up living on the streets, but he had been unable to secure himself any sort of job. That was out of his understanding for, even when he had left his home, he had been engaged at the first hiring fair he'd gone to. But now there was no help for it and he left the lodging house with regret, keeping back a couple of shillings for, even if he had nowhere to live, he had to eat and what he would do when that money was gone if he still hadn't any employment didn't bear thinking about.

He mooned around the area that day carrying all that he possessed in the bag he had strapped to his back, too dispirited to look for work. When hunger gnawed at him, he bought four stale buns at the bakery in Erdington Village. Not knowing how long they had to last he allowed himself to eat only two of them. They barely satisfied his hunger and left his mouth as dry as a bone. He wandered aimlessly though his steps were bringing him back to Grange Road and he was wondering what a body did to slake their thirst when there was no accommodating stream tumbling by. He had always made up his mind to knock on someone's door and ask for a drink of water when he came to a park. 'Pype Hayes' it said on the sign outside and he went in, knowing he would feel better anyway with a bit of grass beneath his feet. Following the path round, he came to a children's playground that had a drinking fountain to the edge of it and he was able to satisfy his thirst at last.

That first afternoon passed in a blur as he walked and walked for miles trying to acclimatise himself with the area. He saw there weren't many factories around the place where he could find any sort of job that paid enough to rent a room or, failing that, enough to keep body and soul together would do for now.

As he retraced his footsteps back to the park he was determined to look in some other area the following day. He remembered one of the lads on the boat telling him Birmingham was known as the 'city of a thousand trades'. If that were true he had seen pretty little evidence of it so far. He ate more buns washed down with water from the drinking fountain and then lay down on a nearby bench, glad of the warm dry night. He knew though he would find life on the streets hard, though he was well aware he was by no means the only one forced to sleep where he could because he had seen down and outs sleeping in shop doorways, under railway arches and a variety of unsuitable places.

But enough was enough he decided. He would seek out Henry the next day to take up his offer of employment that he initially refused because of his stiff-necked pride.

The early morning cold woke him just as dawn was breaking and so he had a basic wash using water from the drinking fountain, combing his hair, smoothing down his crumpled clothes and generally making himself look as respectable as he could before he set off for the house. He didn't want Celia to catch sight of him before he had secured employment, so he decided to see Henry on his own at first as he left the house on his way to work.

He hadn't been waiting that long when Henry emerged and strode down Grange Road, making for the tram stop on Chester Road, and Andy only waited for him to turn into Holly Lane, where there was no possibility that he would be seen from the house, before he called to him, 'Lord Lewisham.'

Henry stopped and looked back and waited for Andy to approach. He wasn't sure who it was at first and, as if Andy knew this, he said, 'I'm Andy, Celia's brother.'

'Yes I know,' Henry said. His first thought was that Andy had got some sort of job and had come to take Celia away and if he did that everything Henry had planned to protect Annabel would fall apart. So he said in clipped tones, 'What can I do for you?'

Andy heard the tone and gritted his teeth yet continued, 'I would like to take you up on your kind offer?'

It was the last thing Henry expected him to say and for a moment he didn't know what he was on about. 'My offer? What offer was that?'

'Of employment,' Andy said. 'You offered me employment too when Celia went to be your sister's lady's maid.'

Henry remembered and remembered also it was a made-up position so that Celia would stay with his sister. And it was an offer the man had thrown back in his face by disappearing the way

210

he did without a word to anyone and now he had an old man keeping the garden tidy. But Andy had done him a favour in a way, for Celia was a compliant girl and anxious to please and easily persuaded to change her name and miss Mass, but he doubted her brother would be so agreeable. In fact he might blow the whole thing clean out of the water and Henry couldn't risk that.

It might be that Celia would want nothing to do with him after he had run out on her without a word and, if she felt that way, it might make life really awkward for her if Henry offered him employment. And so he looked at Andy rather scornfully and said, 'As I recall, you weren't that keen on the employment offered at the time. In fact you had disappeared by the following day.'

'Yes,' Andy said and, because he badly needed the job, he added, 'I'm sorry. There were reasons. I can explain.'

'Explanations are not necessary,' Henry said. 'You may be sorrier still though, for the offer of employment is withdrawn.'

'But...'

'The position has been filled,' Henry said. 'I cannot wait about for people to change their mind.'

Andy stood and stared at him as if he couldn't believe his ears, for now he really didn't know what to do and he was filled with fear for the future. His mouth was suddenly so dry he could barely speak so his voice was like a growl as he said, 'So that's it then?'

'Yes that's it, I'm afraid,' Henry said and he inclined his head slightly as he said, 'Good day to you.'

Andy watched Henry walk away and had the urge to pick up a large stone and throw it after him and then go and get Celia out of that house. Luckily he did no such thing. As he shambled away he told himself he doubted he could have stuck working for the Lewishams for very long for he wasn't used to being anyone's lackey, but he was only fooling himself because he knew in his heart he would be anyone's lackey if they paid him a wage and he had three good meals a day.

He wandered around listlessly all day, sticking to Erdington Village where he helped clear up the market stalls and was given a sixpence and, rather than make it last, he bought a meat pie. He thought he hadn't tasted anything so nice in an age. The crust was thick and crispy on the top and juicy underneath, the meat was succulent and he felt the warm gravy dribble down his throat.

But away from the market, he was aware that cold rain was falling, darkening the sky prematurely, and he made his way to Station Road just on the edge of the village because in his wanderings he had spotted a bridge there that the railway ran along the top of

He found that a cluster of men, homeless like himself, all with their packs on their backs, had had the same idea and were squashed under the bridge and they eyed him a little suspiciously as he joined them. However, he smiled and greeted them and from the greatcoats he knew a fair few of them had been soldiers away fighting in the war that had only ground to a halt two years before and they wore their greatcoats like badges of honour to show they had done their bit.

'Not that it made any bloody difference,' one man they called Len said bitterly as Andy commented on this and another growled out: 'Aye, they said we would come back to a land fit for heroes and we came back to bugger all, no job and little prospect of getting one and not even a place to live.'

'Did you expect any different, Bert?' Len said. 'Don't tell me you expected them to keep their promises.'

'No not really,' Bert said morosely

'Yeah, and far too many lads never came back at all,' one man said

'Their bodies left to rot in some foreign field,' another commented.

'Yeah and lots who returned were damaged,' Len added. 'Missing limbs, their lungs buggered up with mustard gas, blinded or twitching with shell shock.'

Another called Fred saw the shock register on Andy's face in the light from the street lamp and said, 'How come you weren't involved in the war?'

'I was in Ireland,' Andy said. 'There was no conscription there.'

'Huh, then you should thank your lucky stars,' Len said. 'Only some silly sods didn't wait to be called up, like me for instance. Couldn't wait to have a go at the Hun. Thought it would be like one big adventure cos I was still a kid, see.'

'How old were you?'

'Sixteen when I enlisted. Told them I was eighteen. They didn't check that hard.'

Andy thought back to his father's likely reaction if he'd done that. 'What about your parents?'

213

'What about them?'

'Well didn't they object?

'Don't know who my parents are, mate,' Len replied. 'I grew up in the workhouse and I was out of there at fourteen and in a job cleaning the streets. Joining the army seemed to offer a better life than that.'

'More fool you,' Fred said. 'Nothing to stop you looking for another job that would have kept you safe for another two years at least. You'd not catch me joining up one minute before I had to. I didn't want to fight in no war that was hell on earth anyway. I grew up in a workhouse too but I had a life before the war, had a job and a girl. We were to be married.'

'What happened?'

'She buggered off with some man who had flat feet so he failed the medical for the army and they put him in charge of an armaments factory,' Fred said and although he spoke almost lightly Andy heard the hurt of the betrayal in the tone of his voice, even as he went on. 'He was here and I wasn't and he had money to spend on her, cos he was far better paid than us poor soldiers. Anyroad, when I saw what I would be reduced to after the war I couldn't really blame her. She was a little smasher and I thought the world of her and I was glad she'd found someone else. I mean, I've nothing to offer her.'

Andy started for though he had left Celia for her own good he didn't expect her to find someone else while he was trying to sort out some kind of future for the two of them.

'What did you do before the war?' he asked.

214

'I was a toolmaker.'

'Well what happened to your job?' Andy said. 'I heard they were holding them for you.'

'Well you heard wrong,' Fred snapped and then went on in a more reasonable tone, 'See the women took up our jobs when we went to war and when I went to see the boss, expecting to be set on straight away, he said that the woman working my machine had been left a widow by the war and she had a couple of kids to rear too and needed the money. And that might be true and everything, but I happen to know my old boss is a tight-fisted bastard and a woman's wage for the same job is probably the half of mine, however many kids she has, so no wonder he wanted to keep her on instead of me.'

'That's true enough,' Bert agreed. 'The women don't want to give the jobs up – sometimes they can't because they are supporting their families in some way because they're widows, or their husbands have come back too disabled to work. The pension for a disabled soldier or a deceased one is not worth having, so the women hang on to the jobs they have been doing through the war years.'

'And you can't blame them either,' Len said. 'I've seen plenty of scrawny, raggy-arsed and barefoot kids hanging about the streets. Look as if they have never had a decent meal in the whole of their lives, some of them. If you have the means to make life better for them, feed them well and get them boots for the winter months, then you're not going to be that keen on giving up a job that provides them things, are you?'

There was a murmur of agreement and Bert

said, 'And it's not only that. There's things you want in war time that are not needed afterwards, like I was a gun maker and who wants that many guns in peacetime? They are laying people off, not taking on.'

'Yeah, it's like the factories making munitions,' Tad put in. 'All closed. Eventually, they might open them up to make other things, but for now they stand empty.'

'I stupidly thought that there might be things set in place for us by the government, because it isn't as if they were taken by surprise,' Len said. 'They knew all of us would be leaving the forces not that long after the Armistice was signed and that we'd need some sort of job and somewhere to live.'

'And instead we were thrown on the scrap heap,' agreed Fred. 'We'd beaten the Hun and so served our purpose. Instead of being welcomed back as heroes like they said we'd be, we're like an embarrassment to them.'

'Yeah. Surplus to requirements now.'

'So then how do you survive?' Andy asked, though he more or less knew the answer. He realised that he had made a big mistake in moving to a country still in recovery from a devastating war that had claimed and damaged so many lives. He felt that these men deserved a job much more than he did and in fact they couldn't help but resent him for seeking work himself when their own chances of any meaningful employment were almost nil. This was brought home to him further when Fred said to him, 'Look, mate, don't take this the wrong way but you might find you're not that welcome here, cos there's already too many of us chasing too few jobs.'

Andy nodded. 'I know now I should never have come here, but it's too late to regret that now.' Sticking to the story they had concocted, he went on, 'I have a young sister to see to.'

'Where is she?'

'She has a job in service.'

'Leave her there,' Len advised. 'They might work her into the ground for they like their pound of flesh do the nobs, but if they have a decent cook she'll be fed right, cos they get more work out of them then. And you just go round knocking the doors of the factories and that and ask if they have any jobs they want doing. The thing is not to go where others are working already because they get right shirty.'

Andy nodded. 'I found that out already. I was walking past New Street Station when this fancy horse-drawn cab pulled up in front of me and the man that got out of it asked me if I wanted to earn some money. Course I said yes and he piled me up with cases and boxes and I followed him into the station and stacked them in the rack of the train carriage for him and he gave me sixpence. I was jumped on as I went to leave the station by two fellows who wrenched the sixpence from my hand and told me in no uncertain terms to sling my hook and threatened what they'd do to me if they saw me there again. I didn't fancy tangling with them,' Andy said. 'They were tall fellows and very broad with it.'

'You did right,' one of the men said with a wry grin. 'No one tangles with them unless they have a death wish. They are two brothers. Name of Foster and between them they have New Street Station sewn up. Can't blame them totally because they have six children between them and they are also helping the widow and children of the brother who didn't make it home.'

'I see that but what shall I do?' Andy asked. 'The last thing I want to do is tread on someone else's toes.'

'Well ignore the big factories for a start, for they wouldn't give you the time of day,' Len cautioned. 'Unless they have any vacancies on the board outside, we all give them a wide berth. I'd try Aston if I were you.'

Andy remembered passing through a place Lady Annabel called Aston the day they arrived. He recalled a big green clock at the edge of the road and lots of shops and a big brewery.

'Daresay the pickings are meagre,' Len added, 'because I heard the bloke who was working the factories down there dropped dead in the street from malnutrition, so you make sure it don't happen to you.'

'Dunno,' Bert said malevolently. 'Might be the best solution all round. Another Paddy wiped off the face of the earth and so more for the rest of us.'

Some of the men shifted uncomfortably and others looked interested, wondering if there was to be a fight. But Andy hadn't the energy to fight anyone, particularly as he thought the situation was of his own making.

'There's a canal down Rocky Lane as well,' Len put in, 'and if you can't get work in the factories, you can sometimes pick up work on the canals.'

218

'How far away is this place Aston?'

'Oh a fair step from here,' Len said. 'And it's coming on to dark so I'd turn in now and go up tomorrow morning.'

Andy took the advice for a lot of the men were settling down now and how Andy envied them, wrapped up as they were in their greatcoats. He found it uncomfortable to be lying on the uneven bricks and, though he closed his eyes and was tired enough, he was too cold, and full of anxiety to slip easily into a deep sleep for he felt an abject and total failure.

He shivered through the night, the cold jerking him awake constantly and he was glad when it was time to get up. When he was pointed in the right direction for Aston he set off at a lick, glad to get the blood flowing through his veins, again warming him through.

Aston was not that far from the city centre and though there were plenty of shops it mainly consisted of streets and streets of small and dingy back-to-back houses all squashed up together. Cheek by jowl with those houses were small and sometimes not so small factories and warehouses that Andy looked upon with some confidence for there were lots of doors to knock on. Surely one of them could find something he could do.

He found Rocky Lane that Len had spoken of and went down it to stand at the side of the oil-slicked torpid water that smelt a little. But the canal's smell only mingled with the other smells. He was to find out later that the slightly vinegary one was from the sauce factory; the malty one from the brewery, the slight whiff of rubber was from the Dunlop factory that he'd passed in Rocky Lane, and the hot metallic smell came from the foundry.

So much was going on here and he ached to be part of it. He stood and watched as the area came to life. He was totally surprised by the colourful boats that ploughed up and down the canal, which he later learnt were barges. He fervently hoped his future, such as it was, lay in Aston.

'So what's this cook like?' Annabel asked her brother the day before she was due to arrive.

Henry shrugged. 'Just a cook, you know?'

'No I don't know,' Annabel said. 'And I think it very bad of you not to say more than that. I mean, is she thin or fat and old or young for example?'

'Oh she's definitely plump,' Henry said with a slight laugh. 'If she hadn't been I might have engaged someone else.'

'Why?' Celia asked.

'Have you never heard the saying, "Never trust a thin cook"?'

'Well I hardly would hear that, would I?' said Celia. 'I was never familiar with houses like these. I mean, cooks and housemaids and parlour maids and lady's maids were not part of my world.'

'No,' Henry conceded. 'But they do say that, because if you have a plump cook it looks as if she likes her food and is likely to be a better cook than some skinny miss.'

'I would have thought references a better indication,' Annabel said. 'I can't see Mother engaging someone because of their physique.'

'I took references too,' Henry said. 'To tell you the truth, I was on the lookout for one who looked a kindly soul. Some cooks can be the very devil and I wanted one who didn't scare the living daylights out of Celia.'

Celia was very pleased to hear that and she said, 'So how old is this plump woman?'

'In her forties I would say,' Henry said. 'Her hair's brown and sort of frizzy though I couldn't see much of it because she had a hat on, but I did see that it was short. Actually she drew my attention to it because she said she wore it short on purpose because she thought it was more hygienic in the kitchen and it meant her cook's hat fitted better. Anyway, you'll see her for yourself tomorrow.'

And they did of course and Celia found there were things Henry didn't mention in his sparse description of the cook, like the fact that her blue eyes were kind-looking and the two rosy cheeks in her wide open honest face made her look friendly.

However, Sadie the cook had worked in a great many establishments before this one and privately she found it an odd set-up, for the sister of the master spoke with that strange Irish accent and seemed nervous about giving orders as if she was unused to it while her friend was much better at it. But for all that, they were pleasant enough girls and she felt quite motherly and protective towards them, especially the one called Cissy, widowed so young, and she was tickled pink there would soon be a baby in the house.

Henry was relieved the cook was installed for, despite the enveloping coat he'd bought, Annabel's little bulge was becoming more noticeable. As they sat around the table digesting the first evening meal made by Cook, Henry said, 'Now Cook is here, there is no need for you to go to Erdington for Cook will probably have most things delivered. In fact I wouldn't like you to leave the house much now, for it wouldn't do for you to be seen by anyone who knows you, for your pregnancy is beginning to show.'

Annabel nodded for she knew that, and so did Celia and she said, 'I do see what you mean, but the doctor suggested a walk every day.'

'Make for Pype Hayes Park then,' Henry said. 'That's even closer than Erdington Village and you will be safe there apart from Saturdays and Sundays. Give it a miss on those days. But mind, Annabel, I don't want you overdoing it.'

'Henry, I feel perfectly well.'

'You look perfectly well,' Henry said. 'And that is the way we want to keep it.'

Celia wondered how Annabel could possibly overdo things when she had nothing to do with her days but lie about, for she had someone else doing the housework and now another doing the cooking and soiled clothes sent out to the laundry and Celia herself did any fetching and carrying needed.

So, though they were going to be allowed to walk in the park every weekday, there were still hours to fill. Celia was not used to being idle and she didn't think it would do Annabel any good at all either and so she said, 'We will have hours to fill now that Cook is doing what we used to do, so what do you think about making a few things for the baby?'

Annabel looked at Celia as if she couldn't believe her ears. 'I have no feelings for this child, Celia. I thought you knew that.'

'Well whether you have feelings for the child or not, he or she will need clothes.'

'Well they can be bought nearer the time, can't they?'

'I suppose they can,' Celia said. 'But every woman I know would make the little vests and nighties that they wear in the early days and would usually also hem the muslin and terry squares that they use for nappies and sometimes embroider the edges of the baby's blankets or bedspread. Your governess must have taught you to sew?'

'She did,' Annabel said and her voice was wistful as if she wished she were back in the schoolroom and none of this had happened and she hadn't got an unwanted baby growing inside her.

Celia caught Annabel's unhappy tone and she saw Henry had noticed too and their eyes locked together for a moment as Annabel went on, 'She said I had quite a neat hand.'

Henry knew what Celia was trying to do and he said, 'There you are then. And I'm sure you'll enjoy it once you start.'

'D'you really think so, Henry?'

'I do, my dear,' Henry said. 'And I've just thought of another occupation for you. The pair of you were probably too intent on shopping when you visited Erdington Village to notice but opposite that green is a public library that's virtually spanking new.'

'What's a public library?' Celia asked. 'I mean,

I know a library is something to do with books but...'

'It is to do with books,' Henry said. 'But these books you can take home and borrow for two weeks and then take them back and get some more out.'

'And... And they don't mind you doing that?' It was Celia who asked the question but Annabel was looking at him quizzically too.

'No, they want you to do that,' Henry said assuredly to both girls. 'That's what it's all about and why it's called public.'

'Golly, I've never had a book to just read before,' Celia said. 'Just ones for school that were usually bits of books that you had to answer questions about. Not that I had the time to read much then anyway.'

Annabel watched the pleasure on Celia's face with amusement. She was no stranger to libraries for she had grown up with one and she'd always thought it as dull as ditchwater. It was dark and oppressive for the only light in it came from one large window at the end of the room and all the desks and chairs arranged around the room were dark too. The shelves were full of dusty tomes with uninspiring titles that she seldom lifted from the shelves. It was the province of the men and her father, Henry and any visiting male would often be ensconced in there. She wasn't exactly forbidden to go into the library, and on the odd occasion boredom had driven her in there to find something to read. If her father was there already, or came in while she was perusing the titles, he always seemed irritated by her presence and so she had used the library less and less.

She doubted she would be allowed to go to this public one anyway because Henry had said she was not to go to Erdington Village, but Celia could go and choose books for both of them. It was true though that if she couldn't shop and cook, which she had seen as a great entertainment, time might hang heavy. That would give her time to think and she didn't want to do much of that for what she thought about in bed at night was how the child growing within her was changing her body. She hated her thickening waist and she was terrified of the birth itself, so maybe as well as reading she might do as Celia suggested and Henry endorsed and sew some clothes for the wretched child she was carrying.

TWELVE

Celia had more to concern herself with as the summer progressed for Henry would read snippets out of the newspaper he brought home with him. Celia and Annabel would usually be at their sewing after the evening meal and Henry seemed quite worried about the violence in Ireland at the time.

'Seems to have intensified since these Black and Tans were sent over,' he said to Celia one day as July was drawing to a close. 'Did you have anything much to do with them when you came over first?'

225

Celia shook her head. 'Not where we were in Donegal. I mean we knew they were there and all. They came to Ireland sometime in March, I think. A lot of the trouble is in Belfast and sometimes Derry, which isn't far from Donegal, but it didn't affect us that much.'

'Good job,' Henry said, 'for no good can come of it. Mind you, it is bad that more than seven thousand Catholics were forced from their jobs in the shipyard in Belfast. No one should have been allowed to get away with that and the fact that they have done, well it was more or less inevitable that there would be reprisals and rioting.'

Celia nodded in agreement for the sectarian killing and reprisal attacks went on from one side or the other till it seemed Ireland was a very unsafe place to be. And she wished she could write to her parents and make sure they were all right, but she doubted they'd even read a letter she wrote, let alone answer.

But really her main concern was to care for Annabel who was growing more agitated and she was eating far less than she had been, which was a worry, and yet she grew more cumbersome as the summer drew to an end and so, despite the news from Ireland, Celia had to push any worries to the back of her mind.

Annabel was very tired at that time and spent a lot of time resting, which meant that Celia too had time on her hands and she didn't like that because it gave her too much time to think. Celia often wished she was busier for thoughts of Andy McCadden would sometimes flit across her mind unbidden and then she would feel the pang of loss for the tentative love they had shared, and she often wondered where he was and what he was doing.

If Celia had caught sight of Andy she might not have recognised him, or at least not initially, for after weeks on the streets he was nothing like the man he had been when he had won Celia's heart and brought her to England. Now he was dirty and unkempt and by necessity had a shaggy beard and he knew that looking as he did, the prospects of any sort of decent job were zero, though he was desperate to take anything going and for the least pay.

Previously Andy had never tasted real hunger, for there had always been enough to put food on the table, however basic it might be. Even when he was a hireling man he had been given three solid meals for Fitzgerald's wife, who was a better cook than his mother, had always maintained that no man could work effectively with an empty belly.

He would have to disagree with her now, because if he was ever given a chance of any sort of employment he worked as hard as he knew how, even when his stomach yawned ceaselessly with desperate hunger and his head was dizzy from lack of food.

Once he worked all day, moving furniture, for a loaf of bread and when he had been given it, he barely waited until he was secreted behind a bush at the edge of the park before he attacked it with as much gusto as a wild animal might. He hadn't eaten for two days and he was too hungry to save any of it and so he began tearing great lumps off it and shoving them in his mouth until every crumb was gone.

However, so much food reaching his stomach that had been without for so long caused it to react. He left the park walking slowly to try and still the rising nausea, but he was unsuccessful and vomited up the whole loaf into the gutter and lay spent on the pavement, hungrier than ever. He lay there for some time, too despairing and weak to get up. A patrolling policeman spotted him and gave his stomach a slight kick with his hard-capped boots and that caused Andy to cry out and curl into a ball as the policeman told him that if he didn't get up and be on his way, he would find himself in the cells for the night.

Andy's head swam and his stomach cried out with emptiness and, with a desperate sigh, he stumbled to his feet and stood there swaying slightly on legs that shook and wondered if it was worth knocking the policeman's helmet off. Then he might be hauled away to spend a night in the cells, which would be no bad thing: it would be warmer for a start and drier than many a place he had laid his head previously and he might even be fed too. His mouth watered at the thought but then he considered that such an action would perhaps give him a criminal record and make an enemy of the police, which was not a sensible thing to do when you live on the streets anyway.

'Go on,' the policeman barked. 'On your way.'

'That might be easier to do if I had some place to go to,' Andy thought as he lurched away. But he said nothing. What was the point?

He was glad that Celia didn't know how low,

he'd sunk and his future with her seemed further away than ever. In this mood he wandered down to the canal and was hailed by Billy Brown, one of the boaties, plying his barge up and down the canal. He was only young for a solo boatie, Andy thought, about the same age as he was, and he had an open, honest-looking face with a mouth that was turned up at the sides so it looked as if he was constantly good humoured. He was dressed like all the other boaties in a moleskin jacket over a muted check shirt, cord trousers, heavy boots and always a cap that covered his light brown hair.

His barge, like all the others, was decorated beautifully with castles and roses and was pulled along by a shaggy-footed horse he called Captain and he reminded Andy of the horses on the farm that used to pull the plough. Most of the boaties had no time for townsfolk who used to look down their noses at them and call them 'river gypsies'.

Andy had neither the right nor inclination to look down on anyone and in fact he often felt alienated himself from the English who were annoyed that there had been no conscription in Ireland. Many thought the Irish, particularly the Catholic Irish, had a nerve coming over to England now the war was over, chasing the too few jobs that should by rights go to those who had risked their lives.

Andy could see their point but he had to eat too and it was hard to have factory gates slammed on him sometimes as soon as he opened his mouth and feel the animosity amongst some of the unemployed he met. The boaties were not a bit like that and so Andy felt drawn to them and picked up casual work fairly often, particularly from Billy, and he had soon learned to 'leg' the barge through the tunnel, which involved lying across the barge and pushing it through the tunnel using his legs on the tunnel sides.

The first time he had done this, he had thought his legs were going to drop off and they shook like mad when he had straightened up on the towpath. He had become used to it, however, and he had also found out how the locks worked and helped Billy operate them and they got on well together.

And even if Billy wasn't around many of the other boaties could find a job for him even if was just leading their horse around the tunnel and securing it on the other side. The good of the barges was that though they were a slow form of transport, they could carry heavier loads than the carts, or even the petrol-driven vans, so most of the barges were loaded down with heavy machinery or bulky heavy foodstuffs. Sometimes coal tenders were attached to them, though never to Billy's because he worked alone, so any work he had was spasmodic. The first time Andy was asked aboard it was because the delivery Billy had to make would involve negotiating several locks, and that was when he had his first glimpse of below deck.

It was very clean and tidy and had to be for it was extremely small and when Andy remarked on this Billy told him it measured ten foot long and just six wide and he showed him how the table folded to the wall so that the bed that his parents had used could come down.

'So where did you sleep?'

'Here,' said Billy, crossing the small space to a bench on the opposite wall. 'It opens out, see.'

As Billy unfolded it and Andy saw the mattress inside it he said, 'Oh that's like the settles we had at home. They were for unexpected guests really and it was where the children slept, so that adults could have the proper bed. In the daytime, covered with cushions, it doubled as extra seats. Used to be a bit squashed in there as I remember.'

'I remember that too,' Billy said and Andy saw the shadow pass over his face, but he said nothing more then and they went back up to the top and Billy stayed there to steer the craft and Andy jumped onto the towpath and walked alongside the horse.

Andy had never been this way before and he looked about him with interest. They passed an inn that seemed to be doing a roaring trade and a blacksmith's before Billy swung the barge away from the bank slightly and they went forward slowly as he searched for the wharf he needed, and once found, he steered the craft in with ease.

Once the delivery had been made, Billy said to Andy, 'Do you fancy faggots and peas and, some chips for your dinner? I reckon we both deserve it.'

Andy felt the saliva in his mouth at even the thought of such delicious food. 'I'd love it,' he said. 'But where?'

'The hostelry we passed does that and more,' Billy said. 'Unshackle the horse because I'll be turning here where the canal is wider.'

Andy did as he was bid and watched Billy turn the barge and then he refastened the horse and they were on their way again before Billy said, 'There's a stove below and Ma used to cook some great grub on it, but I don't bother just for me. Anyway they have facilities at the back for the horses here as well and we can have a pint with it, but I seldom drink more than the one, two at the outside. Some of the boaties drink far more but Dad used to say it was madness. He always said drunkenness and deep water were not good partners.'

'And I'd say he was right,' Andy said.

'He was,' Billy affirmed. 'Fount of wisdom was our old Dad and we all listened because none of us were big drinkers.'

Andy didn't answer because they had reached the inn where the smell of the food was making him feel light-headed. Billy leapt from the barge and began unshackling Captain.

'Must get the horse seen to first,' he said. 'That was another bit of advice Dad instilled in us, that we had to see to the horse, because he's dependent on us. He always said that if you treat your horse right and feed him properly you will get more work out of him without using the whip.'

'My father used to say the same about the horses on the farm,' Andy said. 'Always made plenty of sense to me.'

Billy finished unbuckling the horse and stood up holding him lightly by the halter as he said, 'Does to me as well, but all boaties don't seem to see that and I don't like the way some of them are with the horses. I suppose it comes from not owning their own horse.'

'Oh, I thought they all did.'

'No,' Billy said. 'Some of the boaties work for haulage companies and the like and the horses are in a pool and they just pick one to pull the load.'

'Why?'

'Well it is a little bit more secure,' Billy said. 'Sometimes times are hard, and there isn't much to eat. Anyroad me granda wouldn't hear of it apparently and warned my dad off. Dad always says it's a swizz anyway cos these firms don't pay you that much when you are working and if the work slows down they cut the wages anyway. I was approached when my parents both died but I said no, more for Captain's sake than my own. And,' he added with a wry grin, 'I reckon my dad and granda would have left their graves to haunt me if I had even seriously considered it. Anyway, this is not getting us fed, is it?' he said, seeing the longing on Andy's face. He dropped some coins in his hand and said, 'Get the drinks in and I'll be along as soon as I get the horse settled.'

When the food came the smell was so appetising Andy had trouble not falling on it like some sort of savage animal, but remembering where he was and what had happened to him after he had eaten a loaf that way, he forced himself to slow down and chew his food properly. He was enjoying every mouthful and the beer slipped down his throat too and tasted like nectar.

As Billy watched the almost blissful look on Andy's face as he ate, he realised just how hungry he had been and for all that he had worked as hard as Billy had that day. 'All right is it?'

'Much more than just all right,' Andy said. 'The

food is wonderful.'

'Steady on,' Billy said with a grin. 'They'll put the prices up if they hear you praising it too much.'

Andy grinned back and then a few minutes later he said, 'What happened to your family, Billy? You speak about them with such, I don't know ... love, I suppose.'

'Well I did have a family once,' Billy said. 'Look, see my grandfather came from farming stock and lived on land in a cottage and his parents were forced off with the railways coming. Only thing for them to do was to follow what others had done and live on one of the barges on the canal. My grandfather was just a young boy then and so he grew up on a barge and married the daughter of one of their neighbouring farmers who had done the same thing as they had. I never knew either of them. My two eldest brothers, George and Bert, did, but John didn't cos he was only two years older than me.'

'What happened to your brothers?' Andy asked though he thought he knew the answer.

'All of them were killed in the war,' Billy said. 'Ma sort of died a little bit with each one. The nearest to me, John, wasn't called up till 1916 and was killed first. The other two followed and, not long after, Ma developed this cough. Course the damp air didn't help that and they wanted to take her to the hospital and she wouldn't go and then she died in the end. Pneumonia, they said, and it was a couple of months before the Armistice was signed. As for my dad, he was lost without Ma. I was too and I still miss her now, cos she was lovely, my old Ma. The final straw for Dad though was

234

when I received my call-up papers as well. It was as if he had just given up. They said he died of a heart attack, but really I thought it was heart ache. And the point was I never did get to join up because then the Armistice was signed and that was that.'

Andy felt great sympathy for Billy and acknowledged that he had had almost as difficult a life as he had. 'So you just stayed on here?'

Billy shrugged. "What else was I to do?" he asked. 'It's all I know. At least I have a roof over my head and make a living of sorts, though because I'm on my own I never get regular work nor am I able to tow the coal tenders and stuff that pays the better money. But then from what I hear I'm doing better than some for the country's in a state. You wouldn't think we'd won the war.'

'You would not,' Andy said. 'Gangs of unemployed men are on nearly every street corner.'

'So why did you come here from Ireland?' Billy said. 'Was it to get away from the fighting?'

Andy shook his head. 'Not really,' he said. 'There wasn't much fighting then, not where I was anyway. I know things are much worse now. An experienced old lag told me to use newspaper to cover myself because it's warm and it is surprisingly so, but I also get to read the news first.' He gave a rueful smile and went on. 'So a life on the streets is giving me an education of sorts.'

'So you can read good then?' Billy said.

Andy shrugged. 'I suppose. Can't you?'

Billy shook his head. 'Lots of us that work on the barges can't read or write well. We don't go to school, see. I was taught to read and write my

235

name and to reckon up enough to understand the toll tickets and that's about it really as far as education goes.'

'Do you miss not being able to read?'

Billy shook his head. 'Probably never use it if I could,' he said. 'More important to me is learning how to steer the barge and understanding how the locks work and concentrating on getting strong enough to leg the barge through the tunnels.'

'I can see that, but it must be difficult on your own.'

'Sometimes,' Billy agreed. 'But the canal people I've known all my life and they'll always help if I'm stuck. You have been a godsend though and to tell you the truth I'd offer you a job straight up, but working on my own sometimes I make a bit of money and sometimes I don't. It's not regular or anything.'

Andy understood that but knew if ever the opportunity should arise he would prefer to work on the barges on the canal than anywhere, but homeless, destitute people like him hadn't the luxury of any sort of preference.

Andy didn't see Billy for a few days after that for he couldn't spend time looking for him when he needed to eat; he had to try and earn money elsewhere too. Any work he picked up was mainly cleaning up or loading or unloading wagons and he seldom got much more than sixpence, however long it took. So a few days later, when he went down Rocky Lane and Billy hailed him from the barge, he went forward eagerly.

'I've been offered a job,' Billy said. 'It's taking

236

heavy machinery down to Gas Street Basin. It will be on a large tender so I hesitated about taking it as I doubt I could do it on my own and I wasn't sure I'd see you.'

'Can Captain pull that much weight?' Andy asked as he fondled the old horse's ears.

'Oh yeah,' Billy said confidently. 'Strong as an ox he is. Won't go quick like, but then you can't go quick on the canal anyway. Captain takes everything slow and sure. Anyway, there's half a crown in it for you, so are you interested?'

'You bet I am,' Andy said, and took hold of the horse's bridle.

'So what brought you to England if it wasn't to escape the fighting?' Billy said after a few minutes as the barge glided through the water.

Andy hesitated for just a moment but then, as Billy had been so open and honest with him, he told him the truth.

'So let me get this right,' Billy said. 'You both run away because your girl's father doesn't think you are good enough for his daughter. What is he, some sort of lord or summat?'

'No, just a farmer,' Andy said. 'See, I was a hireling boy and he didn't think my prospects were good, or at least not good enough, and he was shooting her off to America and so we headed for England.'

'And you said you was brother and sister?'

'That's right,' Andy said.

'And you never touched her, like – you know what I mean?'

'No,' Andy said.

'Well,' said Billy, looking at him with admiration. 'I think you're one royal gent cos there aren't many would do that.'

'I love Celia,' Andy said simply. 'I had her reputation to think about.'

'And now she's with these toffs?'

'Yes. I told you about meeting Annabel Lewisham on the boat and now they are staying in Henry's house.'

'And Henry is?' persisted Billy.

'Henry Lewisham, her brother.'

Andy hadn't been aware of the curl of his lip, but Billy had seen it and he said, 'You don't like him?'

'No I don't,' Andy said firmly. 'He thinks far too much of himself and looks down on the lower classes. I don't mean looks down on me now, for half of Birmingham could claim to do that. I mean at the start when I was respectable.'

'Is he a handsome sort of chap?'

'He's all right, I suppose,' Andy said. 'Tell you the truth, I don't really notice if fellows are handsome or not. One thing in his favour is that he appears to be very fond of his sister and so as she has taken so well to my Celia she will probably be all right.'

'She might be better than all right.'

'What do you mean?'

'Andy, he thinks you are her brother and you have disappeared out of her life. She's bound to be upset despite the letter you left and I bet he would be on hand to console her.'

'Celia wouldn't...'

'Are you sure?' Billy said. 'Those types can be real charming when they put their mind to it and

238

no matter how much her mistress likes your sister she is still a servant girl and from what I've heard they think servant girls are fair game for them. Think of it from Celia's point of view. She has no idea where you are and the only other people she knows in Birmingham are these Lewishams. I bet she's more than lonely at times and a girl like that could be tempted if anyone showed her kindness.'

Andy knew every word Billy spoke was true and he cried, 'But what am I to do? I can't take her away from there to a life on the streets and I can't even see her. If she saw what I am reduced to now she would almost certainly throw me over and congratulate herself for the lucky escape she had. I would never see her again, I know that.'

'It's a problem all right,' Billy conceded. He hadn't a solution and his brow was puckered in thought and Andy was too despondent to talk either and the only sound was the lap of the water and the plod of Captain's giant feet on the towpath.

And suddenly when the silence had stretched out before them for many uncomfortable minutes, he said, 'Well it's not ideal. But if you can read so well, can you write?'

'Yeah, they sort of go together.'

'Well write her a letter,' Billy said.

'I haven't the wherewithal to write,' Andy snapped. 'I'd need paper, something to write with, a stamp.'

'I have paper and a pen,' Billy said. 'My mother could write, she went to this dame school when she was a child and she used to write to her sister in America and we never chucked her stuff out when she died so it's still there.'

'It is a thought all right, Billy,' Andy said excitedly. 'But what about a stamp? How much is a stamp anyway?'

'Haven't a clue,' Billy said. 'Personally though I wouldn't bother with a stamp at all. I'd get a child to take it for me, especially as it's Saturday tomorrow and we'd soon find some urchin will do it for you, especially if you offer a thruppenny bit.' And then as Andy still hesitated, Billy went on, 'You are getting half a crown for this job. Surely you can spare three pence out of that to at least let your girl know that you're still in the land of the living even if you can't have her with you just now.'

'I can, of course I can.'

'Come on then,' Billy said. 'Let's get this lot unloaded as quick as we can and you can get started on that letter.'

However, nothing can be done at speed on the canal and so it was late afternoon before they were free and both were starving hungry and Billy treated them both to fish and chips. Andy felt the warm chips and delicious fish slip down his throat and fill his stomach for the first time in ages and hoped he would be able to hang on to it. His stomach did heave a bit but he managed to keep the food down and a full stomach can put a new complexion on problems and he felt confident that the letter might achieve something.

It was evening by the time they got to the place Billy birthed his barge and so Andy began his letter in the snug little living space downstairs by the light from the paraffin lamp. He poured out his heart in that letter, telling Celia how much he loved her and missed her and so wished they could be together, but getting a job was proving harder than he thought it would be. At last he had it finished and Billy said he might as well stay the night as it was so late.

In fact Billy was thinking that Andy might as well stay on the boat for good, it would be a darn sight better than the streets now that some mornings had the nip of autumn in the air. He said nothing about it then though and they had a bowl of porridge before they set off the next morning in the direction of Erdington.

There were plenty of children playing in the streets before they got as far as Erdington Village and Andy approached one standing on his own who was more than willing to take a letter for thruppence.

They walked with him as far as Grange Road and then they got to the corner opposite the farm. Andy took the thruppenny bit out of his pocket. 'This is yours if you go along this road till you reach number twenty-five and take this letter to the lady there. Now there are two ladies and you must give it into the hand of a Miss McCadden. You got that?'

The boy nodded 'I've got to ask for Miss Mc-Cadden.'

'Right,' Andy said, clapping him on the shoulder. 'Good lad. Wait a while in case there is a message, then hightail it back here and the thruppence is yours. Can you do that?'

The boy nodded his head vigorously and Andy placed the letter in his hand and he set off.

There was only Annabel and Janey in the house for it was Cook's day off and she had taken herself out for the day and, as Celia took over on those days, she had gone to Erdington Village for any special ingredients she needed and also to change her library books and Annabel's. So, when Janey opened the door to see a scruffy young boy on the steps, she said, 'Clear off.'

'I won't then,' said the boy and added, 'I have business here.'

'What business could you have?'

'I have a letter for a Miss McCadden.'

'Mrs McCadden,' Janey corrected. 'Give it here then.'

The boy thought of the thruppenny piece and shook his head. 'Shan't. The man said I had to see only her. I wasn't to give it to anyone else.'

'What man?'

'This man,' the boy said with a shrug. 'He d'aint tells me his name or owt, but he said that I weren't to give the letter to anyone else but Miss McCadden.'

Janey didn't bother correcting the boy again, but said instead, 'She's supposed to be resting. I'll see if she's willing to see you.'

Annabel though was a little troubled when Janey told her what the boy had said. She blessed the fact that Celia was out of the way because the fact that the boy had been told to ask for her in particular made her think the letter might be from Celia's lover, Andy, who had pretended to be her brother and if so it was important to know what he had to say.

'Shall I send him packing, ma'am?'

'No, let him in,' Annabel said and she spoke in a bored tone. 'Probably someone begging for money for their pet charity but I had better speak to him.'

Janey was surprised, but she summoned the boy in.

'My maid said you have a letter for me.'

'If you are Miss McCadden I have.'

'Of course I'm Mrs McCadden,' Annabel said, extending her hand. As soon as she saw it she knew she was right, it was from Andy because she recognised the handwriting. 'Thank you,' she said, but the boy still stood in the room 'You can go now.'

'He said to wait a bit to see if there was any reply.'

'No, there's no reply,' Annabel said and then she reached into her purse and extracted a few pennies and gave them to him.

'Thank you, miss.'

Annabel rang the bell for Janey and the boy had barely left the room before she had the letter ripped open. In it Andy expressed his deep, heartfelt love for Celia and said he was earnestly searching for work and he would fetch her as soon as he could. He said how sorry he had been to leave her in the lurch the way he had and he hoped the letter had explained a little of why he had to go.

Annabel felt a stab of remorse for she had spirited that letter away and she didn't relish explaining that to Celia and if she gave her this letter she would have to tell her, even show her what he had written, when she had let her think he had gone without a word. What if Celia resented her for that? She might easily and when she read this latest missive she might decide to set about finding this Andy because the letter was so full of love and written so sincerely, reading it had brought a lump to her throat and she hardly knew Andy. Celia might easily up and leave her just when she needed her and she didn't think she would cope with the birth without Celia by her side because she was so calm and practical. No, she couldn't let Celia know about this letter and so she ripped it into bits and threw them into the fire that Janey had lit that morning.

'No reply?' Andy repeated to the young boy, bitterly disappointed that Celia hadn't sent him some sort of note, however short.

The boy shook his head. 'She never even opened it.'

'Never even opened it?' Andy repeated incredulously. 'You sure it was Miss McCadden you gave the letter to?'

'Course it was,' the boy cried. 'I said so, didn't I, and she's having a baby, ain't she?'

Andy was totally shocked and he said, 'No, no, you're mistaken there.'

'No I ain't,' the boy maintained. 'Cos my ma looked like that afore she had my little brother. Can I have that thruppence now?'

Andy gave the boy the money and he scampered away and Billy put his arm around Andy. 'She's done the dirty on you, mate.'

Andy nodded as an agonising pain of loss spread through his whole body.

'All those times we were alone together,' he said to Billy. 'And like I said I never touched her and yet for pregnancy to be obvious she must have given herself to Henry almost straight away.'

'Are you sure it was this Henry?' Billy said.

'Course it was,' Andy snapped. 'Who else could it be? She knows not a soul in Birmingham and even the short time I was there I could see the way Henry Lewisham looked at her, but I thought she was too respectable for any of that carry-on. You know,' he added, 'I was talking to a man a few months back and his girl threw him over when he was at the front for a man who dodged the call-up because he failed the medical with flat feet.'

'Christ!'

'Yeah, as he said, this man was here and he wasn't and it's a bit the same with Celia except that his girl married the man – this swine didn't marry her, though she is carrying his child or she wouldn't still be calling herself McCadden. When this man told me that I felt sorry for him, but I wasn't that worried something similar might happen to me for never in a million years would I have said that Celia was that type of girl. Well, it just shows that one person never really knows the heart of another. And that's the finish of her and me for I don't take another man's leavings.'

THIRTEEN

Billy knew that Andy was far more upset than he was letting on and he didn't blame him. It hadn't been his fault that he had no job. God knows he wasn't the only one. And she had waited no time to get another to warm her bed because Andy was right, if her pregnancy was so obvious then her and that Henry must have been at it from the beginning. What a dreadful thing to do to a decent man like Andy. Billy also knew that it was better to work than mope and so he said, 'Are you all right, Andy, cos we really need to be on our way?'

Andy was far from all right, his head was reeling and he realised Celia must have changed totally from the girl he once knew, or thought he knew. Dear Christ! In one way he could thank God he'd had a lucky escape. But in the meantime Billy had a living to make and he nodded his head and said, 'Couldn't be better. Let's go.'

He jumped down as he spoke and held Captain's head and the barge started to slide through the water. And the rhythm of the steady walk along the towpath as he held the halter of the uncomplaining horse eventually began to slow down his racing heart and heal his bruised and battered soul. He knew only time would help him cope with this and until then he wanted to work and work hard so that he was tired enough to sleep each night.

Completely unaware of Andy's misconceptions, Celia seldom thought of him now for other concerns were encroaching on her mind. The Troubles in Ireland were infiltrating into all areas and she couldn't help worrying about her family, wishing dearly she could send a letter and have news of them. However, that wasn't to be and meanwhile she had concerns about Annabel who seemed listless and lethargic so that even a gentle walk seemed beyond her and she'd been that way since the day Celia had been out changing the library books and shopping. She put Annabel's anxious state down to the impending birth, and was very gentle and patient with her.

Cook was very concerned that she was not eating properly, for she often only picked at the meals. 'I can't eat,' Annabel said when Celia encouraged her. 'I'm filled with misery.'

'I know,' Celia said and she also knew when, to please her or Cook or Henry, Annabel ate more dinner than she wanted, she often brought it all back again.

'You must think about the baby,' Cook admonished, as she collected plates one lunchtime to find Annabel had eaten nothing. 'It's not just about you any more. You must force yourself to eat.'

Celia knew Sadie was as worried as she was and she was also a little affronted because she had never had food refused before. She made little fancies and pastries to tempt Annabel's appetite, but often she couldn't stomach those either.

'What does she know?' Annabel said one day

when Sadie, with a click of disapproval, had taken her virtually untouched dinner back to the kitchen.

'We are all concerned about you, that's all,' Celia said. 'And Sadie is worried about the baby too.'

'But I have no desire to think of this baby,' Annabel said. 'To tell you the truth, I wish it didn't exist at all, but as it does I'll have to give birth to the wretched thing and then I don't want to see it, or have any dealings with it whatsoever. I want it taken away, out of my life.' She caught sight of the look on Celia's face and she said, 'Poor dear Celia, I've shocked you, haven't I?'

'A little,' Celia admitted. 'I do understand why you feel that way because what happened to you should never have happened. And by rights that man should be horse-whipped at the very least and admit his responsibilities as regards the child.'

'But none of that has happened or is going to happen.'

'No.'

'Then why were you shocked?'

'Because there is another one blameless in all this business too,' Celia said. 'And that is the child. What a sorry welcome to the world that little mite is going to have.'

'You make me ashamed,' Annabel said. 'You are a much nicer person than me.'

'It didn't happen to me, my lady,' Celia said slipping into her old way of addressing Annabel. 'Maybe if it had I would be feeling the same as you.'

Annabel shook her head. 'No you wouldn't,'

248

she said with certainty. 'In all this, when I have thought of the child, I only ever thought of it as a burden and how it would affect my life. I never thought of it as a little person with thoughts and feelings and I am ashamed of that. We must make sure that whatever we do for the child is the very best solution we can find.'

Celia smiled. 'Glad to hear you say that,' she said. 'But it might not be possible to do that immediately.'

'I know that and if the child has to stay here longer than I intended, then that's how it must be.' She suddenly clutched Celia's hand and looking deep into her eyes she pleaded, 'You will stay and help me, won't you, dear Celia, for I know nothing of babies?'

'I have no qualifications,' Celia said. 'You may be better getting a proper nanny or nursemaid. The only things I know about babies I learnt from my mother when my brother and sister were born.'

Too late she realised that she had told Annabel about her real family. Annabel knew too. She was well aware that Andy was a lover, not a brother, as she had read the letters, but Celia wouldn't have a clue about that so she said, 'I thought there was just you and Andy?'

Celia sighed. 'You'd better hear the truth,' she said and she told Annabel everything. But Annabel wasn't that surprised, but one thing did puzzle her.

'I don't understand why you said you were brother and sister.'

'To protect my reputation,' Celia said. 'For

although Andy and I were lovers, we have only ever kissed. Doesn't look like I'll ever do any more than that now either.'

'So you are still a virgin?'

'Yes and likely to remain one,' Celia said. 'I will be in no hurry to trust another man any time soon with Andy doing the dirty on me the way he did.'

'Well you can stay with us,' Annabel said. She knew her action of not even telling Celia of the existence of the letters had given her friend a jaundiced view of men and what she saw as Andy's abandonment had hurt her deeply and Annabel felt remorse for her actions strike her in the heart so that she gasped as she felt heat flow through her.

'Are you all right, my lady?' Celia said, moving closer and taking up her hand again. 'You've gone so red.'

'I'm fine,' Annabel said almost impatiently. But she needed assurance. 'I want a promise from you, Celia, that whatever happens you'll never hate me.'

'The very idea, Lady Annabel.'

'Promise.'

'All right, if it pleases you so much I'll promise,' Celia said, 'though I can't envisage what you could do to make me even mildly dislike you.'

Annabel sighed and then said, 'Prove it then by becoming my nursemaid. I don't want one of those stuffy nannies and it will only be for a few months until the baby's future is sorted out.'

'I'd be glad to if you're sure,' Celia said. 'I love looking after babies, to tell you the truth. And with all that sorted; now let's give this baby a fighting chance and make he or she as strong as they can be and the first step to that is for you to start eating properly.'

'I see what you're saying,' Annabel said. 'And I will do my best.'

However, her best wasn't good enough for though she did try to eat more she ended up being sicker than ever and eventually when this had been going on for almost a week Henry asked the doctor to call. He was very concerned for Annabel had so obviously lost weight and at that stage of her pregnancy he said that was not good news at all. The doctor was also worried about dehydration and would have liked her to go into hospital, but she became so distressed he didn't insist.

'Celia can do whatever is necessary,' Annabel maintained. 'Can't you?'

Celia felt she had to say she could, but in actual fact she was gravely concerned, for she was no nurse. She knew any hospital Annabel went to would be a private one and the care she would receive from committed and dedicated staff would be tiptop. Celia would have much preferred her to go there, even for a short time, and maybe they would be able to find out what was making her so sick. Henry would have preferred it too.

'Help persuade her this is the best course of action just now?' he pleaded as he let the doctor out.

Celia tried, but Annabel was adamant that she was going nowhere.

'But why, Annabel?' Celia asked. 'What are you

251

afraid of?'

'You know what I'm afraid of, the birth.'

'But they may be able to give you something for that,' Celia said. 'Maybe there's some sort of pain relief or something. And in any case, they might find out what is making you so sick.'

'I'm sick because I am so scared of what is ahead of me,' Annabel cried and her eyes looked haunted and incredibly sad as she added, 'It's all I think about and no hospital can help me with that.'

Celia's heart wrung with sympathy, for this young girl forced to go through with the ordeal before her that was not of her choosing.

'Oh Annabel!' she cried and then felt incredibly humble as Annabel went on, 'It's you I need, because you are so strong and you help me cope.'

Celia had never thought of herself as a strong person and could not remember anyone describing her that way before, but she had to admit that she was a very different person now from the compliant near child she had been in Ireland. Making the decision to come to England with Andy had been the bravest thing she had ever done, but when she'd had to deal with his betrayal she had grown up incredibly quickly. She had more confidence than ever before and if that confidence was helping Annabel then she was glad.

'I won't leave you, never fear,' Celia told her and saw her friend sag in relief for a moment.

And then Annabel suddenly sat bolt upright and said again, 'And you'll never hate me, whatever I do or have done?'

'I have told you before I won't,' Celia said

252

firmly, wondering at Annabel's anxiety.

'No, but listen,' Annabel said urgently. 'I'm going to tell you something that I think about all the time and when you hear it you will know just how wicked I am.'

Celia knew that sometimes people regret telling another their innermost thoughts that are often much better left unsaid.

'Make quite sure that you really want to tell me this, especially if I can't do anything to help,' she warned.

'It will help me to tell you,' Annabel said and reached for Celia's hand and held it tight.

'All right then.'

'I hope the baby dies,' Annabel said and her grip became tighter as if afraid Celia might pull away.

She didn't do that and managed to contain the gasp of shock, but her eyes grew as wide as saucers as Annabel continued. 'See how wicked I am? Are you not disgusted? You are. I can see by your face.'

'I'm not disgusted,' Celia said. 'But I am puzzled. Why do you wish that?'

'Oh, Celia, do you have to ask?' Annabel said. 'I have no feeling for this child and if it lives Henry said it will probably be reared by one of the workers on the estate. And it will always be there, a constant reminder, but if it dies then in time it will be as if it never happened. Then my parents might accept me into the fold again and my life will go on as before. Don't you see that this will be the best outcome all round?'

Celia was a little time answering and when she

did it was to say, 'I see that it would be best for you, Annabel. I do understand how you feel but to wish a poor innocent child's death would deprive him or her of the gift of life.'

'Oh I see that,' Annabel cried in distress. 'You see now. I am not just wicked but also selfish.'

'Don't be so hard on yourself,' Celia advised. 'Those were your innermost thoughts, not actions. Is that why you thought I might hate you?'

'Sort of,' Annabel said. 'And something else I can never tell you about.'

Celia nodded 'Sometimes it's better to keep these things to yourself. Now,' she said. 'I think it's time for you to have a wee rest.'

'I could never sleep.'

'Then I'll read to you until you are tired,' Celia said. 'Let's go up to the bedroom and then if you do drop off it won't matter.'

Just moments later, Annabel was in bed and Celia was sitting beside her reading *Northanger Abbey*. And though Celia knew Jane Austen was one of Annabel's favourite writers, she hadn't gone far into the book before she saw Annabel's eyelids flickering shut as if they were too heavy to keep open and eventually they closed altogether. She lay back on the pillows with a sigh and was soon fast asleep.

Celia had a close look at Annabel as she tucked her in and knew she didn't look anything like a woman just weeks away from giving birth. Even her beautiful face looked a little gaunt, the cheeks sunken in so those high classic cheekbones were prominent and her nose looked rather pinched. She thought Annabel looked sick and she hoped the birth would be sooner rather than later for she didn't think she would improve until then.

Andy, on the other hand, was in a good place for Billy had been able to employ him full time on the barge because he had picked up the contract for taking the Dunlop workers from Rocky Lane to Fort Dunlop by canal when Stan Bridges, the man who had been doing it, had been taken ill. Stan's barge was berthed not that far from Billy and he was sorry to hear that Stan was ill because he had done him many a good turn since his parents had died.

So when he had berthed his barge that afternoon he went aboard Stan's to see how he was. Mabel, Stan's wife, was on deck and when Billy enquired after Stan she shook her head.

'Not too good,' she said. 'He's been in pain, and he said to call the doctor today.'

Billy gave a low whistle because few boaties called the doctor unless things were really serious. 'Must be feeling bad to have the doctor out.'

Mabel nodded. 'He is,' she said emphatically. 'He's more comfortable now because the doctor gave him something for the pain. And he'll be all the better for seeing you, Billy. You go on down.'

Billy went down the steps calling out to the man in the bed as he did so, 'How you feeling now, Stan, you old skiver?'

The smile died as he looked at Stan fully and saw that his face seemed to have shrunk since he had last seen him. It was ashen white and very lined and wrinkled with deep creases on his forehead and down each side of his mouth and his eyes were rheumy and bloodshot and he seemed to have no colour at all in his lips.

Billy knew he was looking at a dying man and yet when Stan said, 'It's the end of me, lad,' he replied, 'Get away out of that, Stan. You'll be as right as rain in no time.'

Stan shook his head and Billy said, 'What did the doctor say?'

'Just confirmed what I already knew, that I have a tumour in my stomach.'

'What can they do?'

'Nothing,' Stan said. 'He said I had less than six months.'

'Oh, Stan!' Billy said and his eyes filled with tears.

'Now don't you be roaring and crying, young Billy,' Stan said. 'One way or another I've had a good innings and while my life on the canal is over, yours is far from it and I may be able to help you there.'

'How?'

'To transport the Dunlop workers like I've been doing,' Stan said. 'This tumour hasn't just happened. Been coming on for months. It was just today when the pain got bad enough to have the doctor in.'

'Well if the doctor can control the pain, can't you carry on a bit longer?' Billy asked.

Stan shook his head. 'Been too much for months but I was too stubborn to admit to it and the old girl can barely manage the locks now and she's been getting bronchitis every winter for the last few years with the damp and all.' He stopped and then went on with a catch in his voice, 'I

256

mean, it isn't as if I have anyone to take over with my family wiped out with TB before they reached double figures.'

'So where will you go?'

'Wife's sister,' Stan said. 'It was always on the cards when we retired anyroad and she is not a bad old stick. Mabel can't wait.'

'God, Stan, I'm going to miss you.'

'I ain't going a million miles away,' Stan said and then gave a rueful smile and said, 'Not straight away anyway. I'll still be in Aston. Albert Road, Mabel's sister lives this side of the park. If you've time you can pop along to see me now and again. I'd like that.'

'I will,' Billy promised.

'Now about this job transporting the workers,' Stan said. 'They need someone to take it on quick, like, because the people can't get there else, unless they walk the length of Tyburn Road and that's a hefty walk when you have a day's work in front of you and it would be worse at the end of the day. Anyway, one of the other boaties did it today.'

'Maybe he might want to take it on permanent,' Billy said. 'Anyone with any sense would cos they would get regular money, like.'

'Maybe he would, if I'd told him what was up,' Stan said. 'But I took care not to let him see me and Mabel just said I was a bit under the weather but would probably be all right in the morning.'

'But—'

'Look, Billy,' said Stan. 'You are a plucky young man and so far you've been dealt a bad hand in life. 'Bout time someone gave you a hand up. I'll write you a letter of recommendation and you take it into the management when you take the workers in tomorrow morning. Oh, and it will need two cos you'll be pulling the tender along with all the workers on so can you get hold of that fellow I've seen helping you a time or two?'

'Oh, yes,' Billy said confidently. 'I imagine he'll be fairly easy to find. And he likes the life on the canal as much as I do.'

And that's just how it was. Billy found Andy sheltering from the sleety rain under the bridge by Aston Station and he was both gratified and relieved at Billy's news and they walked down towards Aston Cross together to seal their new venture with a pint in the Gunmakers' Arms.

By the end of October Andy had been working with Billy for a month and. thought in many ways he had never been happier. There was a tug at his heart though every time he thought of Celia and he would wonder afresh what had happened to change the nature of the girl he thought he had known so completely. He never confided in Billy and so Billy thought he was over any romantic thoughts he'd had about the girl who had ended up betraying him and thought Andy too sensible a man to waste time or effort thinking about that little slut.

Andy was just glad that he was too busy to think about Celia much in the day, but when he was in bed at night thoughts tumbled in his head and disturbed his sleep. He could have done with sleeping deeper for they had to be up early to get the workers to Dunlop's so that they could clock in by half past seven. And before they could set out, one of them had to collect the horse from where he was stabled and feed him and shackle him to the barge, while the other would cook up a pan of porridge for breakfast.

He didn't mind the early morning or the wintry weather for, as he said to Billy, you didn't just farm on good days. He was easy and relaxed with Billy and there was no task on the barge that Andy hadn't learnt to do and each night he bedded down on the bed that Billy had shared with his brothers while Billy slept in the bed his parents had used. Andy was now once more clean-shaven because although water wasn't plentiful in a barge, for it had to be collected from the taps along the towpath, there was a damn sight more than there was when he lived on the streets.

In fact life was so much better and he said so once to Billy and thanked him and coloured in embarrassment. 'Oh give over, man.'

'All right,' Andy said with a grin. 'I just want you to know that I appreciate everything you've done for me and so settled do I feel here that I am going to do something I have been promising I would do as soon as I could and that is write to my parents and let them know I am alive and give them my news.'

'Do you think that wise?' Billy said. 'Thought you said this was all hush and hush. If you give them this address they might trace that Celia too.'

'Well I'm not with Celia now, so that hardly applies any more,' Andy said. 'Anyway we live the other side of Killybegs and it is highly unlikely they would even hear about me running off with Celia Mulligan from Donegal Town. I never said a word about her in my letters home when I worked for the Fitzgeralds, not that I wrote home that often, but when I did, I mean that's hardly the sort of thing you write to your parents, so they'll likely know nothing about it. Anyway it was months ago. Someone else will be in the headlines by now.'

'So are you going to mention Celia at all?'

'No, course not,' Andy said. 'That would set the cat among the pigeons. I will just tell them of the canal and all and about the work I do and I will start tomorrow for it's Sunday and so I will have more time.'

Andy took his time over the letter. He didn't give any reason for leaving Ireland other than the fact that he wanted to try his hand in England and apologised for not writing earlier but said he hadn't any permanent address. He said nothing about the lines of the unemployed nor how many months he had been one of them, but said he was lucky for he had met a young fellow like himself called Billy Brown who owned a barge but who was alone in the world after his brothers had all been killed in the war and his parents succumbed to illness afterwards.

He said how difficult it was to work single-handed on the barge and so now they worked together and he explained the work they did, including ferrying the Dunlop workers.

Writing that though made him think and when Billy came back, for he had taken the chance to see Stan, who he said was fading fast, Andy said, 'I know it's doing us good and everything ferry-

260

ing the Dunlop workers but wasn't it a damned stupid thing to do to build a factory and not have the road built leading to it?'

'It was, I suppose, but that was the war, wasn't it?'

'Was it?'

'Course,' Billy went on. 'Think, if it hadn't been for that, the road would have been built this long while. I mean, they knocked down buildings that would be in the way of it and all but when the war was declared most building of anything stopped.'

'I suppose it would be costly,' Andy said. 'To fight a war, I mean.'

'I'll say,' Billy agreed. 'Cos every bullet fired costs summat and so do the guns to fire them, not to mention tanks and stuff.'

'The road will be built eventually now though,' Andy said. 'I mean, we see men working on it.'

'It will,' Billy agreed. 'And it will be finished and tarmacked and tram tracks laid and trams will run all along the road and we will have to find another source of income but, until then, let's not worry about it for it won't happen today or tomorrow. Anyroad, did you get your letter finished?'

'Yeah.'

'And did you give them an address to write back?'

'How could I?'

'Mmm, difficult,' Billy said. 'As long as we're still doing the run you could have letters sent to the office at the locks where we drop the Dunlop's people off.'

Andy shook his head. 'I just wrote to let my parents know I was still in the land of the living, particularly my mother because I know she worries about me and never wanted me to leave home in the first place.'

'Yeah,' Billy said with feeling. 'It's mothers do the worrying all right.'

'I'm not interested in replies though,' Andy said. 'They might ask me awkward questions I would rather not answer.'

'Like about that Celia?'

'Not specially her,' Andy said. 'Cos I doubt they will know anything about that, but anything I'd rather not discuss with them, like why I was working on a barge for example.'

'Why wouldn't you?'

'That's exactly it,' Andy said. 'You know, when we were coming over here I thought I would end up working in a factory somewhere because people said Birmingham was the city of a thousand trades and so I thought there might be more factory jobs going. Now I've never worked in a factory and though I would have taken a job there, taken a job anywhere if I'd been offered one, I doubt I would have been as contented as I am at the moment.'

'Glad to hear it,' Billy said with a satisfied smile on his face. 'Because I am too.'

FOURTEEN

As Andy was writing his letter, Annabel's pains began. There had been more than a few false alarms in the last month and the doctor had been a regular visitor for he'd insisted they send for him as soon as Annabel's labour started. Celia told Henry to tell the doctor she thought it was the real thing this time. He'd had the phone fitted a few months before, primarily for just such an occasion, but Celia was too nervous of it to ever think of using it so in a way she was glad that it was Sunday and Henry was home.

However, the doctor was not at home and all his housekeeper could tell Henry was that he had gone off with his wife and she didn't know where, but she said he would be back at tea time. However, it was a long time till tea time and Celia was glad Cook offered to forgo her day off to give her a hand and Janey said she would take over Sadie's duties in the kitchen because Annabel refused to release Celia's hand, which she gripped so tightly when the pains came that Celia felt the bones grind together.

Never had time appeared to go so slowly. Celia talked to Annabel of all manner of things in an effort to take her mind off the griping pains. She knew they were in for a long haul because after three hours the pains were still coming twenty minutes apart and so the birth was nowhere near

263

imminent. She knew too the pains had to get a lot stronger and closer together before the baby was anywhere near ready to be born and she did wonder how Annabel would cope because she was finding the pains hard to bear now.

Henry had been woken up early because of the unusual activity in Annabel's bedroom and when Celia came into the kitchen, having eased her hand from Annabel's to make them all a cup of tea, it was to see Henry seated at the table, an unread newspaper in front of him. Celia saw the anxiety reflected in his deep brown eyes as he said, 'God, Celia, I heartily wish Annabel had agreed to do as the doctor wanted that time and gone into the hospital. I mean, I'm not decrying what you have done or anything but...'

'I know you're not,' Celia said and though she was concerned herself about Annabel she knew it would be no good loading that onto Henry too, so she continued, 'And really so far everything is as it should be. These pains are normal so don't let's worry before we have to.'

'I suppose,' Henry said, but he still looked doubtful. 'And then the bloody doctor is out after he expressed such concern and said we must send for him the minute she started.'

Celia gave a slight laugh. 'Henry, you can hardly blame the man for taking a few hours off. He's hardly been away from the house this past month and he only saw and examined her the day before yesterday and there was no indication then that Annabel was going to start the minute he left the house. Anyway,' she went on, 'it will be some hours yet before the baby is born and by then the doctor will be here should she need help.'

'Oh God!' Henry exclaimed. 'Have we got hours of this?' For now moans were coming from the bedroom.

''Fraid so,' Celia said. 'And I must make this tea and get back to her.'

Later when she brought the tea up, she said to Sadie, 'Have you attended many births before?'

'Bless you, ducks, over the years I've delivered many babies,' Sadie said. 'Funny that when I've not chick or child of my own. Course my young man was killed in the Boer War.'

'I never knew that, Sadie.'

'No need for you to know, ducks,' Sadie said. 'Just explaining like and there ain't never been anyone else. I love babies though and each birth seems like a little miracle somehow.'

'Some miracle,' said Annabel with a grimace and Sadie smiled as she said, 'When you hold this wee one in your arms all the pain won't matter any more. Seen it time and time again.'

Celia had heard that said often and even from her own mother and yet she didn't think this might be the case with Annabel ... but only time would tell.

Another hour went by and then two and Sadie went down to the kitchen and brought more tea along with a plate of hot, buttered toast. The food put new heart into Celia who had been flagging.

'Come on,' she encouraged Annabel. 'You must eat too for there's a lot of work ahead.' Annabel was only able to nibble at the toast though, but she gulped gratefully at the tea.

'Everything all right in the kitchen?' asked Celia

Sadie nodded. 'Janey is making a good fist of putting a meal together for this evening for Lord Lewisham will need to eat even if we don't have time.'

'Yes, what about his lunch?'

'Oh, I advised him to go for a long walk and get his lunch while he is out,' Sadie said. 'I mean, he's sitting there like a spare dinner and really it's no place for a man. I said he could take his time for there will be nothing happening for hours yet.'

'What do you mean?' Annabel gasped from the bed. 'I can't take much more of this.'

Sadie smiled but in a kindly way. 'No way round it I'm afraid, my dear.'

Sadie was gentle with Annabel but when she threw the covers back to examine her she was surprised how small her stomach was with the birth so close.

'She hasn't eaten properly for weeks, you know that,' Celia said.

'Didn't know she was this small though,' Sadie said. 'Let's have a look at you anyway.'

She took her time, going round and round the small mound pressing firmly but gently here and there, while Celia found she was holding her breath.

'Is everything all right?' Annabel asked, reaching for Celia's hand as another pain gripped her.

'Coming along nicely,' Sadie said. 'Don't know what the doctor will say, Miss Cissie, when he sees the size of you.'

'How's she really doing?' Celia asked Sadie

266

quietly as she moved away from the bed.

'She's doing well considering,' said Sadie, 'but from what I could see the cervix hasn't moved.'

However, as the hours ticked by the pains grew suddenly stronger and closer together and sweat stood out on Annabel's face, which Celia constantly wiped away. Her hair was fanned out behind her on the pillow and it looked dull and dank and in her eyes Celia read raw, naked fear.

Some time later Sadie toiled up with a dinner that Janey had cooked. Annabel couldn't eat but Celia and Sadie were grateful for the food and it was as Celia carried the plates back down again that Henry called out to her, 'How's she doing?'

'She's very frightened now and is finding the pain hard to bear.'

'I think I would too,' Henry admitted. 'I would have said that I am as brave as the next man, but I don't know how you women stand it.'

'That might be because we've no alternative,' Celia said.

'I suppose,' Henry said and then went on, 'I wanted to ask you something anyway. Do you think that I should tell my parents that Annabel is in labour?'

'Would they be interested?'

'I don't know,' Henry admitted. 'But have they a right to know?'

'Leave it till the baby is born and then you can discuss what's to become of the child as well,' Celia advised. 'You never know but the sight of a baby might heal the rift. I've seen it happen before and, however the child was conceived, he or she is still their grandchild.'

'Yes you're right, of course,' Henry said. 'The point is I feel so useless.'

'We all do,' Celia confessed. 'All we can do is make Annabel as comfortable as possible.'

When she returned to the bedroom it was to find Sadie had tied a towel to the bedhead.

'For when the pains get bad,' she told Annabel and Celia remembered her mother being told the same thing. Annabel though was staring at Sadie with horror.

'What d'you mean when the pains get bad?' she demanded in almost a shriek. 'They're bad now. They're tearing me in two as it as. I don't want your stupid towel. I'll hold Celia's hand.'

'If you hold Celia's hand any tighter than you are at the moment she could easily lose the use of it,' Sadie said. 'Anyway you'll have to push soon and the towel may help then.'

'And I'll still be here,' Celia said soothingly as she wiped the beads of perspiration from Annabel's face with a damp cloth. Annabel sighed and Celia's heart bled for her.

'I'm so tired,' Annabel complained.

'Well neither of us got much sleep last night,' Celia said. 'That ache in your back meant you couldn't get comfy in bed. Why don't you close your eyes between contractions?'

'Why should I? I'll hardly sleep.'

'You may rest though,' Sadie said.

'I just want it to be over, the pain to stop,' Annabel said. 'Does it always hurt like this?'

'I believe so.'

'How do women bear it?' Annabel said. 'Some have big families. Fancy going through this over

268

and over again.' She looked across at Sadie and said, 'Can't you hurry it up a bit?'

Sadie shook her head. "Fraid not,' she said. 'Babies come when they are ready and not before.'

Annabel sank back on the pillows, too exhausted to talk any more, and as the minutes and hours slipped by she eventually closed her heavy eyes and Celia sat back on the chair by the bed with a small sigh of relief.

'Let her sleep while she can,' Sadie advised. 'She'll have plenty of work to do soon and if I were you I would close my own eyes too.'

Celia was feeling very jaded, but didn't think she'd sleep on the uncomfortable chair, but she lay back as far as she could and closed her eyes.

She was woken with a jerk by a scream that went on and on, bouncing off the walls as Annabel writhed and thrashed on the bed, arching her back as the pain gripped her and pulling on the towel tied to the bedpost with such vigour that she threatened to pull the bedhead crashing down on top of her. The pains were not coming in waves any more but were relentless and unremitting like a wall of pain and Annabel would only pause to take a shuddering breath before the heartbreaking screeches began again.

Sadie threw back the covers. 'I can see the head,' she yelled over the noise, but Celia doubted Annabel heard her for she seemed incapable of hearing anything much. 'Nearly there, bonny girl,' Sadie continued unabashed and then suddenly a cascade of water burst from Annabel with such force it hit the bedhead. 'All right,' Sadie said. 'Now you have to push.'

The screams had stopped as if Annabel had no energy left to scream but she was giving agonising moans and at Sadie's words she shook her head vehemently from side to side. 'I can't.'

'You can and you must,' Sadie said and Celia joined in to encourage and cajole her to give one more push, and one more and again, over and over until the head was eased out by Sadie and a thin puny body slithered after it and lay still between Annabel's legs. 'It's a girl,' Sadie said, just as the doctor tore up the stairs.

He had no time for the baby. 'I would say this wee mite is too small and puny to survive,' he said, handing the child to Sadie and Celia saw the tears glistening in Sadie's eyes and felt a lump in her own throat as she gazed at the perfectly formed, tiny, wrinkled child.

Annabel was too far gone to be aware of anything wrong with the child.

'Something else for her to come to terms with,' Celia said and she remembered Annabel had wished the child to die, but it was one thing to wish it and quite another for it to happen. She might feel guilty about those thoughts now.

The doctor had witnessed the women's distress and he said, 'It's always sad when a child dies, but if I do not tend to the mother now, she might go the same way.' And both Celia and Sadie knew they had to swallow their sorrow in order to help the doctor as he said, 'I really wish she had gone to hospital when I suggested it months ago for if she is to recover, hospital is her only option now.'

Annabel seemed only semi-conscious after the birth and the doctor noticed this too. He was

270

pressing on her stomach to help her deliver the placenta and said to Sadie, 'Keep her with us if you can. Gives her more of a chance that way.'

Sadie laid the baby in the cradle ready prepared and took her place beside Annabel, holding her hand and speaking to her in a fairly loud voice and Annabel's eyes flickered open for a while, but showed no recognition before they closed again. Suddenly, the afterbirth was expelled, followed by a gush of blood.

'Almighty Christ!' the doctor cried and Celia stood almost transfixed at the scarlet stream pumping from Annabel and soaking into the mattress. The acrid stink of it was filling her nostrils when the doctor yelled at her, jerking her out of her appalled reverie. 'Fetch towels for Christ's sake and plenty of them and I'll need use of the phone.'

Celia ran to do the doctor's bidding, glad to be doing something and also glad, if she was honest, to be away from the very sick young woman and wee dead baby, for every time she thought of them, tears prickled her eyes. But there was no time for tears, they were a luxury she couldn't afford. As she came back with virtually every towel they possessed in her arms, she met Henry at the head of the stairs.

'What is it?'

Celia shook her head. 'She's bad, Henry. Very sick.'

'Has she had the baby?'

'Yes, it was a little girl, small and puny. She didn't survive. I must get these towels for the doctor. He needs use of the phone, he said. I think he's calling an ambulance.'

Henry nodded briefly. 'I'll wait out here for him.'

Celia didn't answer but hurried from him and when she went into the room it was to find that Sadie and the doctor had raised the base of the bed on books.

'May help a little,' the doctor said gruffly as he packed the towels around Annabel. 'But she is haemorrhaging and needs to be in hospital if she is to have any chance at all.'

'Lord Lewisham, my br ... brother, is waiting outside to show you where the phone is,' Celia told him and it was as the door clicked behind the doctor that she heard the splutter from the cradle. So did Sadie and she lifted the child out and gave her a little shake.

'The child may be small,' Sadie said. 'But despite all she is alive and I think she should have a chance.'

Celia nodded. 'And me.'

Sadie parted the folds of the shawl and gave the baby a slap on the bottom and the baby roared in outrage and, as the newborn's wails filled the room, Celia burst into tears.

'Might be small but her lungs seem to be in full working order,' Sadie said. 'Let's show Miss Cissy the beautiful daughter she has given birth to. It might give her the strength to fight if she has something to fight for.'

Celia knew Annabel might not feel that way at all, but Sadie didn't have to know that.

Annabel lay as still as a stone and Celia initially thought the rigours of the birth had tired her out and she had fallen asleep. However, the room

272

was quiet, too quiet, and Celia was handed the baby, whose screams had given way to small, hiccupping sobs. Sadie stepped forward and put her fingers on Annabel's neck. Then she laid her head on her chest. She sprung away from the bed suddenly with a cry and said to Celia, 'We have to have the doctor back in here quick and your brother better come in too,' and she ran to the door and shouted for help.

The doctor arrived first and he didn't need to be told what the problem was. He began immediately pumping at Annabel's chest and even the baby was quiet, slumbering in Celia's arms as she stood like Henry and Sadie and willed Annabel to begin breathing again. She didn't, however, and eventually the doctor stepped away from the bed and he spoke to them all as he said, 'I'm sorry, she's gone.'

'Gone?' Celia repeated and although the word hammered in her brain she couldn't quite believe it. Women had babies all the time and they didn't die from it. Sadie stepped forward to take the baby, but Celia held on to it. She could see that though Henry was heartbroken at the death of his beloved sister, he was struggling to control himself for to show such abject grief at the death of the friend of his sister might have sparked some speculation. So to distract him as much as anything else Celia said, 'The baby rallied. She's alive.'

Henry took little notice. But the doctor was surprised. 'You might lose her yet,' he warned. 'She is very small and undernourished because her mother wasn't eating properly. You must take great care of her.'

273

Henry looked at the baby for the first time and saw how small and frail she appeared and said, 'You don't have to take that on board on your own, Anna. I can engage a nurse.'

Celia brushed the tears from her eyes and swallowed the lump that threatened to choke her and said, 'Cissie wanted no nurse and I promised that I would help her. Now I would like to care for the baby in her memory.'

Everyone was impressed when Celia said that and, though she meant what she said, she thought it would be a temporary arrangement until a foster family could be found for the baby. It did mean that she had to put aside her grief at the loss of Annabel to care properly for her child.

FIFTEEN

It was Sadie who bought bottles for the baby and showed Celia how to make up the National Dried powdered milk and stressed how important it was to properly sterilise the bottles and advised that she rub the teat with salt first to remove any residue of milk. This was a strange thing for Celia and she had never bottle-fed a baby because her younger brother and sister, like most of the babies around, had been breast-fed.

Sadie also showed Celia how to line the crib with cotton wool so that the baby would be kept extra warm and knew where the best suppliers of baby clothes and equipment were and wrote out a list of the child's requirements for Henry to buy. Celia was immensely grateful to Sadie for her help and advice; Sadie thought, like Celia, that the best way to honour Annabel's memory was to care for her child in the best way possible. The day-to-day care though was down to Celia and as the baby had to be fed little and often Celia's days and nights were fully occupied.

Henry had sent a telegram to his parents to inform them of Annabel's death for he quite reasonably thought they might like to be involved in seeing the final resting place of their only daughter. But in their reply they said they would leave all arrangements to him and that they wouldn't be attending. Henry was angered and shocked to the core that Annabel was not forgiven even in death for something that had not been her fault anyway.

But one way or another his sister had to be buried, though it was a sad little funeral that took place at Erdington parish church a few days later. There was only Henry and Celia there as Janey and Sadie had stayed behind to look after the baby and make refreshments on the vague chance that someone might come back with them.

Celia knew she had to attend that funeral to be some support for Henry so she didn't bother explaining to him that Catholics were not allowed to attend services at other churches. She knew her soul would already be as black as pitch because she had missed Mass for months so one more transgression hardly mattered. Anyway, those at the house still thought she was Henry's sister and would have thought it mighty odd if she hadn't gone to the funeral of her dearest friend.

Celia thought the service very short and quite shabby for a vibrant young girl not quite seventeen. The vicar delivered the eulogy and when he prayed for the young widow, Cissy McCadden, taken in childbirth, it gave Celia a shock, for all she had been semi-expecting it and she lifted her eyes and met Henry's bleak ones. She knew she would have to speak with him soon about the subterfuge they had concocted, which surely wasn't important now that Annabel was dead. As it was she thought it decidedly odd to follow the vicar in prayers for her own soul when she was alive and well.

Later, they stood at the open grave for more prayers to be said and then they watched the coffin lowered into the hole dug ready. Henry threw the first clod of earth in and she followed suit and as her clod of earth landed with a dull thud she said her own private goodbyes to the girl she had become so fond of, tears stinging her eyes.

Many times in the couple of days after the funeral she wondered where her future lay now. The plan had been that she would stay with Annabel and help her care for the baby until it was taken to its new foster home and then they would assume their correct names. Annabel would return home if she was let and Celia would go with her as her lady's maid. Celia had often wondered if it would come off as Annabel wanted. She had no idea how things like this were done among posh people in these big houses.

Annabel's death threw their plans into disarray anyway and she wondered if Henry had thought of this. She needed to talk to him about the baby's christening as well, despite the fact that he often seemed burdened with grief.

Henry was in actual fact taking a long time to get over both his sister's tragic death and the mean way she had been buried and two nights later he sought out Celia in the nursery after dinner. She had just laid the baby down after her feed and was surprised to see Henry at the door and she saw at once that he had been drinking heavily.

'What is it, Henry?' she said. 'What's the matter?'

'You can ask that after that fiasco of a funeral we both attended recently?'

'Oh Henry.'

'Don't "Oh Henry me",' Henry said. 'Annabel should never have been buried in that pitiful way. And maybe it's my fault?'

'How can that be?'

'Well if I had announced who she was after she died,' Henry said, 'then Annabel would have had the proper funeral that she was entitled to. It would have been conducted in the family's parish church and afterwards her body would have been laid in the family vault. Relations and friends would have come from far and wide to lament the cutting short of a young life and their sympathy might have been something of a comfort for all of us. And people would have expected my parents to be organising it and any reception to be at their house. They would have hated every minute of it, but been forced to do it because not to do so when it's your own daughter who has died would look so odd. But it wasn't their reaction that stopped me saying anything.'

'So what was it?' Celia asked.

'It was the thought that everyone would want to know how she died and I couldn't bear the thought of her memory being besmirched when she isn't even here to defend herself. Especially if my parents had intimated that it was all her own fault, as they might. In fact her abuser might attend for he is a man my father tries to keep on the right side of. I couldn't have borne seeing him there, knowing that it was his fault my sister died.'

'I know it was,' Celia said almost impatiently. 'But there is no point in going over and over it. It won't help or solve anything. It's like poking a sore tooth.'

'Dear, dear Celia,' Henry said and she felt his deep dark eyes boring into hers and his voice was thickened by the tears that, as a man, he was unable to shed. 'Whatever would I do without you?'

She swallowed deeply as she said, 'There are other things we must do and the first of these is a name for the baby for she must be christened.'

Henry knew Celia was breaking off any tentative intimacy between them and sticking to practical things and she was right to do that. Anyway, she had a point for the baby couldn't be called that for ever.

'Did Annabel have any names in mind, do you know?'

Celia shook her head. 'Annabel tried not to think of the baby as a living, human being and didn't discuss names at all.'

'What about Grace?' Henry said. 'Her governess told her the story of Grace Darling when she was quite young and it fascinated her. She told

278

me Grace Darling was the bravest woman she had ever heard about and one with the nicest name and after that, if ever she was playing some sort of pretend game, she always called herself Grace.'

'That's lovely,' Celia said. 'I'm sure that Annabel would like her daughter called after someone she so admired, but what of a family name as well? What is your mother called?'

'Catherine.'

'Well Grace Catherine goes well together,' Celia said. 'Would your mother like the child named for her or would she be affronted?'

'I don't know what would please or offend my mother because just at the moment I feel I don't know her at all, nor my father either. You know, Celia, when I was growing up and living at home I never thought for one moment that there would ever come a time when either Annabel or I would do something bad enough to be cast out of the family so completely. The way they have treated Annabel, even after her life was snuffed out, beggars belief.'

'It probably wouldn't happen to you, the son of the house,' Celia said. 'In Ireland the sons generally have a much easier time. Anyway, you couldn't have a child out of wedlock and that seems to be the worst thing any girl can do and yet the father of the child is seldom blamed in the same way.'

'I know,' Henry said. 'It's not at all fair, is it?'

'No, but all the talking in the world won't change it,' Celia said. 'Meanwhile Grace Catherine is a lovely name and if that offends anyone then that's just hard luck.'

So with no pomp and very little ceremony Grace Catherine was christened in the same church that had held the funeral service for her mother just days before. By necessity, for there was no one else, Henry was her godfather and Celia her godmother.

Henry thought the child should have been wearing the Lewisham family christening gown that had been handed down through the family for years but Celia refused to let him dwell on that and reminded him that the child was two weeks old, and wouldn't care if she was christened in a sack.

'Christening her and giving her a name is far more important than the clothes she was wearing,' Celia said.

'So let's go home now and never give the Lewisham christening gown another thought.'

Andy wasn't to know when he sent the letter that his brother was courting a girl from Donegal Town and that she knew all about Andy Mc-Cadden running off with Celia Mulligan. Most of the young chaps were not that surprised for they had seen the behaviour of the two of them at the dances and they were prepared to be understanding for both Andy and Celia were well liked.

Once the Guards had been informed to try and apprehend the pair before they went to England, there was no way their disappearance could be kept secret. Then there was the tale Seamus Docherty had come back from England with, saying he had bumped into Andy on the platform at the station in Liverpool.

'Told me he was going to try to get set on in the building trade there,' he'd tell anyone who wanted to hear and more especially if they bought him a pint to lubricate the throat. 'Pack of lies of course for if he was biding in Liverpool why did he then take a train bound for Birmingham and that Celia Mulligan along with him?'

Now there was this letter just out of the blue from Andy that Maeve, Chris's girlfriend, told Norah about when she met her in the town. 'And you say that he never mentioned Celia once?'

'No, that's what struck Chris as so odd,' Maeve said. 'I mean, according to Seamus Docherty – and there's no point in him lying – they travelled to Birmingham together, or at least in that direction, so where is she now? Puzzling, isn't it?'

Puzzling and damned worrying, Norah thought as she made for home later, all the way worrying about Celia and where in God's name she could be. She knew that Andy McCadden was the key to it, but according to Maeve he had no address they could write back to and, as he claimed he was working on a canal boat, which she supposed was going up and down all the time, Norah could see that that could be the truth.

She wished she could talk over her concerns with someone, but her father had said that Celia's name was not to be spoken of and though Norah might have sneaked a quiet word with Dermot he was off to America shortly and she felt it unfair to load a problem on him when he could do nothing about it.

She knew the only solution was to travel to Birmingham and somehow find her sister, though she had no idea how to get there in the first place and once there how she was going to go about finding her sister in the busy bustling city she imagined Birmingham to be. She had money her parents knew nothing about, sent to her by her brother, Jim, when the plan had been that she was to join him in America.

Keep the dollars I have enclosed in this letter to buy yourself some decent clothes almost as soon as you land. Tell you I felt like a right country bumpkin at first and I imagine it's worse for a woman.

Norah smiled at her brother's thoughtfulness and, without saying a word about it, hid the letter with the folded dollars inside it in her underwear drawer. So she had more than enough money to travel to Birmingham. But what then? She knew she was more or less responsible for her sister making the journey in the first place; Celia would never have gone without her encouragement and making the arrangements and all. It would have been better to let her go to America. She would have got over McCadden in time as apparently she had in Birmingham and at least she would be looked after and safe and still in contact with the family as Jim was.

The harvest was in and everyone was drafted in to help with that. A fine harvest it was too and Sammy was taken to the peat bogs to collect the peat for the winter for the first time. Dermot smiled as he watched him standing in the cold earth in his bare feet, seeing the black water ooze between his toes, for he remembered doing the self-same thing when he was Sammy's age. It was strange to think that it would be the last time he would collect the turf.

All the jobs he had previously done automatically had a certain poignancy now for it was the last time he would clean out the well with lime, renew any worn thatch and give the farmhouse and barns a coat of whitewash, and with each passing day his excitement grew. He tried to hide it from Norah, quite unsuccessfully for she saw it almost bubbling inside him and his glowing eyes when he spoke and she pushed her resentment way down so that she could speak naturally to her young brother, knowing full well it wasn't Dermot's fault she had been such a fool.

And then a window of opportunity opened up for Norah to leave the farm unnoticed. To get to America from the north of Ireland Dermot would have to go first to the pier in Moville in Inishowan, where he would await the tender to take him out to the big liners bound for America that would be anchored out in the deeper waters of Lough Foyle. Inishowan was a fair distance away and Greencastle, where her sister Katie lived with her husband and son, was the next village to Moville.

No one had been able to visit Katie since the wedding because of the distance and Peggy decided that she would seize the chance to see her daughter as well. Provided Tom could cope, they could all go and stop at Katie's for a day or two once they had set Dermot on his way. Norah was overjoyed to hear this, but told her mother she would stay behind and say goodbye to Dermot in the house.

'But don't you want to see your sister?' Peggy asked.

Norah certainly did want to meet Katie and see how she was and play with her baby son, Brendon, but she was seriously concerned for Celia and knew she could not pass up this chance of slipping away and making for England. And so she said to her mother, 'I'd love to see Katie, but I think I would be upset seeing Dermot boarding that ship and sailing off to America. I would hate to make a holy show of you all.'

'Leave the girl be if that's how she feels,' Dan said when Peggy told him this as they prepared for bed. 'It was supposed to be her sailing off for the States, not Dermot, and she is bound to feel it.'

So Norah's explanation for her decision was accepted and so over the next few days until they would leave Norah made her own preparations. She wrote the letter she intended posting when she reached Belfast, telling her parents what she was doing and why, and her clothes she took out a bit at a time and put them into a bass bag she had hidden in a hollow tree just past the head of the lane. Tom had to think she had changed her mind and gone with the family so that he wouldn't miss her too early. She waited until the last night to tell him, offering to help with the milking and cleaning out the byre, as that was the only way she was more or less guaranteed to get him on his own. Her parents thought she was being considerate because there were a lot of last-minute things still to do, but Norah knew they wouldn't feel the same about her when they discovered what she had done, but she knew she had to carry out her plan of action for the sake of her sister.

They were nearly finished in the byre before she told Tom that she had decided to go with her parents to Moville to see Dermot off after all.

'You do right,' Tom said. 'I can understand that it might give you a pang to see Dermot making for the country you really wanted to see, but moping around here will not help. Going to see Katie afterwards will probably take your mind off it a bit too and Dermot will go with an easier heart, for he knows how much he has upset you and it has concerned him.'

That gave Norah a bit of a jolt, for she hadn't fully appreciated how her decision had affected her brother, and she decided that she would tell him the real reason she couldn't go with the family to see him off. The point that he would be unable to do anything about it seemed suddenly to matter less than him thinking badly of her.

So, after they had eaten the meal and she had helped Ellie wash the dishes, she asked Dermot if he wanted a last look at the farm to see what he was leaving behind. He hadn't thought about it and knew by the wink Norah gave him, which no one else saw, that it wasn't to do with that – she wanted him on his own. He had felt sore that she wasn't coming to see him off and hoped she was going to tell him why and so he stepped into the black night readily enough, only stopping to lift his thick jacket from the back of the door.

The air was icily cold and there was no moon but the stars were twinkling merrily once they were away from the lights of the farmhouse, showing the lack of cloud in the midnight sky and auguring a cold morning the following day, not an ideal day to be crossing the Atlantic Ocean. In fact, not a good night to be abroad either and Norah gave a sudden shiver and wrapped her shawl around her tighter as Dermot said sneeringly, 'Come on then, out with it. I know you wanted to get me on my own. "Bon voyage" might be good, but that's probably beyond you?'

'Don't be like this, Dermot,' Norah said. 'Or I will regret trying to give you some sort of explanation. I do wish you well, but I have far more to say than bon voyage.' For the first time she told him everything about helping Celia to flee that time and about the sighting of them in Liverpool by Seamus Docherty, which he hadn't known about, and the strange letter McCadden had sent to his family.

'You see how worried I am?' Norah said. 'When Seamus saw them they were together and just a few months later Andy writes a letter and doesn't mention her at all.'

'I see that's a bit odd, right enough.'

'It's more than odd,' Norah said. 'I am worried sick that something has happened to her and because it's my fault she's there I have to go to Birmingham to find her, using the trip to see you off to cover my tracks. For with us not being able to mention Celia's name, I can't just come out with it in the general way and ask for permission to try and seek her out.'

'No, I see that,' Dermot said. 'And I think Daddy is wrong to put a blanket ban on talking about Celia. Well I mean, all right, she did wrong

286

but not to be allowed to say her name is like she never existed.'

'I agree.'

'And they were harsh, locking her in her room the way they did,' Dermot went on. 'Make anyone want to take off, that would, and what's wrong with this bloke McCadden anyway?'

'Essentially nothing,' Norah said. 'He's like you or Jim or Sammy. He is the second son of a farmer and, as his older brother inherits the farm, he was making his way as Jim is and you must.'

'So what's wrong with that?'

'Nothing and if Daddy was to lose some of his stiff-necked pride and stop trying to live our lives for us, he might have talked to McCadden instead of fighting him. Then he might have found that he's not the devil incarnate, but a hireling man through no fault of his own, who cares for Celia. If that had been done this might not have happened because Celia never wanted to leave Ireland.'

She looked at Dermot, though it was too dark to see his face as she went on, 'There's the rub though. I gave Celia into his keeping and at the time I would have staked my life on the fact that he loved her and would care for her always.'

'So if she's not under his protection...'

'I need to find out where she is and check that she is safe,' Norah said. 'Do you see that, Dermot?'

'Of course I see,' Dermot said. 'I'm not a child and you are doing the right thing, the only thing, and I only wish that I was not going to America just yet and I could come with you and help you.'

'Daddy would never allow it.'

Dermot smiled ruefully and, though Norah couldn't see it, she could hear it in his voice as they turned back to the house. He said, 'Mad, isn't it? I am allowed, encouraged even, to leave my home and go to another continent entirely, because my father wishes it, and yet not allowed to search for a sister in England who might be in trouble.'

'When we inherit the world and all the old ones have died off we may be able to change things,' Norah said. 'Till then we are stuck with their rules and can only try and bend them if we disagree. Now though, as we are both up very early tomorrow morning, I think we had better hit the sack.'

Dermot had no problem with that but before they went in he turned to Norah and said, 'Will you write and tell me how you get on? I know I'm miles away but I'd like to know and you can write what you like for Jim says Aunt Maria gives him any letter unopened.'

'I will, Dermot, I promise,' Norah said. 'As soon as I have news.'

It was hard for Norah to say goodbye to Dermot the following morning and she shed bitter tears as she hugged him tight and so did he and she could only be glad that Tom, after saying his goodbyes and wishing Dermot 'Godspeed', had gone out to the field to collect up the cows for the milking, or he might think it odd that Norah was so upset when she had told him she'd be going to see Dermot off with the family.

Dan had put the canvas cover over the cart in case of inclement weather and to keep them a bit warmer and there was a flurry of activity as Peggy, the children and the luggage were packed inside. Dermot took a moment to look back at the farm-house before climbing up beside his father and they were off, the cart rattling along the cobbles pulled by the sturdy horse, Bess. Tom came out of the byre to give a last wave, unaware because of the darkness and the cover that Norah wasn't aboard with the others, but hidden away waiting till Tom returned to the byre and she could steal away.

It worked like clockwork and so, only minutes after the family had left, Norah, dressed in her warmest clothes and with her thickest shawl and strong boots, crept down the lane, collected her bag and set off to Donegal Town. There was no moon to help to light her way and she felt frost scrunch beneath her boots. She had to watch her step for she had no desire to slip and spread her length on the frozen ground.

She was glad to reach the town still in one piece and there the going got easier, but as she made her way to the station she was quite dismayed to see that the town seemed to have a fair few Black and Tans looming out of the darkness, even at that early hour. They were meant to be intimi-dating and they were and so even if a person had done nothing wrong, they were made nervous by their presence – and with reason, Norah thought.

She hoped that none of them would stop and question her, though they had no reason to, not that that mattered. She couldn't help feeling nervous as she passed them, though she tried not to show it even when she felt their eyes boring into her back as she went down to the station.

However, she reached it without incident and as she bought her ticket for Letterkenny she expected a barrage of questions about where she was going and why from the old stationmaster who knew all the Mulligans and therefore thought he had a perfect right to know their business. She was ready with a tale of some fictitious relative taken ill in Letterkenny, but it wasn't needed, for the lad who issued the tickets that morning was someone Norah had never seen before. He seemed half asleep and not a bit interested in the few passengers who were travelling that time in the morning in early December.

They had a little wait for the rail bus and Norah kept a low profile as she would have hated to bump into someone who knew her, but she was relieved when she realised not one of the handful of passengers was known to her. By the time the rail bus pulled into the station she felt butterflies start in her stomach. She paid no heed to them and boarded the rail bus and took a seat as if she had been doing it every day of her life. For good or bad, on this day, Saturday 4th December, she was making for England.

Henry had written a letter to his parents telling them all about the baby, Grace Catherine, and said he was awaiting their instructions regarding the child's future. Meanwhile, despite the doctor's misgivings, the child, while still small, thrived for though Celia was inexperienced she loved the child as if she were her own and cared for her tenderly.

She felt such compassion for the child, growing up without a proper mother, and for Annabel, who was not there to see the child developing as the weeks passed. Janey and particularly Sadie, who had delivered her, took a great interest in her and even the doctor came a couple of times to check on her and yet no news came from the Lewishams. As for Henry himself, he was intrigued by the baby, but she was so small and delicate looking he was afraid to handle her, though he spent a lot of time in the nursery. He was there one evening when she was five weeks old and she smiled for the first time. Celia had just finished feeding her and she was still lying in her arms when it happened. It was a heart-stopping moment and Henry was amazed how it affected him and for the first time he saw Annabel's baby as a little person.

'She is lovely, isn't she?' he said. 'She's so help-less and vulnerable.'

'She is,' Celia agreed. 'And she's such a good little baby.'

'Don't you think it odd that my parents, even my mother, are not the slightest bit curious about her?'

'Not really,' Celia said. 'I think that they are pretending she doesn't exist just like they did with her mother. They seem totally disinterested in the whole thing and I think you have to come to terms with the fact that they have no intention of coming here to see the baby.'

'Well then,' declared Henry. 'If Mohammed won't go to the mountain, the mountain must go to Mohammed.'

'What's that mean?'

'Well in this instance it means that we must take the baby to my parents. If I just left her there, they would have to at least acknowledge her.'

'And then what?' Celia demanded. 'What's to stop them having her delivered post-haste to the nearest children's home? You have said yourself that she is helpless and vulnerable. Leaving her with your parents after they have indicated they want nothing to do with her is like throwing her to the wolves.'

'Do you think they would send her to a children's home?' Henry said. 'Oh surely not. After all, Grace is their granddaughter.'

'They won't see it that way if they have already disowned their own daughter,' Celia almost said but stopped herself as Henry went on, 'We'll go up on Sunday mid-morning when they will have returned from any church they might attend. We're more or less sure to get them together then – unless you think Grace too young yet?'

'She is young and small certainly, but I suppose if she is well wrapped up she will probably be all right.'

'Well dress her in her finery and when my parents see her I bet they will be as smitten as the rest of us,' Henry declared.

SIXTEEN

In all the churches in Ireland, many times they cited the foolhardiness of young girls leaving their homes alone for England, especially without any job or respectable place to stay organised, which Norah thought was exactly what she was doing. Grave danger lay in wait for such young women, they had been told: men on the lookout for naïve, country girls to lure them under the guise of friendship to a life of immorality there was often no escape from. Or there were even reports of girls that had disappeared altogether and it had been assumed they had been abducted for the white slave trade.

Had Norah been a nervous type of girl, she might have been a little frightened by these alarmist predictions, but she was made of sterner stuff. She thought girls mad to go off with perfect strangers anywhere, however friendly they appeared, and that they deserved all they got. She decided the safest plan was not to look as if you didn't know what you were doing or where you were going, even if it was a sham – as it would be in her case. She had had a good deal of time to think as she took the train from Letterkenny to Belfast and eventually she decided the best thing was to make for a Catholic church and ask the priest's advice about respectable lodgings. She knew that he would also have to be told some tale as to why she was there and on her own and that it couldn't be the truth.

She was slightly unnerved by the teeming docks at Belfast, but told herself Birmingham would likely be larger, noisier and even more hectic. As she had a wait for the ferry, she forced herself to leave the docks and go out into the streets. She had at any rate to find a post box to send the fateful letter to her parents that she'd promised herself she would post in Belfast.

The noise hit her first when she left the station, the raucous sound of so many people, their voices rising and the stamp of their feet as they scurried quickly for the day was icy cold and murky too. There was the sound of the horses' hooves and the clatter of the wheels of the carts they pulled over the cobbled streets and the drone and occasional splutter of the petrol-driven vehicles, where the noise of drivers honking their horns impatiently and shouting warnings for people to move out of the way added to the general cacophony.

Norah found it all just a little disconcerting initially, but as she wandered around the city, though not straying too far from the docks, she became used to it. She didn't have the nerve to enter any of the more inviting looking coffee houses though, but she wished she had because the smell emanating from them was tantalising her and it had been many hours since she'd eaten and she was very hungry. But, she told herself, she had limited funds and was not at all sure how long they would have to last her and, besides, she wouldn't know what to order to eat in a place like that. She'd never even entered a café in her hometown and it might be very expensive. She had also never tasted coffee and, though it smelt very nice, what if she spent precious money on something she didn't like and couldn't drink? She'd just have to hope that food was served on the boat and she wouldn't get so seasick that she wouldn't be able to eat it.

She asked directions to a post office as she made her way back to the docks and found it hard to understand the woman she asked as her accent was so strong. She worked it out, however, and it was as she popped the letter in the pillar box she faced the fact that, despite the time and effort she had spent on the letter, it was extremely doubtful that she would be made welcome in her home ever again. She had worded it with care and apologised for what she had felt driven to do, but there was no way of lessening the blow that another daughter had fled their home.

The post office also changed her dollars into pounds. She thought there were probably facilities on the boat to do that, but couldn't take the chance of arriving in England with money she couldn't use. She felt more secure leaving the post office with some pound notes in her purse, knowing that she could support herself for quite a few days if it took a while to locate Celia.

She turned for the docks again and joined the queue to board. She had been told the canteen would not be open straight away so she decided to stay on deck for a while and she stood at the rail and watched the choppy grey waves slapping the side of the boat, causing it to list from one side to another. Then came the call for those not travelling to disembark and she watched people scurry down the gangplank. And when the last was off, the gangplank was raised, the thick ropes around the bollards were unwound, the ship's hooter gave a screech and black smoke billowed from the funnel as the engines began to throb. Norah found she was more excited than nervous as the boat pulled away from the dock and headed off to the open sea. She turned and watched the shores of Ireland recede and wondered how long it would be before she was ever to see her homeland again and knew it might be never if her parents chose not to ever forgive her. That thought did sadden her, but she told herself firmly that there was nothing she could do about her parents' reaction and she didn't want to start out on the most exciting journey of her life full of trepidation.

'I'm hungry that's all,' she thought to herself and she knew life was always viewed in a more positive light when one had a full stomach, so she headed off to the canteen as the boat picked up speed and sailed into the open sea. The canteen at least was warm and welcoming and she ordered Irish stew and a pot of tea. And how she appreciated that delicious meal and felt almost content at the end of it, which was strange as she had been unhappy for ages. Without Celia, she had been incredibly lonely and when she lost the chance to go to America she had felt very desolate.

She had also lost the love of Joseph O'Leary too, for when he realised Norah had helped Celia escape, he knew straight away why she had done it – to prevent her sister from going to America, hoping to leave the field open for her. He'd felt amazed that she would go to such lengths, even endangering Celia, for McCadden was not that well known to them, just so she should have her heart's desire. It pointed to a flaw in her nature and a heartless one, the one that had rejected his love time and again. He also knew that if Norah's plan had worked she would have thrown his love back in his face once again and left for America without a backward glance and he suddenly felt that she had made a fool of him long enough, just as his friends had been telling him for ages. This time the humiliation and hurt had gone too deep for him to forgive her and he told her so when they met in the town the Saturday after Celia left.

His words had shaken Norah, for she couldn't remember a time when Joseph O'Leary hadn't loved her and so she'd thought he would continue to love her whatever she did. His friends said he did right to finish with her and it was about bloody time. Not long after, Norah saw him walking out with Siobhan Clancy, the big buxom daughter of a farmer who had been a school friend of hers, and she was surprised that she had been so hurt by that.

The point was all the other chaps thought she had done the dirty on Joseph once too often and they weren't to chance their hands themselves, so she had been snubbed by more than one or two, which was just what Peggy had prophesied would happen. Even some of the girls were no longer friendly when she met them in Donegal on Saturdays, so when Dan vetoed her going to the dances any more, she scarcely cared, for she didn't want to risk sitting by herself all night and never being asked up to dance. It did mean though that her life was very mundane and boring and then, when that worrying letter had come from Andy, she had been filled with guilt and knew whatever happened afterwards to her didn't matter half as much as finding her sister alive and well.

She left the canteen warmer and replete and rejected the now rain-washed deck, which was peopled mainly by those who were not such good travellers as she was proving to be, and she turned into the first saloon. It didn't smell very sweet for there was a certain odour from many bodies in damp clothes closeted together. Mixed with this there was also a tangy smell of whisky and the malty smell of Guinness and even a slight whiff of vomit from the unfortunate few who hadn't made it outside quick enough. But the most prominent stink pervading everything else was the smoke from many cigarettes that hung in the air like a blue-grey fug.

Almost from the minute Norah came on board the boat, there had been speculation about her from many of the other mainly Irish passengers for few young girls travelled alone. Norah was well aware of it, had even semi-expected curiosity, but some of the single men were looking at her in a way that she found quite perturbing and it brought the priest's words into focus. Peering through the smelly miasma she saw with a little dismay that there were a fair few of these ogling single men in the saloon she had stepped into. For a moment or two she was unsure what to do, for she had an idea that wherever she sat they could home in on her and even the thought of that made her feel quite intimidated.

However, her progress was also watched by three Irish sisters. It was obvious to them that Norah was a country girl from her boots and her shawl and Mary, the eldest sister, reasoned it was probably her first time of travelling for she looked nervous and unsure of herself and so she called her over. Norah was pleased to see three such respectable women and approached them eagerly.

She wasn't a bit surprised that they were sisters for they all had vibrant red hair and green eyes and looked really similar. They introduced themselves as Orla, Bridget and Mary and Norah worked out that while Orla might be near her age the other two were older. They told her they had been in Ireland at that unseasonable time to attend a family funeral.

They were openly curious as to what she was doing travelling the Irish Sea alone – and unmarried, they were quick to notice. No way could Norah admit the whole truth, not to these women who would be shocked to the core, so she told them instead the tale she was going to tell the priest when she arrived in Birmingham later.

'I have a younger sister, Celia, living with an aunt in Birmingham,' she said. 'But she has fallen ill and our aunt wrote and told us, but our parents were away in Inishowan when the letter came, seeing my young brother off for he was bound for the States.' And then, noticing the puzzled looks on the listening women's faces, she explained, 'They have to go out in the tender from Moville pier for the liners are anchored in the deeper water of Lough Foyle.'

Mary nodded. 'Ah yes, I did hear tell of that. Never seen it myself, but Inishowan is the back of beyond, isn't it?'

Norah nodded. 'It is even from us in Donegal Town, for all it's still classed as Donegal.'

'Ah but Donegal is a big sprawling county, isn't it?' Bridget put in.

Norah nodded. 'You're right, but I have another sister, Katie, and she married an Inishowan man and is now living in Greencastle, which is apparently the next village up the hill from Moville, and no one has seen her for ages, well not since the wedding, and now she has a wee boy that none of us have seen either. So Mammy said that going so far they could go a little further and stay with Katie for a day or two. Even Daddy could be spared from the farm this time of year, especially with my eldest brother Tom there anyway. She even took my little brother and sister as well so they could meet their nephew and she was so excited about it and I knew it would help her to see Katie and her grandson for it would be hard for her to say goodbye to Dermot.

'And so, when the letter came, not long after they left, we deliberated a bit but then knowing that it was from my auntie in Birmingham, where my younger sister Celia is staying at the moment, we thought it might be important and opened it. It told of the illness of Celia but gave no details and so, rather than sending a telegram to my sister for Mammy, which would have frightened her to death and sent them all running straight back again, Tom and I decided that I would come first and see how my sister was before telling Mammy.'

'I think that is very brave of you to come alone,' Mary said. 'And I suppose no point worrying your mother unnecessarily.'

'No indeed,' said Orla. 'Your sister might be well over what ailed her by now and could be as right as rain when you get to see her. And you're bound for Birmingham now you say?'

'Yes,' Norah said.

'Well now isn't that just grand?' Mary said. 'For that's the very place we're going to as well so we can go together. More fun and safer than travelling on your own.'

'It is,' Norah said. 'And thank you, I would be glad to travel with you.'

'You're welcome,' Mary said and Orla put in, 'Tell you, I'll be glad to be off this boat though, cos I am frozen to the bone. And I can't help feeling a wee bit sorry for your brother too for early December is no time to cross the Atlantic.'

'No I suppose not,' Norah said. 'But we have a farm, you see, and his help was needed through the spring, summer and autumn.'

'If your father needed his help so much I am surprised he let him go at all.'

'Oh, Daddy was all for it,' Norah said. 'Told him he had to take the opportunity offered to him. Because he'd have to make his own way eventually as only my eldest brother, Tom, will inherit the farm.'

'Aye, that's the way of it all right,' Mary said, nodding her head in agreement. 'Women in Ireland wear themselves out rearing big families. I mean, there were nine of us. I was the eldest and well remember how my poor mother was run ragged with us all and one by one she saw her children take the emigrant ships, me included because there is nothing for us in Ireland. Only my eldest brother is left.'

'Nothing much there for people wherever they go these days,' Bridget remarked. 'For England and the States are going through a slump as well. And it breaks my heart to see clusters of the unemployed everywhere.'

'And the homeless bedding down wherever they can,' Bridget said. 'There are so many of them and I think it's scandalous.'

'Think the government will lose any sleep over that?' Mary burst out. 'If a few freeze to death there will be less for them to worry about. "Land fit for heroes", my arse.'

Icy fingers of trepidation trailed down Norah's spine as she said, 'So I take it it's difficult to get work in Birmingham at the moment?'

'Difficult!' Mary exclaimed. 'Bloody impossible more like.' And then she peered a little closer at Norah and said, 'You've gone very pale all of a sudden. Are you all right?'

Norah was far from all right. 'No,' she said as she struggled to her feet. 'I'm feeling a little sick.'

'Maybe you need some air,' Orla said. 'I was just thinking how muggy it is down here.'

'Yes, I think I'll go on deck for a bit.'

'See if you can spot land yet,' Orla called and Norah waved her hand as she opened the saloon door and stepped out onto the blustery deck.

Although drizzly rain was falling and the wind was fierce, Norah was glad of the cold for she hadn't lied when she said she felt sick but it wasn't

302

seasickness, or even the stale air in the saloon, but the dreaded fear she had of what had happened to her sister if the job situation was as bad as Mary said it was. She crossed to the rail and held on to it so tightly her knuckles showed white and she peered through the deepening dusk, for the short winter's day was almost at an end, but she could see a blurred landmass in front of her and she was glad. The sooner she could reach Birmingham and start searching for her sister the better she would like it. She knew if anything bad had happened to Celia she would never ever forgive herself for as long as she lived.

'Well, you look as if you have lost a pound and found a sixpence,' said a voice beside her and she swung around to see Mary standing there looking at her in a concerned way. 'I was a bit bothered about you,' she said. 'Have you been sick?'

Norah shook her head and Mary said, 'You often feel better if you can be. Do you still feel queasy?'

'A bit,' Norah said. 'But the fresh air helped a lot.'

'It would,' Mary said. 'And is that all that's bothering you?'

'Why? What do you mean?'

'Well something's upset you,' Mary said. 'You're looking right miserable at the moment.'

Norah had a great desire to confide in this motherly woman, telling her everything and feeling sure that she would understand much better than her own mother would. But she knew she could tell no one. It was her burden to carry and yet, she had to say something and so she said, 'I'm a bit concerned that I did the wrong thing in not telling my mother about Celia's illness. It seemed such a simple decision at home and Tom agreed with me, but what if it is serious? The sooner I see Celia the better I'll feel.'

'I understand that,' Mary said. 'And it won't be long now till we land.'

Norah lifted her head and saw that Mary was right. Land was much closer, close enough to see the twinkling lights in people's houses like pinpricks in the darkness.

'We'll be standing out in this again to disembark soon,' Mary said, indicating the rain coming down heavier. 'So if it doesn't make you feel too sick it would be better to go back to the saloon and stay dry as long as we can.'

'I feel better now anyway,' Norah said. 'And my shawl is quite soggy enough. You go ahead and I'll follow you.'

The train to Birmingham sped across the now dark night through countryside, vast areas which were black as pitch or murky grey and then they would run by the sides of towns and see the lights in houses and dull lights flickered in the carriages as the train pulled up at dimly lit stations. Norah was tired and more anxious than ever and just wanted the journey to be over. The three sisters were aware of her melancholy and, though not truly understanding it, they still did their best to keep her entertained by telling her about the city her sister had lived in for some months.

They spoke of the shops. 'More than you would ever see,' Orla said. 'And a fair few of them on many floors.'

'And the traffic,' Bridget said. 'That got you in a right spin as I remember?'

'Haven't you been in Birmingham that long then?' Norah asked Orla.

Orla shook her head. 'A year,' she said. 'And getting a job was the best thing I ever did too, because it gave me money in my pocket for the first time in my life.'

Norah could so identify with that because she never had money of her own: collection money was doled out to her before Mass as if she was a wean and even when she went into Donegal Town on Saturday for her mother, Peggy knew to the penny how much things cost and how much change she might be due. And so Norah said, 'I can see the attraction of that. I don't know what it is to have money in my pocket. Was it easy for you to get a job? I know on the boat you said it could be difficult.'

'Lots of people struggle,' Orla said. 'But Bridget spoke up for me.'

'That's how a lot are set on these days, unless you had a good employer before the war and he saves your job for you, like my Pat,' Bridget said. 'He worked at Fort Dunlop and he was called up and they promised him that they'd keep his job for him. Well, he was one of the lucky ones and when he came back, sure enough his job was waiting for him and he goes up by canal barge.'

A memory stirred in Norah's brain about Mc-Cadden taking the Dunlop workers to work and back every morning and night and thought at least McCadden might be easier to find than she'd thought.

'Is the canal far?' she asked.

'It isn't from where we live,' Bridget said. 'See, we're in Upper Thomas Street by the HP Sauce works and you just have to cross the Lichfield Road and go down Rocky Lane. Just a step away.'

Norah stored all this away, determined to try and seek McCadden out as soon as possible the following day.

The three sisters began regaling Norah with the delights to be had in Birmingham for young people with a bit of money in their pockets and they talked of things beyond Norah's ken, like the bargains to be had in the Rag Market, the free entertainment on a Saturday night in a place called the Bull Ring and the music hall, which hosted a variety of acts and moving pictures.

'They tell stories, you know?' Orla said, seeing Norah's confusion. 'Terrible things happen, like girls tied onto railway lines with a train coming, oh all sorts of things happen.'

'Goodness!'

Mary laughed. 'The girl never gets crushed by the train or anything. She's always rescued just in time.'

'Oh.'

'And there's no voice, just the piano thumping away and you know when something dreadful is going to happen by the music played and the way it's played.'

'I heard they're going to be putting voices on soon,' Orla said. 'They are going to call them "talkies".'

'Well they are not here yet,' Mary said firmly.

306

'And I'm sure Norah would be entertained enough at the silent ones we have now as I bet she had nothing like it in Donegal.'

'Oh no I didn't,' Norah said. 'All told there wasn't much at all in the town. Don't know whether I will get to go to any in Birmingham as my first priority is seeing my sister.'

Norah had told the three sisters that she would be getting a taxi to the fictional address where her aunt lived as the train slid into New Street Station.

The platform was teeming with people, much worse than Belfast, Norah thought as she alighted from the train and hugged Mary, Bridget and Orla, for she had been immensely glad of their company but now she was on her own and knew she must be on her guard. She saw a few odd people in raincoats and though they might have been perfectly respectable, she thought her best bet was to walk in a purposeful way with her head lowered and make for the taxi rank as confidently as if she had been going to it all the days of her life. There were horse-drawn cabs and petrol-driven ones but going in a cab pulled by a horse was no treat to Norah and she made for the petrol-driven ones. The driver of one was out of his cab having a smoke and so that was the one she approached.

In the light from the street he knew Norah was a country girl by her dress and not the sort of person that usually used taxis, but he doffed his cap and said, 'What can I do for you, miss?'

'I need to go to the nearest Catholic church please?'

'Oh, that would be the cathedral then.'

'Oh, does Birmingham have a cathedral?' Norah asked, for though she knew all cities had cathedrals she didn't know in England whether they would have a Catholic cathedral as well.

'Birmingham has two cathedrals,' the taxi driver said. 'St Philip's is the Anglican and St Chad's the Catholic one, so it's St Chad's you want and I can't take you to either.'

'Why not?'

'Because I wouldn't take the money off you.'

'I can pay. I have money.'

'I'm sure you have but I won't take any money for a journey that is so close. Look,' the taxi driver said, pointing. 'That road there is New Street. Turn left there and cross the road on your right-hand side and you will come to Bennetts Hill and that will lead to Colmore Row. You will see the Council House and Town Hall to the right of you, but you turn right again and walk straight down that road. You will pass St Philip's on the left and the Grand Hotel on the right, but you keep straight on until you come to a road to your left called Whittall Street and you turn into it by a big square building that until quite recently used to be a workhouse and St Chad's is at the end of that short road. Now you got that?'

Norah nodded but it was done so hesitantly the taxi driver told her again and then he said, 'Now you're all right and no one will harm you, but you keep your head down and don't talk to anyone.'

Norah set off with great trepidation, glad at least that the rain had stopped but it had rained a good deal and she walked well away from the road, for some of the vehicles sent up spray and the glow from their headlights gleamed and the wheels swished on the wet road and she pulled her cloak tighter around herself.

She kept her head lowered as the taxi driver advised but as people passed her she could see them illuminated in the street lights and saw that she was totally wrongly dressed for Birmingham. The women's clothes were generally shorter and most wore coats and if they had boots they had fashionable ones, nothing like the clodhopping work boots she wore and she understood why Jim had sent her the money for a new wardrobe when she got to America for she imagined they were even more fashion-conscious in New York.

However, there was nothing she could do about it and maybe her clothes would help convince the priest that she was who she said she was, because if he disbelieved her or refused to help, she wouldn't know what to do, for she had not form-ulated a plan B. She was walking along beside the shops the three sisters had told her about that probably sold the clothes the women about wore, but she could see nothing but vague grey shapes in the windows because the shops were all closed.

Bennetts Hill was easy to find and she gave a sigh of relief when she turned into it. No shops in this road, she noticed, just lines of shiny wooden doors of buildings that opened on to the street and at the top of it she saw the majestic Council House to her right as the taxi driver had said and another building resembling a picture she had once seen of a Roman temple and she imagined that that was the Town Hall and she turned right and carried on.

She passed the Grand Hotel opposite St Philip's with its white paths weaving through the gardens, and so she knew she was on the right road, and in fact it was no distance then to Whittall Street and she saw the cathedral straight away at the end of it but she approached slowly, nervous now she was at her journey's end.

SEVENTEEN

The door to the church stood open because the priest had just finished benediction and Norah waited till the small congregation had left the church and then she entered the porch but hesitated to go further. The lights had been dimmed and there was only one woman there setting out the hymn books, for the morning Norah supposed, and no sign of the priest who was at that moment taking off his vestments in the sacristy. Then the woman looked up and saw Norah. Eileen Hennessey was the priest's sister who had lost her husband in the early months of the Great War and, as she was childless and the priest's housekeeper had left his employ for more lucrative war work, it had seemed sensible that Eileen move in to look after him. She took her job very seriously and could sometimes be impatient at the many demands put on the priest, for he was generally a kind-hearted man and didn't like to refuse if he could help in any way.

However, when Eileen saw Norah standing in

the porch, looking so incredibly nervous and somehow vulnerable in her slightly shabby and out-of-date clothes, she felt a tug in her heart and she stepped into the porch towards her, saying as she did so, 'Can I help you?'

Norah's voice was little above a whisper as it seemed the courage and determination that had brought her this far had all but deserted her and so Eileen had to strain to hear her words. 'Yes, please would it be possible to see the priest?'

'He's changing,' Eileen said. 'Can I help you?'

'Oh maybe,' Norah said. 'You see...' and she told Eileen the same tale she had told the sisters on the journey over. During the telling the priest, John Mortimer, known as Father John, finished changing into his normal garb and came back in the church from the sacristy, but neither woman noticed him. He heard the tail end of what Norah had said, but it was enough to alarm him and he was gratified to hear his sister say, 'I do understand the urgency you must have felt to ascertain your sister wasn't too ill and yet it was still very foolish for you to travel quite alone and without booking respectable lodgings before you left Ireland.'

Eileen had taken the words out of his mouth, Father John thought, for that would have been his initial response as well to the girl's tale and as he approached he saw that she looked suitably chastened, even more so when she turned and spotted him. So did Eileen.

'Oh John,' Eileen said and with a slight nod in Norah's direction went on, 'this young girl by the name of Norah Mulligan from Donegal in Ireland has travelled here alone because of the

311

illness of her sister and—'

Father John raised his hand. 'I know, Eileen, I heard the general gist of it and the question is, young lady,' he said, facing Norah with a frown puckering between his eyes, 'what are we to do with you now?'

Norah was exhausted and tense with nervousness and worried about what she would do if the priest was unable to help her. She felt tears prickling behind her eyes and knew she couldn't let them fall if she was to convince the priest that she was fully capable of looking after herself and so to keep those tears at bay she spoke more sharply than she intended.

'You haven't to do anything with me,' she said. 'I am not a child and I have money. I know not all lodgings are respectable and I just want directions to one that is. I may need one for a few days depending on how my sister is.'

Far from being offended, the priest was relieved by Norah's spirited response for he realised that she was not as young as she appeared – the country clothes hadn't helped her there – but despite them she seemed an upright young woman who had genuine concern for her young sister. However, he said to her, 'I really don't know how to advise you, my dear. We have Catholic hostels in the town but I know they're full. There might be room at the hostels run by the Girls' Friendly Society, or the Birmingham Mission, but I couldn't possibly be certain. They are not ideal because although they are basically Christian they are not Catholic, of course, but at least there you would feel safe. It will be Monday before their offices are open.'

'Have you no emergency hostels?'

The priest nodded. 'We have,' he said. 'But I would strongly advise you against trying to use those, for you would meet the dregs of society as well as those just down on their luck. They are for the homeless, most of them.'

'And shortly I might be joining them,' Norah thought wryly as Eileen spoke up, 'John dear, as it is only for a few days why can't Norah stay with us – at least until after the weekend when a temporary place might be found for her in one of the places you mentioned?'

'Oh, that's so kind of you.'

'Not at all,' Eileen said dismissively. 'It's the only thing to do, the Christian thing to do. We can hardly throw you onto the streets.'

'Eileen is right as usual,' Father John said. 'We always have a spare room made up for a visiting priest or the bishop who might come to stay, as St Chad's is a cathedral, so you are welcome to make use of it.'

'And I'll tell you something else,' Eileen said as they began walking towards the presbytery, which was next to the church, 'I don't know why it is, but if I am on a long journey anywhere I always arrive as hungry as a hunter. Does it affect you the same?'

'Oh yes,' Norah said fervently.

'Well I always leave supper for John after benediction and it is a little bit of stew that won't take a minute to heat up. Will that suit?'

'Oh yes, it will suit very well indeed.'

When they arrived, Eileen took her shawl from Norah and bid her lay her bag down and sit before the fire. She had left it banked up but now poked it into life and shook a few nuggets of coal on it for good measure and as Father John, in the chair on the other side of the fire, seemed engrossed in a paper, Norah had nothing to do but feel the warmth seeping into her very bones As she watched the flames flickering up the chimney and smelt the delicious smells coming from the pan she had seen Eileen put on the range in the kitchen she felt saliva gather in her mouth. She closed her eyes with a slight sigh and didn't stir even when Eileen came in and took a shovelful of glowing embers from the fire and put them into a copper pan.

'I think our guest has gone to sleep,' John remarked to his sister a little later as she came in with their bowls of stew.

At the sound of the priest's voice Norah awoke with a start. 'I'm so sorry,' she said but he looked amused rather than annoyed and Eileen said, 'Nothing to be sorry about. Come and take your fill and then I will show you the room you'll be using. The bed's not been slept in for some time so I've put the warming pan in to air the sheets and warm it slightly and you can go up whenever you want. Generally we don't keep late hours here.'

'No, we didn't on the farm either,' Norah said as she took her place at the table.

'What livestock did you keep in the farm?' Father John asked.

Norah answered him and he asked another question about the farm and her family and Norah stuck to the truth as far as she could. It was easier and also, if she showed the slightest hesitation, he

314

could easily contact their parish priest to check a few things and then the cat really would be out of the bag but she thought it would be easy to make a mistake with her head fuzzy through lack of sleep.

Again she was saved by Eileen who said, 'Enough, John. Can't you see the poor girl is dropping with tiredness? Further questions will have to wait.'

The priest didn't argue with his sister and a short while after this Norah was in the room. As Eileen said, the bed had been warmed by hot coals in the copper pan and Norah found it more than comfortable and cosy and she sighed in contentment. And yet she doubted she would sleep easy for so much had happened that day, but when she closed her eyes she dropped off almost immediately and was soon in a deep and dreamless sleep.

Sunday dawned icily cold and Celia was glad to have so many pretty, warm things to dress Grace in. This was the first sight Henry's parents would get of their granddaughter and she guessed that they were probably quite shallow people who would be more amenable to a pretty, sweet-smelling and well-dressed child and that's what Grace would be, Celia decided.

And so she put on the terrycloth nappy squares she had hemmed before Grace had been born and popped the rubber pants over that before she pulled the wool vest over the baby's head, followed by a petticoat and white crocheted dress with a line of little blue rosebuds on the neck and around the hem and matching lace-trimmed

315

pantaloons. She chose a matinee jacket the same pastel blue as the rosebuds on the dress and she had to admit the baby did look gorgeous. Celia smiled as she planted a kiss on her forehead and took her downstairs to see if Henry approved.

He did very much. 'She looks so lovely,' he said, taking her in his arms. 'Surely she would melt the hardest heart?'

Celia wasn't sure about that and Henry held her tight and was rewarded with a beaming smile and he felt his heart constrict with love for Grace and he really didn't see how his mother could fail to be captivated by the child.

'And what of you, Celia?'

'What about me?'

'You know what I mean,' Henry said. 'Annabel had so many clothes just hanging there and she has no need of them now. I know she would want you to have her things.'

Celia knew she would too because Annabel often sorted something out for her to wear and Celia had never felt so bad about that because it was Annabel's choice. But after her death, it hadn't felt right to rifle through her personal possessions. Now though, with Henry's urging, she left him minding the sleeping baby and went into Annabel's room. Janey cleaned this room along with the others and the furniture gleamed and the three mirrors on the dressing table had no marks on them and even the fire was laid in the cleaned grate.

Remembering why she was there and aware that Henry was waiting for her, she opened the wardrobe and ran her fingers along the many, many

316

dresses hanging there. Some she rejected out of hand as being too fancy but eventually she settled for a winter-weight dark blue dress that came midway down her calves and a short matching jacket. And in the drawers she found silk underwear, including corsets and black stockings.

She was unused to the button boots and so she sat on the chair in front of the desk to fasten them. Although she had seen the desk many times before, she'd never taken that much notice, though she knew that it was modelled on one that Henry's father had in the library of the family home. He said that Annabel had been to stay with him often before this last time especially after he was de-mobbed when the war had ground to a halt two years before. 'When I saw this replica of the one my father has, I knew Annabel would be tickled pink to have it in her room,' Henry had said.

'Why particularly?' Celia had asked.

'Because my father's had a secret panel,' Henry explained. 'Annabel used to open it and put things inside.'

'What sort of things?'

'Letters mainly, little notes, you know,' Henry said. 'Sometimes when I was visiting I'd check it and if there was something in there I would add to it. She loved that. I often thought Annabel was very lonely growing up and as I was ten years older and at boarding school from the age of seven I was no companion for her. I think she would have been happier going away to school and if she had stayed until she was eighteen, she would have been safe from Timberlake's advances and might be still alive today and looking forward to a bright future.'

'Of course,' Celia said. 'I never thought of that and you're absolutely right.' She turned to study the desk now. It was indeed beautiful and gleamed like everything else in the room. The pen holders above the main desk were delicately carved and there was a pad of leather inlaid on the top of the desk to write on and blotting paper was secured in a brass holder.

She wondered if there was a secret panel in this desk. Henry hadn't said there was and Annabel had never mentioned it, so Celia doubted there was because she was certain Annabel would have told her if there was and taken delight in showing her how it worked, for she had been quite childlike in many ways. So not really expecting to find anything she began running her fingers over the top of the desk gently and wasn't that surprised when her search was fruitless. And yet she started underneath and eventually her probing fingers came into contact with a small lever and when she pressed it to the right, a panel slid open. Celia gave a small cry of surprise and delight, but it wasn't empty as she had imagined it would be. She remembered what Henry had said and smiled sadly at the thought of Annabel still writing letters to herself and lifted it out. She wondered for a moment if she should take it to Henry and got to her feet to do that, but curiosity got the better of her. She saw that the envelope had already been opened once and she withdrew the sheet of paper and began reading and her legs shook so much with shock that she sat down, afraid they wouldn't hold her up.

My dear, darling Celia,

I'm heartsick to leave you this way, my darling girl, but you seem set with the Lewishams and if you stay there, will have a guarantee of food to eat and a roof over your head and a wage, while I at present can offer you none of those things. I need to establish myself in some sort of job and find somewhere to live as well, so please bide there with patience, believing that we will be together very soon and then the future will be ours to savour. Never doubt my love for you. I am leaving you because I love you and I will be in touch again as soon as I am financially secure so that I can care for you properly.

Your ever loving Andy

The words danced before Celia's eyes but burned into her soul for she knew that this was the letter she should have received months before, the letter that Andy had left for her that for some reason she had been prevented from seeing.

'Promise you will never hate me,' Annabel had begged and now Celia understood why. But even now she didn't hate Annabel – she understood her desperation and all she felt was a deep and profound sadness for herself and also for Andy. She wondered if Henry had been party to this deception and whether he knew where Andy was now so she could find him and explain about the missing letter.

And yet she didn't move, she sat with the letter still in her shaking hands, unshed tears burning behind her eyes while thoughts tumbled about her head. She had no idea how long she had sat there before Henry knocked discreetly on the door. 'Celia, are you all right?'

Celia heaved herself to her feet and staggered to the door and opened it. Henry didn't notice the letter at first, he was more concerned with Celia's bleached face and her hurt eyes which seemed to stand out in her head. 'Celia, my dear. What ails you?'

'You had better read this,' Celia said, handing Henry the letter. 'Unless of course you already have knowledge of it.'

Henry took the letter from Celia's trembling fingers and she watched his eyes go wide as he read and knew that it was the first time he had set eyes on it and she felt glad about that. She would have hated to feel that he had been party to that deception.

He raised his eyes and said, 'What can I say? Andy is obviously a lover, not a brother, and when he left here he left behind a letter which you never received?'

Celia nodded. 'That's about it.' And then she went on, 'Before Annabel died she asked me more than once if I could ever hate her. Of course I always assured her that I could not ever envisage a time when I would hate her.'

'And do you hate her now?'

'Not hate exactly, more... Oh I don't know. I believed that she thought a lot of me and I did a great deal for her and gave up a lot, my faith for instance, and yet she saw me distraught over Andy's disappearance. I thought he had left me high and dry and without a word. I would never let someone I cared about go through so much pain and despair if I could ease things for them and Annabel knew what was in the letter because it had already been opened when I got it.'

Henry shook his head, distressed that his sister could knowingly hurt this girl they owed so much to. 'I can only apologise on my sister's behalf,' he said. 'And assure you I knew nothing about any of this and the first time I saw it was when you handed it to me.'

'I saw that in your face,' Celia said. 'And I am so glad that you weren't involved, but I am not sure what to do now.'

'Well we must find him and explain certainly,' Henry said and then suddenly flushed guiltily as he remembered rebuffing Andy when he came asking for the job he had offered him initially.

Celia though had seen the flush and said, 'What?'

Henry was ashamed though and scared of admitting what he had done to Celia and so he said, 'It's nothing.'

'Yes it is. What else am I not being told?'

'All right,' Henry said. 'And I feel bad enough about this already. Andy came to see me a few weeks after he left. He looked in pretty poor shape actually and he asked me if he could take up the job I had offered him originally and I refused him.'

Celia stared at the man she thought she knew and said, 'I don't believe you. You know what the unemployment is like. Andy wouldn't have come to you unless he was desperate.'

'I know,' Henry said. 'But at the time I thought he was your brother and he had abandoned you. I didn't know whether you'd want to see him.'

321

'Shouldn't I have been given the choice?' Celia said testily. 'And is that the whole reason you refused him?'

'Well there was also the subterfuge we had engaged,' Henry said. 'You know, you changing names with Annabel and agreeing not to go to Mass. I didn't know if your brother, as I thought he was then, would agree to that.'

'So you refused Andy employment to potentially protect your sister's name?'

'Yes, I suppose.'

'There is no suppose here,' Celia said. 'That is what you did. All this has been about you, your family and your sister's name. Your name was more important than holding out your hand to help a man who you'd once offered to employ.'

'I know,' Henry said. 'I'm sorry. That's all I can say now but if ever I am able to make amends to Andy I will do so.' Celia had made him face uncomfortable truths and he remembered guiltily the satisfaction he had felt telling Andy he had no job for him. He had seen the desperation on his face and he was bitterly ashamed of his behaviour.

'All right,' said Celia. 'I may hold you to that, but for now we must away to your parents, for Grace's future relies on it.' And so saying, Celia put on a coat in grey Melton cloth with a fur collar and a trim of fur around the edge, with a matching fur hat and fur-backed mittens.

'You look as pretty as a picture,' Henry said. She blushed at the compliment, making her look more attractive than ever, but she knew she looked well for she hardly recognised herself when she saw her reflection in the mirror.

'Are you ready?' Henry asked and Celia gave a brief nod. And with another blanket wrapped around the baby, they set off.

EIGHTEEN

Eileen had said the previous evening she always went to the children's Mass at nine o'clock. Norah was not in a position to argue about anything and she just nodded her head and the following morning she woke from a lovely long sleep in the very comfortable bed. She felt well rested and full of confidence for the task of finding Andy McCadden. She wasn't sure how many boatpeople inhabited the canal, but she couldn't see it could be so many that they wouldn't know one another.

There was no rush for the presbytery was only a step away from the church and she washed herself first in the cold water in the ewer Eileen had placed on the chest of drawers the night before. The coldness of the water set her teeth chattering a bit but she felt better to be a little cleaner and was soon dressed in her best dress, though she thought the effect was spoilt rather by the shawl and big boots. But when she followed Eileen into the church later she was to find that she wasn't the only one dressed like that.

The church was impressive inside as might be imagined for it was a cathedral. Celia hadn't seen its splendour the evening before as she had only gone as far as the porch so she looked about her with interest and the first thing she noticed were the white marble pillars supporting the beautiful arched roof and the decorative screen dividing the choir stalls from the nave and an even more elaborate one to the side of a small altar that Eileen whispered was the Lady Chapel or the Chapel of the Blessed Sacrament. Eileen knelt down, put her hands together and was soon deep in prayer and though Norah knelt beside her she was too excited to pray. The statues were some of the finest she'd ever seen, she thought, especially the one of Jesus on the cross above the altar, and the altar itself was stunning and suddenly lit with a myriad colours from the winter sun shafting through the stained glass windows either side of the altar.

Then the organ began to play and people got to their feet; the Mass had begun. Normally Norah liked the Mass – the Latin singing and responses always soothed her – but that morning she couldn't wait for it to be over. However, Eileen was a very influential woman, having the ear of the priest and all, and many wanted a word with her. In the end, sensing Norah's impatience and the reason for it, Eileen told her to go home and put the kettle on the range for the porridge.

Norah would have forgone the breakfast, anxious to be on her way, but Eileen wouldn't hear of it. Later Norah was glad of the warm porridge as she stood at the tram stop that bitterly cold morning. She had told Eileen her aunt lived in Aston and she'd advised her to take the tram.

'Go down Whittall Street, turn right at the end into Steel House Lane, and a line of tram stops are there and any tram will take you to Aston.'

'Steel House Lane is a funny name for a road.'

'Not when it houses a police station,' Eileen said. 'You'll see it from the tram stops. Now you know where you're going. You won't be on the tram long, but the conductor will tell you where to get off. If you were more familiar with the city Aston is close enough to walk from here.'

Norah, standing at the stop, watching a rattling, clattering monster approaching, wished she could walk. She had passed many trams on Colmore Row the previous evening and was very nervous of them and the thought of actually travelling in one filled her with alarm and so she boarded with great trepidation. She asked the conductor straight away if the tram went to Rocky Lane and he assured her it did and that he would tell her when it was time to get off. Despite this her nerves didn't improve much when the tram set off either, for it clanked and swayed in such an alarming way she was sure it would come flying off the rails at any moment.

However, no one else seemed to be the slightest bit worried and so she tried to still her pounding heart. It was only minutes later the conductor was telling her it was time to get off and she stood on the pavement opposite the green clock. There were lots of shops too on both sides of the road, all shut because it was Sunday, and she walked along until she came to Rocky Lane as the conductor had told her to.

Rocky Lane was only a shortish road on an incline packed with small factories and warehouse units but closed and quiet because it was Sunday

325

and Norah carried on down it. Then suddenly the canal was in front of her, filled with barges of all shapes and sizes, all painted beautifully with elephants and castles, she noted, and she stood and stared. For she had never seen anything like it before and had never dreamt that the barges would look so pretty. There were a lot of them too and she wondered which one Billy worked on and how she could find out, for most of the barges looked closed off. And she could hardly climb aboard one uninvited and knock on the hatch and she stood undecided about what to do, annoyed with herself for having come all this way to be scuppered at the first post.

Then suddenly the hatch opened and a woman climbed out with a bucket in her hand and looked with curiosity at Norah and so she said, 'Excuse me. I'm looking for a man called Andy McCadden.'

'He's further down,' the woman said and shouted, 'Someone here for McCadden' and this call was taken up by others as Norah began walking along the towpath.

About the sixth boat down, Andy popped his head up through the hatch and cried, 'What's all the bloody row about?' Then he saw Norah standing on the towpath looking a little lost and he vaulted from the boat and was in front of her in seconds and grasping her shoulders he held her gaze. 'Almighty Christ, Norah, what are you doing here?'

Norah shook his hands off and said angrily, 'What d'you think I'm doing? I'm looking for you and hoping you can tell me what you've done with my sister.'

'Me?' Andy said bitterly. 'I've done nothing with your precious sister. Every bloody thing she has done to herself. Threw me over for a bloody toff she did and having his baby as well.'

Norah felt as if she had been kicked in the stomach by a mule and yet she said, 'She wouldn't do that.'

'But she has done exactly that,' Andy maintained. 'I was looked down on because I was a hireling man and yet I never touched your sister and you know what I mean by that. I had too much respect for her but she opened her legs for that bloody toff and he took her down and now she is expecting his baby. You think he'll care for her and look after her? They don't marry our sort and she'll be tossed aside when he has finished with her. And she needn't come crying to me because I don't take up with another man's leavings.'

Norah's head was reeling. She knew whatever had happened, her sister had inflicted deep hurt on the man beside her now. 'How did she get involved with this man that you say is a toff anyway?'

'Oh that came about because of meeting his sister, Miss Annabel, on the boat coming over,' Andy said and described what had happened and how Celia came to be working at her brother, Henry's, house now.

'And he's the toff.'

'That's him,' Andy said grimly. 'And one thing I will say in the toff's favour was that he seemed very fond of his sister and she had taken to Celia and while that situation between them continued she would be well looked after while I looked for work. I explained all that in a letter I left when I slipped away the next morning before she woke. I asked her to be patient, assured her of my love and said I would be back for her as soon as I could,' and here he glanced at Norah.

'We both knew that we couldn't marry until Celia was twenty-one, but I wanted to be in a position to look after her before that. I feel a right bloody fool now, I can tell you. Anyway, I always thought that while I had a pair of hands, a willing heart and was prepared to do anything I would get a job with no trouble. I had taken no account of the massive slump the country was experiencing after the Great War, which was made worse by the returning and returned servicemen. Added to this, Irishmen were not welcome because many people believe we were too friendly with the Hun.

'In the end, with my money exhausted and no sign or sniff of a job, in desperation I sought out Henry bloody Lewisham and apologised for running out on him and asked if the job was still available. He said, no, the position had been filled – and he said it with a smirk, you know?'

'It might have been filled though,' Norah said.

'Norah, there wasn't a real job,' Andy said. 'It was made up by Henry on the spur of the moment so that Celia would stay as lady's maid to his sister. No, the reason he didn't employ me a few weeks later was because he was having it away with Celia and knew I wouldn't stand for it.'

Norah was still shaking her head. 'If all you say is true then Celia is much changed from the young girl who came here some months ago.'

'It is true,' Andy said. 'But I suppose you won't believe it till you see it with your own eyes. I will take you to the house. I suppose that's what you want anyway – to see her?'

'Of course it is,' Norah said. 'I want to make sure she's all right.'

'Oh, you'll see just how well off she is in a little while, but I can't just take off like that. Come and meet Billy and we'll tell him where we're bound for.'

'Will he mind?' Norah asked as they walked back towards the boat.

'Why should he mind?' Andy said, surprised. 'I'm not married to him. He usually goes to see Stan on Sunday afternoon anyway. He was the one recommended Dunlop's to give us the contract, ferrying the workers up and down the canal. Billy is very fond of him and poor Stan is nearing the end. Anyway, come and see what you think of the space we live in.'

Norah was enchanted when she went onto the boat and she was amazed at how space was utilised and when Norah asked Billy if he had always lived on the canal he told her of his life and his brothers being killed in the war and his parents dying just afterwards.

'That is so sad,' Norah said.

'Well I ain't the only one lost loved ones in that bloody war, beg your pardon, miss,' Billy said. 'But it was a bad time for me and the boaties helped me a lot at first. I knew I couldn't rely on them for ever though and I had to either work or starve. It was a godsend meeting Andy.'

'Yeah, I came down first looking for work,'

Andy said. 'But I was drawn to the place. They're outsiders too in a way.'

'Yeah, many of the townies look down on us,' Billy said. 'But people wouldn't be able to have lots of things in the shops, heavy machinery for the factories and coal to warm their houses if it wasn't for the canal folk. Not that I was getting much of that sort of work on my own and I wasn't making enough for Andy to work permanently and live on the boat, which was warmer and softer than the streets, until we picked up the contract from Dunlop's. Now we've sort of proved ourselves we pick up loads of work after we've delivered the workers off.'

'Did you really live on the streets?' Norah asked Andy.

Andy nodded. 'I couldn't afford even the cheapest lodging and I couldn't have borne Celia to have suffered like that and though it hurt like hell to be without her I thought she was best left where she was.'

Norah did see and she knew Andy had been badly hurt and yet she said, 'How do you feel about her now, Andy?'

'How d'you think I feel?' Andy almost snarled. 'What would you have me do? Hang around till Lewisham has finished with her and take her back as if she had done nothing wrong and spend my life bringing up another man's child?' Andy shook his head and went on. 'Sorry, Norah, I'm not made that way. I wish things were different and with hindsight that we hadn't come here. But we have come and so we have to now deal with things as they are. I don't know what's going to happen to Celia in the end and I will try not to care though I do hope she survives to make something of her life.'

Norah felt her heart plummet for she had felt deep sadness in Andy and she had seen the glitter of unshed tears in his eyes. She had to see her sister and ask what she was playing at throwing away the love of this good man. Guiltily, she knew she had done just that to poor Joseph O'Leary. She wondered when he had realised it was finally over – had he felt as bad as Andy did now? – and guessed he did because he had loved her so much. No wonder all the young fellows and many young women were cold towards her and she vowed to treat men with more respect and compassion in future. But now it was imperative that she saw her sister without delay.

'I think we really should be off now,' she said to Andy.

'Couldn't agree more,' Andy said and then, as they walked to the tram stop, he said, 'Why are you still here? I thought you would be living the high life in America by now.'

'Huh and so did I, but my father knew Celia wouldn't have left home without help and knew it was me helping her and so I wasn't let go and Dermot went instead.'

'Dermot? Isn't he only a child?'

Norah smiled. 'It wouldn't go down that well if he heard you saying that. He's sixteen and thinks himself a fine figure of a man. Remember he is going to our Aunt Maria and our brother is already there and will look out for him. Anyway he has only just gone because his help was needed

331

till after the harvest. I think one of the reasons Daddy was so keen to get him away was the tale of all the young fellows joining the IRA to fight the Black and Tans.'

'Sixteen year olds?'

'Oh yes, sixteen year olds and younger still. Daddy always said he doesn't want a united Ireland won by children. Anyway when Dermot's friend, Jerry Maguire, who had been in our house many times and seemed a fine sensible young man, joined too, Daddy wanted Dermot well out of it.'

'Do you think he'd be caught up in it himself?'

'He says not, but it's hard to know what pressure he'd be under,' Norah said. 'They say things like anyone not for us is against us – and what if Jerry was to call upon the bonds of friendship? Anyway Daddy didn't dare risk it and Dermot went yesterday.'

'And you came here?'

'Well yes, but not like you would do in a normal family, saying "I'm off to England to see my sister" and going with my parents' blessing and money in my pocket. No, none of us were allowed to even speak Celia's name in the house and I had to wait till they were all gone to see Dermot off and sneak away.'

'Did they all go to see Dermot off?'

'All except the eldest, Tom. He was left at home to see to things and he thinks I went with the others and they thought I had stayed in the farmhouse. They went not just to see Dermot out from the pier in Moville but to visit Greencastle, the next village where my married sister Katie lives, and they will likely stay a day or two with her because living such a distance away Mammy never gets to see her and she has a wee boy now, so he will be a great draw.'

'So she doesn't know you're here?'

'No one but Dermot knew what I intended to do, but I wrote to Mammy and posted the letter in Belfast telling her everything,' Norah said. 'I didn't want them worrying too much or maybe setting the Guards after me like they did with you and Celia.'

'They set the Guards after us?'

'They surely did,' Norah said. 'To all intents and purposes you left without telling Dinny Fitzgerald and in effect stole his horse. He was wild about that and only slightly mollified when he got the telegram. The Guards were on the case by then and they retrieved the horse and questioned the people at the stables but they could tell them nothing. They didn't know you and you had given them no indication of your future plans and they didn't see Celia at all. I think they put a watch on the port at Belfast.'

Andy nodded. 'I did wonder when I saw the police watching as we boarded but I didn't know if I was being over-cautious because I didn't know if that was the usual practice or not. Anyway, once on board I said we were brother and sister.'

'Why?'

'To protect Celia and for propriety's sake she became Celia McCadden, my younger sister, come to England in search of work after the death of our parents.'

'She agreed to that, I presume?'

'She welcomed it. Could see the sense of it.'

'Yes I suppose so,' Norah said.

'We weren't together anyway,' Andy said. 'Because she met up with Annabel Lewisham and she was so incredibly seasick that she stayed with her for the rest of the journey.'

The tram pulled up to the stop and Andy led the way to the top deck and Norah followed him fearfully holding tight to the rails and sat beside him with a slight sigh of relief. Andy didn't notice her unease because he was thinking of something else and she had barely sat down when he said, 'What made you come now to see Celia?'

'Basically the letter you sent.'

'The letter?'

'Yes,' Norah said, 'the letter. Before that came, all we knew was that at a station in Liverpool, you boarded a train heading towards Birmingham.'

'How did you know that much?' Andy said and suddenly slapped his hand to his brow. 'I know, it was Seamus Docherty, wasn't it? Christ, I thought I'd given him the slip.'

'Not well enough apparently,' Norah said. 'He was telling all that would listen.'

'He would.'

'Well you can't blame him,' Norah said. 'See, he hadn't been there when the hullabaloo went up about the two of you taking off because he'd been at some funeral or other in Liverpool. When he came back and you two were the talk of the place and he knew the next chapter, so to speak, he was bound to say, wasn't he?

'Anyway, what we did know was that you and Celia were together. Then you sent the letter to your parents telling them about the canal and the job you had on it and didn't mention Celia once.'

'She had thrown me over by then. Anyway I didn't think they'd know about Celia. I'd never mentioned her in my letters home. I was leaving anyway when I was with the Fitzgerald's because for all I loved Celia I thought the obstacles were too great and she was being punished and I had decided to go away and try to forget her for her sake.'

'Surely to God, Andy, you haven't been away from Ireland long enough to forget how it operates?' Norah cried. 'Your brother Chris is dating a girl from Donegal Town but I should imagine that, even if that wasn't the case, your names are known throughout the whole country over what you did. There was no one I could discuss my concerns with because Celia's name cannot be mentioned in the house and I felt quite alone. And I knew I had to be the one to sort it out. I suppose my name will be mud as well now.'

'I'd say you have a chance.'

'And I would, but no matter. As it was, I was filled with shame because I had arranged for you to slip away and encouraged Celia and if anything had happened to her it would be all my fault, so I took the chance to leave as soon as I could. You had given clues, you see: no address, but you said you were on a canal boat taking Dunlop workers from a place called Aston. I thought you might be here today as I knew you wouldn't be taking workers over on Sunday.'

'And here I am,' Andy said. 'And you will soon see that Celia is the one you should have the least worry for. She is sitting pretty and this is our stop.'

It was countryside, Norah thought as they alighted from the tram and began to walk down the road. 'How much further?' she asked.

'Nearly there,' Andy said. 'See we're coming to Pype Hayes Park on the left side of the road?'

Norah nodded and Andy went on. 'Well, when we come level with the entrance of that we turn right and Grange Road is just there and that's the road Henry Lewisham's house is on.'

The houses in Grange Road were set well back from the tree-lined road and looked quite imposing, Norah noted, and Henry Lewisham's was no exception. Surveying the sweep of drive and the three white steps to the oak studded front door, Norah was struck by shyness. She knew a woman of her social class wouldn't normally knock at the front door of such an establishment.

'Go on then.'

'I can't.'

'Course you can,' Andy said. 'Have you come all the way from Ireland to look at the door?'

'No, but...'

'But what?'

'Well who shall I ask for? Celia?'

'Best ask for Lewisham,' Andy suggested. 'Ask for Lord Lewisham and go from there.'

'Aren't you coming with me?'

'No fear. I'm the last person either of them will want to see,' Andy said and added, 'But I'm not hanging round all day either, so are you going or aren't you?'

'I'm going,' Norah said and she couldn't

336

control the slight tremor in her legs as she heard her feet crunch on the gravel as she walked down the drive. Once she reached the door she pushed the bell pull and heard it jangle inside, before her courage deserted her. The door was opened by a maid in black and white who lifted her chin slightly at seeing Norah and that put Norah's back up straight away. Willing her voice not shake with nerves as well as her legs, she said, louder than she intended, 'I need to speak with Lord Lewisham.'

The maid's face plainly said the likes of Norah would have no business with Lord Lewisham, but what she said was, 'Both Lord and Lady Lewisham are out.'

Norah was stunned by her words but she said, 'Have you any idea when they will be back?'

'I'm afraid not.'

'Oh.' Norah was completely nonplussed.

Not so the maid. 'Will that be all then?' she said and at Norah's brief nod she closed the door firmly and with a definite click and left Norah standing on the steps and she retraced her steps to where Andy was waiting for her. Everything he had said about Celia was true. That man Lewisham couldn't have married Celia, but she was using his name and that could only be because she was living with him as his wife.

Henry's parents' house, Manor Park Hall, where Annabel and he had been born and reared, was in the middle of the countryside set behind high hedges and an ornate set of gates opened to a long curving gravel drive. Celia's mouth dropped open with surprise for the house was huge, like a mansion. It was set in its own grounds and was three-storied and of honey-coloured brick. There were a great many castellated chimneys and mullioned windows. A balustrade ran all the way around the front of the house, finishing at the marble steps that led up to the oak studded door. It was the sort of house normally Celia would be nervous of entering. But her emotions had been in such turmoil that she had followed Henry blindly.

The door was opened by a maid in a spotless frilled white pinny over a black dress and a hat matching the pinny was atop her curls. She knew Henry, of course, and greeted him and so did the butler who came to take their coats, but this Henry declined. 'We won't be removing our outer things, thank you, Mannering. We don't intend to stay long.'

'As you wish, sir,' the butler said, though Celia could see both he and the maid were very curious about her role and where Grace fitted in. She also knew though that servants have eyes and ears and would often know far more of the lives of the people they served than they would be aware of. She was sure if the servants put two and two together they'd know whose child she was carrying.

'Lady Lewisham is in the drawing room, sir. She is expecting you.'

It had been Celia who had insisted that Henry phone ahead for it was an awful long way to his family house and a wild goose chase if they were out. He had said nothing of the child but said there were matters concerning Annabel that he

338

had to discuss. The maid led the way through the oak-panelled hall past the gong and in front of the large and imposing staircase. She felt her feet sink into the carpet and noted that the stairs were carpeted the same way and fastened with shining brass stair rods and hanging from the ornate and sculpted ceiling was a beautiful chandelier.

The maid announced Henry but she didn't know who Celia was so she said nothing and Celia slipped in behind Henry as he was explaining about the child The room screamed opulence, beautiful upholstered easy chairs before the fire dancing merrily in the marble hearth, probably quite priceless ornaments arranged on tables and more in a glass-fronted cabinet. Two more crystal chandeliers were hanging from the moulded ceiling and there was a bureau against one wall and a grandfather clock in the corner and the room seemed bathed in light from the winter sunshine shining through the large window overlooking parkland.

Suddenly Celia's attention was taken from the room by Henry. She saw his blazing eyes were fastened on his mother's as he snapped out, 'What do you mean Grace is nothing to do with you? She's your granddaughter, for God's sake.'

Celia wasn't a bit surprised by Lady Lewisham's response – unlike Henry, it was what she had expected all along. If she'd had any thoughts for Annabel at all she would have been along to see her when she was alive and arranged a respectful funeral at her death. She looked at the elegant woman before her but the clothes didn't make up for the discontented face, thin cruel lips, long aris-

339

tocratic nose and hard gimlet eyes. She was heavily made-up and her hair was beautifully coiffed and decorated but it made no difference for her mean spirit made her look almost ugly. Why would a woman like that care what happened to Annabel's child when she cared not a jot for the mother? And she proved this by saying, 'I disowned my daughter when I lost respect for her because she brought shame on the house when she propositioned Timberlake.'

Henry took a deep breath and Celia knew that he was trying to control his temper. She was standing apart from them both, still by the threshold of the door rocking Grace, who was becoming restless as she picked up the tension in the room. It was like electricity sparking between Henry and his mother as Henry spat out, 'Timberlake totally abused your hospitality and rather than Annabel propositioning Timberlake I was told it was totally the other way round and Timberlake broke into Annabel's room and violated her, your own daughter, and yet the man went unpunished.'

'Timberlake is a gentleman,' Lady Lewisham said. 'As he said to me, he had no need to force her door open for it was already ajar and she was inside, naked and waiting for him like some sort of wanton. He said that she had been tormenting him and teasing him all evening and promised what she would give him if he was to come to her room that night and, as he said, a man is only made of flesh and blood. He'd had a lot to drink and he said he allowed himself to be beguiled by her charms that he might have resisted sober. He

340

said she was more than willing, begging for it in fact. Annabel was a very beautiful girl, but obviously lacking in any sort of moral fibre.'

Celia felt sick. She remembered the horrendous tale Annabel had told her, how she had sobbed and her eyes looked haunted because for a while she was back in that room, battling with the man intent on raping her, and that even though she struggled she knew there was no way she would be able to stop him. And then, when it was obvious there were going to be consequences, she had gone to the people who should have protected her. But they believed the man's version of events and, instead of admitting he had done this terrible thing, he had made Annabel out to be some sort of immoral slut, a girl that bore no resemblance to the one she had lived with for some months before Grace's birth.

She saw Henry didn't believe in this man Timberlake's version of events either and he said to his mother, 'So if Annabel was tormenting and teasing him all night surely you would have noticed and so would many others. There would have been talk and there was none. Did you actually see them canoodling yourself or maybe Father did?'

Lady Lewisham looked vague. 'Your father has no recollection of the night in question and even I ... I'm afraid I too imbibed a little unwisely.'

'So you saw nothing, or if you did you can't remember?'

'No, but ... well I'm sure Charles Timberlake would have acted in a discreet manner.'

'Oh are you?' Henry said with heavy sarcasm. 'I don't think there is much discretion about breaking down a young girl's bedroom door to ravish her totally against her will, because that's what really happened.'

'You always took her part.'

'Someone had to,' Henry said. 'Neither you nor Father had much time for Annabel... But this isn't whether you believe her or not, is it? You know the type of man Charles Timberlake is, everyone knows, and Annabel isn't the first girl he's raped and I would take a bet she won't be the last. I did think the daughters of friends might be safe, but obviously I was wrong. If you tried to hold him the slightest bit responsible, he would have maybe pulled out his offer of finance that Father is relying on. Or else, he might have spread abroad the story of Annabel's wantonness you believed so completely. Either or both of these would have ruined you as far as respectable society goes. I think that it would serve you bloody right. I can't believe that you still consider that man a friend.'

'How dare you talk to me like this, Henry? Whatever has come over you?'

'Nothing has come over me,' Henry said. 'Such a terrible injustice has been done here and nothing will happen to the man who caused the death of the sister I loved so much. But both you and Father destroyed her before her death and I find that hard to forgive because you did it just so your lives would go on as before.'

'Henry's right,' Celia put in, unable to be quiet any longer.

'And who are you, pray?'

The caustic tone was lost on Celia. She was too angry and agitated to take any notice of it and had no intention either of lowering her voice as she cried, 'I am a friend of Annabel's. Tell me, did you enjoy calling her vile names and falsely accusing her of things she hadn't done? In the end, as Henry said, you destroyed her as much as Timberlake and she was filled with a shame she had no right to feel.'

'I don't know what you mean.'

'Oh yes you do,' Celia said. 'I don't believe even a person like you is that stupid. You don't like facing the truth, or hearing what the consequences were of what you did, but I will tell you anyway.'

'How dare you?' Lady Lewisham shrieked, pulling the bell rope agitatedly to summon assistance. 'Get out!'

Celia stood her ground and said, 'I dare because of Annabel. I stayed by her side for months and she was lovely and kind and very, very frightened. She was a young girl facing the birth of a child she did not want and she was terrified of the birth itself and worried what would happen to the child and her afterwards.'

The butler entered the room and when he put a hand on Celia's arm to eject her she shook him off. 'Get your hands off me. I will go when I'm ready. Till then I'll say what I've got to say.'

The butler made a move towards her again and Henry stepped forward. 'You put one hand on her again and you'll have me to deal with. Let her speak.'

The butler looked towards his mistress for he didn't know how to deal with the situation now and she said, 'Fetch Lord Lewisham.'

'Oh do,' said Celia. 'Then he can hear too,' and

343

she turned back to face Lady Lewisham and went on, 'Annabel said the future was like a big black hole. As the pregnancy progressed she stopped eating because she said she was full up of misery. You could have eased that for her – a note from you or a visit would have made all the difference. She felt abandoned by all except Henry.

'Then the labour was long, arduous and very painful and I was with her through every contraction. I saw her weakening but there was nothing I could do. And then just after she had eventually given birth to Grace, she haemorrhaged. Do you hear that? Can you even begin to imagine her despair and anguish? For your daughter Annabel, who you wouldn't even acknowledge, bled to death. You have lost a daughter that you should have valued, Henry a beloved sister, me a dear friend and poor Grace has lost a mother.'

'What is this?' blustered Lord Lewisham, coming into the room at a rush for such was the volume of Celia's voice raised above the keening of the baby, he had heard some of what she'd said and imagined the servants would have too and would be agog, especially when the brazen girl, whoever she was, went on, 'Ah Lord Lewisham, I'm glad you could join us. I have come to show you little Grace. She is your granddaughter and the result of the brutal attack and rape that happened under your roof by a houseguest at the time, a Charles Timberlake.'

Lord Lewisham looked stunned. His face was very red and glistening with sweat, despite the cold of the day, and his rheumy eyes opened still wider and even his moustache seemed to bristle as Celia went on. 'It was entirely his fault, but he wasn't man enough to admit that. Not content with filling Annabel's belly with his bastard child, he went on to blacken her name and you believed him over her. I wondered about that at the time because if you knew anything about your own daughter you'd be well aware she wasn't at all like the woman Timberlake described. She wouldn't have had the least idea how to entice and tease a man for she had led a cloistered life here, so where would she learn such things? Ah, but then I learnt that Timberlake was a wealthy man and one with influence and realised that those things are more important than the truth and if that meant casting your daughter aside when she needed you more than ever then so be it.'

Lord Lewisham knew he was beaten. He would tell the servants that if they gossiped about this they would lose their jobs, but he knew that would only fan the rumours and there was no way they could hope to keep it secret now. He would lose his respectability over this and so would his wife. Her stricken eyes met his across the room and he sighed.

He'd thought they could get away with keeping Annabel's pregnancy a secret, even after she'd wrecked their plans for her to bide at Aunt Agatha's. Henry had agreed to hide her away and, God forgive him, he had been relieved when she had died. It had been neater that way, drew a line under it, and he felt ashamed of that now because he had to acknowledge that much that the vixen had said had been true. He had also thought it a pity that the child had survived. As it had, he'd presumed Henry would have it housed in some children's home.

Never in a million years had he envisaged Henry appearing at Manor Park Hall with the child tended by some virago who berated them soundly and shouted their business to the world. She had dealt them both a mortal blow.

'You had better go,' he said in defeated tones to Celia. 'You've done your worst.'

'Yes,' Celia said. 'I'll go now.'

'But the child...' Henry said.

Celia looked at the now quiet and sleeping child as she said, 'Henry had this idea that you might have made arrangements for this child to be fostered by someone here on the estate. I can plainly see from your faces that such a possibility had never entered your heads. In a way I'm glad. This child is doubly precious because Annabel lost her life giving birth to her so I would like anyone who'd look after her to love her too like Henry and I do. Even if you were willing to take care of your own flesh-and-blood grandchild, you love yourselves too much to make a good job of it. In fact I would hesitate to leave you in charge of a goldfish.'

NINETEEN

Henry had arranged for the taxi that had brought them to wait and as they settled back into it Henry looked at Celia with amazement. 'I can't believe you said all that to my parents.'

346

'Why?' Celia said. 'It needed saying. There isn't one word I said back there that I will ever regret saying.'

'No, but...'

'I believe in straight talking,' Celia said.

'You most certainly do,' Henry said with a wry smile. 'I have never seen my father so lost for words. I suppose you know you've destroyed them.'

'I don't much care if I have,' Celia said. 'The way they treated their daughter was unforgivable. Anyway, they will only be destroyed if they allow themselves to be. They cannot be held responsible for what happened to Annabel though from what you say, if Timberlake was invited to their home, then greater care should have been taken of her, because Timberlake's reputation had gone before him. What people may castigate them for is the way they behaved towards Annabel when the dreadful news was broken to them. The servants would have been aware of much and I was glad to at least set the record straight with them.'

'You did that all right,' Henry said. 'You didn't see because you were ahead of me but as I left the butler clapped me on the shoulder. He had never done anything like it before and he said, so quietly I had to strain to hear, "Good on you, sir. We always thought that Timberlake a bad lot and we never blamed Miss Annabel. She was little more than a child."'

'See, they knew everything already,' Celia said. 'And it will be all over the county in no time because whatever restraint your father puts on the staff will only work in the short term and really in my experience a tale grows in the telling, so when it starts seeping out in bits, it will be added to. It would be best to make a clean breast of everything, and take the censure and criticism. When the dust has settled true friends will still be there.'

'Timberlake won't.'

'No loss there then,' Celia said. 'Seems to me I've done everyone a favour. Oh, I know all about his money and influence, but how many fathers will be willing to take an investment from Timberlake when they know that the price he might exact could be their daughter's virginity and loss of innocence?'

'Not many, I'd say.'

'I'd like to think none,' Celia said. 'Anyway, straight talking means for us as well. There is to be no more false names and me pretending I am someone else. I understand why it was done but that reason is no longer valid.'

Henry nodded. 'I know you've often felt uncomfortable.'

'Well I'm not used to bossing people about, I think you have to be born and grow up in that kind of life to be comfortable with it. Annabel for example was much better at it than me. So we will tell Janey and Sadie first and then I have to try and find Andy and explain that I never received the letter and why and you can tell him the real reason you rebuffed him when he came asking for the job you offered him initially.'

'And what are we to do with the baby in all this?'

'Why should we do anything with her?' Celia asked. 'Isn't she fine where she is? I know you

348

probably were kept in the nursery but I don't like that way of going on and if I am dealing with her that's the way it will be.'

'All right,' Henry said. 'I won't argue, but you must tell me if it gets too much for you. She will have money of her own anyway for the sum Annabel would have received at eighteen, probably to fund her season in London, reverts to Grace and when I was going through her papers I also came upon the tickets for the jewellery she pawned in Belfast before boarding the boat. I never fussed her about it, but always assumed she'd just thrown them away and those too belong to Grace and I will retrieve them as soon as possible.'

'Oh, I'm glad she will have some money at least,' Celia said. 'It might smooth the path for her when she is older. Maybe give her more choices in her life.'

The taxi drew up in front of the door as Celia said, 'And talking of Grace, my nose tells me she needs changing and she could probably do with a wee feed too so our talk with Janey and Sadie will have to wait.'

'A few more minutes won't make any difference,' Henry said as he paid the taxi driver. 'Sadie is probably busy with the dinner anyway. She said she'd have it all prepared and put it on when she heard us arrive back. If you change Grace now, I'll go and get her bottle organised.'

So Celia had Grace clean and sweet-smelling and Henry had just returned from the kitchen when there was a knock on the door. They never had visitors and with Janey busy in the kitchen, rather than call her, Celia, still with the baby in her arms, opened the door herself, but cautiously, and then she screamed in delight and surprise.

'Norah,' she cried. 'Oh Norah.' And she threw her free arm around her sister while tears rained down her cheeks as she realised how much she had missed her. Henry, carrying a baby's bottle in one hand, came in upon the distressed sisters still in the hall, for Norah was crying too. Knowing it would all be explained later, he scooped the baby from Celia's arms and carried her away.

'Come in,' Celia urged Norah, throwing the door wide open. 'Please come in.'

'I will but I must tell Andy first.'

'Andy? You mean Andy's here?'

'Yes, waiting till I check you are in this time because we came before, but you were out.' And Norah wrinkled her nose as she added, 'Don't think your maid likes me much. Looked at me like something that had crawled out from under a stone and definitely would have no dealings with the likes of Lord Lewisham, who I asked to see.'

'Janey is all right when you get to know her,' Celia assured her sister. 'She's a bit protective of us. So where's Andy now?'

'Just up the road,' Norah said. 'We took a turn around the park before I came to try the house again.'

'Not really the weather for parks,' Celia said. 'Why didn't he come to the house with you?'

'He said that he didn't know you'd want him here.'

'What nonsense,' Celia said and then, remembering that Henry had sent him away before when he had come to ask him for the job he had offered him initially, thought he might have reason to feel unwelcome. 'There have been so many misunderstandings and so much to explain it's important that I see Andy. I thought I would have to go searching for him. Let me go and tell him he must come to the house. I'll just get my coat.'

'No,' Norah said and it came out louder and sharper than she intended. She saw Celia recoil slightly and went on more gently, 'You might frighten him to death with your fine clothes, or at the very least make him uncomfortable.'

Celia looked down at her tartan plaid dress and jacket and smart leather boots. 'D'you think so?'

'Yes I do,' Norah said emphatically. 'Celia, Andy is a boatie and though he has a suit on today under his overcoat because it's Sunday, both have seen better days. I imagine it will be hard enough to get him to come through the front door of an establishment like this.'

Celia nodded. 'You're right and I felt a bit like that myself initially, but please tell him I really need to see him. There are things I must explain to him.' As Norah scurried down the road, Celia was able to go into the sitting room and tell Henry, who was feeding the baby, who Norah was and she also said Andy was waiting for her down the road. Henry quite agreed with Celia that they be brought to the house, though he felt a little uncomfortable meeting Andy again for he knew the first thing he had to do was apologise to the man.

In the meantime he popped into the kitchen to

see if Sadie could magic up some sort of meal for their unexpected guests. However, Sadie had been used to much bigger establishments before she came to work for Henry and had got into the habit of always keeping a stock pot on the go that she could use as a base to rustle up soup in a jiffy and she told Henry so.

'I don't want to put you out.'

'You haven't, sir,' Sadie assured Henry. 'In fact I would like the opportunity to cook for a houseful.'

Celia expected Norah to return with Andy in a matter of minutes but Andy was proving reluctant.

'You saw her then,' he said, when he saw the smile on Norah's face.

'Yes, I saw her and she wants to see you too.'

'Huh, and what if I don't want to see her?' Andy said slightly belligerently. 'She has no right to order me about any more.'

'I don't think she means it that way,' Norah said. 'She said she has a lot of explaining to do.'

'Well she's right there, she does.'

'Well she might tell us about the baby for one thing, because whatever you think it can't be Celia's.'

'And you've seen the baby?'

'Yes.'

'Well why can't it be Celia's?'

'Because you didn't arrive in Birmingham until late on in May and babies take nine months to be born. This one is here. I've seen her and though she is small she is a few weeks old.'

'Are you sure?'

'Course I'm sure,' Norah said. 'Now are you coming or not?'

'I can't go in there dressed like this.'

'Look, this is Celia we're talking about. She won't care how you're dressed.' But she remembered her conversation with Celia and knew he had a point. 'Come on, Andy, she said she had things to tell you, to explain.'

'Explain, huh?' Andy exclaimed. 'Maybe she can explain why that Henry Lewisham likes treating ordinary people like shit.'

'How he behaves is nothing to do with her.'

'She must know about it though. How can she stay working for a man like that?'

'Oh that's not fair,' Norah said. 'You must know better than anyone that jobs are not ten a penny. Anyway, if he has done nothing to her she might even like him. I mean, all right so he did something nasty to you once, but before that it was all right. He offered you a job, didn't he? But you thought jobs were easier to get than they were and your stiff-necked pride wouldn't let you accept it, but you didn't stay and explain, you just took off. In a way, you were throwing his offer back in his face and, yes, maybe he was cross and wouldn't have you back on principle.'

'Well if he makes one snide comment to me, just one, then I will punch him on the nose.'

Norah almost bounced on the ground in temper. 'Andy McCadden,' she cried. 'I am not going into that house with you when you are threatening to assault the master of it. He would have you arrested and you would badly hurt Celia. She'll definitely be upset and might find herself out of a job because of your actions. Is that what you want?'

'Course not.'

'Well come on then,' Norah said. 'And behave while you are there, for heaven's sake.'

Norah thought for a moment Andy was going to wheel away from her and return to the canal, and he did think of it. But the need to see Celia was strong and with a shrug he fell into step beside Norah and she sighed inwardly with relief, and as they walked he said, 'If it's not Celia's baby it has to be Lady Annabel's.'

'It might belong to neither of them.'

Andy shook his head. 'No,' he said. 'The boy who delivered the note said she was expecting a baby, only he got the wrong person. No wonder there was no message back. Wonder how it happened for I told him he had to give it into the hand of Miss McCadden and no other. Point is, if it is Miss Annabel's, I'm pretty certain that she's not married.'

'Oh that would set the cat among the pigeons.'

'Even with the gentry?'

'More especially with the gentry, I would say,' Norah said.

In the house Celia was wondering what had happened to them and would have gone looking but Henry advised her to wait and so when the knock came on the door it was Janey who answered it, but Henry had told her they were guests invited to dinner and she blushed with embarrassment as she remembered the rude way she had spoken to the woman just an hour or so before. And so the first thing she said to Norah was how sorry she was for the way she had spoken to her earlier.

'It's when you asked for Lord Lewisham,' she said as she led the way to the sitting room. 'I couldn't think what you could want with him.'

'Well I did think of asking for Celia but I thought I should ask for the master of the house.'

Janey had her hand on the handle of the door of the sitting room when she turned with a slight frown on her face and said, 'I think there has been some mistake, miss, for we have no Celia here. The mistress's name is Lewisham, Anna Lewisham.'

Andy looked from one to the other in total confusion. 'Maybe,' he thought, 'that was another thing to explain,' but Norah stated firmly, 'I don't understand this and why Celia has chosen to call herself another name, but I do know that the young woman I spoke to just a few minutes ago is my sister Celia that I lived with for eighteen years.'

There was no arguing with that and Janey really didn't have the right to argue anyway and she opened the door and then went back down to the kitchen to tell Sadie the latest developments.

Celia wasn't in the sitting room and so Andy and Norah came face to face with Henry, who crossed the room and said they were more than welcome. He shook hands with Norah and said how lovely it was to meet one of Celia's sisters and then turned to Andy with his hand outstretched. There was a slight hesitation before Andy took it, but if Henry noticed this he did not remark on it but just shook Andy's hand warmly as he said, 'Andy, I owe you a sincere and heartfelt apology for the way I treated you last time we met. There were reasons, which I will explain to you, but the reasons will not be good enough and I am very sorry if my actions caused you hardship in any way.'

Andy was impressed with the apology for he thought it took guts and especially to do it in front of Norah and not make some bumbling half apology when they were alone. He hated apologising himself – he imagined most people did – and so it shifted his opinion of Henry slightly. So he didn't say that Henry refusing him work could have easily been the death of him, but said instead, 'That's water under the bridge now.'

'It is,' Henry agreed. 'But it was very wrong of me so if ever I can make amends for that I will do. In the meantime we would very much like you both to stay and enjoy the superb Sunday dinner that Sadie is cooking at the moment.'

Neither Andy nor Celia had known what to expect from this meeting and Andy at least had been filled with anxiety and to be invited for a meal, to sit around the table with them, was something he never envisaged. But he was hungry, he had to own, and he saw Norah was little better and the delicious smells coming out of the kitchen were making his mouth water and he said, honestly, 'Well, sir, I never expected that and I thank you very much for we'd love to stay for dinner and I'm sure I speak for Norah too.'

'Oh, yes please,' said Norah. 'It's a long time since breakfast.'

As Norah was speaking, Celia came into the

room with the baby who had snuggled into her drowsily and she handed her to Henry.

'Will you put her in the crib in the dining room?' she said. 'She's half asleep already.'

And she turned and first embraced her sister and then turned to face Andy. When Celia just that very morning had read the letter Andy had left she had felt a rush of love for him, for she saw that he had left for her own sake. She appreciated and understood why he'd done what he had and she had imagined she would run into his arms when she saw him again and tell him this. But he didn't know that she had just read the letter.

And so Andy was cautious because, even though the baby wasn't Celia's and he could now see that for himself, it was no guarantee that there was nothing going on between her and Henry because he thought they seemed very easy with one another. So there was a constraint in him so strong that Celia could feel it and it stopped her going any closer and holding him tight as she wanted to. Had she been able to look into Andy's mind she would have seen that he was holding back with difficulty. He thought he had been able to forget about her and had told Billy he had, but seeing her again and so close, he knew he loved her more than ever and he had the urge to crush her to him and tell her so.

'Hello Andy,' Celia said as the silence stretched out and added, as if he was some casual acquaintance she used to vaguely know, 'It's good to see you again.'

Andy opened his mouth to make some sort of reply but it was so dry he doubted he would be

357

able to speak at all, so when he eventually said, 'Good to see you too,' it came out like a growl. It was a totally unsatisfactory meeting for both of them and Henry, coming back into the room after tucking Grace into the crib, saw the awkwardness between them.

However, he could do nothing about it and so he said, 'Would you all like to come through to the dining room? Dinner is about to be served.' He led them into a sizable room dominated by a large table laid up for dinner and when at that moment a buxom woman entered carrying a steaming tureen, the smell from it wafting in the air made Andy feel quite faint as he realised just how hungry he really was.

'We would like you and Janey to join us at the table today,' Henry said as Janey came in with two baskets of bread.

'Oh no, sir,' Sadie protested as she moved around the table ladling soup into the bowls. 'Janey and I would be much more comfortable in the kitchen.'

'No doubt,' Henry said with a smile at them both. 'But there is a lot to talk about, explanations given, and some of that includes you and Janey. The arrival of Norah and Andy means those explanations are long overdue and as I don't want to repeat myself I would like you to eat with us today. Janey, would you please lay up two more places?'

Janey gave a glance at Sadie before she did what Henry asked and Celia saw the cook give a shrug that plainly said, what choice have we? And if she was honest, Sadie was intrigued by what Janey had told her and she would like to get to the bottom of that. She hadn't long to wait for just a little later, as they sipped the hearty soup mopped up with the equally delicious bread, Celia began her tale.

TWENTY

'The first thing I have to tell you is that I am no great lady,' Celia said. 'I'm sure you both have been confused for I am just the daughter of an Irish farmer. I was born Celia Mulligan eighteen and a half years ago,' and she went on to explain that she had fallen in love with a hireling boy named Andy McCadden. She explained her father's reaction when he had found out, which had culminated in locking her in her room. Sometime in the telling, Celia's hand snaked across the table towards Andy, who was sitting opposite.

Andy still didn't know what the situation was between Celia and Henry and did wonder if she was playing some sort of game with him and yet almost of its own accord his hand stretched to meet hers as Janey asked, 'What's a hireling man?'

'It's a man who is employed by another,' Andy said. 'I was forced to make my way in the world because I was the second son in our family. But Celia was a farmer's daughter and I was not good enough for her in her father's opinion.'

'Seems very harsh,' Sadie said. 'The class system is very much in operation here too. I did think that the only good thing that might come from the Great War, when as many officers as men were killed, was that it might have brought about some sort of levelling off of the class system, but the old order soon established itself again and girls from the gentry usually have little choice in their life partner.'

'That's not all though,' put in Norah. 'As well as locking Celia in her room, Daddy tried to bribe Andy to stay away from Celia and when that didn't work he had him beaten up. Isn't that right, Andy?'

'Yeah, and they needn't have bothered because I had already decided to leave. Not because of the bribe – I wouldn't touch the man's money – or the threat of violence, but because I thought Celia might have an easier life if I moved away.'

'Had you really decided to do that?' Celia asked.

'Yes,' Andy said. 'I loved you too much to see you suffer because of me and anyway it was a sort of agony to have you so close and not be allowed to even speak to you.'

There was a pain in Celia's heart because Andy had used the past tense. He'd said he loved her. She longed to ask him if he still loved her but how could she ask such an intimate question in front of so many people?

'Well,' Cook said, as she collected up the bowls, 'I think it's all very sad if you want the truth and I'd like to hear the rest, but we must get the dinner out now or it will spoil.'

'We'll all help,' Norah said, leaping to her feet and catching up the bread baskets.

'Good idea,' Celia said, withdrawing her hand from Andy's.

Immediately Cook looked uncomfortable and disapproving. Until a few minutes before she had thought Celia to be Lady Lewisham and as such it was unthinkable that she would do anything so demeaning as clear the table. Celia, however, laughed when she said this.

'Have you forgotten already?' she said. 'I was born Celia Mulligan and, despite all the times my name has been changed, I am still Celia Mulligan, born of good farming stock, but not gentry and not one afraid to get my hands dirty.'

'Celia's right,' Henry said. 'Anyway, today is a sort of special day so you girls do that and I will get the joint and start carving it and maybe Andy can get the dinner plates. It's best to get the telling and the meal out of the way before Madame wakes up demanding attention.'

'What do you call the baby?' Andy said, returning from the kitchen with the plates and the girls ran round putting steaming tureens of vegetables and jugs of gravy on the table.

'Grace Catherine,' Henry said. 'Catherine after my mother, for all the good it did.'

'Is she Annabel's child?'

A shadow passed over Henry's face but he nodded and added, 'But I will tell you all about that in due course.'

A few minutes later, everyone was sitting down to eat and for a moment there was silence broken only by the coals settling in the hearth and the snuffly, gentle breathing of the baby. Suddenly Janey said, 'And then what happened? How did, you get away?'

Celia began to tell of her escape and Andy

361

added to it now and then and Norah told them of her help in Celia's escape and then the aftermath of it that they hadn't been aware of. Celia told of meeting Henry's real sister Annabel on the boat and tending to her when she had become very seasick and how Annabel had asked her to be her lady's maid.

'I knew summat was up,' Janey said to Celia. 'Because you always looked uncomfortable telling me what to do, as if you wasn't used to it. You were the same with Sadie. We often spoke of it.'

'There's a good reason for that,' Celia commented grimly. 'And that's because I have never done anything like that before. I was at the beck and call of everyone else. That being the case I had no problem accepting the post when Annabel asked me to be her lady's maid. I mean, Andy and I had made no plans as such, had we?'

Andy shook his head. 'There was no time really.'

'We did wonder why Annabel was travelling without any sort of attendant,' Celia said. 'Because she was of the class that doesn't usually travel alone. She told me that her previous maid had been taken ill and she had to travel without her because she had to get back to England urgently. It was untrue for there was no lady's maid and the truth was she shouldn't have been on the boat returning to England at all.'

'Where should she have been?' Sadie asked.

'On a train travelling to the west of Ireland to Aunt Agatha,' said Henry grimly. 'Our aunt is a religious fanatic who sees sin in the very air we breathe and she's also nasty and vindictive and

362

would have made Annabel's life hell on earth. Annabel had obviously decided she couldn't take it. She had written to me already telling me what had happened and our parents' reaction. When she heard I was on the way back home she pawned her jewellery to raise enough money for the fare and travelled back on the next boat.'

'And before any of you think badly of Annabel for the condition she was in,' Celia said, 'with Henry's permission I'd like to tell you what terrible thing befell that poor girl and I want to tell it exactly as she told it to me. That all right, Henry?'

Henry nodded. 'We agreed no more lies,' he said and so all there heard of the brutal rape of Annabel Lewisham, daughter of the house, by a man called Charles Timberlake who at the time was a houseguest of her father's. However, Celia said, 'Henry, you told me he was a well-known profligate rake. I take it your father would have known that too?'

Henry nodded his head. 'Unless he went round with his eyes shut. The man made no secret of it, for Christ's sake. But because most of his conquests were servant girls and the like, I can only think Father assumed his daughter would be safe from his attentions, but an alley cat has more morals than Timberlake. That being the case, when they discovered Annabel was pregnant, why believe Timberlake's claim that it was all Annabel's fault? He said she had teased and enticed him and drew him into her bedroom where she was waiting for him naked!'

'Begging your pardon, sir,' Sadie said. 'I only

knew your sister for a short time, but I would never believe that she would do that sort of thing. Despite the fact she was pregnant there was a kind of innocence about her. In fact, I said to Janey that I was surprised she was pregnant at all and imagined her husband would have had to be very understanding and gentle with her. She seemed younger than she really was in that way, sir.'

'Yes,' said Henry. 'She was, I suppose, because she was given little experience of life. She saw no one and wasn't even allowed to go to school and so to be taken by force must have been dreadful and yet Timberlake was believed and Annabel banished.'

'Did you change Annabel's name to protect her?' Andy asked.

Henry looked a bit sheepish as he answered, 'Yes, Celia became Anna Lewisham and Annabel became Cissie McCadden.'

'But why did Annabel become McCadden when I thought Mulligan was Celia's maiden name?' Janey asked.

And then it was Andy's turn to explain why on the journey they had discussed it and decided that for the sake of Celia's reputation it might be better if they travelled as brother and sister. 'That was done to protect Celia because, although I loved her and was prepared to take her to England, I couldn't risk sullying her reputation in any way.'

Henry knew what Andy was saying and that was that he hadn't really touched Celia and he was impressed. Few men would have shown such restraint and he thought Celia's father mad for

364

going to the lengths he had to keep the young people apart. Owning a farm or business didn't automatically make a man a good husband and he thought her father should have at least got to know Andy better instead of dismissing him out of hand, though he knew he hadn't the right to say any of this.

Andy didn't know what Henry was thinking but he did know that he was thinking deeply about something so he asked quite gently, 'Where is Miss Annabel now, sir?'

'She died giving birth to Grace,' Henry said.

Andy was shocked and so was Norah. Andy remembered the beautiful young girl, because that's all she was, and he felt sad that her life should have been snatched away from her so cruelly. He also saw Henry was still badly affected by his sister's death, and he thought that understandable, and Celia too who had worked with her so closely. 'That was a terrible thing to happen,' he said sincerely to Henry. 'I am so very sorry and you must miss her too, Celia.'

Celia nodded, unable to speak for a moment as the sympathy in Andy's voice caused tears to flood her eyes. And then she swallowed and said, 'I did and it was quite an intense friendship for we were together so much. She was very scared of the future – she spoke of that often.'

'The birth, d'you mean?' Norah asked.

Celia nodded. 'Oh yes,' she said. 'She was worried about that, but she was also worried about what would happen after the birth.'

'What could happen?'

'Well this doesn't happen very often,' Henry

365

said. 'But sometimes, even in the upper classes, if a lady has been less than discreet and a child is the result, that child is then usually given to someone on the estate to bring up as their own They don't lose by it, they are well rewarded.'

Norah stared at Henry as if she couldn't believe her ears. 'Everyone loses by it, can't you see?' she said. 'The baby is taken from the mother. Does anyone ask her how she feels about that? Is she given a choice?'

'Not usually, I suppose,' Henry admitted. 'Like I said though it very seldom happens.'

'Even once is too much,' Norah maintained. 'Quite apart from the mother, think of the couple. I would hazard a guess that that child wouldn't get the best of upbringing foisted on people who didn't want a child. But they could hardly say for they couldn't risk upsetting the gentry who they often rely on for employment and a roof over their head.'

The baby began to fidget and protest in the crib and Celia picked her out and with the baby in her arms said, 'And what of the child? Think, if it had been Grace lodged with some cottager, would she have the sort of schooling to fit her for society? And what would that society be? Would she ever be told who her true parents were, and if so, mightn't she resent the upbringing she had and the fact that she would have to travel rootless through life?'

'You know, I never thought of any of this and you are so right,' Henry said. 'And really I don't know what the answer is because if it is common knowledge that the woman has had a child out of wedlock then her life's over.'

Celia nodded. 'Annabel once said to me that she hoped her child would die. I was shocked and she said she thought it was the only way she would be accepted back home and have any sort of life, any future at all. She didn't think of the child or even see it as a flesh-and-blood little person who would have feelings of its own. Point is,' she went on, 'I don't think it would matter what she did, she would never be accepted back. In their eyes she had sinned and that was it, or maybe in their heart of hearts they knew she was innocent and to allow her to live back at the house again would have reminded them what they had done to their own daughter on a daily basis. We went up to the house today because Henry had this crackpot idea that his parents might have made some arrangements for the child.'

'Did you think it a crackpot idea?' Henry said.

'Course I did,' Celia said. 'Why, didn't you? Think about it, Henry. All the time Annabel was here they never seemed to care about her at all. I would never have left a vulnerable young child in their care.'

'I don't blame you,' Henry said and added bitterly. 'The way they treated my sister, they don't really deserve to be called parents. I mean, Celia and I had to become godparents to Grace because there was no one else we could ask.'

Andy didn't like the sound of that. 'Celia couldn't be the child's godmother,' he said. 'She shouldn't even have been at the service, though probably the funeral was all right, but not a christening. She's a Catholic.'

'At least I worship the same God, Andy,' Celia retorted angrily. 'Who would you want to look after the child's immortal soul – some random woman from the street outside, or maybe the one who cleans the church or the one who arranges the flowers?'

'No but...'

'There isn't a but,' Celia snapped. 'This is how it was and how we had to deal with it and we may as well get it all out of the way at once. Because I was pretending to be Henry's sister and they are not Catholics, I couldn't go to Mass. I haven't been for months. In fact I have never been near the church.'

Andy was shocked and so was Norah and Henry said, 'That's why I couldn't risk employing you that time you waylaid me in the street. I thought you might have objected to what Celia had agreed to do. And I was cross with you for taking off like that without a word and upsetting Celia so.'

'I didn't go off without a word,' Andy growled. 'I wrote a letter.'

'Yes, I know you did now,' Celia said. 'But I didn't see that letter until this morning.'

Andy's mouth dropped open. 'You are joking?'

'Am I likely to joke about something like this?'

'I suppose not. But how...'

'Don't look at me,' Henry said. 'I didn't see it till this morning either.'

'It was Annabel,' Celia said and she told Andy how she had found the letter.

Andy was silent for a minute and then said softly, 'You must have felt totally abandoned

368

when I just vanished like that.'

Celia just nodded briefly. But Henry cried, 'Celia was so upset she collapsed and I had the doctor called. At the time I thought you were her brother and as such couldn't understand how you could have run out on her without a word after bringing her to a strange country and everything.'

'That would be another reason not to give me another chance on employment.'

'Yes,' Henry agreed. 'Your actions pointed to you being unreliable, not a good trait in an employee. Then, as well as the subterfuge that Celia had agreed to which you might object to, I wondered how she would feel even seeing you when she thought you'd abandoned her once and how she would react if you were just to take off again.'

Andy nodded. 'I can see that from your point of view I was not an attractive prospect.'

'No,' Henry said. 'But if I had taken the chance on you, I know the existence of the letter would have come to light and everything would have been different.'

'Annabel was afraid of me leaving her,' Celia said. 'And God knows what would have happened to her if I had for she had no one else. I'm not taking anything away from you, Henry, when I say that.'

'I didn't think you were,' Henry said. 'And I agree with you, Annabel needed someone who cared around her, a friend.'

Andy nodded. 'Though I knew in my head it was best for Celia to stay where she was, my heart felt differently for I was aware that I'd left her with virtual strangers.' His eyes fastened on Celia then as he said, 'After a few days fretting about you, I sneaked back to Grange Road. I was too afraid to come up to the house so I hid behind the big oak tree beside Freer's farm hoping to catch sight of you. But when you left the house it was with Annabel.'

Celia remembered when she had first come to the house, she and Annabel would go up to Erdington Village every day and she felt a sudden tug in her heart for the young girl's life snuffed out before she had even begun to live. Sadness flitted across her eyes at the memory but she spoke to Andy, 'Why didn't you make yourself known to me?'

'I wanted to,' Andy said. 'You'll never guess how much, but I didn't want you to see the state I had been reduced to. You looked so clean, wholesome and you were wearing clothes ... well, I'd never seen you wearing clothes like that before.'

'They were Annabel's,' Celia said. 'Remember we had swapped our names and, as Annabel's sister, Henry said I had to dress to a certain standard.'

'I understand that now,' Andy said. 'But I had no idea then what was happening. You seemed alien to the girl I had travelled from Ireland with. You were laughing at something Annabel had said and you went up the road arm in arm, not a bit like a lady out with her maid. Your evident happiness eased my mind and I knew you could bide there safely and I could put all my energies into securing a job, which I found soul-destroying.'

'I could have helped there,' Henry said.

'Yes, and I could have allowed you to help me in the first place if I hadn't been so stubborn,' Andy said. 'There were faults on both sides.'

'Maybe, but I'll look out for you now,' Henry promised. 'See if I hear of anyone setting on and get you a better job than working on a canal boat.'

Andy felt the hairs on the back of his neck stiffen with indignation at the slight scorn in Henry's voice, but he swallowed his anger and spoke respectfully enough. 'If you please, Lord Lewisham, there is no way that I could give up life on the canal boat just now. I'd be leaving Billy right in the lurch if I did.' He told Henry a little of Billy's life history and when he had finished, Henry nodded and conceded, 'Well, all right, I see that you might have a measure of responsibility towards this man but really–'

'No, Lord Lewisham,' Andy said more firmly. 'Not to put too fine a point on it, Billy saved my life.'

'And you his by the sound of it,' Henry said. 'Didn't you say he was struggling on his own?'

'Billy didn't want to give up the boat he had been born and grew up on, probably because it was the last link with his mom, dad and brothers. It meant he could only handle small spasmodic deliveries and was unable to pull tenders, but if he had failed altogether, someone would have taken him on and someone would have bought his boat to give him some ready cash. My joining him meant he could go for the big jobs with all the rest and start to make a decent living, but I

371

think I might have starved to death. So I can't just run out on him now.'

'Your loyalty to your friend is commendable,' Henry said. 'But surely to God you don't expect Celia to live on a boat?'

'Why not?' Celia demanded. 'I am not some precious hothouse flower, you know.'

Andy made no remark to that but addressed himself to Henry. 'Lord Lewisham, what sort of man do you think I am?' he snapped. 'I have no notion of taking Celia anywhere and certainly not to a cramped boat that she would share with two men she is not related to. I can't marry Celia until she is twenty-one and no longer needs her parents' consent to the wedding and that will be over two years away and one hell of a lot can happen in that time. I don't believe in crossing bridges till I come to them. I sort of took it for granted that Celia would stay here until we married. I think you owe her at least that much with all she has done for you.'

Henry coloured slightly at the implied criticism, but he had to admit privately that Andy had made a legitimate point and he was in Celia's debt and the least he could do was offer her security of employment. He had also got used to seeing her around the place and she was the only one who had really got to know his sister and he knew he would miss her greatly when she did eventually marry Andy.

And yet, he said to Andy, 'I wasn't fully aware of the barrier to your marriage until Celia turns twenty-one. But that being the case, mightn't the gossips be just as active in their disapproval if she

372

was to stay on her own with me, even though we have Sadie and Janey here as well a lot of the time?'

'They might indeed,' Andy said. 'Seems to me some people appear to have too much time on their hands and they use it making mischief for others and finding fault where there is none. I take it you are keeping the child here or are you planning on putting her in an orphanage somewhere?'

'She was my sister's child and so of course I'm keeping her.'

'So you'll need nursemaids?'

'Yes and as you see Celia is fulfilling that role now, and now I know your marriage isn't imminent I hope she will continue.'

'Of course I will,' Celia said and at her words the baby, who had fallen asleep against Celia's shoulder, began to whimper and draw her legs up and Sadie remarked as she got to her feet, 'I'd say that little one wants a feed. Want me to see to it?'

'If you would, please.'

Andy waited until the cook had left the room before he said to Norah, 'Did you have plans for what to do after you located Celia? I mean, are you going straight back to Ireland now?'

Norah shook her head. 'Whether I ever go back to Ireland again is more or less determined by my parents and primarily my father, but I have no immediate plans to return soon. Why?'

'Because if Henry is agreeable you could be another nursemaid,' Andy said and Celia clapped her hands in delight.

'Oh say yes, Henry?' she begged. 'It would be

lovely to have Norah here with me.'

'Yes and Celia can't do it all,' Andy said. 'She'll need proper days off and Norah's presence in the house will protect all of you from malicious blathering.'

Henry smiled. 'I have no trouble with Norah coming here and helping Celia, but we really have to ask Norah how she feels about it.'

Norah was thrilled with the proposal because she'd known that to stay in Birmingham she would have to get a job of some sort and somewhere to live as well, but she answered with a smile. 'It was hard to get a word in edgeways,' she said. 'But yes, I am happy to accept your offer and would I live in as well?'

'Of course,' Henry said. 'We have rooms to spare and you may have to share the nightshift. I'm sure we will be able to sort out the arrangements between you.'

Just at that moment, Sadie popped her head around the door to say the bottle was ready. Celia began getting to her feet with the fractious baby but Norah forestalled her. 'Let me?' she pleaded and Celia gave the child into Norah's arms.

As the door swung shut behind her, Henry said to Celia, 'Lovely girl your sister.'

Andy saw the spark of interest in Henry's eyes with relief, for he hadn't been totally sure that Henry hadn't had his sights on Celia, but it was Norah who had taken his fancy.

Celia had not noticed Henry's speculative glance and agreed happily that Norah was lovely.

'I'm sorry that she seems to have fallen out with Mammy and Daddy as well. I was thinking may-

374

be the two of us should write them a letter for after all Christmas is not far away.'

'Huh,' Andy said. 'I don't think I'm going to write another letter in the whole of my life.'

'Why on earth not?'

'Well they have caused me nothing but trouble,' Andy said. 'It was writing the one to my parents that caused Norah's headlong dash here and I wrote you two and you only read the first this morning and the second you haven't clapped eyes on.'

'Yes,' Celia said. 'Funny if it was Annabel who took that too that she didn't put it with the first one.'

'Yes. It must have been Annabel for I told the boy to only give it to Miss McCadden and that meant he gave it to Annabel.'

'You gave it to a boy to deliver?' Janey asked, coming in at that moment to tend the fires.

'Yes.'

'Then I know what happened to it,' Janey said. 'I've just remembered. Cissie, as we called her then, was in the sitting room and I thought she was trying to rest, but she agreed to see the boy who specifically asked for her. After he left she told me she was going for a proper lie-down in her room and I went into the sitting room to check the fire that I had lit earlier. It had burnt down to a few glowing embers and that's where she had thrown the letter that she had ripped into pieces. Any bits touching the coals had burnt to ash, but some bits were just lying on top of the edging stones at the sides of the grate and, though the edges were brown and crinkled, you could still see what it was.'

'So that's what happened to it,' Andy said. 'Meanwhile I felt upset that you had sent no answer back when I had laid my heart bare in that letter and then the boy said you were pregnant and I didn't know what to think.'

'What d'you mean, you didn't know what to think? And why did a letter that you wrote to your parents have anything to do with Norah appearing in Birmingham?' Celia asked, puzzled.

Andy said, 'You and I need to talk and though it's not the kind of day for lingering in the park, at least it isn't raining.'

But Celia didn't want to go anywhere on her own with Andy because she still felt awkward with him and she wanted others around her to cover the self-consciousness she felt.

Andy knew how she felt but he knew if the situation was to be remedied then he had to see Celia alone. So when she said, 'Don't see why we have got to go out anywhere on this bitterly cold day. Why can't we say what we have to say right here?' he glanced across at Henry, who sensed his need to be alone with Celia and so he urged her too: 'I think it would be better if you go,' he said. 'You needn't be out that long.'

'What about the baby?'

'Surely to God there's enough people in the house to look after one small baby?' Andy said, slightly exasperated. 'Anyway, if Norah is sharing her care then it's about time she got her hand in so let's go while we have the light at least.'

TWENTY-ONE

There wasn't any light, all told, Celia thought for the clouds were heavy and grey and ringed with purple and though she was warm enough in her good thick clothes she worried Andy would be chilled, for his clothes were not really suitable for the intense iciness of that winter's day.

They had walked up Grange Road side by side, but once they had crossed Chester Road and were inside the park, Andy reached for Celia's hand. She hesitated for a fraction of a second and Andy said, 'Please?'

Celia took up Andy's hand and again felt the tingle run up her arm but this time it seemed to fill her whole body with heat. She looked at Andy in wonderment as he remarked, 'D'you know, I think this is the first time we have ever been alone together, apart from when we travelled to Letterkenny by horseback and we could hardly say anything of importance then.'

Celia knew that Andy was right. There had always been someone with them or they had been in a public place. 'Did you still want to ask me something important?'

Andy nodded. 'Just about the most important thing in the world and that is how you really feel about me now?'

Celia had guessed that was what Andy would say and she had dreaded it. She couldn't tell the truth and say she didn't know how she felt, for that would hurt him so much, and yet she couldn't let him think they could just slot back into the same places where they were before.

So she chose her words with care. 'Andy, I think we need to get to know each other all over again, not in some hole in the corner affair either. There has been so much deception and so many misunderstandings and now we are two different people.'

'Have you feelings for anyone else?'

'No,' Celia said emphatically. 'And even if I was that way inclined,' she added, 'when would I have had the time or opportunity to meet anyone?'

'I meant Henry,' Andy said.

'Henry?'

'Yes, Henry,' Andy said. 'Don't look so surprised. Have you feelings for Henry Lewisham?'

Celia was just about to ardently deny she did, but then decided Andy deserved the whole truth; there had been far too many lies already. So she said, 'I admit I was dazzled by Henry at first for I had never met anyone like him, so well-dressed and self-assured. And then when you disappeared, I thought you didn't care for me any more and Henry was there to lean on.'

'What do you mean by that?' Andy said through gritted teeth.

'I mean, to depend on and that was all,' Celia retorted. 'Remember, I was completely alone.'

'You're right, quite right,' Andy said. 'I must take some responsibility for this anyway. I see now that I should never have just disappeared but told you face to face what I intended doing.

I should have given you that much respect.'

'Yes,' Celia said. 'I would have tried to talk you out of leaving, even though I didn't know how hard it was going to be for you to get a job.'

'Nor did I,' Andy admitted.

'I was so cross when I found out you had come to see Henry about a job and he had turned you away,' Celia said. 'Because he knew how bad the unemployment was. He didn't tell me that until today, after I found the letter, and probably for the first time I realised how selfish he was and so devoted to his sister that he would have done anything for her.'

'He did apologise and explained why he didn't want to employ me.'

'Don't get me wrong,' Celia said. 'I thought a great deal of Annabel but Henry, in trying to protect her reputation, had me change my name and even give up my religion without a thought as to how that might affect me. All this misunderstanding with you wouldn't have happened if I had received the letter you left and retained the name we decided on the boat.'

'If you didn't want to do it, why didn't you refuse?'

'Because at the time they asked me I thought that you were out of my life forever,' Celia said to Andy. 'And they were my employers, so I couldn't be that picky about what I did and didn't do. But I swear on my mother's life that there was never any hint of a relationship between Henry Lewisham and me.'

'You have no idea how much lighter my heart is because of those words.'

'You really did think there was some sort of carry-on between us?'

Andy gave a brief nod and Celia said, 'I'm not the sort of girl to go running into another man's arms. In fact, what you did put me off men for ever. I thought, if a man I thought I knew could go off without a word, how could I ever trust another? I'm surprised you didn't assume Grace was mine as well.'

Andy was suddenly so still that Celia cried, 'You did didn't you, you thought Grace was my child? How on earth could she be?'

Andy said, 'All right, it was mad and I am sorry for thinking that you had betrayed me that way, but the boy who brought Annabel the note said you were pregnant and because of the change of names I thought he meant you and when there was no reply I suppose I thought the worst.'

'I'll say you did,' Celia said tersely. 'Now tell me what Norah has done to upset Mammy and Daddy so much.'

And Andy dropped Celia's hand and wrapped his arm around her and Celia thought it much more than just pleasant to be snuggled that way and she leaned against him as she listened as he began to tell her the tale that Norah had told him and Billy in the boat. Celia was surprised that Dermot had gone to America, that her mother had agreed – that he might be influenced, coerced or even bullied into joining the IRA, like so many young fellows apparently had been.

Celia could only think of her mother and the wrench it would have been to see her young son set sail across the foam, knowing the likelihood

380

was that she'd never see him again. And then this loss would be compounded when she arrived home to find that her daughter was gone too. She could understand why Norah felt she had to come and see that she was all right though, as Andy had sent the letter to his parents making no mention of Celia because of a misunderstanding after Seamus Doherty had seen both of them boarding the Birmingham-bound train.

'What made you come to the canal for work?' she asked Andy.

'Well that was originally born of necessity,' Andy said. 'When I with factory doors continually slammed in my face, it used to make me feel pretty bad at times and coming down the canal made me feel better about myself. There was always something useful I could do.'

'And why were you accepted so easily by the boaties?'

'Because the boaties are considered social outcasts anyway because of the way they live, yet they'd no choice, because they'd been farmers once and were turfed off the land because they were bringing the railway through. And Billy of course knows no other life. And they make a living and that's what matters in the end.'

'And why didn't people like you?'

'I'm Irish.'

'So?'

'Listen, Celia,' Andy said. 'Some of the survivors of that devastating war were told that they were coming home to a land fit for heroes and they came back to poverty and deprivation and the dole queue. The last thing these poor battered veterans want is young, fit Irishmen coming to England to chase the few jobs there are.'

'Many Irish boys fought anyway because they were promised Home Rule if they fought for England,' Celia said.

'Yeah and that hasn't happened and I never really expected it to,' Andy said. 'But it wasn't till I came here that I fully appreciated the fact that it's not just the Irish the English let down, because they have also let down these poor souls that have fought through the blood and gore of the trenches. Look at people like Billy who had three brothers killed in the war and his parents dead as well of heartache, he says.'

'I'd love to meet Billy and see his boat and the canal and everything,' Celia said. 'It seems so much part of your life now.'

'So why don't you come over next Saturday afternoon?' Andy said. 'It's a different place on Sunday, but after we bring the Dunlop workers home at lunchtime on Saturday we are free for the afternoon. If you come then I could show you everything, introduce you to Billy and then if you like we could go to the Bull Ring.'

'What's the Bull Ring?'

'It's a big market,' Andy said. 'In the early days, searching for work every which way, I picked up a bit of work there, mainly running with the barrows to claim the best spot, setting out the goods and sweeping up at the end of the day and that.'

'Won't the market be closed at night though?' Celia said, cutting across him.

'That's just it,' Andy said. 'Maybe every other

night in the week it would be, but Saturday night there is great entertainment to be had. I've never seen it myself, but Billy said it's well worth a visit. We always intended to go but never did. What d'you say?'

'I'd love to go...'

'I sense there's a "but" coming there.'

'It's the baby.'

'What about her? She's not your responsibility.'

'Yes she is.'

'Not totally.'

'Andy, I was with Annabel until she breathed her last and I took on the care of the baby because there was no one else. Until a few hours ago I didn't know whether you were alive or dead, whether our relationship was over and with it my future. For Annabel's sake, I loved and cared for her child the best way I knew, so I was with her nearly every minute of the day and she slept by my bed at night and over the weeks she's twisted her way into my heart and become my life, my reason for living if you like. I love her as if she was my own and when Henry's parents said they had made no arrangements for Grace's care, I was glad. Not that I ever believed for one minute that they would have done.' Celia looked at Andy, but the light was fading in that short winter's day and so her face was half hidden in shadow, but her voice was plaintive as she said, 'I can't just turn that love off.'

'Darling,' Andy said. 'I'm not asking you to turn anything off, but just share it a little. Every word you have just said tells me what a wonderful person you are and what a loyal friend. Now your sister is here so let her share the load, for Grace's sake as well as your own. I want to walk out with you properly, a thing we never could do in Ireland, and get to know you again after so many months apart. Don't you feel that too?'

The pleading tone in Andy's voice struck a chord in Celia's heart and she said, 'Oh yes, Andy. Yes I do.'

Andy turned Celia to face him and pulled her tight and so close that she felt his breath on her cheeks and then their lips met. This was their first real kiss and it was so powerful it nearly took Celia's breath away and as Andy teased, her lips apart, she moaned as strange stirrings flowed through her body. Andy heard the moan and felt her body responding to his and his heart soared for he knew then he hadn't lost Celia as he had feared, but to win her totally he knew he would have to proceed slowly but that was all right. He was a patient man.

When he released her he said, 'Now we must go back to the house for you must be frozen and I don't want you taking a chill.'

Celia felt as if a furnace was burning inside her, but she didn't say this. She didn't say anything for it was enough to be held close to Andy, to hear his heart beating in his breast.

When Andy and Celia returned to the house it was obvious to Norah, who knew her sister better than most, that something had happened between them and she was glad. She was totally in agreement with Celia going to the canal to see the boat Andy was working on and also to see Billy.

'You'll like Billy, Celia,' Norah said. 'He's ever

so nice and the boat is as pretty as a picture, brightly painted outside and all spick and span inside. It's small though,' she went on. 'Billy's mother must have felt she was working in a doll's house.'

'She wasn't a big woman by all accounts.'

'Just as well,' said Norah. 'But Billy is not exactly a small man, is he, and if his brothers were built like him can you imagine the four of them being there together?'

'Billy always said it was often a bit of a squash and yet, you know, I think he would give up all that space he has now willingly if even one of his brothers had survived.'

'I would say you're right,' Norah said.

'You know, till I came here, to England, I never realised how many men that Great War took,' Andy said. 'I mean, I saw the casualty figures, but they were just numbers and it only really hits home when you relate to the people. Billy told me it isn't just him lost all his brothers, for nearly every boatie family had someone belonging to them conscripted and a fair few never came back. He said they had what they called Pals regiments when all the men would be collected up from one area. Small towns with surrounding villages and farms or parts of larger towns.'

'That's right,' Henry said. 'Dreadful idea.'

'Why was it?' Celia asked. 'Wouldn't it be better to be all together? They could look out for one another.'

Henry shook his head. 'I was an officer and I can tell you that in a war of that magnitude no one can look out for another. It wasn't some jolly

385

boy scout camp they were going to. There was colossal loss of life and those that stayed together, died together, which meant that whole areas were stripped of men, in every city and town in Britain. It was stopped in 1916 when most of the damage had been done. Tell you, working and fighting alongside those men made me rethink the class system we have in this country. What with boarding school and then university, I'd never had much to do with the working classes, except for the estate workers and their families. I saw men with true courage and heroism and many still retaining a sense of humour in spite of everything.' He shook his head from side to side and then said, 'When you've relied on one another and shared so much together you can never think of people the same way again.'

Celia was silent. Everyone was silent. They had all heard the passion in Henry's voice and knew every word had been wrung from him, and also that every word was true and then he gave a short bitter laugh and went on. 'Well aren't I the doom and gloom merchant? When we were in the thick of it, before any chaps might go home on leave, we were always warned not to share the horrors of war with our loved ones because it would cause them to worry needlessly. How right they were, so I'm sorry for that little display. It's just that sometimes memories catch me unawares.'

'I can quite understand that,' Andy said while Celia cried, 'I didn't know you were in the army, Henry?'

'There was no need for you to know,' Henry said. 'It wasn't a big issue at the time. Our country was at war and so young men and some not so young, if they proved fit enough, were drafted into the services.'

'I suppose. Strange Annabel never mentioned it.'

'It barely made a dent in her life,' Henry said. 'She wasn't at school, don't forget, and so her education was in no way interrupted and she had no school friends to discuss things with and her poor governess would only speak of things Mother approved of and war talk wouldn't have been considered a suitable topic for polite conversation.'

'Didn't your parents' servants leave you in droves like we heard was happening?' Andy asked.

'No,' Henry said. 'It wasn't what you would call a stampede: the stable lad, two farm hands and the young gardener were all called up. But my father called the old man who used to do the garden out of retirement and asked him to serve for the duration and he agreed. The old stable hand said the stable lad was worse than useless and with me off as well there would be less to do and he would be happier on his own. The farm hands were, I grant you, more difficult to replace and in the end my father was forced to take on a couple of land girls. The others were too old to be called up or too settled to want to move. My parents' and Annabel's lives were barely affected by that devastating war. There was always plenty of food in the house too and my father's cellar was as well stocked as ever. They still held dinner parties and my mother her soirees.'

Andy was shaking his head almost in disbelief. 'It doesn't seem right that they should go on as if none of it is any concern of theirs and they don't seem to spare a thought for the dead, the dying and the disabled, especially when you could have been one of those casualty statistics.'

'Oh they didn't want me to go to war,' Henry said. 'We argued about it, my father and I, and my mother wept crocodile tears all over me. My father said he could fix it so I didn't have to go.'

'How could he do that?'

'Oh, there are a number of ways,' Henry said. 'He could have bribed someone who maybe had a dicky heart to pose as me so that on paper I failed the medical. I don't know if that's what he intended because I didn't listen but you can get most of what you want if you are prepared to pay the price.'

'That's true enough,' Andy said with feeling.

It was a little later over tea that Andy talked about taking Celia to the Bull Ring on Saturday evening after she had been to see the boat.

'Oh there'll be some entertainment there I'd say,' Henry said.

'Like what?'

'I haven't the slightest idea.'

'What!' Andy cried. 'You mean you've never been?'

Henry shook his head and Norah said, 'But why if it's as good as you say it is? I mean, you must have asked people about it to know that much.'

'I think I know why,' Celia said. 'I bet Mama didn't think it quite the thing.'

'Probably not,' Henry said. 'But you can't help

what class you are born into, can you?'

'Well no,' Celia conceded.

'No need to go along with such outdated notions when you are an adult though,' Henry said. 'So I have a great idea. Why don't all four of us go together?'

Andy's heart sank because that wasn't what he had envisaged at all, but he could hardly say anything and it was Celia who cried, 'How can we all go out and leave the baby?'

Sadie was clearing the table and had heard a lot of the discussion and said to Celia, 'You won't be leaving the baby on her own. I'll be here to see to her.'

'You won't mind that?'

'Why would I mind?' Sadie said. 'I'm going nowhere and she's a little angel about going to bed. What I do mind is that you never seem to go out and enjoy yourself. Since I've been here you've seldom been across the threshold unless you can count the strolls you used to take in the park with Miss Annabel till she got too big and ungainly.'

Henry felt guilty for he knew Sadie spoke the truth and he said, 'Sadie's right, you should be going out more, and from what I've heard Saturday night at the Bull Ring is as good a place to start as anywhere else. What do you think, Andy?'

Andy thought he might as well tell Henry exactly what was in his mind. 'Well what I think, sir,' he said, 'is that while I don't mind the four of us going to the Bull Ring this time I don't want it to be a regular occurrence that we go out in a gang. Celia is my girl and I want to court her

389

properly. And after being apart so long we need to get to know each other again and we won't do that if we always go out in a party.'

'Oh, well said,' Sadie said before anyone could say a word. 'Andy has hit the nail on the head.' She then looked from Celia to Norah and said cryptically, 'You two are grand girls so your parents must have done something right, but I must say your father's attitude towards Andy is totally wrong because he's a decent and honest young man. A fine fellow altogether.'

'We'll have to send you over to Ireland as a special envoy to plead Andy's case,' Henry said with a grin, but in all honesty the more he saw of Andy the more he liked him. 'Just now though I must get Norah back to the priest's house to collect her things.'

'What will you tell them?' Celia asked.

'A small lie, I'm afraid,' Norah said. 'See, when I arrived not knowing where you'd be, or how long it would take to find you, I told the nuns that you were staying with an aunt and had been taken ill but as Mammy was away from home saying goodbye to Dermot and visiting Katie, that she seldom sees, I thought I would come across to see how you were before we alerted Mammy.'

'And now?'

'Well now I'll tell them that you have been ill and are recovering but not yet able to take the position you had secured to look after Lord Lewisham's orphaned niece and so I am taking your place until you are fully fit. It's as near the truth as we could get it.'

'Yes,' Celia agreed as she lifted the complaining

baby from the cradle.

'And I'm going along to add credence,' Henry said.

'Oh yes,' Celia said, looking him up and down with a smile on her face. 'You look, sound and appear so respectable that not even the priest will worry that you might be abducting Norah for the white slave trade.'

'I'd better be off too,' Andy said, 'before Billy sends a search party out for me.'

'Well I'm going to telephone for a taxi,' Henry said. 'And I'm quite happy for you to share it.'

It was on the tip of Andy's tongue to say that he was all right and walk up to the tram stop, but he caught Celia's eyes and she raised them slightly to the ceiling and he knew that look was warning him not to keep fighting Henry. And so he said, 'That's very good of you, sir, and thank you. If you drop me at Rocky Lane I will be very grateful.'

'It's not even out of my way,' Henry said, as he made his way to the telephone in the hall. 'And do you think you can drop this "sir" business now? I will be Henry as you are Andy?'

'If you say so, sir, I mean Henry,' Andy said.

Henry laughed. 'You'll soon get used to it,' he said.

The door had barely closed on Henry when Norah found something urgent to do in the kitchen, taking Grace from Celia's arms as she passed. Celia guessed it was to give her some time alone with Andy to say goodbye. Andy thought the same and he drew her into his arms and she sagged against him with a sigh of contentment and the kiss seemed to ignite a light inside Celia and she knew it was the promise of wonderful things to come.

The journey to Rocky Lane took little time in the taxi and, once Andy was away from all the gas lights at Aston Cross, Rocky Lane seemed dark as pitch for there were no lights until they reached the canal side. Few stars were seen to twinkle in the murky Birmingham skies, but there was a full moon peeping now and then around the winter clouds and in its light Andy saw someone in front of him. He guessed it was a boatie, for Rocky Lane led nowhere else, and when the moon peeped out again he saw it was Billy. He almost called out until he realised his friend wasn't alone. He could only see in short bursts but in the moon's orange glow he saw enough to know the figure beside him was shorter than he was, a woman, and that Billy had his arm around her.

His initial thought was that Billy was a sly old dog and the second was to wonder where the hell he met her, where he had a chance to meet her, because she was obviously more than a mere acquaintance he was pally with – that much was obvious even with limited light. Anyway, this impression was compounded when Billy suddenly drew to a halt and pulled the girl into the doorway of a small factory and when they kissed Andy realised he was close enough to hear the girl, whoever she was, moan.

He felt guilty, as if he was spying, and Billy did have a perfect right to see anyone he wanted. After all he had his Celia, and he turned on his

392

heel and went back up to Aston Cross and didn't return to the boat for almost an hour.

Billy was polishing up the tack for the morning and he looked up as Andy came in.

'I didn't expect you to stay out this late,' he said. 'And I must say you have a dirty, big grin on your face, like the cat that's got the cream.'

'Oh well, you see I found out about a few things today,' Andy said and he told Billy about the name switch and how it was that Celia didn't get his first letter at all and the other one had been given to the wrong person because of the name switch and that it had been burnt before Celia had seen it. 'And there is a baby, a girl, but it was Lady Annabel's not Celia's, and she died giving birth to her so Celia and now Norah are caring for her. Henry thought his parents might have arranged for someone on the estate to bring her up, but they wanted nothing to do with Annabel's child, even after her death.'

'Can't see that happening in my family,' Billy said. 'So, who was the father?'

'Oh that's the best yet,' Andy said. 'It was some houseguest who charged into Annabel's room and raped her. And then when there were consequences he put all the blame on her and it couldn't have been her fault. I mean, I have met her and she was like a child. She was only sixteen and she'd also had a very sheltered and lonely upbringing.'

'A right rotter then.'

'I'll say,' Andy said. 'But if she hadn't died what sort of life would she have had?'

'I know what you mean and it is wrong that the

woman always gets the blame,' Billy said. 'Still, now you know your girl's in the clear. I presume you are together again?'

'Sort of,' Andy said. 'I mean we are, but we are taking it slow because we have both changed since we arrived in England first. I've asked her to come over next Saturday afternoon. She wants to meet you. Can't think why.'

'Why not?' Billy said with a grin. 'Irresistible to women I am.'

'Yeah,' Andy remarked sarcastically. 'I have to fight my way through the throng waiting for you on the towpath every day.'

Billy's laughter pealed out and Andy said with a wry grin, 'You just see you behave yourself next Saturday. You try your so-called irresistible charms on Celia and you might find yourself lying flat on the towpath with a busted jaw. Celia is spoken for.'

Billy wasn't a bit bothered by Andy's threat because it was just banter between them and it continued in this vein for some time. At any minute Andy expected Billy to tell him about the girl he had been with that night but when he didn't he thought there might be some sort of problem. Anyway, Andy told himself as he turned in that night, it was Billy's business and he was sure he would tell him in his own good time. And he fell asleep thinking of Celia.

TWENTY-TWO

Both Celia and Norah were surprised to see a van pulled up in front of the house on Wednesday and Henry sitting beside the driver.

'Henry, what is it?' Celia cried as she went to meet him with Norah behind her.

'I've bought a Christmas tree,' Henry said as the driver jumped down from the van and opened the door. He handed Henry garlands of ivy and holly with its bright red berries and shouldered the tree with apparent ease.

'Where you be wanting this, guv?'

'In the hall,' Henry said, going ahead of him. 'I'll show you where.'

'What you made you buy a tree?' Celia asked as the man took his leave and Janey and Sadie came for a look.

'Well it's not that far from Christmas now.'

'I know, it's just...'

'You think we should still be in mourning for Annabel?'

'Yeah, I suppose,' Celia said. 'You don't think that it's a bit disrespectful?'

'I did,' Henry admitted. 'That's exactly what I did think but then I remembered how Annabel loved everything about Christmas and every year she would decorate the tree and I thought if we do it in her memory that would be showing her respect.'

Celia nodded. 'Yes, Henry,' she said. 'I can see that.'

'So after dinner I will go into the attics and bring down the tree decorations that I have and the streamers for the room and we will get prepared for Christmas, if only for Grace's sake.' He was quiet a minute and then said, 'Annabel has gone and she will always be missed and there will probably always be an ache in my heart when I think of her, but not celebrating Christmas will not bring her back.'

Everyone in the house took their cue from Henry and while he saw to the tree, starting with a big pot of earth to sink it in, Grace was put to bed and Celia and Norah began to decorate the room and hallway. Sadie, coming in with a hot drink for them both just as they were finishing off, was very impressed for the room was festooned with streamers, swathes of holly decorated the fireplace while the ivy garlands were fastened to the walls and paper lanterns dangled from the ceiling where they spun in the heat from the fire.

Henry too had made the tree very beautiful. He had a lot of shiny balls in different colours and glass animals and bows of silver and gold ribbon tied with red satin cord, a shimmering star had been placed on the top and set into every outer branch were candles and Celia knew when those were lit the tree would be transformed.

'Well what do you think?' Henry, asked, standing back to admire his handiwork.

'It's beautiful, Henry,' Celia said. 'Wait till Grace sees it. I think you have made the right decision to decorate the house.'

With the house decorated, Christmas seemed nearer than ever and the following morning, after feeding and changing Grace, Celia went into the dining room and decided to write to her mother. When Norah came in she explained what she was doing.

'She'll probably throw any letter you send away unopened.'

Celia gave a slight shrug. 'Can't help how she will react when she gets it,' she said. 'But I have to try. In the letter you sent to Mammy before you hightailed it to England, did you say that you were worried about me and why?'

'Course,' Norah said. 'I didn't want her to think I had left on a whim.'

'I see that,' Celia said. 'But if I don't write Mammy won't know that you found me and that I am fine.'

'Oh, yes,' Norah said. 'Never thought of that. In fact I'll write too and explain why I am not coming back just yet.'

'Do,' Celia urged. 'Because Mammy is bound to miss you too, finding out you had left when she's just said goodbye to Dermot. I mean, on Christmas Day she will just have her and Daddy and Ellie and Sammy because Tom will probably go to Sinead's house for at least part of the day.'

'In a way you know Mammy has brought this upon herself.'

'You know it's Daddy makes the rules.'

'More fool her accepting that state of affairs,' Norah said. 'You'd not catch me agreeing with my husband if I thought he was wrong.'

'You'll have to get one for yourself before you can be that categorical,' Celia remarked cryptic- ally. 'Now are we going to discuss this all morn- ing because Grace will soon be awake and that might mean at least one of us doesn't get their letter written at all and I think Mammy would like to hear from both of us.'

'You're right,' Norah said. 'And I must write to Dermot too for I promised I would when I had news.'

Celia took her time over that letter, issuing first a sincere apology for upsetting them all, but stressing that she truly cared for Andy McCadden and did not want to leave him and go to America.

But as you wouldn't listen or try to understand and had me locked in my room I had no option but to leave in the way I did. I would like you to know that Andy behaved like the gentleman I knew him to be and we have done nothing wrong. I actually secured live-in employment before I left the boat.

She explained about meeting Annabel Lewisham and deviated from the truth slightly by explaining that she was a young widow and pregnant and so she was travelling from Ireland to her brother's house as he was going to look after her. She made no mention of either her parents or her husband, nor of how long it took Andy to find work. She went on:

Andy meanwhile got work on one of the barges and lives on board with the owner. Meanwhile my mistress died giving birth to her daughter, Grace, who I have been caring for ever since and that's where Norah found me, but I'm sure she would tell you all in her letter. I would just like you to know that I love you all very much and think of you often, but though I regret leaving the way I did, I don't regret leaving Ireland, because here I can meet with Andy openly. Please don't be upset at this letter but you must try and see that when I marry it will be for life and I cannot tie my life to someone I don't love and Andy McCadden is the one who holds my heart.

This is written with all my love
Celia

The girls posted their letters that same day and Celia, at least, waited with great trepidation to see if their mother would reply.

Both girls would have been surprised if they could have seen into their mother's heart that day. Peggy had arrived home from Katie's house on Tuesday evening and Norah's first letter, which she had posted in Belfast, had arrived that morning and so was waiting for her behind the clock on the mantelshelf.

She read it out with a heavy heart and while Dan raged about Norah's selfishness and deceitfulness, Peggy wept for her and the burden she had carried alone. She knew why she had been so concerned about her sister – she would have been more than concerned herself if she'd had the information Norah had – but she hadn't known because Dan had decreed Celia's name couldn't be mentioned in the house. So it had been up to Norah to devise a plan to travel to England alone and try and find her sister. Peggy sincerely hoped she did find her and that Celia was all right and she hoped that Norah would write and tell her for she wouldn't rest till she knew both of her daughters were safe.

Oh, but there were going to be some changes around here, she decided then and there. For one thing there would be no ban on talking about Celia or Norah. She loved them with her heart and soul and would not disown them just because they were doing something she didn't necessarily agree with. Surely they had a right to make decisions about their own futures? Look where trying to deny them that right had got them and if she ever got the address of where they were living she would write and tell them so.

There was another thing she had decided as she had bid a tearful goodbye to her daughter Katie earlier that day. Katie had hated seeing them ready to leave as she had missed them greatly and especially her mother, and said she felt so isolated from them all. And, thought Peggy, there was no reason for her to feel that way for it wasn't as if she was in darkest Africa. A rail bus travelled all the way from Donegal Town to Letterkenny and Katie said either she or her husband, Roddy Donahue, could pick Peggy up from there. Roddy, who she got on with very well, said he would be delighted to see her; it would help Katie, and Peggy would get to know her grandson. And so it was decided and it was just one more thing she had to hit Dan with. He would be astounded at her determin-ation, she knew, for he'd had things his own way for long enough, but she wasn't going to let herself be browbeaten any more. Dan's decisions were not always just and sensible ones and he had to be made to realise that.

Celia dressed warmly for her visit to the canal on Saturday afternoon as Henry had said it was bound to be colder nearer the water and the Bull Ring would be no warmer. Henry wanted to phone for a taxi as the day was icy but Celia refused, though she did say, 'You might see that Norah has a coat. Her shawl might not be adequate and, though there are two or three in your sister's wardrobe, she thinks you may feel she has a cheek to wear one of Annabel's coats. I can't really understand it because she is quite happy to share Annabel's indoor clothes. If you tell her it's all right she will be fine about it, I'm sure.'

'I will,' Henry promised. 'And,' he added, 'warmer footwear wouldn't come amiss either. But to be honest it is about time you had clothes of your own. I'll get that seen to by Christmas.'

'Oh Henry,' Celia breathed in awe.

'That suit?'

'More than suit,' Celia said. 'All the time I was growing up all my clothes were hand-me-down, apart from my outfit for Mass. We just didn't have many new clothes.'

'Well not a word to Andy or Norah either,' Henry said. 'It's our own little secret. And talking of Andy, isn't it time you were on your way if you won't accept my offer of a taxi?'

'Keep your money, Henry,' Celia said with a smile as she closed the door behind her and made her way to the tram stop.

Andy was waiting for her at the tram stop at the top of Rocky Lane and Celia thought he seemed a little preoccupied. 'Penny for them,' she said as they began walking down Rocky Lane hand in hand.

'What?'

'You seem worried about something?'

And if Andy wasn't exactly worried, he was concerned and puzzled at Billy's odd behaviour. Twice that week he had gone out in the evening after they'd eaten, to see Stan he said. Andy didn't doubt him at first.

'Is he much worse then?'

'Mm,' Billy said vaguely.

He had been even more vague the next day when Andy had asked questions about the ailing old man, so much so that Andy wondered if he had even seen Stan at all. But because Billy was being so elusive, Andy had decided not to tell him of the visitor he'd had: Henry Lewisham, who had offered him the opportunity to train for a good well-paid job in the brass industry, the sort of trade he had dreamt of, and the sort he would have bitten his hand off for if it had come six months earlier. But now it was just too late.

Two nights later, when Billy had left the boat with the same excuse, Andy followed him. Billy did go into Stan's house all right but he was in it no time before he came out again hand in hand with a young lady, the same young woman Andy had seen Billy with before. He couldn't understand why his friend had never said a word about it. Andy would have said they never had secrets from each other and it bothered him that Billy

402

appeared to – so much so that Celia had noticed Andy's mind was elsewhere.

And it wouldn't do, he told himself firmly. Whatever ailed Billy was his business and Andy had been apart from Celia too long to waste any of the scant time they had together by letting his mind wander to other people and their potential problems. So he pushed Billy and the girl to the back of his mind and forced a smile to his lips.

'Sorry, pet, but my thoughts are not even worth a farthing,' he said. 'And I'm worried about nothing. I was just thinking of a particularly large load we have on Monday and working out how to load boat and tender so we can do it in one journey.'

'Oh, is that all?'

'That's all,' Andy assured Celia. 'But that is Monday and today is today so let's chase the wind.' And they ran down the hill together, hand in hand, and laughing at their foolishness. Like Norah, Celia was enchanted with the pretty painted barges but because the winter days were short they didn't go in straight away. Instead Andy led her up the towpath till she could see the tunnels that they legged the barge through and the locks with the sluice gates. And they were lucky enough to see a barge approaching so Celia could actually see the locks in action. Then Andy took her back to meet Billy.

Celia knew of Billy's sad history and she thought him a lovely young man and hoped he would find someone special very soon. She was a little dismayed by the size of the living area, though Norah had warned her. And while she thought the space-saving innovations very clever, she still didn't see how anyone could raise a family in such a small space.

People did, though Billy said most lads married boatie girls. It wasn't a rule or anything like that, but a woman not raised to a boatie life would usually find it hard to settle. Then the couple could either stay on the canal and the woman would be unhappy or they could leave the canal and the man would be unhappy. Billy's words made Celia wonder about her future with Andy if he stuck with the canal. But she refused to worry about it for she told herself any marriage between them was two and a half years away and a lot could happen in that time.

After a feed of fish and chips that Andy bought, they set out for the Bull Ring as the evening darkened. When they alighted from the tram, the darkness was complete but street lamps threw pools of light in front of them. There was also light from the shop windows for most shops were still open and very inviting they looked. Celia would have loved a wander round one or two of them, but Andy was on some sort of mission.

'This is High Street,' he said. 'And at the end of here there's an incline and that leads to the Bull Ring so let's see if it's as good as people say it is.'

They walked down the incline and just stood still and stared. Stalls and barrows, full of produce of various sorts, stretched out as far the eye could see and each one was lit up by spluttering gas flares so it was like fairy land. Andy knew he would have Celia for himself for a couple of hours before they would be joined by the others so they wandered around the stalls and waited for the promised entertainment.

It began with stilt walkers dressed in long, long striped trousers and black jackets and top hats, walking seemingly effortlessly among the people and stalls, now and then proffering their hats for the watching people to put money in. They saw a prize-fighter promising to beat anyone foolish enough to take up his challenge to fight, but the five-pound prize should a man beat the champ might be a great temptation to many, Celia thought. Then they came upon another man dressed in what looked like an oversized nappy and a turban, lying on a bed of nails on that bitterly cold night just as if it was a feather bed, and another trussed up in chains.

And while they were sampling these delights of the Bull Ring, Henry and Norah were in the taxi travelling to the city centre and Norah was saying, 'And he refused the job opening that you had for him? What reason did he give?'

'He didn't want to leave Billy.'

'Well it might have something to do with you doing the asking,' Norah said. 'Andy is a very proud man, but the real reason is probably that he doesn't want to do the dirty on Billy because they get on well together and Andy owes him a lot.'

'I know he does,' Henry said. 'But I don't want Celia to start her married life in a barge.'

'She can't, not that one, Andy told you that. But maybe he thinks he has plenty of time yet.'

'And unemployment might be as bad as ever and this offer will not be on the table for long,' Henry said. 'It only came about because one of the owners banks with us and when he came in for the Christmas bonuses he happened to say that the father of his apprentice has been left a farm in Ireland and they're all going over to see if they can make a living at it. Point is, it's left the man who was training him in a bit of a fix. I told him about Andy and he said he was willing to see him on my recommendation, but he's up to the neck with Christmas orders now so he wants this signed and sealed as soon as possible. He can only give Andy till Monday and then the advert is going in the *Evening Mail*.'

'What business is it?'

'A brass works,' Henry said and Norah remembered the conversation with the three sisters on the boat and how they said speaking for someone was the only way to get a proper job these days. She knew that Andy would be mad to pass this up.

'And it's only in Aston,' Henry went on. 'So if he lived in our place he could take the tram every morning and it's a particularly good apprentice-ship because there are three brothers side by side, all making different things in brass, so he will have the maximum experience. If he wanted to move in a couple of years when he'll be through training, he will find it a lot easier to get a job as an experienced brass worker.'

'It sounds good all right,' Norah said. 'What did Billy make of all this?'

'Billy wasn't there,' Henry said. 'He'd gone to see that old man that left the canal because he was ill and Andy and Billy took up the contract he had to take the Dunlops workers to the Fort and back. That's why I was late home the other night, you remember. You and Celia were almost ready to send out a search party.'

Norah smiled. 'I remember,' she said. 'You came home in a very funny mood. We thought you were cross about something.'

'Not cross, more preoccupied,' Henry said. 'And nervous because I was worried Andy would do exactly what he did do.'

The taxi dropped them at the top of the incline and they were as impressed as Andy and Celia had been, but looking at how full it was Henry thought they never might find the others.

Henry offered his arm and Norah thankfully linked her arm through his, for though Henry had sorted her out a warm coat and boots and a scarf and mittens, she was a bit chilled leaving the warm taxi. They wandered around searching fruitlessly for Andy or Celia and then Norah spotted Billy walking with a girl snuggled into him and she hailed him.

'It's Billy,' she said to Henry. 'Come and meet him.'

Billy didn't look best pleased to see Norah and before she had time to say who Henry was, Billy said urgently, 'Hello, Norah. Don't tell Andy, will you?'

'Don't tell Andy what?' said a voice behind him and Billy wheeled round. In the light from the flares Norah saw him flush crimson in embarrassment. 'H ... hello Andy and you too, Celia.'

'We'll go into what you don't want me to know later,' Andy said. 'Aren't you going to introduce me to your girl?'

'This is Emma Wilson and through no fault of her own she is linked to what I didn't want you to know just yet. Look, is there somewhere quieter to go and I'll tell you all.'

'The Royal George isn't far,' Henry said. 'Let's go there. Better than trying to explain anything in the melee.'

It was Celia and Norah's first visit to a pub and Celia did wonder if they would be let in, but Henry had such an air of authority that no one said a word to them.

Once they were seated around the table with drinks in front of them all, Billy said, 'Right, first thing is Emma is my girl and we were going to wed after the war. And then my brothers died and for my parents and me it was a very bad time. I was hurt that Emma hadn't been to see us, couldn't understand it. Then Ma went and Dad was... Well, I couldn't leave him and when he went as well I felt like I was in some dark hole and couldn't do anything for ages. In the end I went looking for Emma and when I felt able to call on her, none of the family were there.'

'What had happened?' Celia said, for she could see that the love light shining in Emma's eyes was all for Billy.

'I caught Spanish Flu,' Emma said. 'And they said I had to get off the boat and away altogether to avoid infecting others, but the Birmingham hospitals were full and I was sent to a hospital in Wolverhampton and Dad moved the whole family over and began to work on the Wolverhampton Canal so they could see something of me.' She caught up Billy's hand and held it tight as she said,

408

'No one gave poor Billy a thought because my life hung in the balance for weeks, so they say. Anyway they couldn't send him a note because they can't read and write and neither can Billy.'

'Nor you?'

'I can now,' Emma said. 'I was at the convalescent place and there was a schoolteacher there and she taught me. It's really easy once you get the hang of it and once we're wed I'll teach you if you like, because it's a good skill to have. When I recovered, I didn't know what had happened to you, see, whether you had been called up and died like your brothers or whether you were dating another girl. So I came to find you and when I heard about Stan I went to see him and he told me how you go every Sunday and Mabel said she'd have got to hear if you were walking out with someone else and so that first Sunday I waited for you to come to their house. And,' she added, 'we meet there every week now.'

'How long have you been seeing each other?'

'A month now.'

'And why was you seeing Emma such a big secret?' But even as he asked the question, Andy knew the answer. 'Because you couldn't wed with me on the boat,' he said. 'If you got married I would have to leave.'

'I'd never just chuck you out, Andy,' Billy said. 'We'd work something out.'

'But, Billy, how will you manage without Andy's help?' Henry asked.

'Emma's brother is coming over,' Billy said. 'He has a small boat of his own and he will berth it by mine and use it to sleep in.' Then he turned to

Andy and said, 'And that's all right and that, but I feel a real heel because I know you really like canal life. You said only a while ago that you have never been happier.'

'And I meant it,' Andy said. 'It's been great and I will never forget what I owe you, and once the idea of leaving you and trying to find employment elsewhere would have filled me with panic, but Henry has thrown me a lifeline.'

'What?'

'When I left Ireland I only knew farming and those skills aren't that useful in a city and so I wanted to learn a trade, something I can hold up to Celia's father to show I am looking after her properly. In the boat coming over, I was talking with a young fellow who was going into the brass industry and his uncle had spoken for him. Seems that's how it's done in a slump like this – you need someone in the know to give you a bit of a leg-up.'

'Are you telling me Henry has done that for you?'

'Yes, well, he got me an interview and gave me his recommendation.'

'Which Andy initially refused to even consider because of the fix it would leave you in,' Henry said to Billy. 'So now you and Emma can plan your wedding with an easy conscience. Seems to me you have waited long enough.'

'Couldn't agree more,' Andy said.

Billy's face was one large beam of happiness and Emma seemed incapable of speech but her radiant smile spoke volumes as Billy said, 'I will do that, sir, and thank you. And, Andy, I would like you as my best man.'

Andy was a little choked by that, which he hadn't expected for they hadn't known each other that long, but he gave, a brief nod of his head and said sincerely, 'I would be honoured, Billy, truly honoured.' He looked at Henry and said, 'I don't think I have thanked you properly for thinking of me in relation to this job but I am very grateful.' Then he gave a rueful smile and said, 'Seems as if I am making a habit of throwing job offers back in your face initially.'

'For a different reason this time,' Henry said. 'And loyalty to a friend is always commendable.'

'Oh, isn't it wonderful how everything is working out?' Celia cried in delight and no one disagreed with her.

Celia was happy, so happy that she felt she could burst. She loved Andy with a passion and she could tell him and show him, which was much more than they could do in Ireland. And then it was like she got the icing on the cake in the form of a loving and understanding letter from her mother, acknowledging that there were faults on both sides.

Peggy had been so happy to get letters from both her daughters and such lovely ones. Celia was doing a good and worthwhile job caring for a motherless child and now Norah was helping her. In her heart of hearts she knew Celia was a good girl, but she couldn't help worrying when she had run away with a man she had not been married to, but it appeared all the time they had been living apart at their different places of work. And

411

she knew exactly what Celia had been saying when she said that Andy McCadden had behaved like a perfect gentleman. When Peggy read that, she knew it was time for her and Dan to swallow their pride and meet the man her daughter had chosen. She acknowledged that neither she nor Dan had really listened to Celia or tried to understand and she expressed regret over that:

But it is not too late, my darling girl, and if Andy McCadden is the man for you then we must accept it. But if he is to join our family we must get to know him and so we must meet him as you urged us to do before you left and we refused. So, my darling girl, come for Christmas, all of you – Norah, Henry that you speak so warmly of and I would love to see Grace.

Celia was ready to turn cartwheels but she knew her mother would probably have to stand against her father to send that letter and she was right. Initially Dan had forbidden Peggy to write back and had been astounded that she said she intended inviting their two disobedient daughters home for Christmas as if they had done nothing wrong. But Peggy stood firm and said it was their own actions that had caused Celia to go. 'And then,' she said, 'because you decreed that no one was to speak Celia's name, when Norah thought Celia might be in trouble, she had no one else to discuss it with, no support at all, and she went all by herself and travelled to England to find her. I think that was commendable and if you don't then there is something wrong with you. Now here is the ultimatum, you either relent and let

412

those girls come home for Christmas and behave like a normal human being for the duration of their stay or I will spend Christmas with them instead and take the young ones with me. It's up to you.'

To say Dan was astounded would be an understatement, he was completely flabbergasted that Peggy had spoken to him in that way and in front of the children too, but looking at her anguished and anxious face he realised that he had pushed her to her limits and she meant every word she had said. Deep down he had wondered if he had dealt with Celia correctly. He knew many of the townsfolk had thought he had been too harsh and some had told him so. It wasn't in his nature to apologise and he didn't now but what he did say to Peggy was, 'Oh bid them come if you must.'

'No, not if you say it in that begrudging way.'

'All right,' Dan conceded. 'Maybe it's time to build bridges. Bid them come and welcome and I promise I will behave myself.'

Norah however didn't know about this confrontation between her parents nor the promise forced from her father and she said, 'Andy won't go. Why should he?' Celia felt her heart plummet and Henry saw it and though he thought Norah was right, he said, 'Let him speak for himself. I will take a taxi now and fetch him. He will have finished for the day now.'

They were back in no time and Andy scanned the letter and looked up and said to Celia, 'You'd like me to go to your house for Christmas? To the house where I was vilified, where you were locked up to keep you away from me, and sit with the man who beat me and the other who endorsed and encouraged the violence?'

Celia didn't speak, she couldn't speak. She was asking too much. It was not the right time for Andy. It might never be the right time.

'And what of you?' Andy said.

'What about me?'

'Well you never wanted to leave Ireland. If you go home for Christmas would you want to stay?'

'No,' Celia said. 'I know what I said and I meant it at the time. But I did leave Ireland and I'm glad I did and would never go back to live. You would always be the hireling man there ... but we don't have to go to Ireland. It doesn't matter.'

'To you it matters a great deal. I can see it in every line of your body,' Andy said.

'No.'

'I think the answer is yes,' Andy said. 'We'll go. It matters to you so much and I want to please you, so we'll go.'

'What about all you said, what about all my family have done to you and to me because of you? Does it not matter any more?'

'Look,' Andy said, 'I love you and I would go through that and more if I could have you at the end of it. I really wouldn't care if I washed my hands of your family altogether but then you would be unhappy. I don't want the person I love to be unhappy because I can't put the past behind me, especially as I have come away with the first prize anyway.'

Everyone was impressed by what Andy said and

414

tears were trickling down Celia's cheeks. Henry vowed that if ever he got to see Celia's parents he would stress what a fine man they were getting as a son-in-law.

Andy put his arm around Celia and said, 'I will be starting to learn the brass industry in the New Year and I have a yen to stand before your father and tell him that. And with my head held high I will ask him for your hand in marriage in the correct and proper way and I will assure him that I will be earning enough to provide for you and any children we may be blessed with.'

'Oh Andy!'

'Really though I know one person should be asked before your father.'

'Who?'

'You, of course,' said Andy. 'You may not want me at all for I have never asked you.' And then and there, without any lead-up to it, he dropped on one knee and said, 'Celia, will you do me the honour of becoming my wife?'

'Oh Andy!' Celia said again and burst into tears. She wanted to marry Andy, there wasn't a doubt in her mind, but there was a lurch to her heart when she thought of leaving Grace behind when that happened. She wasn't Andy's responsibility, she was another man's child and her rightful place was with her Uncle Henry.

'What's the answer?' Andy demanded.

And despite the tears coursing down her cheeks, Celia cried out, 'Yes, Yes. Yes and as soon as possible!'

With a shout of joy, Andy leapt to his feet, put his arms around Celia's waist and spun her round the room. And Celia thought that, despite everything they had endured, their love had proved strong and true and her joy was complete.

The publishers hope that this book has given you enjoyable reading. Large Print Books are especially designed to be as easy to see and hold as possible. If you wish a complete list of our books please ask at your local library or write directly to:

Magna Large Print Books
Magna House, Long Preston,
Skipton, North Yorkshire.
BD23 4ND

This Large Print Book for the partially sighted, who cannot read normal print, is published under the auspices of

THE ULVERSCROFT FOUNDATION